THE
WIZARDS
OF
CENTRAL PARK WEST

Ultimate Urban Fantasy

ARJAY LEWIS

MIND
BENDER
PRESS

Cover Design: Marianne Nowicki, PremadeEbookCoverShop.com
Editing: Brandi Salazar; www.brandisalazar.com

ISBN-13: 978-1983636417
ISBN-10: 198363641X

Published by:
Mindbender Press
474 South Main Street
Phillipsburg NJ 08865
www.mindbenderpress.com

BOOKS BY ARJAY LEWIS:

PARANORMAL DETECTIVE:
(In The Mind Series)
FIRE IN THE MIND
SEDUCTION IN THE MIND
VIOLATED IN THE MIND (Novella)
REUNION IN THE MIND
HAUNTED IN THE MIND
DEVOTION IN THE MIND
ASYLUM IN THE MIND
SPECTER IN THE MIND
VENGEANCE IN MIND

HORROR:
THE MUSE: A Novel Of Unrelenting Terror
KEPT IN THE DARK

ROMANTIC MYSTERY:
A STUDY IN MURDER

ULTIMATE URBAN FANTASY:
THE WIZARDS OF CENTRAL PARK WEST

FOREWORD

This book is not entirely an original concept. In fact, the title was coined by a good friend, Louis Garcia Blake. Lou and I met in the 1970s when we were both young magicians. We were trying to write a musical together, but it never came to fruition.

However, both Lou and I became writers. Lou had a natural talent and had several articles and stories printed in newspapers, as well as magazines. When I showed him some of my early scribblings, he had an uncanny knack for polishing my words until they gleamed.

What Lou lacked was the ability to shut down his inner editor and just write. A novel is a marathon, and it is often difficult to reach the finish line. Many never even get out of the starting gate.

However, he would talk about his stories to anyone who would listen. This is actually not a good idea for an author. My writing mentor Parke Godwin noted that you can talk a story out and end up not writing it at all. I have always felt this to be true, and I am quite secretive about a book until it is ready to be shown to my first reader. (Usually, my wife.)

Lou passed away suddenly more than a decade ago, suffering a massive heart attack, surprising all of us who knew him. When I helped clean up his computer for his bereaved mother, I located a few pages of attempts to write his book concept.

In it, the lead character, Marlowe, was a cross between Buffy the vampire slayer and an all-powerful wizard. Lou had also listed the minor characters of a little ghost named Bob, and a vampire, Daniel Kraft.

One day, walking through the woods near my apartment in Dover, New Jersey, I was unexpectedly inspired by the idea to write a novel about wizards and began to envision the tale I wanted to write. I decided to do this as a tribute to an old friend who enjoyed fantasy as much as I do and helped inspire my own writing in my early attempts.

It is my wish that you enjoy the book, and I also hope that somewhere Lou is looking down and smiling.

Arjay Lewis
January 2018

DEDICATION:

To Louis Garcia Blake
"For of all sad words of tongue or pen,
The saddest are these:
'It might have been!'"

"In a way, we are magicians. We are alchemists, sorcerers, and wizards. We are a very strange bunch. But there is great fun in being a wizard."

—Billy Joel

"And the most unusual and surrealistic place in New York City is Central Park."

—Christo

PROLOGUE

The old man pushed his shopping cart over the cobblestone sidewalk, past the brightly lit facade of the Tavern on the Green. An immaculately dressed doorman wearing a long, gray frock coat and a top hat watched his progress with disdain.

As the bearded man made his way toward the park, the doorman approached him, anger flashing in his eyes.

"Take another route," the doorman spat. "If I see you here again, I'll call the cops."

"Yes, sir, yes, sir!" the old man replied, and quickened his pace.

He was used to this reaction; it happened often. His bedraggled clothes, dirty face, and the smell that accompanied him evoked either anger or pity.

Neither reaction bothered him.

He reached the roadway and turned left, staying on the gravel bridle path. This took him away from the grounds of the Tavern, covered with glittering white Christmas lights even in June.

He faded into the majesty of Central Park, as he followed the street lamps. Here in the dark-green of the park, the spaced wrought-iron lamps provided pools of illumination.

He reached the huge bust of Giuseppe Mazzini, and there he stopped to observe the treetops. A small, cooing noise warbled from between his lips.

There came a chittering reply from a nearby oak, and a small creature darted in and out of sight as it spiraled down to the ground.

"Quiptail," the old man said, his voice a husky whisper as he went down on one knee. "Hope I didn't wake you!"

He reached into his pocket and pulled out a crumpled bag of nuts.

The squirrel boldly left the safety of the tree, moved to the man, and unabashedly reached into the bag, pulled out a peanut, shelled it with his clever paws, and popped the tasty treat into its mouth.

"You can take the whole bag, Quiptail. No need to store it in your cheeks." The old man smiled at the furry creature's antics. "Anything to tell me this night?"

The small creature turned his head left and right, as if to scan the darkness. Then it made another series of noises.

"Really?" the old man said. "You're right, my friend, the pigeons are truly acting inappropriately. But you know how they are."

The squirrel nodded his head in agreement then made more sounds. The old man's face grew solemn as he lifted his head to peer into the darkness. "That is most interesting. A red snake, you say?"

Again the small rodent nodded its tiny head in agreement.

"I shall watch for it. Warn your friends. If they see it, they must not approach it."

The squirrel chittered.

"Yes, the pigeons, too. All should beware," the old man added. "Thank you for your help. You may take your prize."

The squirrel reached out and picked up the small paper bag, placed the top in his teeth, then with a blur of movement, it scaled the tree and disappeared from view.

"So now it begins," the old man murmured to himself.

He rose and began to push his cart forward. It was filled with a collection of the useful: his cane and other paraphernalia. It also held the useless: old newspapers, bits of cloth, and aluminum cans. The trash was a necessary part of his disguise, as much as the rags he wore.

He headed for the 72nd Street entrance for West Drive. Central Park was the first major city park built in America and was well planned. Four transversal roads cut through it every ten to twenty blocks, linking East Side to West. At the same time, a curved roadway wound its way circuitously the entire fifty-block length in one huge circle.

He started downhill where there were few street lamps. Ahead of him, the entrance to Riftstone Arch gaped like an open maw. It was a stunning span, built of huge, carved stones, artfully arranged to hold up the twenty-foot tunnel without mortar. Though four lanes of vehicles passed over it every day, it took the weight without even a quiver.

It was a structure worthy to bear his name.

He passed under the roadway and into the unlit tunnel, pushing the cart with his right hand as he felt along the stone wall with his left. All he needed to do was touch the correct spot and he would pass easily through the huge stones and into his hidden lair.

He stopped suddenly.

There was an odd noise that made the hairs on the back of his neck rise.

Something was wrong.

He knew it wasn't some mugger preying on the homeless. This foe was like himself.

More than mere mortal.

He turned suddenly, his eyes aglow with a bright red light, his hands up protectively as rosy illumination surrounded each of his outstretched palms.

"Who dares confront Riftstone?" he demanded, his voice booming with an unnatural timbre as it echoed off the curved walls of the tunnel. "Show thyself!"

A deep, foreboding chuckle was the only reply. The sound came from everywhere and nowhere.

The bearded man blanched, his body seeming to shrink away from the noise. The fiery glow in his eyes faded, and his hands lost some of their brilliance.

"By Zoroaster!" the man murmured like a prayer. "Abraxas?"

He took a step backward, turned, and attempted to lunge for his cart.

The metal-wired conveyance was pulled from his reach. The bearded man fell into a puddle and drenched himself.

Another ghastly chuckle came forth around him, so loud the walls seemed to rumble with the reverberation.

He rose up, wet and dripping. His safe haven had become a trap, one that he'd walked right into.

His anger flared, and the scarlet glow blazed, not only around his hands but his entire body. He chanted in the ancient language, calling power to him.

"Thou art an annoying little man," the disembodied voice snarled, and the bearded man's head fell back as his tongue was ripped—still quivering—from his mouth. It hovered in the air then was cast aside.

The glow ceased as his concentration was broken. His hand went to his mouth, shock clouding his face.

His only chance was his staff.

He reached out his arm toward the cart at the far end of the tunnel. Energy flowed in waves as he willed his weapon to him.

Something unseen grabbed his arm then pulled with inhuman force. There was a cracking noise, as the limb was torn from him. The pain was excruciating, but all the old man could do was make mangled grunts with his tongueless mouth.

The arm hung suspended for a moment, and then sailed off, like a discarded part of a rag doll.

The man looked at the remaining stub of bone protruding from his shoulder, watching his life's blood gush out.

He still had a chance, but he must act quickly.

A foot landed in front of him, hoofed and scarlet red, the legs covered with curly fur. Riftstone stared up at the figure. The creature was finely muscled: red skin, bright as fire; its arms extending into powerful claws; the head embellished with huge horns that would be oversized on a large bull. The creature was stooped over to fit the twelve-foot-tall tunnel.

"Remember me, old man?" the demon asked, the claw-like hand grabbing Riftstone's throat. He lifted him close, hot breath against his bearded face. "I'm back, and I have an ally."

The demon turned and peered into the darkness at the other end of the tunnel. Someone moved out of the shadows, dressed in long, flowing robes covered with stars and moons and holding aloft a wooden pole. A pale gray light hovered over the hooded figure.

Fighting not to swoon, Riftstone extended his remaining arm beseechingly.

The figure stepped closer and held up the staff, the gray light glinting off the patterns on the robes and the stone walls. "It had to come to this, Riftstone. You should have listened."

The old man's head fell forward, and his body hung limply as he lost consciousness.

"Do with him as you will." The cloaked figure stated with a dismissive wave and turned to walk away.

"Oh, I shall." The demon's face broke into a huge grin.

ONE

Edward Berman pulled his cell phone from the pocket of his suit jacket and announced "HOME" to the small box.

"You want coffee, Eddie?" Luis Vasquez asked as he aimed his thumb at the Starbucks on the corner of 86th Street and Columbus Avenue behind their parked vehicle. He wore a cheap suit with a tie that didn't match it or anything, except perhaps industrial waste.

"Sure," Eddie pulled several bills from his pocket. "Pay for it this time."

Vasquez took the money and shrugged. "Can I help it if some well-meaning citizens want to treat two hardworking detectives to a free cup of coffee?"

He flashed a grin, his teeth uneven, yet unnaturally white. It was a strong counterpoint to his coffee-with-cream colored skin and straight black hair. The sparse mustache over his lip never fully grew in, but his heavy-lidded bedroom eyes drove women wild—at least that was what Luis bragged. He was large and heavyset but not flabby. He was built like a fireplug carved from stone—solid.

Eddie heard the phone pick up on the other end, turned his attention to the call, and leaned against the unmarked police car.

"Hello?" came the throaty female voice.

Eddie's heart sped up. Fifteen years of marriage, and every time was like the first time.

"It's Eddie."

"Hello, sugar." Her voice dripped of smokey cafés and whiskey as her slight accent teased his ear as if she nibbled it.

Eddie focused on the business at hand. "I just wanted to check on Momma."

"Your momma is as well as can be expected," Cerise said. "We're going to the doctor in a half-hour."

"I want you to call me as soon as you know anything."

"I will, sugar." Cerise lowered her voice to a murmur and went on. "Don't get your hopes up. Doctor Ramsen said there might not be much that can be done."

Eddie felt a lump in his throat. He knew what the doctor said; he'd been there. The idea of his mother's mortality was difficult for him to accept. "I just want to be kept informed, y'know."

"Edward," Cerise chided, "expressions like 'y'know' are incorrect English, which sets a poor example for your sons."

"Did Momma just come into the room?" Eddie asked as he picked up on the tone under his wife's lecture.

"That's right," she said, too cheery.

"Then sorry I didn't get down wid dat," he said to annoy her.

"Don't start. It's bad enough the boys listen to that rap music."

"Hip-hop, honey. Our sons like hip-hop."

"It's all the same to me."

Eddie grunted a reply. He never could understand why Cerise was so strict with their two sons. Her number-one concern was poor English. He remembered his own youth in the '90s, when he wore stupid clothes and spoke as if he came out of a jive sitcom. Kids went with fads, and Eddie felt his kids should have some latitude.

But there was no point arguing on such a stressful day.

"You'll call me as soon as you know anything?" Eddie said.

"Of course," Cerise replied. "Be safe on those streets. I want you to take care of my big, black man."

This made Eddie smile. It was a pet name she'd used since the days they started dating. Eddie was so light-skinned he could almost pass for Caucasian. But his short, kinky hair, full lips, and African nose gave full credence to his ethnicity.

Cerise was a different matter. The daughter of Africans who emigrated to the United States from Botswana when she was a child, she was so dark her skin was almost ebony. She was beautiful and possessed the exotic quality of the foreign-born. She also talked with a light accent from speaking Setswana growing up.

For dark-as-night Cerise to call Eddie her "big, black man" when he was just six feet tall, slender, and so much lighter, made him laugh the first time she'd said it. Now, it was one of those running jokes that married couples amused each other with while strangers looked on questioningly.

Eddie told her, "You take care of Momma."

"Will you be home for dinner?"

"Should be. Luis and I are spending the day catching up on paperwork. We needed to get out of the precinct for a break."

"I love you, Eddie."

"I love you too, baby." Eddie shut down the phone. He raised his head to see Vasquez with two cups of coffee.

Luis shook his head as he handed Eddie his coffee.

"What's wrong with you?" Eddie inquired.

"It's disgusting."

"What, the coffee?" Eddie took a sip. "Tastes fine to me."

"Not the coffee, you." Vasquez leaned against the police car next to Eddie. The car shifted from the added weight. "You talk too nice to your wife. I never speak like that to Maria."

"According to you, you haven't said two words to her in three years."

"Sure I have. We have an argument every Saturday night."

"Some people just go to the movies."

"It's cheaper than HBO," Luis shrugged as he imbibed his coffee.

"If all you do is argue, how come you got six kids?"

"We have to make up some time," Luis smirked.

"So, if you fight all the time, what's the attraction?"

"My wife cast a spell on me," Luis suggested with lifted eyebrows.

"Say what?" Eddie replied with an incredulous look.

"She went to this place in the Village—Magickal Cherub— down on Eighth Street. She bought a kit and put a love spell on me."

"You have *got* to be kidding me."

"It worked. I ain't ever gonna leave her."

"If only for the fact that the child support would wipe you out," Eddie said as his cell phone made its unique musical ring. "Besides, I like your wife, and one of your kids is named after *my* wife."

"Maybe she put a spell on you, too." Luis took another sip.

"No one believes in spells." Eddie touched the button on his phone. "Berman."

Luis watched his partner's expression grow hard.

"Where?" Eddie listened intently.

Luis exhaled heavily. Time to go to work, but he knew not to get his hopes up. Since he and Eddie had been transferred to the Central Park Precinct, they didn't get any interesting cases.

"Probably a damn cat stuck in a tree," muttered Luis. "Or a frickin' pigeon swiped somebody's wallet."

"Got it," Eddie said to the phone. "Give us five minutes."

Luis moved to the passenger side of the vehicle as Eddie put away the phone and unlocked the doors. They got in, and Eddie pulled the car out from the illegal parking space which blocked a fire hydrant.

"What's up?" Luis tried not to get his hopes up.

"A homicide."

"A homicide?" Luis repeated, excited. "A full-blown murder? They goin' to let us work the case?"

"I don't know. Someone offed a homeless guy in the park, and we got the call." Eddie drove carefully into traffic.

"Why would anyone want to kill one of them?" Luis said.

"Whoever did it wanted him *very* dead."

"What do you mean?"

"His body was torn to pieces."

"*Madre de Dios*," Luis murmured as he quickly crossed himself.

TWO

Traffic in Manhattan was light for an overcast day in the middle of June, and they were able to get from 86th Street to the 72nd Street entrance quickly.

They drove down Park Drive West and quickly pulled off the roadway and onto the gravel bridle path. Several uniformed officers were milling about, putting up yellow crime scene tape to keep the area free of the curious.

Eddie and Luis got out of the car and approached on foot.

They flashed their shields to a short, chunky, African-American policewoman just outside the tunnel. A youthful blond officer was sitting on a rock nearby, his hat in his hand. From his color, it looked as if he'd not only lost his breakfast, but all the food he'd consumed in the previous week.

"Hey, Taylor," Eddie said to the woman. "I'm Lieutenant Berman, and this is Sergeant Vasquez."

The policewoman nodded. "I've seen you around. This is Young. He found the body—Well, the pieces."

"You all right, man?" Vasquez asked Young.

The blond boy—he couldn't have been more than twenty-two —nodded and swallowed hard. He looked as if he might vomit again.

"Sorry, sir." Young attempted to stand.

"Just stay where you are, Young." Eddie put a hand on his shoulder to lower him to his rock seat. "No point in pushing your luck."

"Or throwing up on us," Luis added. "You didn't mess up the crime scene, did you?"

"No, sir," Young said. "I made it out here to the bushes."

Eddie turned to Taylor. "What can you tell us?"

"Routine patrol," Taylor said. "We go through here every morning. Young likes the tunnels. That's where we found…" She gave a nod of her head in the direction of the archway. "Sir, it's a mess—"

"The blood," Young interjected. "All the blood…"

The youthful officer looked like he was about to pass out.

"Young, put your head between your legs." Eddie placed his hand on the back of the blond's neck. "Now push up against my hand. Keep pushing. Good."

It was an old trick to keep the blood flowing to the brain. Young wouldn't be of any help unconscious.

"Okay, now raise your head." Eddie looked questioningly at the officer. "Better?"

Young nodded weakly.

Eddie returned his attention to Taylor. "You called this in? Forensics? The medical examiner?"

"Yes, sir," Taylor stated. "They're on their way. Uniforms got here first, then you."

Eddie nodded. "Okay. Stick with your partner and help secure the scene. We'll want full reports later."

"Yes, sir," Taylor said.

Eddie turned to Young. "Your first homicide?"

"Yes, sir," Young sounded, at best, unenthusiastic.

Eddie nodded. "You do get used to it."

"I could never get used to…*that*." Young swallowed hard.

Eddie looked to Luis. "Let's go, sergeant."

Luis nodded, and they began to walk through the opening.

Eddie lowered his voice. "We need to show the rookies how a pair of experienced detectives handle a homicide."

"So I shouldn't throw up?" Luis asked.

Eddie smiled. "You'll mess up our rep."

"Okay, then I won't."

They had left the dim daylight and entered the shadow of the darkened, artificial cavern. The tunnel was as long as the roadway over it was wide, but dark inside, bathed in an artificial twilight.

The first thing to hit them was the smell of urine combined with the iron stink of blood and rotting meat.

"Man, what a smell." Luis waved his hand in front of his face.

"Great, and after that coffee, I need to take a leak," Eddie snapped.

"Just do it here. No one will notice."

"Bad enough Young almost puked. I'll pass."

"Eventually, you will," Luis smirked, "but not on the crime scene, LT."

Eddie blinked, trying to adjust his eyes to the gloom. He could see what looked like brown paint spattered efficaciously on the walls and floor.

"Blood," Luis stated aloud, as he followed Eddie's gaze.

"Did you bring that penlight of yours?"

"Oh, yeah, right here." Luis flashed on a small light and moved from the walls to the floor in front of them.

"What's that?" Eddie said.

Luis shifted the light back to where Eddie pointed. The beam rested on a bare leg.

They approached carefully.

Eddie crouched and looked at the detached limb. The bone stood out from it, and the flesh was unevenly sheared.

Luis pulled a pair of latex gloves from his pocket. "What happened? We get the New York version of the '*Texas Chain Saw Massacre*?'"

"Can't be sure without forensics, but I don't think this was cut," Eddie explained. "See the way the muscle is torn—and the ligaments—so uneven? I would say this leg was ripped."

"Jeezus!" Luis pulled a glove on his other hand. "How would you do that?"

"Got me." Eddie shook his head. He tried to stare into the shadowy gloom and saw a metallic glint. "Touch as little as you can."

"Well, thank you, lieutenant," Luis grumbled. "It's been a few months since my last murder scene, but I do remember. Hey, you need to glove up."

Eddie nodded and extracted latex gloves from his pocket. He started to put them on as he walked through the tunnel, his eyes fixed on the flicker of light.

"What do you see?" Luis shone the small light ahead of Eddie.

"I dunno, let me check it out." Eddie snapped the glove on his left hand. The object was vaguely familiar, and there were wheels that pointed toward him. Then he saw the metal basket.

"It's a shopping cart," Eddie assured as he finally recognized it. It sat upside down, dented and damaged.

He drew closer to see a small silver ball protruding from the back of the cart. It glowed, almost as if it generated its own luminescence.

Without thinking, Eddie reached out with his ungloved right hand and touched the silver ball.

There was a blinding flash of red light and a loud "*Crack*."

Eddie fell back to the gravel path as fireworks went off in his line of vision.

Luis ran over and pulled Eddie upright. "Eddie, you okay?"

"Yeah," Eddie muttered, dazed. "Damn."

Eddie shook his head to clear it and struggled to get back on his feet. He felt wobbly, as if jolted by a Taser.

"What the hell was that!" Luis exclaimed.

"Got me. It happened when I touched that thing." Eddie pointed at the silver ball.

Luis shifted his penlight and flashed it on the disfigured shopping cart. A whistle escaped his lips.

"Look at that!" Luis declared. "It's beautiful."

With his gloved hand, Luis slowly drew out the silver handle. A handsomely tapered stick came with it, made from a wood so dark it almost disappeared in the shadows of the tunnel. Luis shined the light the length of the walking stick.

"Is that a cane?" Eddie asked, his vision clearing a bit.

"It's silver. And this wood, what is it? Mahogany?"

"I think it's ebony."

"Kinda weird, huh?" Luis looked from the cane to his partner's face.

"What do you mean?"

"Where did a homeless guy get a cane like this?"

Eddie put the glove on his right hand and hesitantly took the stick from his partner's grasp. No flash this time. It was only a piece of wood with a fancy top.

But it was exquisite. The silver was decorated and beautifully shaped with sweeping grace. The stick wore coat upon coat of wax or varnish, so it felt smooth, well-balanced, and not too heavy.

Luis flashed the light a few feet ahead.

"Lieutenant?"

"Yeah?" Eddie replied, finding it hard to take his eyes off the walking stick.

"I think I found the head."

Eddie pulled himself away to follow the beam of the penlight. He expected to see a head lying sideways on the ground. But it sat upright on the stub of its neck, as if the owner was buried in the dirt and might at any moment rise up out of the ground.

Eddie stepped closer and used the cane for support as he crouched down. The head—obviously male—wore long hair and a dirty, gray beard. The eyes were closed, and the head was leaning back on the neck with the mouth agape enough to show strong, white teeth with a flicker of gold.

Luis gawked. "It's like it was posed for us."

"May have been," Eddie agreed. "Look at the teeth. You ever see a homeless guy with such good dental care?"

Luis flashed the light into the mouth. "Looks like he got them bleached, like me."

"And there!" Eddie pointed at a tooth that shined brightly. "He's got a gold crown."

"Go figure," Luis said.

"Lieutenant?" a female voice echoed in the manmade cave.

"Yes, officer," Eddie acknowledged, and took the penlight to shine it on the head from different angles.

"The coroner and crime scene unit are here," Taylor said from the mouth of the tunnel.

"I'll bring them in, Eddie," Luis volunteered as he rose and stepped away.

"Thanks." Eddie leaned closer to the head.

Unexpectedly, the cane quivered in his hand. He turned his head to peer at the stick. The silver orb grew warm as it jiggled from its own internal tremor.

Then it stopped.

Eddie returned his attention to the head.

The eyes were open, and it watched Eddie as he moved.

With a shriek, Eddie fell back and tumbled into a puddle. He wanted to run, to crawl away, but was frozen in terror as the cane vibrated in his hand, and the disembodied head's eyes bore into him.

The mouth began to move, and a voice whispered hoarsely, "You are summoned!"

Eddie shrieked again as he lost control of his bladder.

THREE

Outside in the open air, Eddie shivered as he sat next to Officer Young. He was wet, smelled bad, and held the ebony shaft in his gloved hand with a death grip.

Crime scene investigators were all over the hillside and tunnel like a small army of ants. The click of cameras and the flashes of strobes brightened the tunnel as if it were distant lightning.

Young looked better now, but he watched Eddie with a combination of pity and understanding.

"You all right, sir?" Young asked tentatively.

"I'm f-fine, officer," Eddie stammered, his jaw tight to keep his teeth from chattering.

Young rose. "I'll help secure the scene, sir."

"You d-do that, officer," Eddie said.

Young nodded and walked away. Luis walked over with Eddie's cup of now-cold coffee.

"Drink this," Luis suggested.

Eddie accepted the drink and took a trembling sip.

"Guess you don't need a bathroom anymore."

"Oh, you f-funny, man," Eddie responded.

Luis glanced over at Taylor and Young, who chatted with the other uniformed officers.

"So much for impressing the rookies. They think you are *mucho loco*."

"It t-talked. I saw it. I *heard* it," Eddie protested.

Luis crouched and kept his tone low. "Look, Eddie, maybe it did. Maybe it jumped up and did the *lambada*. Nobody but you saw it. Now, you're the lieutenant, and I'm just some wetback sergeant. But, partner to partner, it might be a good idea not to mention this on your report."

"Yeah." Eddie inhaled deeply and nodded.

Luis relaxed. "We just say you slipped and fell into a puddle —a smelly puddle. It happens."

Eddie regarded his partner. "T-thanks, Luis."

"For what?"

"For not calling Bellevue," Eddie confessed.

"It isn't the cool, calm approach you suggested," Luis mused.

"I have a change of clothes at the precinct."

The Twenty-Second Precinct building was located on the access road that linked East Side to West Side on 86th Street. It served as the center for all park police activity from 59th Street all the way up to 110th Street, making it the largest precinct in Manhattan.

"You relax for a minute, and I'll talk to the coroner and CSU, then we'll go." Luis walked back toward the tunnel.

"Relax," Eddie moaned to himself. "After all, I'm only losing my mind."

"You okay, lieutenant?" a voice spoke.

Eddie started and looked up at a black man standing over him. He had a kinky, gray beard that clung to his face like lamb's wool. The hair surrounded his head like a cloud. He wore military fatigues and carried a dented, aluminum broom handle.

"Sorry, you startled me." Eddie recognized the newcomer as one of the homeless who called the park home. Eddie had often seen him, as he walked about and held conversations with the empty air. The only downside was the stink of stale body odor he wore. "You're Troy, right?"

"Trey, folks call me Trey," the man explained, as he leaned casually against his broom handle. "Bad things happening, lieutenant?"

"Very bad things. Looks like one of your own was taken out," Eddie warned.

"One of my own?" A look of suspicion touched Trey's face.

"Yeah, a homeless guy," Eddie said.

Trey looked at the tunnel sadly. "You don't say."

"You should move into a shelter until we catch who did it," Eddie suggested. "For your own safety."

A grim smile crossed Trey's face. "A shelter won't protect me from what did this. You're a good man, lieutenant. I hope you can rise to the occasion."

Without another word, he walked off toward a grove of trees using the broom handle to help him along.

That was odd, Eddie thought. *I wonder what he was talking about?*

"Ready to go?" Luis stepped in front of Eddie and pulled him to his feet. "I'll drive. There's some trash bags in the trunk. I don't want you making the seat wet. After all, that's where I sit."

"You're all heart, Vasquez."

"Hey, you can't bring this." Luis took hold of the cane in Eddie's hand.

Eddie looked down at the foreign object. "Forgot I had it…"

"It's evidence! I'll put it back where we found it. You go up to the car."

Eddie nodded wearily. He glanced at his watch. It was only eleven AM, but he felt exhausted. That head looked at him— those eyes, that voice—and then Luis pulled him out of the tunnel as he screamed like a crazy man.

"Having fun, Berman?" a familiar voice sneered.

Eddie looked up to see Agent Jason Wilcox as he glared down at him.

"You are not what I need today, Wilcox," Eddie said, and felt grounded by having to confront the bigger man. "In fact, I can't think of any day I need you."

"I'm devastated, Berman." Wilcox ran a hand though his brown hair and flexed his huge biceps.

Eddie sighed. Wilcox was a part of the FBI Urban Crime Task Force in the New York branch and often found ways to push his authority over the NYPD.

In the business of policing New York, homicides in the park automatically fell under the auspices of the Manhattan North Precinct's homicide division. However, the task force could insert itself, whether NYPD liked it or not. Eddie felt that in Wilcox's instance, that was usually any crime that would promote his personal career.

It's about numbers, Eddie thought. *He solves cases. Ultimately, that's all anyone is interested in.*

"I thought you weren't pursuing homicides since your transfer," Wilcox went on. "Disciplinary situation, if memory serves me."

"You're the one who made the big stink, Wilcox," Eddie said, stone-faced.

Luis was suddenly at Eddie's side. "Everything okay, lieutenant?"

"Hey, now the United Nations is complete," Wilcox smirked with a glance to his own partner, a thin, white-haired man named Sam. Sam wasn't as nasty, but he gave Wilcox free rein. Sam smiled and sucked on the cigarette that smoldered in his mouth.

"*Graçias*, Wilcox. I love to start my day listening to your racist diatribes," Luis said.

"Just a joke, Vasquez. Get a sense of humor," Wilcox advised.

"Word from the expert," Eddie muttered sardonically.

Wilcox returned his gaze to Eddie. "And I love your look. I hear wet and rumpled is very chic. Not to mention your cologne. What is it, Eau de Toilet?"

Sam broke into loud guffaws, and Luis glared daggers.

"Don't mess up my crime scene, Wilcox," Eddie warned.

"*Your* crime scene?" Wilcox scoffed. "It's Manhattan North's crime scene. Of course you two worked there *once*."

"Until you showed up," Luis grumbled through clenched teeth.

"You involved yourself in *my* case, after I told you to back off." Wilcox pointed his finger at Luis like a weapon. "As it is, I caught the creep."

"While we almost got killed," Luis argued.

"You were grandstanding," Wilcox jeered. "You should have been happy to share information—"

"Save us the Fed bullshit. You're not supposed to get involved in a city case unless you're *asked*," Vasquez snapped. "On this case, forensics is still trying to locate all the body parts."

Wilcox brightened up. "Really? This one is sure to get headlines."

"It's not about credit, Wilcox." Eddie felt himself grow hot under the collar.

"That's right, Berman, it's about catching the bad guys, and a few headlines are good for advancement," Wilcox pointed out. "I mean, for those of us who don't get affirmative action."

Vasquez turned his even larger body toward the muscled Wilcox. "You want to know how a *Chicano* fights, I'll be happy to show you."

"Anytime," Wilcox spat back.

Sam and Eddie ran between their respective partners and attempted to pull them in separate directions. They might as well have tried to move granite.

"Luis, let's go," Eddie said.

Luis shifted his eyes to Eddie and relaxed. "Yeah, we got reports to fill out. You might try it sometime, Wilcox. Oh yeah, I guess you gotta learn to read first."

"I'll try not to fall into anything," Wilcox gloated.

The big man lumbered away with Sam behind him, like a well-heeled lapdog. Vasquez opened the trunk of their police car and took out the trash bags. He fumed as he brought them to the passenger side and began to line the seat with them.

"That *gringo* is going to get in my face one time too many," he muttered, "and then I'll show him how a real man fights—one who doesn't pump up with steroids."

"My hero." Eddie got into the car.

"Whatever." Luis hopped in the driver's side and gunned the engine.

*   *   *

A figure, neatly arrayed in a suit and tie, stood in the grove of trees watching the vehicle depart. His long, white beard gave him the appearance of a skinny, springtime Santa Claus.

He returned his gaze to the crime scene as his mouth tightened into a hard line.

There was a sound, and he turned so quickly, it was as if he'd jumped into a new position, the slim cane in his hand raised.

"Marlowe?" a voice asked.

The nattily dressed man lowered his stick.

"Trefoil, is that you?" He exhaled in relief.

"You heard?"

"Quiptail witnessed the entire event and came to me," Marlowe said. "I was too late to help."

"As was I," Trey sighed and stepped closer. He leaned against his broom handle. The two men stood next to each other and watched the police at work.

"I hope you don't mind, old friend," Marlowe grimaced, "but your disguisement—"

"Good, ain't it?" Trey boasted.

"Yes, very effective. It is just…well, the *odor.*"

"Oh, of course," Trey acknowledged and raised his broomstick to give a small wave. "Better?"

Marlowe inhaled deeply and smiled. "Much, thank you."

"Gentlemen," another voice announced behind them.

"I know who that is," Trefoil noted as he gazed up at the heavens.

"He had to show up. It was inevitable," Marlowe agreed bleakly.

The two men turned slowly in unison to face the short, thin man behind them. He stood about five feet four and wore a tightly buttoned tweed jacket, a bow tie, and round horn-rimmed spectacles on his face.

"Good morning, Bankrock." Marlowe forced a smile.

"Gentlemen." Bankrock adjusted his spectacles nervously then glared at the leather-bound notebook in his hand. "There was a serious, and may I add unauthorized, use of high levels of mystical energy in this area within the last twelve hours—"

"We are well aware of that, Bankrock," Marlowe stated.

"Well, I for one want to make sure all protocols were followed." Bankrock checked his pad. "Were there any witnesses to this event, and what was the cause of such an enormous shift in —"

Trefoil gestured to the crime scene. "Riftstone's dead."

Bankrock stopped speaking and looked from one man to the other. He swallowed hard. "What?"

"Murdered," Marlowe intoned.

"Murdered?" Bankrock repeated and grew pale.

"Torn limb from limb," Trefoil explained.

They stood silent.

"Who could have done this?" Bankrock gulped. "He was a prophet!"

"You detected mystical energy. Don't you know?" Marlowe asked.

"My own oracular abilities are limited," Bankrock demurred. "I'm no seer."

"You just a damn bureaucrat," Trefoil muttered.

"I can tell you that a level nine magickal disturbance occurred," Bankrock offered, a bit testy.

Marlowe turned back, his eyes wide. "Level nine?"

"Damn," Trefoil added.

"As you well know," Bankrock continued, smugly, "anything above a level three must be investigated."

"A level nine," Marlowe murmured. "Such power."

"You can see why I was concerned," Bankrock said.

"It is times like these I miss Greywacke," Marlowe mused.

"As many of us do," Bankrock commiserated. "What is the current situation?"

"The police are here," Trefoil said. "Found his body. Well, the parts."

"This is terrible!" Bankrock adjusted his collar, as if to get more air. "Who could attack Riftstone? He was one of the Five— a seer. You couldn't just sneak up on him."

Trefoil stared. "My guess is the Great Evil."

"What?" Bankrock quavered and checked his notebook. "Him? Are you mad?"

"Bankrock has a point." Marlowe's face was lined with concern. He turned to his taller companion. "What makes you think so? He has never manifested near New York. Besides, would he dare attack one of the Five?"

"Maybe he's changed his style," Trefoil implied.

They stood in silence for a moment.

"He could never manifest at a level nine," Marlowe declared, his eyes still on the police.

"Only a power level of three or four." Bankrock checked in his notebook. "At most."

"You know the ancient prophecy," Trey said, his eyes still focused on the police in the distance. "One day, he is supposed to bring about the end of the world. It's his destiny."

"And yet, he has been stopped again and again by the Five," Marlowe said. "He has grown weaker with each defeat."

"Well, I still think it's him," Trefoil pointed out. "'Cause the first one he would go for is Riftstone."

"Aye," Marlowe replied with a nod. "Riftstone dispatched him numerous times."

"Riftstone made it his business to track the Great Evil down anywhere he showed up," Trefoil commented.

"If you are correct, this is terrible," Bankrock interjected. "We can't have the Great Evil showing up here, unannounced—"

"Like we got a choice," Trefoil sneered.

"Maintaining secrecy will be impossible." Sweat broke out on Bankrock's forehead. "Haven't you two both fought him before?"

"We have defeated him," Marlowe insisted. "Each of the Five possess the power to cast him out."

"Sometimes, it's taken two or three of us to do it," Trefoil proposed. "Right now, there's Marlowe and me."

"Good!" Bankrock pleaded. "Then you must bind him, cast him out at once."

"It is more complicated than that," Marlowe reckoned. "Riftstone's staff has touched my consciousness."

"Of course it has," Bankrock whined. "You must decide who will receive it and its power. I have a list of appropriate apprentices that might be suitable—"

"I cannot," Marlowe said.

"Of course you can…" Bankrock began and checked his list a second time.

"You lead the coven," Trefoil assured. "It's up to you."

Marlowe, his face as still as a statue, said, "One has been summoned."

"Summoned?" Bankrock repeated, his mouth agape.

"Summoned?" Trey grunted. "That still happens?"

"Desperate times have their own energy," Marlowe expounded.

"Yeah, your mama," Trey said. "Does this guy know?"

Marlowe sighed. "It falls to me to inform him."

"This is terrible!" Bankrock croaked, agitated. "We have an unsanctioned summoning! I shall have to consult several grimoire on the proper way to handle this!"

"Calm yourself, Bankrock," Marlowe boomed, his patience wearing thin. "None of us asked for this. We must accept the circumstances we have been given."

"But *you* are the coven master. You are linked to Riftstone's staff until a bearer is initiated," Bankrock fretted.

"You sayin' we should fight the Great Evil with a Newling?" Trefoil bounced the bottom of his broom handle against the ground. "You are losing it, m'man,"

Marlowe shook his head and began to walk. Trefoil followed close at hand, as did Bankrock, who had begun to scribble in his pad.

"The Staff of Fire made the selection; we must abide by it," Marlowe consoled. "I believe the pair of us can defeat the beast. We will merely bring the Newling to assure our success."

"Provided he ain't in the way," Trefoil cautioned.

"In the meantime, we have much to do." Marlowe snapped the fingers of his free hand. "Bankrock!"

"Yes, Marlowe!" Bankrock stepped forward.

"All must be told of Riftstone's death and Trefoil's belief that Abraxas has returned," Marlowe advised.

"I'll get on my mirror right away," Bankrock acquiesced.

Marlowe raised his cane to stop Bankrock in his path and gazed intently into his eyes. "Nay, do it face to face, so none of the Dark Forces can intervene."

"But that would require so much traveling," Bankrock groused.

"It *must* be done in person," Marlowe intoned. "And warn all that none should go forth alone at night if they are near New York. Once the sun sets—"

"There has been an increase in Vampire activity of late." Bankrock took another glance to his notes.

"This takes precedence. One of our own has been slain."

"I'll stay at your townhouse tonight, if thass all right," Trefoil said.

"Of course, my friend," Marlowe replied.

Trefoil nodded. "We need to find the other two. Last I heard, Ahbay was in China."

"I believe Eugenia is in England," Bankrock interjected.

"As we travel, leave word that they are to contact me—and not by the standard techniques," Marlowe warned. "If you are right, Bankrock—"

"And I usually am—"

"A level nine disturbance could disrupt some of our abilities. My only explanation for Riftstone's death is that he was caught unawares."

"Unawares? A prophet?" Bankrock worried. "How is that possible?"

"There are ways to cloud second sight," Marlowe stated. "All of us must be on our guard."

Trefoil nodded gravely. "Damn straight."

With that, Marlowe and Trefoil each stepped into a separate grove of trees and disappeared.

"What about the paperwork?" Bankrock demanded to the empty air.

FOUR

Eddie rubbed the towel over his naked body as he stepped out of the shower stall and strode barefoot to his locker. There, he dressed in fresh underwear and socks and put on a new shirt, pulling it loose from its wrapper. He put his dirty suit in the plastic bag and slipped it into a small duffel.

He put on a different tie and returned to the sink to examine himself in the mirror. He was coming up on the big four-oh, forty years old, but he still carried himself well. He made sure to jog around the Central Park Reservoir and lift weights regularly.

He scrutinized his reflection and opened an eyelid with his fingers to examine the orb.

Not too bloodshot.

In the mirror, Eddie saw the glint of metal in the corner of the room behind him.

He turned and approached his open locker. There was an object in it…with a gleaming ball of silver on top.

"It can't be." Eddie reached in to extract the ebony wood cane. "How the hell…" The wood felt alive in his hand, as if it pulsed.

Eddie thought about it for a minute and felt his temper rise. This was some wise guy's idea to make the lieutenant squirm.

He held onto the cane and threw his duffel and toiletries into the locker, then slammed the thin metal door. He went up the stairs two at a time, until he reached the second floor, the level of the "double-deuce" detectives' bull pen.

He walked into the large, open room where several detectives had individual workspaces. There were no walls between desks, so there was little privacy. At the far end of the room were several walled offices—one a conference room, the other two for interrogation. They were lined with one-way, mirrored glass and the latest in audio and video equipment.

He strode up to Vasquez's desk where Luis leaned with his chair balanced on the back legs.

Eddie rammed the cane against the back of the chair, and the big man tumbled to the ground with a *thump*.

Looking up from the floor, Luis was shocked. "What the hell?" was all he could manage.

"I bet you think this is funny." Eddie brandished the cane. "You say you're leaving this at the scene, then you bring it back with you and stick it in my locker! Very funny!"

"Wha…?" Luis pulled himself off the floor.

"It's a good thing you are a damn good detective and the best partner I ever had, because if not, I'd get you transferred to a beat on the Lower East Side until you were so old you'd need a walker."

Luis' clouded face brightened. "You think I'm a damn good detective?"

"Your idea of a practical joke stinks! I've had a bad enough day—"

"I'm the best partner you've ever had?" Luis smiled from ear to ear.

"Yes, yes." Eddie held the cane right in Luis' face. "This was *not* funny!"

"Isn't that..." Luis puzzled, finally aware of the walking stick.

"The cane from the crime scene!" Eddie raged. "The one you brought here."

"I brought?"

"Come on, just admit it. Ha, ha, you're a comic genius."

Luis opened his hands in innocence. "I din't do it, Eddie."

Eddie stopped, stunned at Luis's reaction. The man couldn't keep a secret. Eddie knew of his upcoming surprise party Cerise had planned for months because of Luis.

"Look, the gag's over," Eddie said, calmer now.

"I stuck the cane back into the shopping cart, like I tol' you," Luis insisted.

The two men stared at each other.

"Well, if you didn't," Eddie wondered, "and I didn't..."

Luis snapped his fingers. "Wilcox! That son-of-a-bitch—"

"Wilcox couldn't walk into this precinct without being noticed." Eddie inspected the wooden rod in his hand. "Today is getting weirder and weirder."

"You're tellin' me." Luis stared at the stick as well.

"I'm taking this to evidence." Eddie exhaled deeply and twirled the stick between his fingers. "I want to make sure it's locked up tight."

Luis nodded. "Eddie, you got to make sure we don't lose this case to Manhattan North. We can handle it."

"It's the captain's decision." Eddie was unable to take his eyes off the round top of the cane. Why did it intrigue him so?

"Come on! This is our first real case since we got here," Luis whined. "When the Metropolitan Museum of Art was robbed last month, we didn't get anywhere near it."

Eddie forced himself to meet his partner's stare. "Luis, we have no experience with robbery division, and we don't know anything about South American Pre-Columbian artifacts."

"That's not the point!" Luis sat heavily on the edge of his desk. "It happened in the park. We're detectives, and we weren't part of the investigation. The FBI got in on that one as well with their FUCT task force."

"It's UCTF: Urban Crime Task Force. The way you say it would be Force of Urban Crime Task."

"Yeah, well, every time they show up, we're FUCT."

Eddie shook his head. "You have a point, and they haven't a clue who did it, anyway."

"This case is right up our alley," Luis said. "Talk to the captain? Convince him?"

Eddie sighed. "Do we have any leads?"

Luis shrugged his massive shoulders. "The uniforms are casing the neighborhood. We should have something to start with by tomorrow."

Eddie sighed again. "All right, I'll ask."

"And you can share the case with the best partner you ever had." Luis smirked.

"I take that back. It was said in a moment of weakness." Eddie headed for the stairs to go up to the top floor and the evidence room.

The third floor was the same size as the floor below, except there was a crisscross of metal fencing that created a small lobby, with only a locked gate to get in or out. Behind the fence was a collection of files, tagged items, and small locked rooms that resembled a huge garage sale. Framed by a three-by-five, window-like opening, an aged officer sat on a tall metal stool.

"Hey, Hank," Eddie said.

"Hey, Lew," Hank responded, using verbal shorthand for lieutenant. "What d'ya need?"

Eddie handed Hank the walking stick. Hank whistled in approval.

"That's a beaut. Where did you get it?"

"From a very dead homeless guy."

Hank's face wrinkled up in puzzlement. "What would a homeless guy be doing with this?"

"One of many questions," Eddie pointed out. "Can you put it where no one will play with it?"

"Under lock and key." Hank handed Eddie an evidence form to fill out.

"Good." Eddie began to scribble the necessary information. "I *really* need you to keep your eye on it. I don't want that turning up any place it shouldn't be."

"You suggestin' I misplace evidence, lieutenant?"

Eddie could tell he'd rubbed the older man the wrong way. "No way, Hank. I trust you better than my bank." Eddie ripped the yellow copy off the evidence form for himself. "It's this cane… I don't know, strange things have been goin' down since I found it. I figure if you hold onto it, it'll be secure."

Hank nodded grimly. "You can bet on it, Lew."

"Thanks, Hank."

Eddie returned downstairs, the odd stick no longer his concern.

FIVE

Captain Jacobs was a big man in a small job. He'd worked his way up the ranks and earned his own precinct. His one failure was how he played the game of politics. He wasn't a kiss-ass, and more than once he told a city commissioner his true opinion of their poor decisions. But he possessed a spotless record and needed to be put somewhere. So they gave him the "22." He made it his own little piece of the NYPD and took the misfits he was assigned and treated them as if he was the mayor of New York or a dictator. It all depended on the day and his mood.

When Eddie knocked on his door, Jacobs opened it and broke into a warm smile.

"Hey, lieutenant, you all right? Heard you had a little incident this morning." Jacobs shook Eddie's hand firmly.

"It was nothing, sir." Eddie hoped he didn't look as uncomfortable as he felt. "I'm here to ask that my partner and I be assigned to the homeless guy homicide."

"Straight to the point!" Jacobs grinned. "That's what I like about you, LT."

"Can you swing it, sir?"

Jacobs blew air out hard. "Homicides always go through Manhattan North—"

"This took place *in* the park," Eddie said. "With the record I have with Luis—"

Jacobs held up his hand to stop Eddie. "You don't have to sell me, lieutenant. I know you two are good. But you do realize you were assigned here for disciplinary action because of the Viper case, right?"

Eddie sighed. "We think this is a case we could solve."

"Look, Eddie, you and your partner followed a lead without backup, and your partner got shot. You're lucky you didn't lose rank or seniority. Now, I am sure these last three months have been as dull as dishwater—"

"Yes sir. I mean, no sir." Eddie sulked.

Jacobs went on. "I think you are also looking for a chance to get back in good with Manhattan North Homicide."

"Well, sir—" Eddie said, but Jacobs held up his hand again.

"How's your caseload?"

"Light. Just got to catch up on paperwork."

"Clean it up today, and I'll talk to Captain Seville at Manhattan North." Jacobs considered it for a moment. "What the hell, I've got a homicide and two homicide detectives. *We* should work it."

"Thank you, captain."

"Just make me look good. That means no screw-ups!" Jacobs jabbed the air with his finger as Eddie left the office.

Eddie returned to his desk and gave Luis a thumbs-up as he sat.

Luis spun in his chair, raised his hands over his head, and quietly cheered, "Yessss!"

"Paperwork." Eddie turned his attention to his desktop computer. Luis gave a nod and followed suit.

Hours went by as Luis and Eddie worked to cross every "t" and dot every "i" on report after report. It wasn't exciting stuff: a petty burglary; a purse snatching; people attempting sexual liaisons in the Rambles, the wooded section of the park. They filled out enough information to keep a bevy of bureaucrats happy.

In this way, five o'clock came and went. Finally, at about seven, Eddie reached overload.

"Let's call it a night, Luis. My head is spinning."

Luis nodded. He looked tired, and his cheap suit was now a mass of wrinkles. "Yeah. We're pretty much done. We only need to write up our notes on the new case."

"Hopefully, tomorrow forensics will have a list of what was in the shopping cart and the uniforms might have some leads." Eddie pulled his tie back into place. He rolled his head, which made his neck crack. "See you in the morning."

Eddie walked to his locker and pulled out his duffle bag, taking an extra look to make sure the cane had not returned.

He walked up the stairs and out the front door into the cool spring air, as he headed for his car.

New York in the late spring was beautiful. Memorial Day was only a few weeks past, and Eddie was already wearing short sleeves and light suits. Soon, the nights would be hot and humid as the year moved fully into summer.

He left the square, steel building that was the temporary location for the "22," past a fanciful group of small buildings and former stables. Those quaint edifices had been the precinct headquarters in the past, but the city didn't possess the funds to restore the dilapidated structures.

As he walked across the 86th Street transverse road and up a wooden set of stairs to the parking lot for the police and maintenance vehicles, he noticed a sign which read:

AUTHORIZED VEHICLES ONLY

ALL OTHERS TOWED

Once in the car, he gunned the engine, pulled onto the transverse road, headed west, and drove to the West Side Highway using 96th Street as he headed north toward the George Washington Bridge.

It was a short drive from Manhattan to his home in Teaneck, New Jersey. When he couldn't make it home in time to join the rest of the family, Cerise always made up a plate of dinner and kept it warm in the oven for him.

The ride gave Eddie a chance to unwind and reflect. He was now convinced that he'd imagined the talking head. After all, a body ripped apart could make even the most seasoned cop start seeing things.

And the bizarre cane was locked safely away. It was time to get out of the Twilight Zone and just be a plain old father and husband. Eddie thought about his job. Nineteen years from a young rookie of twenty-one to a detective lieutenant. It was a long road, but one he was proud of.

Despite Wilcox's comments, Eddie knew he didn't get there by favoritism or government programs.

He'd earned it.

Eddie was driven by the memory of his father, a beat cop in the seventies, eighties, and nineties. Lawrence Berman started in Harlem, raised his son there, and told him again and again to get an education. Eddie learned that becoming a cop was a hard career for any man, especially a black man.

But the day Eddie graduated from the police academy, and he saw the pride in his father's eyes as the big man fought to stem the flow of tears, he knew he'd made the right decision.

His dad didn't last many years past that day. His big heart that cared so much for the world, coupled with excess pounds and a two-pack-a-day smoking habit, killed him when Eddie was twenty-four.

But his father was still his guiding light, an incorruptible man who cared about justice. Eddie drew inspiration from his memory and sought to make sure that if his father was looking down, he'd still be proud.

As Eddie pulled into the driveway, he wondered why Cerise didn't phone him after the doctor's appointment. His hand went to his jacket pocket for his cellular phone…but it was empty.

Eddie shut off the car and cursed. Where had he left the phone? Cerise must have been trying to get him for hours!

He remembered the duffle with his other clothes. Eddie reached into the back seat and felt around for the bag.

His hand touched wood.

His mouth fell open in shock and disbelief. He grabbed the wooden rod and lifted the walking stick, its silver handle sparkling in the dim light.

"Son of a bitch," he muttered, even as he fought to understand what happened. This cane was locked away in the evidence room. It could *not* be here!

He looked at his lit house for reassurance that he was still in Teaneck and not Wonderland, quickly got out, walked to the rear of the car, opened the trunk, threw in the cane, and slammed the lid.

He found he was breathing hard as he picked up the duffle and opened the zipper. The scent of stale urine struck him as he felt around in the bag and gingerly recovered his phone.

He zipped the bag closed, plodded to his front door, and activated the device to look at the screen. It happily lit up to let him know he'd missed five incoming calls.

He opened the door and Douglas, his youngest son, sat on the stairs with a book open in his lap. Small and dark like his mother, but with more of his father's features, he was about to turn eleven.

"Hey, Dad," Douglas said nonchalantly.

"Hey, kid." Eddie rubbed his son's short hair affectionately.

"I ain't no kid."

"I'm *not* a kid," Eddie corrected.

"Yeah, you an old man." Douglas smiled at his own joke.

"How you doing, Douglas?" Eddie said.

"Doug, Dad. You hate when grandma calls you Edward. I don' like Douglas."

"Excuse me if I call you by the name I picked."

"I learned a new trick."

"Show me."

Doug put down the book and rose from the stairs. He reached into his pocket to extract a half-dollar.

"Okay now, you gotta watch," Doug said.

A bit clumsily, Doug held the shiny coin in his left hand between the thumb and fingers. He appeared to grab it with his right hand, and with a showy gesture, opened it to show that the coin was gone.

"Hey, pretty good!" Eddie marveled. "Where did it go?"

Doug touched his father's ear with his left hand and pulled it back into view to reveal the coin at his fingertips.

"How do you do that?" Eddie said with a huge grin.

"First rule of magic, Dad." Doug returned the coin to his pocket.

"Oh yeah, that's right," Eddie recalled. "Never reveal the secret."

He sat back on the carpeted steps and picked up his book. "Mom's been callin' you."

"I just found out. Where is she?"

"Kitchen." Doug was already engrossed in his reading.

"Eddie?" Cerise's musical voice called out as she came through a door into the living room. "I've been calling and calling, then I spoke to Luis—"

"When did you call Luis?" Eddie led his wife back to the kitchen.

"A half-an-hour ago," Cerise said. Her eyes were large, and Eddie could see that a storm brewed within. "He told me you fainted at a crime scene—"

"I did *not* faint," Eddie growled too loudly, then lowered his voice. "I slipped in a puddle, that's all."

"I've been calling—"

Eddie moved close, putting his arms around his wife. "I'm sorry, baby. When I changed clothes, I didn't move my cell phone. It's been in my locker all day." He gently kissed her short, curly hair, which tickled his nose.

She looked up at him, her face a mask of concern. "You know I worry when I can't reach you."

Their lips met.

"I'm fine," Eddie hummed as he pulled back.

For a moment, they gazed into each other's eyes, until Cerise broke into a grin.

"Okay, I'll forgive you—this time."

"Be still my heart." Eddie smirked.

"I won't say that, 'cause you make my heart beat fast." Cerise went to the nearby oven and pulled out a dinner plate covered with foil. She placed it on the kitchen table where a napkin and utensils waited.

Eddie became serious as he sat. "So, what happened with Momma?"

Cerise leaned against the kitchen counter and sighed. The kitchen wasn't large, and the cabinets and countertops were not new, but the entire room was immaculate and comfortable. "Lived-in" is how Eddie liked to describe it.

Cerise's face was very still. "It's not good, Eddie."

Eddie stopped pulling the foil from his meal. He rose and went to her.

"How bad?"

A small, thin voice spoke up from the doorway. "I'm dying, Edward."

Eddie looked over to where his mother stood. As he grew up, she was always larger than life. His ample, tough momma, who made the rules and smacked his butt if he broke one. She'd shrunk with time and age, but now she seemed tiny to him. The force of her personality once made her appear larger, and now even that was shrunken.

Cerise spoke to her mother-in-law. "Shouldn't you be in bed, Momma?"

"It don' make no difference now, dearie." The older woman shambled into the room.

Eddie approached her, got down on one knee, and took her hand. "What is it, momma?"

"The cancer, it's spread," she said casually, as if they spoke of the weather.

"Isn't there something they can do?" Eddie rose and turned to his wife. "What did Doctor Ramsen say?"

Eddie's mother piped up. "He said, 'more chemo and radiation', but I said no."

"Momma!" Eddie pleaded.

"I mean it. The chemo almost killed me the last time." Her hand went to her white hair. "My hair all fell out, and I wanted to die, bad as I felt." She adjusted the ample glasses that made her eyes look huge. "Besides, it's spread, and there is too much to cut out."

"But, Momma, you can't just give up—"

"Yes, I can, Edward," she said. "Besides, I'm not giving up. I just want to die in one piece."

Eddie looked helplessly from his mother to his wife. His stomach felt as if it had been removed and replaced with a knot of wiggling creatures, each one with sharp teeth.

"H-how much time?" he stammered out.

"Three months," his mother said.

"Momma, what can I do?"

Eleanor Berman reached out and tenderly touched her son's cheek. "You always feel so responsible for everybody."

"I want to take care of you," Eddie mumbled, as tears stung his eyes. "I love you."

Eleanor shook her head sadly. "Edward, I love you, too. But sometimes there just ain't nothin' you can do."

SIX

Eddie couldn't bring himself to eat, and when he went to bed, found he was too wound up to sleep.

"Sugar?" Cerise said groggily as he got out of bed. "What's wrong?"

"Can't sleep," Eddie stated flatly.

She reached out to him and touched his arm. "Can I help?"

"No." Eddie drew her into a clumsy embrace. "I just need to clear my head."

Her hand went up to caress the back of his head. "Do you want to make love? It always relaxes you."

He took her hand and kissed it. "I just need to think."

"Oh-kay." She fell back into bed.

Eddie walked downstairs and into the hall. The room was silhouetted as light poured in from the small windows on either side of the front door. It colored the room with a bluish tint, and in the dim light, Eddie spotted his cellular phone.

He picked it up and touched it so the screen lit up. It still read "5 MISSED CALLS." He retrieved the incoming calls, each numbered in progressive order.

As he moved to the back of the house, he began to delete them. The fifth was his home number, as was the fourth, the third, the second, and—

There was a number he didn't know.

It began with a "212" area code, which meant it was from New York. The only numbers to follow were "18." This made Eddie frown. It should have been ten numerals. There was no such thing as a five-digit phone number.

He closed down his phone as he entered the kitchen and slipped it in the breast pocket of his pajamas. Walking over to the stove, he lit a fire under the teapot.

He glanced over at the microwave. Its illuminated clock glowed "11:58" in bright green.

He rubbed his eyes, which stung with fatigue. Maybe what he should do is throw on some clothes and go for a jog. It would clear his mind and tire his body.

Glancing over at the back door, he caught the glitter of metal. Instantly awake, a film of cold sweat covered his body.

Next to the back door stood the walking stick.

It was almost hidden in shadows, but there. The graceful silver ball, the thirty-six inches of ebony wood.

Eddie's mouth fell open. He tried to think of any way the cane could have escaped the car trunk to be in his kitchen in the middle of the night.

He couldn't conceive a single one.

It was like an out-of-body experience. His limbs still operated under his guidance, but he was outside of it and watched himself. He crept to the door and gingerly picked up the stick.

He heard a noise and turned, raising the cane like a weapon, the silver handle poised to strike.

Eddie realized the noise was his phone ringing.

He looked at his breast pocket, and his cellular phone was vibrating while making its pathetic electronic ring.

He lowered the cane and pulled the phone out, took another peek at the clock on the microwave. It read "12:00."

Midnight.

An involuntary shudder crept down Eddie's back. He looked at the phone still chiming in his hand. The screen read "212-18."

He hit the button. "Hello?"

He spoke with a strained voice.

"Lieutenant Berman?" a man's voice asked. It was a deep, and for some reason reminded Eddie of Santa Claus. An odd impression in June.

Eddie cleared his throat and stared at the stick in his hand. It didn't matter what curious events were happening. He was a police lieutenant and needed to act like one.

"This is Lieutenant Berman," Eddie said, his voice businesslike. "Who is this?"

There was a sigh of relief at the other end of the phone, and the man went on. "My name is Marlowe, and you don't know me."

"Then why are you calling me? Hey! How did you get my number? And where are you calling from? Two-one-two-eighteen?"

"You have many questions I cannot answer at this time. You are at home?"

Eddie looked around the room. "Never mind that—"

"In your kitchen. By the way, the water is about to boil."

At that moment, the tea kettle began to whistle, at first fitfully, but then with gathering strength.

Eddie paced over to the stove, put the cane under the arm that held the phone, and shut off the flame. The kettle stopped howling and fell into a hushed, anticipatory silence.

"How did you know?" Eddie felt the out-of-body sensation return. He walked to the kitchen window, glanced out to his backyard, and then lowered the blind.

"I know many things, but I cannot share them over the phone. Is your staff there?"

Eddie drew away from the phone and looked around the room, puzzled. "No one who works for me is here."

Eddie heard an exasperated exhale over the phone. "Not that kind of staff! I believe you are currently seeing it as an ebony cane with a silver handle?"

Eddie took the cane from under his arm and held it with his free hand. "If you know I'm in my kitchen, why can't you see I'm holding it?"

"Because it is a multidimensional manifestation of ancient energies in solid form," the voice stated, as if the answer were obvious.

"That clears that up," Eddie commented sarcastically.

"Lieutenant, I will answer all of your questions, but not tonight. Now you *must* listen. Do not leave your house under any circumstances."

Eddie felt sweat coat his body a second time. It was one thing for someone to call and say you were in your kitchen. All that took was a stakeout and a pair of binoculars. But how did this man know that he *thought* about going for a jog a few short minutes ago?

"How did you know about that?" Eddie's mouth tasted like cotton.

"Your staff—that cane—sensed it. Until initiation, the coven master is linked to the staff. That's why I called. Do not leave your house, and keep the cane with you until I can meet with you."

"I—I can't," Eddie stammered. "This multi—whatever—is evidence in a murder investigation."

"Lieutenant, unless you want someone investigating *your* murder, please heed my warning."

"Are you threatening me?" Eddie felt anger push his fear aside. "Look, buddy, I'm a cop—"

"Lieutenant, I am well aware that you are a peace officer. I am not threatening you. I am warning you, for your own good and the good of many others. If anything were to happen to you, it could be a cataclysm."

Something in the strange man's tone made Eddie sure that he was truly concerned for his welfare. "What the hell did you say your name was? Marlowe?"

"Lieutenant, I'll meet with you tomorrow and explain," Marlowe soothed. "But, please, I need you to do one more thing."

"What?"

"Hold the cane up in front of you, the ball of the cane higher than your head."

"Now look," Eddie adjusted the cane in the midst of his protests, "I don't see—"

Eddie's ability to speak left him, as the cane began to emit a red glow that surrounded first the stick, then his arm and body. Yellowish flashes of light flickered around the room, the stick vibrated in his hand, and Eddie shook so hard his teeth chattered.

As quickly as it started, the resonance stopped, which left Eddie quivering.

"There!" came the voice over the phone. "You should be safe, for now."

"What the—" was all Eddie could manage.

"I'll see you tomorrow, lieutenant. Sleep well."

"I can't— I mean, I'm not tired," Eddie said, sure he'd never sleep after this.

"Ah yes, I understand. It has been a most upsetting day. That I *can* help with."

The man spoke a few words in a tongue Eddie couldn't recognize. The way the syllables combined made it sound barely like a language at all. More like the ramblings of a madman.

"That should do it. Good night, lieutenant." Marlowe ended the connection.

The cane in Eddie's hand began to glow with a much softer, almost pink light and vibrated in his hand again. It shook him gently in a relaxed way, as if he were being rocked in a cradle.

Everything faded to black.

SEVEN

Eddie was still being rocked, as if on a cloud. Then the shaking grew stronger, and Eddie opened his eyes.

Sunlight poured in through the drapes of his living room, and he lay in his favorite lounge chair.

"Sugar," Cerise said. "Come on, you've got to get up."

Eddie leapt up from the inclined chair and immediately fell back again. His sudden vault threw the recliner off-balance, the chair tipped over, and Eddie tumbled headfirst onto the floor.

Cerise jumped out of the way with an "oh!" of surprise, as Eddie somersaulted over and landed flat on his back. She knelt down and gently rubbed her husband's face.

"You all right?" Cerise worried.

"Yeah, yeah, I'm fine." Eddie gingerly got up and untangled himself from the blanket that usually rested on the sofa.

He wondered how he got here; his last memory was in the kitchen. How did he walk into the living room and cover himself with the blanket? His eyes shot around to find the cane lying on the floor next to the tipped-over chair.

Cerise said, "I was concerned when I got up and you weren't there." She and Eddie lifted the chair upright.

"Sorry, I was going to have tea. I guess I fell asleep." Eddie pulled her into an embrace. Even though he'd slept in a chair, he felt more rested than he had in days.

"Don't you want to sleep with me anymore?" Cerise teased.

"If you need verification, I could take you upstairs and prove my love," he whispered into her ear.

She gently slapped his shoulder, smiling. "You're so bad. The boys are up. I have to go to work, and so do you!"

"My first duty is to you," Eddie spoke with a gleam in his eye. "And I *always* do my duty." He was kidding but decided he could be persuaded if his wife was willing. He felt good.

She searched his eyes. "What got into my big, black man?"

Eddie grinned. "Some sleep?"

"If you get home at a reasonable hour, maybe I could take you up on that offer. Now go, get ready."

The spell broken, Eddie felt the weight of all his responsibilities descend back on top of him. "Will Momma be all right?"

"I'm only gone for a few hours, Eddie. If—*when*—she gets worse, we'll hire a nurse," Cerise tactfully pointed out.

"Right, right," Eddie replied, not liking the idea.

"I'll start coffee." She strode toward the kitchen.

"Thanks, baby." Eddie turned, scooped up the cane, and started up the stairs to take a shower.

"What's that?" a voice said as Eddie neared the top of the stairs.

Eddie jumped. "Morning, William. Don't scare your old man like that."

"Sorry, Dad," William said.

His oldest son, now fourteen, stood on a step slightly above him. Like himself, the lanky youth was a morning person, dressed and ready, while his younger brother still failed to rise from the bed.

The boy was not as tall as his father, only about five-foot-seven. But Eddie was sure he wasn't done growing. He possessed a round face and his skin was not as fair as his father but lighter than his brother. He did, however, have his mother's striking good looks, and Eddie knew he would be a "chick magnet" in a few short years.

Just don't get one pregnant, Eddie thought. *Go to college, make a life, then decide to have children.*

"Hello? Earth to Dad?" William teased.

"Sorry." Eddie returned his attention to his son.

"What's with the stick?"

Eddie looked at the cane in his hand as if seeing it for the first time. "It's part of an investigation."

William stared at the stick in surprise. "You bringing your work home?"

"Just this once." Eddie spun the stick between his fingers with a flourish. "Besides, I have a teenager in the house. I might need it to keep you in line."

Doug looked at the stick and whistled. "That would leave a mark. Can I see it?"

"Sure," Eddie said and held it out. As William reached for it, Eddie was possessed by an irresistible urge and pulled it back from the young man's grasp.

"I mean…later," Eddie cautioned, surprised by his own actions. "You have to get dressed."

"I *am* dressed, Dad," William blurted, also startled by his father's behavior.

"I mean, *I* have to get dressed." Eddie sauntered down the hall for the bathroom.

In the shower, Eddie tried to understand his reaction to the cane being touched. He let Vasquez handle it the previous day. Something about that curious man on the phone calling at midnight. What was his name? Monroe? Mordred?

Eddie stepped out onto the bath mat, picked up the nearby cane, and looked at it again. "Marlowe!" he said aloud.

He smiled. That was the man's name. He dried himself with the towel, and then used it to clear the mist-shrouded mirror. He turned the tap on the sink and threw his shaving brush in the basin.

"You called?" a voice said.

Eddie fell back, his rear end smacking the tub as he sat down hard to avoid being completely bowled over.

It was the voice from the phone!

He grabbed his bathrobe and pulled it on and stared up at the ceiling.

"H-Hello?" Eddie stuttered as he studied the white ceiling to see where the voice emanated. He held up the cane, the reassuring weight of it in his right hand.

"I'm over here," Marlowe snapped impatiently.

Eddie looked at the mirror. Instead of his reflection, there was a white man with a snowy beard and hair. His eyes were a beautiful shade of blue and seemed to possess an intelligence as old as the world.

Eddie's mouth fell open. He screwed his eyes shut, shook his head, and tentatively peeked again.

The man in the mirror watched him. Eddie now could see that the background of the room behind the long-haired man was a different room, not a reflection of his bathroom.

A weak "How?" was all Eddie could muster.

"You called me," Marlowe explained. "I hope it was important. I *do* have a full day."

He could see that the old man was wearing a red, satin coat. What used to be called a *smoking jacket*.

"Wha—" is all that came out of Eddie's mouth.

Marlowe nodded, as if Eddie not only stated an important question, but a complete sentence.

"Ah yes, I asked to see you today. How is this afternoon for you?"

"I-I—" Eddie found it hard to draw breath.

"Oh, of course, you don't know your schedule yet," Marlowe said amiably. "I understand. How about five PM?"

"Where?" Eddie still tried to accept that he held a conversation with the man in the mirror.

"The arch where the murder took place. We both know where it is. It should be safe before dark."

"I-I—" Eddie stuttered.

"Good!" Marlowe approved. "See you then, and please make sure to have the cane with you."

No sooner was he done than the mirror glazed over silver for a moment, and Eddie's face reflected back at him.

The bearded man was gone.

The change was so astounding, and Eddie's face, wide-eyed and frightened, startled its owner a second time.

He stood for a minute staring at the mirror, steam rising from the sink where his shaving brush floated.

"I'm losing my mind," was all he could manage.

EIGHT

Eddie ate his breakfast in a dream. Cerise noticed but let it go. She decided it was his way of coping with his mother's illness.

But his mother was the last thing on Eddie's mind. As he got in his car and drove in clogged arteries of traffic. He found his attention was focused on the cane, which lay on the passenger's seat.

If it did any more vanishing tricks, he wanted to see it with his own eyes.

For the cane to show up wherever he went was strange, but the man in the mirror was impossible. A part of him still hoped it was an elaborate hoax. His surprise party was only three days away. Could his wife have set this up? She could've gotten Luis in on it—

He dismissed the idea. Cerise would never do anything this bizarre with his mother sick.

A twinge of guilt smacked Eddie in the gut. He'd been so focused on the strange cane, he didn't even speak to his momma before he left for work. How could he be so damn inconsiderate? His father always insisted that he treat his mother with respect. Now she really needed him, and he was worried about a stupid piece of wood.

He exited off the West Side Highway and down West End Avenue to 86th Street. He soon entered the park transverse road and pulled into the authorized parking lot.

As he climbed out of the car, he grabbed the troublesome twig. He felt an overwhelming desire to throw it into the woods and lifted it above his head to assume the stance he used when he threw javelin in high school. It was well-balanced, and he could probably chuck it a good thirty feet.

He cocked back his arm, took aim at a tree…then promptly stopped dead as an idea struck him.

A small smile twisted his mouth.

There was one way he could figure this out. If there were several of these expensive-looking canes being moved from place to place, then the one he put in evidence would still be there.

He walked into the "22" and strode up the extra floor to the evidence room. There, behind the small opening, looking as if he had never left, sat Hank, who leaned on his bench with an open newspaper.

"Hey, Hank," Eddie greeted.

"Mornin', Lew." Hank looked up over the edge of his glasses, balanced precariously on the tip of his nose.

Eddie rubbed the silver handle on the cane and turned his body so that his leg blocked Hank's view.

"I need to take a look at that cane I brought you yesterday. You know where it is?"

"Sure do, Lew," Hank said. "Safe as a babe in its mother's arms."

"Could you bring it to me?"

"You gotta sign on the line, Lew." Hank took a clipboard to quickly write some numbers then turned it for Eddie to sign.

Eddie waited until Hank turned his back and switched the cane from his right hand to his left, still blocked with his body.

He signed his name and smiled up at Hank, who walked to the far end of the cluttered evidence room. Eddie could easily see him past the rows of metal shelves.

Hank unlocked a door.

Eddie stood nervously and rubbed the orb of the cane. He really *wanted* another cane to be in there. Then there would be a logical explanation.

Hank reached into the room.

Eddie leaned forward into the opening to watch Hank's every move. Hank pulled something out and walked back toward Eddie.

In his hand was the ebony walking stick.

Eddie's mouth twisted into a big grin. He'd been right!

"This the one, Lew?" Hank asked as he drew near.

"No, I think *this* is the one." Eddie raised his left hand with a little "Aha!"

His hand was empty.

The walking stick, which was there a scant moment earlier, was gone. Eddie looked around the floor then patted his legs and suit jacket, as if the cane had folded up like a magician's collapsing wand and was now hidden in one of his pockets, ready to be revealed for the act finale.

"This a joke, Lew?" Hank griped behind the caged opening.

Eddie whirled around, startled. "I guess it is." He forced a smile that felt as if his face was wearing a mask. "Yeah, I'm just playing with you, Hank."

Eddie tried to keep himself from shivering as he turned to walk out of the room.

"Hey, Lew." Hank held out the walking stick. "You want this?"

Eddie shook his head. "No, I don't need it until later."

Hank shrugged his thin shoulders. "Suit yourself." He picked up the clipboard, crossing off the last entry as Eddie left.

Walking back to the locked room, Hank muttered to himself, "The Lew is crackin' up."

Which reflected Eddie's own point of view perfectly.

NINE

"Hey, Eddie," Luis said as Eddie entered the detective's bullpen. "You okay? I got a call from your wife last night."

Eddie waved his hand dismissively. "Why'd you tell her I fainted?"

"Eddie, I meant fell. It just came out that way. My mouth moves faster than my brain."

Luis' eyes reminded Eddie of a big puppy. "No big deal. Cerise was worried about my momma."

"She gonna be okay?"

He met his partner's eyes. "It's not good."

Luis's expression grew dark. "The cancer?"

All Eddie could do was nod. "Luis, let me ask you. If Cerise were trying to pull a practical joke on me, you would tell me, right?"

Luis frowned. "What are you talking about?"

"Nothing." Eddie exhaled heavily. "It's just been a rough twenty-four hours."

"The coroner finished the autopsy." Luis handed Eddie a note from the phone log.

He read it. "She wants to meet with us?"

"Said there was some peculiar shit with this case."

"I don't think Doctor Beverly Warren put it quite that way."

Luis shrugged. "Maybe not, but the message is the same. She won't finish her report until we visit her."

Eddie shoved the note into his pocket. "Okay, you drive."

The morgue for the City of New York was known by the fanciful title, "The Chief Medical Examiner's Building," as if the city's preeminent forensic pathologist was also an investor in Manhattan real estate.

Built in 1960, the six-story structure resided on First Avenue and 30th Street. The building's most striking feature was the side which faced east was windowless. Other than that, it blended in with the neighborhood with little fanfare or attention.

However, it handled more cases in a single week than most city morgues attended to in years. Due to this volume, state-of-the-art computers, X-rays, and medical equipment took up entire floors. There were multiple autopsy rooms and enough refrigerators to hold hundreds of deceased.

Eddie and Luis parked in a special lot assigned for police cars, ambulances, and hearses. They walked into the large building and upstairs to the office of the assistant medical examiner.

Doctor Beverly Warren waited for them, as Eddie had called en route. She wore green hospital scrubs and a white lab coat with an official city ID which hung around her neck. Her hair was chestnut brown and her skin pale. She possessed stunning green eyes that Eddie decided must be enhanced by colored contact lenses.

"Good morning, gentlemen," Beverly said as way of greeting, glanced up from a clipboard then made another hasty pencil mark.

"What do you have, doctor?" Eddie asked.

With her eyes on the clipboard, Beverly smiled. "Quick, to the point, direct. No wonder you're a lieutenant."

Luis piped up. "Why'd we haveta come all the way down here? Couldn't you just e-mail us?"

Beverly gave Luis a smirk. "Whiny and annoyed. Check the attitude or you'll be stuck a sergeant, Vasquez."

"I have to agree with Luis, Beverly," Eddie insisted.

They knew each other well and had worked on enough cases together for almost a decade. Beverly arrived fresh from Ohio to the New York City coroner's office when they met. They had become comfortable with each other over the years and knew when they didn't have to use titles.

"What is so important you wanted a personal meeting?"

With a tiny movement of her head, she indicated her office, and the two men entered the small, windowless enclosure. The fluorescent lights were on, which gave the room a green pallor.

Beverly peeked down the hall, stepped in, and then carefully shut the door.

"You afraid to be seen with us, doc?" Luis was surprised at the stealth.

"No, I was planning to seduce the pair of you, and I hate to have my fun interrupted," Beverly deadpanned.

"Beverly, we have a case to solve," Eddie urged.

She picked up a file from her desk and handed it to Eddie. "This is my only copy. It does not leave this office."

"What's the big deal?" Vasquez muttered.

"This is about the homeless guy who was dismembered?" Eddie asked.

"That's right," Beverly declared. "I have to clean up my report before I submit it officially. I understand it's your case?"

"So far," Eddie affirmed.

"Glad to see you back where you belong. I've actually missed you two the last three months," she said.

"We missed you as well," Eddie assured, unable to contain a smile.

"Read the prelim."

Eddie opened the folder and began leafing through the papers.

Luis peeked over Eddie's shoulder. "Looks like an autopsy."

"Now I know what I missed: your immediate grasp of the situation, Vasquez," Beverly taunted.

"How were the victim's limbs removed?" Eddie pawed through the papers.

"Torn," Beverly stated.

"*Madre de Dios*," Vasquez whispered. "Like you thought, Eddie."

"What was remarkable was how it was done," Beverly went on. "In the Middle Ages, a form of execution was called 'Drawn and Quartered' in which the limbs of the condemned were each tied to separate horses who were sent galloping off in different directions."

"How do you know this stuff?" Luis grimaced.

"Too much free time," Beverly responded without missing a beat. "That technique worked, but it left rope burns on the wrists and ankles."

"I take it there were none on the victim," Eddie speculated.

"And no horses at the scene?" Luis added.

"There were hoof marks, but not from a horse," Beverly commented. "Take a look at these."

She picked up a stack of photos from the desk and showed one of a disembodied arm. There were several small, egg-shaped bruises along the arm.

"What left those marks?" Eddie wondered.

"The closest thing I can guess is that his arm was grabbed by a giant hand. Look at the other side," Beverly said, neatly flipping to a picture of the opposite side of the arm. "There is only one mark here, and it is more oblong."

"Like a thumb," Eddie concluded.

"Bravo, lieutenant," Beverly said. "The evidence suggests that the limbs were torn off by a rather large hand."

"How big?" Luis challenged.

"The hand would have to be…" Beverly pulled a small ruler from her pocket and held it up to the photo. "Bigger than a baseball mitt."

"Big hand," Eddie blurted.

"That's not all. Due to the indention marks, I would say that the hand possessed very sharp fingernails, like claws."

"Claws?" Luis repeated.

"Claws!" Beverly asserted.

"How strong would this guy have to be?" Eddie considered.

Beverly shifted her eyes to the ceiling thoughtfully. "Considering leverage and angles? Tall as well as powerful."

"How big?" Luis chimed in.

"What was the height of the tunnel?" Beverly asked as she observed the section of the drop ceiling directly above her head.

Eddie shrugged. "Riftstone Arch? In the center, about eleven feet—maybe twelve."

Beverly brought her eyes back to the detectives. "I would speculate that the murderer would be about as tall as that tunnel."

Eddie and Luis exchanged a glance. There was a long silence.

"That's not possible," Luis protested.

"It gets worse." Beverly plucked the report out of Eddie's hands and pointed to a specific page. "How does a guy with hands that large walk away without leaving big footprints?"

"No footprints?" Luis said.

Beverly shrugged. "Hoofprints were all CSU found."

"I thought you said there were no horses," Eddie said.

"It is a bridle path, but these prints weren't from any horse. They were cloven hooves, like a pig."

"I got it!" Luis yelped. "We need to look for a really tall pig with big hands."

"The prints don't come in or out of the tunnel. They appear there then they're gone. Both of you left tracks; so did the victim. The only other marks were left by a snake, which was unusual as well."

"Why?" Eddie asked.

"Because the snake moved through the gravel in a pattern that suggests a sidewinder, which is a desert snake. You don't find them in New York."

"Let me get this straight," Eddie griped. "A giant shows up, kills our vic then disappears?"

Luis frowned. "Could the dirt be too hard to take impressions?"

"I double-checked the scene photos and the reports," Beverly said. "That arch is at the bottom of a dip in the road. There are puddles down there, poor drainage. The gravel and dirt are soft, wet, and take impressions very well. Here, see."

She pointed to a photo that showed several body parts and the gray dirt under them. She pointed with her finger to circles that were around indentations in the earth, each one a different color. ""Here are your footprints, which I highlighted in yellow, and Vasquez's green. Then the victim's prints, blue; the cloven hoof marks, red; and these are the snake's tracks, orange."

Eddie shook his head. "How do you sneak in, rip someone apart, and get out without footprints?"

"I have no idea." Beverly picked up another page and held it out to Eddie. "Now, I took a look at his internal organs. How old do you think he was?"

"Hard to say with his head a different place than the rest of him," Luis pondered.

"Anywhere from sixty to eighty, I'd say," Eddie theorized.

"I did a biopsy on his liver, and it was as vital as a twenty year old's."

Luis said, "We *are* talking about the John Doe, right?"

"Yes, and his muscle tone, along with his other organs, suggest a man who wasn't more than thirty and lived like a monk."

"Anything show up on the tox report?" Eddie asked.

"No drugs, no alcohol, though there were trace amounts of Artemisia Absinthium in the digestive track."

"Isn't that a type of liquor?" Luis offered.

"Yeah, that stuff—Absinthe," Eddie suggested.

"The liquor is made from the plant, but he ingested just the herb, also known as wormwood. I'm damned if I know why." Beverly again leafed through the folder to extract a single sheet of paper. "Now for the coup de grâce."

"What is that?" Luis questioned.

"A metallurgist report." Beverly handed the page to Eddie.

"You checkin' the weather?" Luis frowned.

"Not a meteorologist, Luis, a metallurgist—a guy who studies metals." Eddie read the report and shrugged. "So what?"

"Did you read it?" Beverly asked.

"Doctor Warren, this report is very technical. Can you put it in layman's terms?"

Beverly inhaled sharply and twisted up her face. "Actually, I don't know if I can."

"Try?" Eddie grunted.

"Unless it makes things even stranger," Luis added.

Beverly's face relaxed. "Okay, I think if I tell you how I got there—" she paused then started in. "Several of the man's teeth were gold."

"Not too unusual," Eddie said.

"No, except for one thing. I pulled the teeth, and they were not gold crowns or even dental implants. The gold was growing out of his jaw. It was unique, a really rich color I'd never seen before. So I extracted the four in his mouth. All in all, his teeth were in great shape."

Luis shook his head. "So he had gold in his mouth. What's the big deal?"

"According to Hal—he's the metallurgist—it's a very big deal." Beverly picked up speed with excitement. "He told me that this was the purest gold he'd ever seen. Nowadays, gold has to be pulled out of the ground with arsenic. It takes a lot of soil to get a little gold, and it's loaded with impurities," Beverly said, her gaze shifting from man to man. "Not this guy's teeth!"

"I don't get it," Luis conceded.

"According to Hal, the gold in that man's mouth could not have been mined by modern methods. In fact, he has no explanation how this quality of gold ended up in someone's mouth."

"I think I follow," Eddie said. "Gold that pure would be very valuable. How did a homeless guy get it?"

"There's one other theory." Beverly suddenly looked uncomfortable. "I went online, and there are these cults where when the reverend is preaching, gold falls from the air."

"What?" Luis said, even more annoyed.

"It's right here." She held up a color photo of a man with gold teeth. "They also have records of faith healings in which damaged teeth were—ta daa!—transformed to gold!"

"What you're suggesting," Eddie hypothesized, "is that this guy's teeth turned into gold, like Midas."

"King Midas?" Luis frowned. "But that's just a fairy tale."

"Technically, it's a myth," Beverly clarified. "But so far, it's the only explanation that fits."

TEN

Between the traffic and a quick stop for lunch, it was afternoon by the time Eddie and Luis got back to the "22." Eddie's head still reeled from unanswered questions and the dreadful awareness that he didn't have any idea how to even begin to work the case.

Usually, he and Luis used dogged persistence and those sudden flashes of insight that a detective depended on. They would quickly figure out a motive, pursue a suspect, or at the very least get a general direction for the investigation.

He pulled Luis into the conference room near their desks and poured them both coffee.

"Any donuts?" Luis looked over at the coffee table hopefully.

"You need donuts?" Eddie said. "We just had lunch."

"I haveta keep my strength up." Luis took a Styrofoam cup from Eddie.

"I'm telling you, Luis, this case—*this case…*" Eddie shook his head in dismay.

"Nothing is fitting together," Luis sympathized as he took a large swallow. "So what if we don't solve it?"

"What?" Eddie said, surprised.

"A homeless guy ends up dead. It's not like he's got family who want to know what happened."

"Damn it!" Eddie slapped the conference table with an open hand. "I hate to settle. I hate saying the victim wasn't important."

"But, Eddie, I'm just being reasonable," Luis pleaded, his hands open in an imploring gesture.

"Come on, Luis, we asked for this case."

"You heard Doc Warren. What are we gonna do, go looking for a twelve-foot guy with claws?"

"He would be easy to spot," Eddie said, tightlipped.

"Uniforms have questioned people in the buildings that face the park. No one heard or saw anything."

"Then we start over. Did anyone talk to the doorman at the restaurant?"

"Tavern on the Green?" Luis reasoned with a nod. "I could try to talk with him after four. That's when the shifts change."

Eddie caught his reflection in the one-way glass at the far end of the room and remembered the assignation he'd made with the man in the mirror.

Eddie spoke as if in a trance. "I have an appointment with someone who told me he could explain it."

"Really?" Luis brightened as he rose. "That would help."

Eddie shook himself. The bizarre feeling left, and he turned to his partner. "Any other ideas?"

"Hey, how about the homeless in the park?" Luis suggested. "Someone has to know the vic, right?"

"Good thinking," Eddie responded.

"And bring that cane," Luis said as they threw out their cups and returned to their desks.

Eddie was taken aback. "The cane, why?"

"If they'd seen him, they might recognize it and know how he came by it."

Eddie nodded. "I'll go upstairs and sign it out."

Luis caught his arm and pointed. "Isn't that it next to your desk?"

Eddie turned to see the fanciful stick right beside his chair.

"Uh…right." Eddie gingerly grabbed the cane and followed his large partner out the door.

They walked north through the park, the day sunnier than the previous. The air carried the crisp scent of late spring and growing things.

The last few months, working out of the Central Park precinct, Eddie had been given a real chance to explore the urban oasis. He could see the seasons change when spring came alive, and he'd walked through the guilefully devised wilderness of the Ramble, the expansive open space of the Great Lawn, and the rustic environment of the North Woods. It made him feel more at one with nature. He no longer thought of the park as merely an obstacle in the middle of the island that separated the East Side from the West.

People strolled the concrete walkways, some in business suits and power ties, many in shorts and T-shirts. Eddie and Luis headed north toward the Conservatory Gardens. The gardens were a fenced-in section above 103rd Street, a formally designed quadrangle of plants, fountains, and statuary.

It was used for outdoor weddings of every type and denomination. It was not uncommon on a Saturday in the spring to see a white-clad bride pass a Buddhist couple in traditional garb with the bride in fiery-red silk.

Unknown to most of the visitors, outside the fence was a site where the homeless camped out when good weather came around. They were hidden by the underbrush and trees, and the iron fence gave them a modicum of privacy and a place to hang makeshift tents.

Eddie reflected on the difficult life the ragged men and women endured. Often mentally ill or suffering from drug or alcohol dependence, they lived a nomadic existence. They carried their meager possessions in carts or bags and would spend the winter months in shelters. Once spring and summer arrived, they would return to the streets and their self-destructive habits.

You could find them throughout the park, panhandling or just wandering around having animated conversations with invisible adversaries—or perhaps God. Some only muttered to themselves. They all looked unkempt, smelled bad, and were as much a part of the city landscape as the Empire State Building.

Luis pointed at several very large cardboard boxes set up in a remote area not far from a guilefully hidden dumpster.

"Over there," Luis pointed, and they started in the direction of the boxes. Eddie carried the cane and used it as he walked. The handle felt warm and reassuring in his hand.

"Man, how can they choose to live like this?" Luis considered.

"With some it's not a choice," Eddie responded as they drew nearer.

"That's crap," Luis said. "It's always a choice. You *choose* to become an alcoholic or do drugs. That stuff don't force itself down your throat."

"You don't think alcoholism is a disease?" Eddie queried.

"Not on your life. My father was a drunk, and so was my uncle. Me, I only touch the stuff at parties, and I stop at two. I could drink more—I like it—but I just think of my old man and my kids. I know when to quit."

"You didn't know when to quit having kids." Eddie smirked.

Luis grinned as well. "I sure as hell ain't giving that up. Besides, I love my kids—"

"And your wife, repeatedly," Eddie joked.

Both men chuckled as they arrived at the first cardboard box. It was emblazoned on the side with the word FRIGIDAIRE and must have been used to ship the largest refrigerator ever manufactured. It was over seven feet tall, ten feet wide, and just as deep.

"Hello, anyone home?" Eddie yelled, finding a piece of black cloth stapled to a makeshift opening that shielded the resident from the outside world.

"Get thee 'way," a reedy voice muttered back.

"Police!" Luis knocked on the cardboard wall gently.

"You gonna move me?" the invisible resident worried.

"No," Eddie explained. "We want to ask some questions."

"I spoke to the police," the voice grunted. "I know naught." The box jiggled a bit as if the person inside shifted around.

"If you could, just for a moment," Eddie implored.

The box stopped.

"We are trying to find out about a man who was killed." Luis felt his frustration rise. "Look, it's for your own protection. He was a homeless guy."

Luis turned to Eddie and spoke in a low voice, "Man, what a stink. Do they *all* have to reek like that?"

Eddie was abruptly aware of the odor coming from the cardboard abode. There was the stench of urine—that was the strongest—coupled with stale body odor, but there was also something pungent, like burning hay or stinkweed.

"Is it a man or a woman?" Eddie quietly asked Luis.

Luis shrugged.

Eddie knocked on the cardboard one more time, this time using the head of the cane. The box shivered, and a head poked out. The face belonged to a wizened woman with more than wrinkles—crevices—carved into her face. Her hair was short and curled wildly, a combination of gray and white. She looked up at Eddie with a toothless expression of surprise.

"Thee t'aint the man 'twas here earlier!"

"No, ma'am." Eddie stepped back to avoid the fresh gust of redolence that exuded from the box when the woman looked out. "Did he ask about a homeless man who was killed?"

"That be," the woman snorted, yet still remained within the safety of her box.

"What did he look like?" Luis inquired. "Maybe he's from our precinct?"

The old woman cackled an unsettling laugh. "If he t'were, you'd best deny it."

The woman pushed the black cloth away and stepped out. She was average height, wearing shabby clothing that looked piled in layers over a heavy body. A small cloud of gray smoke trailed her out.

"T'was a big, white man an' a most grievous ass-hole!" she spoke the word as if it were two words, with the accent on the first syllable. "Pardon my language, but I speak plain."

Luis and Eddie exchanged a knowing glance.

"Was his name Wilcox?" Eddie ventured.

"Somethin' like tha'." The woman's eyes shifted to the stick in Eddie's hand. "Now, where didst thee get tha'?"

Eddie held the cane up. "It belonged to the victim. We were hoping you might recognize it— and could tell us about the owner."

She stepped closer and shot out a hand to grasp the stick. Eddie started, fought the urge to pull it from her, but held tight as she caressed it. Her hand was like leather, with large veins which popped from it, the fingernails grimy but long and claw-like. She rubbed the ball at the top and closed her eyes for a moment.

"Thou hast been summoned," she rasped, her eyes still shut. Eddie was amazed that this phrase slipped from her.

"I've been…what?" Eddie replied, the back of his neck tingling as if a hundred small spiders crawled up his spine.

"Summoned!" she hissed emphatically. "Come in. Thou must come in."

She moved her hand to his free wrist, took it in a grip of iron, and pulled him toward her box.

"Lieutenant?" Luis, alarmed, moved toward him.

"No," Eddie asserted over his shoulder. "She might know something. If I'm in trouble, I'll yell."

The woman pulled Eddie past the cloth partition and into the box. The inside was pitch black, and smoke misted around Eddie's feet. The horrific odor was overpowering, and Eddie coughed.

"Sorry." The woman waved her hand.

Immediately, the stink was gone, replaced with the ambrosial scent of incense.

"Come, come." She pulled him farther.

Eddie realized that the room around him was much larger than the inside of a cardboard box.

The woman pushed aside another cloth, which slapped Eddie in the face as he went through it.

Before him was a large hall.

Though mist-shrouded with the sweet smelling herbs, it was lit with glowing purple fixtures built into the structure. The walls were elaborately decorated with unusual symbols that glowed yellow.

Before them stood a large table with a heavy, brocade tablecloth. Upon it sat a large crystal ball in a metal holder, glowing with an inner fire.

The woman released Eddie's hand and went to the far side of the table to sit in a large throne-like chair, piled high with pillows.

Eddie stared at the huge room around him. The ceiling ran above his head at least twelve feet, and there were two sofas and a divan hiding in the shadows.

"Where the hell are we?" Eddie wondered aloud.

"Sh! Quiet thou!" the woman whispered and sat forward in the massive chair to stare into the crystal ball. She reached behind her head and pulled up a kind of hood which covered her face with shadows.

Eddie also noticed that her clothes no longer appeared to be rags, but a flowing purple robe that swathed her hefty shape.

"Luis!" Eddie croaked.

"Shush now!" The woman concentrated on the ball.

Eddie turned in a full circle as he tried to fathom how the cardboard box had become this magnificent edifice.

"But…where? How?"

"'Tis merely fourth-dimensional physics. Now be still!" The woman consulted the glowing sphere. Then, almost as an afterthought, she added, "Thou carries Riftstone's staff. It has summoned thee!"

"Who? I mean, yes, I found the cane at the Riftstone Arch," Eddie explained.

"Ah!" The woman left the massive chair, walked over to Eddie, and grabbed his head in her wizened hands. She stared deeply into his eyes. "You know little."

"You're telling me." Eddie grimaced, her grip almost painful.

She let go and backed away, an unhappy expression on her face. "I have shown more than thou shouldst see!"

Then she turned, did what looked like a little jig, and smiled. "Oh well, ye might as well get used to it!" She let loose her cackling laugh and spun again.

Eddie could see that she was now dressed in purple silk adorned with glittering stars and moons.

"I am Frisha!" she stated with a wave of her hand, and a large, wooden spoon flew off the table and into her palm.

So quickly that Eddie thought his eyes played tricks on him, the spoon grew longer and thicker. It became a gnarled wooden staff that stood a head taller than the woman.

"Lieutenant!" a voice echoed as if it was a hundred miles away.

"Luis?" Eddie yelled back, momentarily comforted by his partner's voice.

"You all right in there?" Luis's voice was strangely amplified in the huge room.

"Say thou art fine," Frisha whispered.

"I art fine—I mean, I am fine! Be out in a minute." Then he added under his breath, "I hope."

Frisha nodded her head and smiled her toothless grin. Her dental hygiene hadn't improved.

"When do ye meet Marlowe?" she said.

"Marlowe?" Eddie was shocked that she knew his name. "Uh…at five."

"Do not be late, and goest by thyself." She lowered her voice. "Thy friend does not walk the path."

"I don't know anything about a path." Eddie tried to think how to get answers from the strange old girl. "Look, I'm here about a murder. I want to find who killed…Did you say his name was Riftstone? Like the arch?"

She nodded, and her face bent in a small, warm smile. "What is thy name?"

Eddie experienced that chill on his neck again. "Aren't you the fortune teller?"

"I know all, I see all, and I wash my clothes in All," she said. Then, she cackled at her joke, as if it were the funniest thing ever said. Eddie stood dumbfounded as tears of mirth rolled down her cheeks.

"You see?" Frisha chuckled and fought to regain her breath. "I see all, I use the detergent named 'All.'"

"I get it," Eddie deadpanned.

Frisha's grin faded. "Thou hast no sense of humor."

"Okay, look!" Eddie demanded, his frustration finally getting the best of him. "I'm Lieutenant Eddie Berman. Can you tell me anything you know about Riftstone? I'm trying to find his killer."

Frisha nodded gravely. "Thou will indeed confront he who slew him. There be naught the mortal police can do."

"The *mortal* police?" Eddie repeated.

"Ye shall understand once thou meets Marlowe. I can tell thee no more. Ye must be initiated—"

"Initiated?" Eddie spat back, annoyed. "Into what, the loony bin?"

"'Tis not my place to say. However, Freddie—"

"Eddie!"

"I be a seer known far and wide. Ye may wish to seek my counsel in the future."

She gave a small bow, using the large stick to support herself.

"Lady, I'm after answers right now."

Frisha smiled again. "That is what we all seek. But now, thy destiny seeks thee." She grabbed his arm once again and pulled Eddie across the room. For an old lady, she possessed a remarkable grip.

Eddie went through the curtain, felt the fabric slide against his face, and then exited, blinking into the sunlight back in Central Park.

Luis stood waiting with concern. "You okay?"

Eddie nodded and smiled wanly as he fought an overwhelming sense of disorientation. He looked at Frisha, but the woman was once again the ragged hag. Gone was the fancy cloak, the mysterious hood, and the wooden staff.

"Thank ye, officer." Frisha waved the large wooden spoon she clutched. "I wish I couldst tell thee more, but 'tis all I know." She turned, gave Eddie a wink, and added, "I din't like that other policeman. He din't have manners like thee."

She shuffled back into her box, and the awful urine-body-odor-burning-stinkweed smell assailed Eddie's nostrils.

"You sure you're all right?" Luis asked.

"Yeah." Eddie tried to think of a plausible story. He couldn't tell Luis what he'd seen; it was crazy. An image of himself sitting in a straitjacket, cross-legged on the floor of a padded cell ran through his mind. He quashed the brief fantasy and said aloud, "Maybe it was the stench—"

"Must have been worse in there." Luis began to lead Eddie away toward the fresh air of the North Meadow. "She know anything?"

"Not much," Eddie lied. She knew something but told nothing. She also used that word again: *summoned.*

Eddie glanced at his watch. It was quarter-to-five. "Look, I'm going back to the murder scene. Can you go talk to the doorman at the Tavern?"

Luis nodded. "Sure. I want to see if Wilcox was poking around there, too."

"I don't know, Luis." Eddie shook his head as he held up the cane. "Strange sticks, magic gold teeth, stinky old ladies. It would serve him right if we did give him this case."

ELEVEN

Eddie arrived at Riftstone Arch with three minutes to spare. The crime scene tape had been removed, and the arch was open to the public.

He approached the mouth of the tunnel from the north and peered in. The sun wouldn't set for another two hours, yet shadows lurked within.

He decided to wait outside until the bearded man arrived. He leaned with his back against the cold stone of the tunnel.

"Is it always dark in there?" Eddie muttered.

"Yes, indeed it is," a voice echoed.

Eddie made a sound of surprise that was somewhere between "Wha!" and "Ahh!" and stared into the gloom a second time.

A man stood inside. He was about five-foot-five, with white hair and a trimmed beard. He wore a suit and tie with a black hat on his head set at a rakish angle. In his left hand was a tall staff, similar to the one Frisha had conjured. An unearthly light shone on its top, giving a slight illumination to the tunnel.

It was the man from the mirror!

Eddie glanced about to make sure no one watched, then slowly entered.

"Hello, Edward. It is a pleasure to meet you in person." The man extended his right hand. "I'm Marlowe."

Eddie took his hand and shook curtly. "Bad idea to sneak up on a police officer, Mister Marlowe."

"No 'mister,' just Marlowe," he said as a smile played on his face. "I knew you wouldn't shoot me, Edward."

"It's Eddie. Or if you want formal, lieutenant."

Marlowe chuckled. "I'm afraid your title means little, Eddie. But your name and the name you prefer? There is much power in it."

"Would you mind not speaking in riddles? I'm a little tired of it. First last night, when you phoned me. Then this morning. How did you get into my mirror?"

Marlowe shrugged. "You called me."

"I met a crazy lady, Frisha, and she told me—"

"Ah! You have met the seer?" Delight spread on his face. "How is she?"

"How the hell should I know? One minute she's a hag living in a box, then we're in this huge room, and she's in purple silk."

Marlowe made a clucking sound of dissatisfaction and smiled. "Always a flamboyant one, our Frisha."

"Yeah, well, she didn't tell me anything. Just spoke with a bunch of 'thee's' and 'thou's.'"

"We call that manner of discourse 'Oldspeak', Eddie."

"Great! Then she says I have to talk to you."

"I understand your consternation," Marlowe said, "and I am afraid I am not sure how to proceed. No one has been summoned for almost five hundred years."

"There's that word again. What does that mean, 'summoned?'"

Marlowe didn't turn to him, but instead shifted his gaze to the wall. He gestured with his stick, and a bolt of white light shot from the top and struck the wall. The word "SUMMONED" appeared in phosphorescent letters.

"Whoa!" Eddie gasped.

Marlowe's voice echoed in the man-made cavern. "To be summoned means that you neither sought nor trained to walk the path of the mystic. It is when one is called to it from a state of innocence."

The glowing letters flickered, as if the fuel that fed them was spent, and disappeared, leaving the tunnel lit only by the glow atop Marlowe's stick.

"Eddie, before I tell you anything more, you should know that no one can be *forced* to walk the path. If you wish to join us, it must be of your own free will."

"Join you? How can I do that when I don't know anything about you?" Eddie said.

Marlowe nodded. "We have told you little because the less you know, the safer you remain." Marlowe faced Eddie and spoke in a low voice. "There are many things in this world that are beyond the understanding of the ordinary masses. There is a constant battle between the forces of ultimate good and ultimate evil."

"I didn't see it on the news," Eddie mocked.

"Of course not! Because it is happening in shadows and secrecy. Which is the way it *must* be. Most people live their lives focused on their own little world, but some choose to live a life of vigilance, existing at a higher state of awareness."

Marlowe paced, as he scrutinized Eddie intently.

"What do you want me to become a part of?" Eddie began to pace as well. "You aren't a cult, are you?"

"If you join us, you will no longer merely solve crimes, Eddie. You will have a hand in protecting all of humanity."

"Humanity?" Eddie repeated, dumbfounded.

"Here is what I offer. You can give me back Riftstone's staff, and I shall walk away. You will find the unusual events of the last day will fade in your memory, until they are nothing but a dream."

"That's sounds pretty good," Eddie pondered.

"Or you can join me and others like me. You will begin a difficult training period." Marlowe turned away and sighed, then went on, his back to Eddie. "And you will help vanquish an evil entity."

"How would I do that?" Eddie questioned.

"You must learn of things heard only in legends and master abilities mortal man cannot comprehend." Marlowe met Eddie's eyes. "And you might not survive."

"I could be killed?" Eddie asked to make sure he understood.

"We are fighting a most powerful foe," Marlowe explained. "But to tell you more would be wrong. That is your choice, and I am afraid you must make it—right now. We have much to do this night."

Eddie stood staring at the shorter man. "This is nuts."

Marlowe nodded. "Many lives depend on your decision, Eddie."

Eddie lifted the cane and stared at the silver ball. He could feel an energy hidden within it. He realized that in a way he had known it the moment he touched it.

He thought about his wife, sons, and even his momma. It wasn't fair to them to take such a big risk. But wasn't that what he'd accepted since the day he became a police officer?

He thought back to when he was ten and lived in Harlem. He'd been playing stickball with a couple of friends when his mother ran into the vacant lot more upset then he could ever remember.

"What's with yo' momma?" asked his friend Roosevelt. They stopped playing the moment she walked into view.

"Dunno," Eddie said, afraid he might be in serious trouble, and he racked his brain to remember if there was a chore he'd forgotten.

"Edward!" his mother bellowed, and Eddie ran to meet her. She all but fell into his arms.

"Momma, Momma, what is it?" Eddie said, fear a tight ring around his neck that seemed to suffocate him.

"Your daddy," she wheezed, out of breath. "Your daddy. He's in the hospital!"

Tears sprang into his eyes, not just from the horrific news, but more from the panic in his mother's face. It was the most frightening thing he'd ever seen.

Eddie helped her to the nearest subway station, and the two of them rode to Harlem Hospital Center in silence but clung to each other for support.

They went in, and the smell of ammonia and medicine covered an under odor of sickness and fear. They were given guest passes and rode up the elevator.

In the hall they found Jake Walker, Lawrence Berman's partner, who Eddie called "Uncle Jake."

He came over and hugged Eleanor, repeating her name over and over as she cried into his shoulder, and Eddie felt even more afraid and alone.

"Is Daddy dead?" Eddie was barely able to get the words out, scared that to utter them would make it true.

Jake turned to him and gave a tight smile. "No, Eddie, he's not dead. He got shot, but he'll be fine. They just brought him out of surgery 'bout an hour ago."

"How'd it happen, Jake?" Eleanor demanded. "If I found out he was takin' stupid chances again, I'll—I'll—" And she burst into fresh tears.

"Sh, no, this wasn't his fault. Guy was on PCP. Came into a coffee shop and just started shootin'. Larry took him out, probably saved a whole lotta lives. Your husband's a hero, Ellie."

Eddie snuck past them and looked into the room. There was his daddy, sitting up in bed with his eyes closed and tubes going into his arm and up his nose. He was a strange color, and Eddie thought Jake was wrong, that his father indeed was dead.

He moved to the bed and grasped the big, rough hand. It twitched, and Eddie gazed up to see his father's big brown eyes look down at him through half-closed lids.

"Daddy?" Eddie said, and the tears fell.

"How's my little man?" his father whispered.

"You got shot," Eddie said as relief swelled in his chest.

"I sho' did." He lay back in the bed and shut his eyes.

"Why do you do it, Daddy?" The question burst from Eddie before he could stop it.

"What'd you say, Eddie?" Lawrence Berman said, his eyes returning to his son.

"Why do you do it? I mean, if people are gonna shoot you. Why don't you do somethin' else?"

In response, Lawrence Berman pulled Eddie close in those big arms that could hold the world.

"Protect and Serve, son," he said. "It's the police motto, and I believe it. I take a risk out there, but I make a difference. I got shot, but I stopped that guy so other people didn't."

"I don't want you to die, Daddy." Eddie snuggled closer to his father's side.

"Sometimes you gotta take a big risk to do the most good, son. Remember that."

He always did.

"A big risk to do the most good," Eddie muttered. His eyes met Marlowe's. "I'll do it. I'll join your…whatever it is."

Marlowe nodded. "If that is your decision, then you shall be bound by it." He held his staff aloft, and the light on top of it grew brighter. The walking stick in Eddie's hand began to tremble.

"Hold tight, Eddie," Marlowe said as a beam of white light flew from his staff to Eddie's hand.

Eddie could feel the cane grow warm and start to change. It grew longer and thicker and changed from black to a clear, pale wood. It kept growing until Eddie was holding a staff as tall as Marlowe's, only more gnarled at the top.

"How did that—" Eddie said.

"You now see its true form, Eddie," Marlowe said. "The cane was a shape chosen by the previous owner."

"Riftstone," Eddie said. "The guy named after this arch?"

A sad smile traced Marlowe's face. "Nay, this arch was named for him."

"Get out of town," Eddie said. "They built it a hundred and fifty years ago."

"He was an old friend, and you shall learn that many of the arches in the park are named for our kind," Marlowe said. He stepped back and pointed at the staff in Eddie's hand. "You must choose a new form."

"What?" Eddie was annoyed at how stupid he sounded.

"It was a walking stick; you may choose that. But it should be a configuration that you can carry easily and readily."

Eddie looked up and down the length of the stick. "You mean I can make this look like anything?"

"Correct. It must be a shape you can keep close at hand."

Eddie smiled like a kid in a candy store. "Can I make it a lot smaller?"

"As tiny as a toothpick, if you wish it, or as large as a house, though I would suggest something easier to transport, yet uncommon enough so it cannot be easily misplaced."

"So if I choose a pen or a pencil, it'd be easy to lose."

"You are connected to it," Marlowe assured. "However, you do not want a form that makes you hesitate when you need it. Now, choose quickly, there is much to do."

Eddie nodded. "A credit card," he said, and held out the staff to Marlowe. "Make it the size of a credit card."

Marlowe pursed his lips and nodded thoughtfully. "An unusual request, but not without merit. Very well, close your eyes."

Eddie shut his eyes tightly, the staff in his hand.

"Envision how you want it to look and the size it should be. Make the image as clear in your mind as you can."

Eddie closed his eyes and saw a plastic card in his imagination. The staff in his hand grew warm, and Eddie opened his eyes to see a small card in his hand. It was dark with a wood grain design. In one corner, his name was embossed in gold letters with the words "Member Since" next to it and 06/17 underneath.

"Holy—" Eddie looked at the card a second and third time before he slipped it into his wallet.

"Good! Now we must go!" Marlowe said, and Eddie noticed that he was no longer holding a staff but a fancy walking stick.

The glow was gone, and the tunnel appeared as if nothing unusual happened.

Marlowe walked out the far end with Eddie fast on his heels.

"Where are we going?" Eddie asked. For an old guy, Marlowe was spry, and Eddie had to trot to keep up.

"To your initiation, of course," Marlowe reported.

"Wait a second!" Eddie grabbed Marlowe by the arm. "I have to go back to the station, meet my partner, go home to my wife —"

"Ah, yes, you are married." Marlowe stopped short. His free hand went to his beard to gently stroke it.

"I have responsibilities."

"Not this night. Quickly, make the necessary calls as we walk." Marlowe turned and walked on.

Eddie exhaled angrily, grabbed his cell phone, and spoke the name "Luis" into the box.

"Vasquez," Luis said as he picked up on the first ring.

"Luis, I'm, uh, following up on a lead—"

"Where are you? I can be there in ten minutes."

Eddie thought fast. "It might not pan out, and I don't want both of us to waste our time."

"I'm your partner. Wasting time together is what we do. What if you need backup?"

Eddie exhaled forcefully. "Luis, I don't want to pull rank—"

"But it sounds like you are about to," Luis snapped back.

"I need to do this on my own this time," Eddie implored. The last thing he needed was his partner upset. "Please, work with me?"

There was a long silence as the big man considered.

"If that's what you need, Eddie, I understand." Luis's voice was subdued.

"Thanks, Luis, I owe you." Eddie hit the "END" button then spoke the word "HOME."

They continued walking rapidly, and Eddie noticed they approached the Central Park Lake and the memorial to singer John Lennon known as Strawberry Fields. Marlowe did not slow down but headed determinedly toward a standing group of lush and verdant trees.

"Hello?" came Cerise's voice.

"Hey, honey." Eddie tried to sound upbeat. "I may have a break on my case."

"That's good, isn't it?"

"Yeah, but I've got to do some legwork tonight." He felt ashamed that he could lie to her so easily.

"When will you be home, Eddie?"

He could tell she wasn't happy. "What's wrong?"

"Momma's been asking for you." Cerise sighed.

Eddie stopped cold. "Is she all right?"

"As well as can be expected."

He stood there, trapped by indecision. He'd done his best to be a good son, and now there was only so much time left to be with her. On the other hand, he was pursuing his father's lesson of the importance of serving others. If the whole thing only took a week, he'd have time for her then. But what if—

"Eddie?" Marlowe waited at the entrance to a grove.

"I'm sorry, I don't know how long this will take. I'll call you later." Eddie shoved his phone back into his pocket. He felt a wave of anger and frustration wash over him. What had he agreed to?

Marlowe's eyebrows were raised as if to say, "Can't keep up with an old man?"

"I'm here, I'm here," Eddie wheezed, struggling to catch his breath.

Marlowe glanced about at a throng of people who enjoyed the warm weather. He leaned toward Eddie and said, "You will need your staff."

Eddie reached for his wallet, but Marlowe stayed his hand.

"Not here," Marlowe said. "Once we enter the grove, casually take it out."

He then turned and moved into the shadow of the trees. Eddie followed, reached into his wallet, and extracted the black card. As he watched, Marlowe's cane changed, grew, and became the tall, wooden implement.

Eddie suddenly realized he had no idea how to change the card. Just as he considered this problem, it grew warm. It began to shift, change, and grow, until Eddie held the full-sized wooden staff.

Eddie watched with such utter fascination that he smacked headlong into a tree, which in the tree's defense, stood unaware of his wandering attention.

Eddie lost his footing, fell to the ground, and cracked his head against a large rock. Lights flashed behind his eyes. He felt himself pulled into an upright position, as Marlowe's staff waved before his face. There was a pleasant, pink glow, and his mind cleared.

"Can you *please* be a little more careful, Eddie?" Marlowe chided.

Eddie rubbed the back of his head. The spot no longer hurt, and he found he didn't have a lump.

"Sorry," Eddie apologized. "I'm not used to— All this seems easy to you."

An understanding smile appeared on Marlowe's face. "I suppose it does. It has been a very long time since I was a novice. Come, we are almost there."

Marlowe turned and began to walk again. Eddie used his staff as a hiking stick and followed, on the lookout for any more ill-placed forestry.

TWELVE

Although the sun was still above the horizon as they entered the grove, once among the trees, it was dark as night.

In fact, Eddie noticed that the grove appeared much larger than he'd expected. They kept walking, though he was sure they should have come out next to the Central Park lake minutes earlier.

Eddie examined the trees and noted that they appeared different within the grove than outside of it. He caught up with Marlowe.

Gone was the old man's suit and tie, replaced with a long, flowing white robe with a black velvet over-tunic. Gone was the stylish hat, and in its place was now a full-cut hood that gathered loosely around his neck and head.

"Your clothes," Eddie hissed as he sidestepped another tree.

"Oh that's nothing." Marlowe's eyes were on the path ahead. "Look at yours."

Eddie looked down. Gone were his own suit and tie, and only a simple red robe covered him. He raised the garment's hem to find he wore a pair of sandals.

"Hey!" Eddie moved in front of the old man. "Those shoes cost me fifty bucks!   "

"They are undamaged—merely transformed," Marlowe explained, easily stepping around Eddie. "When one is to be initiated, this is how they are clad. Your rank and your belongings are of no consequence here. We approach the sacred clearing."

True to his word, they walked into an open field. Eddie looked up, shocked to find that the sun was gone and a night sky opened up above them. A huge, three-quarters moon loomed overhead.

"Hey, look at that." Eddie gazed up at the nocturnal firmament. "I've never seen the stars so clear."

Marlowe took a token glance upward and nodded. "I imagine not. The lights of the city keep you from being able to see the sky clearly."

"Wait a minute." Eddie was still fascinated by the view. "We're just a few hundred feet away from those city lights."

Marlowe turned to him. "Eddie, at this moment, we are as far from man-made things as one can be."

"We're in Central Park. We just walked into a grove."

"That is where we started, Eddie," Marlowe told him. "Listen."

Marlowe stood stone still as Eddie did just that.

"I don't hear anything except the wind."

"Exactly," Marlowe agreed. "No traffic, no horse-drawn carriages, none of the hustle and bustle of the city. And do you discern the moon? When we started, the sun had yet to set."

"Now it's night." Eddie looked at his wrist, which was pointless because his watch had vanished with the rest of his attire.

"You are thinking as an ordinary man, so this is strange to you. But to the wise, all becomes clear. We have traveled to a place where it is almost midnight."

"Wait a minute. We entered the woods. How—*when*—did we travel?"

Marlowe turned and gestured with his free arm. "What do you breathe, Eddie?"

Eddie blinked, puzzled by the question. "Air."

"Good," Marlowe approved. "Now, is the air you breathe just New York air, or is it all one air everywhere you go?"

"You're playing with me, right?" Eddie's frowned.

"I am *very* serious," Marlowe replied.

Eddie shrugged. "I've never thought about it, but okay. I guess it's all one air for the whole planet."

"Excellent," Marlowe chuckled. "You are a quick student. Now, the water you drink, is it individual water or one water?"

"There's a lot of different water supplies," Eddie countered.

"But everyone on the planet drinks the *same* water?" Marlowe stated with a twinkle in his eye.

Eddie nodded. "I guess so."

"Very well, Eddie!" Marlowe strode up a small hill as large shadows loomed in the darkness.

"So if everyone breathes the same air and drinks the same water," Marlowe announced as he approached the top, "is it not possible that we all walk through the same woods?"

"Now *that's* a stretch," Eddie pointed out as he followed. "Where are you going with this?"

Marlowe stopped with a huge spectral shape behind him. "It's a new way of thinking, Eddie. If we walk through the same woods, all you need do is come out of that one forest in a different location than where you went in."

Eddie was close enough to see that the large shadow ahead was a stone—a huge standing boulder that towered above his head.

Marlowe sped up his pace and reached a flat rock which rose up two feet from the ground. He leapt on it and planted his staff into a small hole in its center. The top of his staff burst forth with a glittering white light, and Eddie had a clear view of the entire hill. He could plainly see that they'd entered a stone circle.

"Hey," Eddie said. "Is this Stonehenge? Are we in England?"

Marlowe returned to Eddie, silhouetted by the light from the center of the rock.

"No, Eddie, Stonehenge is too public for us. This is a stone circle in a place far from prying eyes. Only we, the wise, know how to find it."

"We?" Eddie inquired. "There's no one else here."

"I have bid them come." Marlowe gestured toward the glowing staff. White and silver energy sparkled around the top like a small cloud buffeted by a tornado. "You are to be initiated."

"So, what does that entail, exactly?"

"All will become clear," Marlowe intoned.

"You keep saying that, and nothing is more clear than it was before—" Eddie turned then gasped!

From the shadows between the large standing stones, small globes of light hovered above the ground. As Eddie watched, robed and hooded figures drew closer, each carrying a wooden staff. On the top of each one, balls of light glowed in different hues of the rainbow.

The figures were an odd collection of shapes and sizes, some round and short, others so tall they passed seven feet. Their robes were different colors and styles, but all were decorated with stars and moons. Some of the symbols were merely cloth, but many sparkled as if tiny lights were sewn into the fabric.

The faces were all very different: Caucasian, African, Spanish, Asian, and Native American, even facial structures that suggested ancestry of Eskimo or the Pacific Islands.

Upon closer examination, Eddie could also see that there were subtle differences in the clothing along the racial divide. A very black man wore robes that suggested African colors and style, and one Native American man wore a robe that appeared to be made from the hide of an animal.

Most of their faces were old and wizened, except for the rare youthful one. Eddie couldn't remember a time when he'd seen so many people past the age of sixty in one place. Sixty? Hell, most were at least eighty!

One shining, purple silk robe caught his attention, and he saw Frisha give him a nod. He looked over the crowd again and noticed a man with a blue light that floated above his stick. He was dark-skinned and had a gray beard that curled on his face like a pelt, and wore long, African-style blue robes.

Eddie pointed to the man and said to Marlowe, "I know him."

"Of course you do. He's been in Central Park for years."

Eddie stopped for a moment and stared at the man. "Trey, right?"

"Trefoil is his full name," Marlowe said.

"Another guy named after an arch?"

"Once again, the arch was named for him," Marlowe corrected.

"Whatever. He spoke to me the day of the murder," Eddie said, and felt as if yesterday was ten years ago. "Is he part of this?"

"A much larger part than you can imagine."

The others drew closer. They all walked at the same pace, so they formed a circle which grew smaller. It was as if they'd rehearsed the speed and tempo of their strides. They progressed until the circle of bodies was close enough for another person to pass between, but only just.

In unison, they raised their staffs, and different colored radiance shone forth from each toward the center and united with the energy above Marlowe's own stick.

A low, soft chanting started from the crowd that soon grew in volume. Eddie heard the words but couldn't understand them, yet they carried a strange familiarity that spoke not to his rational mind, but to some primal force in his soul.

The multiple rays of light from each staff grew brighter, and Eddie glanced at his own to see a red light shimmering on top.

As they chanted, Marlowe returned to the rock and held his staff aloft. The beams of light formed an illuminated canopy over their heads.

The chanting stopped as Marlowe raised his hand to speak.

"Let us all pledge our faithfulness," Marlowe's voice echoed off the huge stones.

"We hear and affirm," the circle of men and women answered.

"Since the dawn of time, there have been those who walk the way of the wise," Marlowe shouted. "They have been known by many names: wizards, shaman, witch doctors, alchemists, faith healers, and countless others in all languages and places on this verdant earth. This night we bring within our fold a new member, the first in many years. He did not choose the path but was summoned."

The assembly broke into quick whispers of surprise. The word "summoned" flashed from person to person with excitement.

"For those who do not know, Riftstone has moved to the higher plane of existence which we all must eventually go. He did not go by choice."

Another chorus of murmurs ran through the group: "Rest his bones"; "May he be at peace"; "Blessed be."

"Tonight we unite to welcome this new member and set him upon the path."

"*Huzzah*!" the crowd yelled as one voice.

Marlowe turned to Eddie, his eyes seeming to shimmer with the reflected light overhead.

"Edward Berman," Marlowe said, "are you here by your own free will?"

Eddie looked around at the group and thought, *This is like a dream—make that a nightmare. I hope they don't want me to drink blood or something.*

"I am," Eddie found himself saying, surprised by the sound of his own voice.

"You have been summoned by the staff you hold. All of the staves we possess came from the same ancient tree. Only those who choose the path or are summoned can wield the power within the wood." Marlowe held his own staff aloft, and the stick glowed with layer upon layer of wax. "Each staff has been polished over long centuries through the blood and sweat of those that seek to improve this world and continue our learning. There have been many that have laid down their lives in this cause."

A muttering of approvals ran through the band.

Marlowe turned to Eddie and stared deeply into his eyes. "Edward Berman, are you prepared to take this heavy burden upon you?"

Eddie looked around at the figures surrounding him and the beams that glowed above his head.

"Can you be a little more specific?" Eddie whispered hoarsely.

"What?" Marlowe murmured back, embarrassed by the interruption.

"Exactly what am I agreeing to?"

"We are asking you, upon your oath and your honor, to be trained in our arts. To use them to protect lesser beings from evil and work with us to serve the good in this world."

Protect and serve, ran through Eddie's mind. *They're asking me to join the metaphysical police.*

"In that case," Eddie turned to the group and announced, "I —I agree!"

"Do you swear by your oath before this honored assembly?" Marlowe said.

"I do!"

"*Huzzah,*" spoke the circle.

Marlowe turned one way, and then the other, and spoke to the crowd. "Do you accept him to join with us?"

"*We hear and—*"

"Wait!" one voice bellowed, and the crowd grew instantly silent.

"Is this what we wish?" A man stepped from the circle. His staff remained freestanding behind him, an ivory beam of light still emanating from its top.

The man pulled back the hood. He was one of the few younger members of the assembly. A tall, white man with strong features and a pointed nose. He was clean-shaven, and his gray-black hair was long but stylish and well-cut. His fingernails shimmered from a recent manicure.

"What say you, Drusilicus Greywacke?" Marlowe huffed, annoyance in his tone.

"Is it prudent to bring one with no training into our fold?" responded Drusilicus.

"He was summoned," Marlowe argued, facing the man down. "The first in centuries—"

"Yes, and the first brought to this circle in decades," Drusilicus announced. "There are those of us with apprentices—fine students—and they are not allowed to join until we pass from this world."

Marlowe nodded. "'Tis the tradition."

"Riftstone had no apprentice, though many suggested he should. He led a solitary life, though many of us reached out to him." He glanced at Eddie disdainfully. "Are we showing wisdom bringing this…this…person to our bosom? There are so many others, trained and ready to take up the fight."

He stood and turned, his arms extended to include the group. Murmurs went through the crowd as they looked to each other and nodded.

"He was summoned," Marlowe declared. "That takes precedence. The staff knows best who is most qualified."

"Also the tradition," Drusilicus cautioned. "However, there are those who say that Riftstone was struck down by the Great Evil."

Another murmur went through the crowd.

"'Tis true!" Frisha yelled out.

Drusilicus observed the crowd like a trained attorney as he sized up a jury. "If that is so, then this is not the time for hasty judgments. We must consider the significance, as only the Five can cast out the Great Evil."

"The Five?" Eddie whispered to Marlowe. "Who are they?"

Marlowe whispered back. "They carry the staffs of those who formed the first coven. They are the most powerful of all."

Drusilicus snorted. "See, he does not know even our most basic history." He turned and faced the tall black man who stood unmoving in the circle. "Trefoil, you are one of the Five. What say you?"

Trefoil planted his staff into the ground with one strong push, its blue beam shimmering from the stick to the circle's center. He stepped forward.

Trefoil did not break eye contact with Drusilicus, as the others listened intently. "I say the idea of confronting the Great Evil with someone untrained scares the crap out of me."

A quick titter went through the group. Trefoil lifted his hand for silence.

"Riftstone was an odd fella, I'll give you that. His solitary ways may have cost him his life." Trefoil walked closer to the center stone. "However, I accepted his habits, and I trusted him. Which means I trust his staff. If Edward Berman was summoned, then he is the one who should take up Riftstone's staff and walk the path."

A buzz of assent rushed through the men and women in the circle.

"Then it is decided?" Marlowe began.

"Wait!" Drusilicus raised his hand again. "Does he know that Riftstone was one of the Five? That he now holds the Staff of the element Fire?"

"He will be instructed thus," Marlowe said.

"I would ask that someone else be considered to take that staff and join the Five. Until the initiation is complete, Marlowe, as you bear the Staff of Spirit, you can give it to any," Drusilicus acknowledged. "A wizard of great power should accept it, and Edward Berman could be given another."

"We can't do that," Trefoil insisted, his mouth stern. "Riftstone's staff chose him! There must be a reason."

"He speaks sooth, Drusilicus," Marlowe maintained. "The Staff of Fire chose Edward Berman."

"How many other wizards must die?" Anger flashed across Drusilicus's face as he looked at Eddie. "Who will save them? Him? As I see it, we are all in jeopardy." He grew calmer and spoke more carefully. "I do not deny him his rights. I merely recommend caution."

The crowd mumbled quietly, and the light on top of the staves began to diminish.

Marlowe raised his hand, and the beams grew brighter as all eyes focused on him.

"The Five always faced risk," Marlowe proclaimed.

"Then I would ask for a long unused codicil," Drusilicus requested. "Give Edward Berman the ability to surrender the Staff of Fire to another if he so chooses."

"That is most unusual, Drusilicus," Marlowe warned. "I do not see how it benefits."

Drusilicus shrugged like an actor playing to an audience. "If he discovers he is not up to the challenge, he may pass the staff to another. Only then will I approve."

Trefoil looked over to Marlowe and spoke in a low voice. "He's got you there. One who is summoned to be one of the Five must be approved by the entire coven."

Marlowe looked at the ground and exhaled heavily. "Agreed."

Drusilicus bowed and returned to his spot in the circle, and then replaced his hood over his head and held his staff firmly. Trefoil looked at Marlowe questioningly and returned to his own place in the circle.

"Do I get the job?" Eddie asked Marlowe just above a whisper.

"That you do," Marlowe replied in an undertone. "The spell I shall add will not affect your powers, but you have the ability to pass your staff to any as you will."

"Lucky me."

Marlowe waved his hand at Eddie's staff, and the red light on top of it flickered for a moment then grew brighter.

"There, 'tis done." Marlowe raised his hands and increased the volume of his voice so all could hear. "He has sworn to us upon his oath. What say you?"

"*We hear and affirm,*" the others responded.

"Do you accept Edward Berman into this circle?"

"*We do!*" came the answer.

"Then, as coven master, I state that Edward Berman is now one of us, to be trained in the path of the wise."

"*Huzzah!*" rose the cry from the circle.

"Who shall take Edward as apprentice?" Marlowe queried.

Drusilicus shifted his staff and leaned forward. "Since Marlowe supports this new member so strongly, I say he should train Edward Berman."

Marlowe looked panicked for the briefest moment, then set his jaw and nodded. "I shall, so mote it be."

"*So mote it be!*" reverberated through the crowd.

Each member of the circle held up their staves, and Marlowe raised his and touched it to Eddie's staff.

"Hold very still," Marlowe said, as energy flowed to Eddie's, the beams of light resting on top.

Marlowe moved from the rock and joined the circle, as two cloaked figures shifted to make space for him. A white beam of light lashed out from his staff and joined the others on top of Eddie's.

A chant began in each throat invoking that strange language as the beams of light grew brighter. A kaleidoscope of color danced atop Eddie's stick. The multicolored illumination traveled down his staff and onto his hand. Eddie watched as his entire body began to glow.

Then, all at once, the light was on him, in him, part of him. He was one with a rainbow which swirled about him. His brain was filled with it, and he felt as if his body was breaking down. It ceased to be skin, bone, and meat and became nothing but light.

Even with his eyes tightly shut, it was dazzling. And in that blissful, blinding effulgence that bordered on nirvana, Eddie lost consciousness.

THIRTEEN

Eddie tried to lift his head, but it weighed three hundred pounds. Fireworks exploded behind his eyes, along with the mother of all headaches.

He lay still and cursed as he attempted to recall when and how much he'd been drinking. It must have been a lot—so much that he'd forgotten everything, including the first drink.

As he rested there, recollection slowly returned. The walk in the woods, the stone circle, the coven. Then that overwhelming light, like something alive that held him in a loving embrace.

He carefully opened his eyes and silently hoped he was in his own bedroom and the occurrences of the previous twenty-four hours were only a dream.

Dreams feel real when you have them, he decided, *and you only know they're not when you wake up.*

This reassuring thought was gone as Eddie realized he wasn't in his own bed.

The room was very dark, but he could fathom the slightly brighter outline of windows on the shaded walls, the crack of light under a doorway, and the green, glowing ball that hovered directly above him…

The last object struck Eddie as something out of the ordinary, and his eyes returned to it. Something was indeed suspended over him, a glowing green, translucent blob that spun end over end. As he watched, a nose began to form, followed by a large pair of eyes, a mouth, and two stunted arms.

"Boo!" the green face trilled with glee.

Eddie's scream echoed inside his own head so loudly that he felt as if it exploded. He fought to get up from the bed, tangled himself in the sheets, and rolled off and onto the floor with a resounding "*thump*."

On the floor, he struggled, which made the bed sheets cover him like a shroud. He rolled and fought to break free as the glowing creature laughed uproariously.

"Bob!" came Marlowe's voice as the door burst open. "Lights!"

Eddie could see a pale illumination through his cloth prison. Then, Eddie felt himself lifted off the ground. He floated, weightless in the air, as the cloth fell from his limbs.

The room stopped spinning, and he was lowered to the ground and onto his feet.

He stood face to face with the green creature, and it reiterated the word, "Boo!"

Annoyed now, Eddie took a swing at it. His hand passed through the green, glowing shape and distorted it for a moment but did no damage.

"Bob, stop this at once!" Marlowe commanded. The old man stood in pajamas and a red silk bathrobe, his head covered with a red night cap, as if he'd walked out of a story book.

The small, misshapen, green glob cast its makeshift eyes toward the old wizard. The distorted mouth opened, and a pathetic "Aw" came out.

"I mean it, leave him be!" Marlowe raised his staff, which made Bob curl into a ball and roll toward the ceiling to pass right through it.

"Forgive me. I should have placed a barrier around your room." Marlowe approached, and Eddie noticed that, besides the staff, Marlowe carried a silver goblet.

He proffered the cup to Eddie. "Here, drink this."

Eddie still felt as if two hundred horses galloped through his cerebrum. He lifted the cup and smelled it.

"Yuck!" Eddie held the cup away. "You cannot expect me to drink this."

"It will help with the pain in your head," Marlowe noted simply.

Eddie looked at the smaller man hopefully. "Really?"

Marlowe said nothing but gave a small nod. Eddie held his breath and downed the noxious substance in one foul-tasting gulp. It tasted worse than it smelled, and Eddie grimaced as the substance went down his throat. He shut his eyes and rubbed his face with his free hand, as if to remove the vile taste.

A moment passed, and Eddie's head cleared. The headache didn't merely fade; it was simply gone. He tentatively opened his eyes to find he felt terrific.

"What was this stuff?" Eddie handed the goblet back to Marlowe.

"My first calling was as an herbalist. You just drank a combination of plant extracts that aid in the recovery from an overwhelming psychic encounter."

"Of course." Eddie wondered if he would always only understand half of what this man said. "What was that…that *thing* that woke me?"

"You mean Bob?" Marlowe asked. "Don't mind him, he's harmless. A bit of a prankster."

"No, no, I mean what is he…or was he?" Eddie looked up at the ceiling at the spot where Bob dematerialized.

"A disembodied spirit. Don't worry, he never incarnated, so you weren't visited by a 'ghost,'" Marlowe explained, his gaze also going to the spot where Bob was last seen. "He's expressed no desire to be in a solid form, human or otherwise."

"What is he doing here?"

"Oh, he lives here, assists me," Marlowe affirmed and met Eddie's eyes. "You know, minor errands, keeps me aware of appointments, incoming messages, that sort of thing." Marlowe lowered his voice conspiratorially. "Nothing too complicated. He's not the smartest fellow."

Marlowe reached into the pocket of his robe and extracted a small, glittering ball. "Now we must to business. There is much to tell."

He handed it to Eddie, who stared at the round glass. "Is that a crystal ball?"

"Yes, a most special crystal, indeed. Focus deep inside the glass, and I shall begin the tale."

The ball began to glow in Eddie's hand, and he saw shapes and images within.

"Since the dawn of time, there have been the wise—those who carried a staff and worked wonders," Marlowe said.

Eddie could see a small figure within the glass wander over a hill of sand as he carried a staff much like his own.

"Each staff is a remainder of the Tree of the Knowledge of Good and Evil."

"Isn't that the tree that Adam and Eve got the apple from?" Eddie wondered aloud.

"Yes," Marlowe agreed, and the image of a mighty and beautiful fruit tree appeared within the glass. "It is told in our legends that the Divine destroyed the tree—" A flash of lightning smashed the image of the tree in the crystal, which made Eddie jump back in surprise.

"But the remnants rained down upon all parts of the earth," Marlowe said. Within the crystal, Eddie could see pieces of wood falling in different lands.

"The wise were drawn to the wood, which they made into staffs and studied to learn their power," Marlowe said, as Eddie watched a dirty, bedraggled man dressed in little more than a loincloth pick up a stick and hold it up to the sky.

"But what about the Five?" Eddie said.

"In time, as staffs were found, the wise began to form groups. The Five started the first coven."

"Why five?"

"Their staffs represented each of the elements: fire, water, earth, air, and the most powerful of all—spirit."

"That's the one you carry, right?"

A smile crept onto Marlowe's face. "I do. Originally, the Five were drawn together from different parts of the planet. They banded their power together and traveled. They taught spiritual concepts to many cultures in different ways."

Eddie could see a man speaking to vast crowds, a staff in his hands, and a loving look in his eyes.

"Thousands of years ago, by mortal reckoning, the world was influenced by many beings who called themselves gods. The Five struck down many of these old gods and their practices of human sacrifice."

The glass in Eddie's hand began to glow, and mist swirled within. He saw a red-skinned demon with fierce claws and huge horns upon his head, towering over much smaller men. "One such was Abraxas. Abraxas was the Supreme God of the Basilidians."

"The who?"

"Basilidians. Don't worry, they all died out."

As Marlowe spoke, Eddie saw thousands of people bowing down to a huge statue that was fashioned like the giant demon.

"Never heard of him before today."

Marlowe nodded. "Oh, you have."

Eddie saw the image of a red serpent as it crawled on an apple tree and spoke to a naked woman.

Eve? Eddie thought. *Could that story be true?*

"According to legend, Abraxas has three hundred and sixty-five different personas."

"One for each day of the year?" Eddie observed.

Different shapes flashed in the glass: reptiles, animals, strange creatures that Eddie could not recognize, all the same dark-red color as the demon.

"Yes, and he has the ability to transform to any one of them at will. It took the combined might of the Five to stop him, and even they could not destroy him, but merely bind him in other dimensions."

Eddie looked into the glass and saw five robed figures as they focused the colored lights from their staffs and made the red demon disappear and the huge temple behind him crumble.

"Each staff has been passed down from master to apprentice. The Five have faced him time and again. He has worn many different names: Satan, Beelzebub, the great dragon, the serpent, the corrupter of souls."

Eddie lowered the glass. "You mean you guys are going to take on the devil? I mean, like the actual devil?"

Marlowe nodded, and Eddie noticed that he suddenly looked old. "Yes," he whispered. "Each time he has found new worshippers who use dark magic to bring him back to this world through the shedding of blood."

"You mean—" Eddie gasped, his mouth falling open.

"That's right. Abraxas gains strength through human sacrifice. People must die to empower him."

"Damn."

"He was very busy during the twentieth century, as you can well imagine. The last time he was imprisoned was a scant seventy years ago at the end of the conflict you know as World War Two."

"Were you there?" Eddie asked.

"Aye, and before we removed him from this dimension, he gave man the knowledge of nuclear weapons. Since then, although he was unable to affect the mortal world, that invention created havoc."

"The Cold War," Eddie considered. "But he failed. We didn't blow ourselves up."

"Due to his banishment and the influence of those who walk the path. I'd hoped we would have a few more decades before we were wont to combat Abraxas again. However, things have changed. Instead of tracking him down, he is hunting us."

"Why?"

"Something has emboldened him greatly. I believe he killed Riftstone in his guise of a giant demon."

Eddie considered the forensic evidence Doctor Warren shared with him. Now, it all fit. "So, he's our killer? And if I'm following you right, he's even stronger because he shed Riftstone's blood."

Marlowe nodded. "Yes, but Riftstone could not have been the first. The Great Evil must find a way into this world, and transcending the barriers would weaken him. He would need a way to increase his power before he would dare strike at a wizard."

"Is there another way he could get power?"

Marlowe looked up from the crystal in Eddie's hand. "I can only assume that he had help."

"You mean someone who got him a sacrifice?"

Marlowe nodded. "There are always those willing to kill for the gifts he can bring them."

FOURTEEN

The ball in Eddie's hand grew dark, and he handed it back to Marlowe who put it into the pocket of his robe.

"So, where am I?" Eddie asked to break the silence.

"My home. Forgive me for not telling you."

"How did I get here?" Eddie turned to examine the room around him. It was decorated with antiques, but each in mint condition. There stood a large bureau and dresser made of a fine-grained wood finished in a dark lacquer and kept in good condition so the wood shimmered in the candlelight.

There was not a spot of dust on the round end table near the bed, which was a huge four-poster monstrosity that enveloped one corner of the room. Several large windows were covered with heavy, burgundy drapes. Artwork adorned the walls, all of it as ancient and well-cared for as the furniture.

"I brought you here. Trefoil helped."

"You're stronger than you look. Is it still dark out?" Eddie asked, gesturing at the heavy drapes.

"I must keep the windows covered, for the benefit of...one of my guests."

Eddie looked down at himself. He still wore the simple red tunic of the previous night, but his feet were bare. He stared blankly at his wrist, trying to ascertain the time. His wristwatch was still gone.

"What time is it?" Eddie asked. He felt rested, in spite of his rude awakening, now that the killing headache was gone.

"It's six-thirty," Marlowe stated.

"Six-thirty?" Eddie said as his jaw fell open. "As in the morning?"

"Yes, as in the morning," Marlowe replied.

"Aw jeez." Eddie felt his robe for a pocket, in a useless attempt to locate his phone. "I gotta call my wife—"

"Eddie, why don't you take a shower?" Marlowe said calmly. "I will make sure your clothes are returned to their former condition while you wash. Speaking with you has given me ideas. I must act on them."

"But—" Eddie decided he really didn't have a choice.

"Bring your staff," Marlowe instructed as he walked out the door.

Eddie shot a look around the room and located the archaic wooden pole near the large bed.

Eddie grabbed the stick and stepped into the hall. It was also dimly lit, with dark wood on the floor and wainscoting. The walls were coated with a very clean and tasteful dusky wallpaper.

Several sconces stood out from the wall. As Eddie drew near, he could see that while three candles burned in each, they were not being consumed. No smoke rose from them, and the wax did not liquefy.

Marlowe stood in front of an open door. He gestured Eddie in. It was a large bathroom, the walls and floor covered to the ceiling with tiny white and black tiles. In the room stood a huge claw-foot bathtub that could easily fit a family of four—with room for a water buffalo. From several chains hung a tubular circle which held a shower curtain.

Eddie entered, awed by the twelve-foot ceiling and the expanse of space.

"Hang your robe on the towel rack, and I'll take care of everything," Marlowe said as he shut the door.

"You'll take care of everything?" he muttered. "How about telling my wife where I've been all night?"

This room was lit with an overhead light, making the candelabrum unnecessary. Eddie walked to the shower curtain and pulled it aside.

"Boo!" Bob said from his hiding place in the shower.

"Ah!" Eddie fell back as he raised his staff reflexively.

Energy crackled and flashed like bolts of red lightning around them. It bounced off the walls and the sink and made the water in the commode leap as it struck.

"NO! NO!" Bob screamed as the voltage discharged, popped, and sizzled around him. "I sorry, I sorry, don't hurt me!"

But one of the fire bolts made contact with his hind quarters, and with a screech of fear, Bob passed through the closed door, his tail smoldering as he went.

Eddie rose, the output of pyrotechnics over as quickly as it started. "Showed you!" He panted as he stared at the staff. "That's what I'm talking about."

He gingerly laid the staff next to the towel rack and hung up his robe.

Eddie got under the hot water, which was the exact right temperature the moment he turned it on. He began to wash, and found his favorite shampoo and conditioner waited on a metal shelf that hung from the curtain rod. He couldn't recall if it had been there when he began to shower, but he used the products gratefully.

He got out of the tub and grabbed a fluffy black towel and began to dry his face. As he pulled the thirsty cotton away from his eyes, he saw that on the rack, the red robe was replaced by his suit of the previous day. It was on a wooden hanger and looked freshly pressed. He also saw his good shoes under a stack of clean underwear and socks.

But, most important, his service weapon and shoulder holster dangled from the hanger in front of the suit. He stepped over, removed the pistol, pulled the magazine, and made sure it was functioning correctly before he returned it to the hanging harness.

He looked at himself in the mirror and picked up the electric razor from the sink. He began to shave, pleased at how well the small machine cut the tough hairs under his neck.

He dressed. As he put on the boxer shorts and tee shirt, he reached into the jacket pocket and felt his cell phone, which lay there unaware that it had disappeared at all.

Eddie quickly hit the button, and his home phone began to ring.

"H-hello?" came a tired voice at the other end.

"Cerise, honey? It's Eddie."

"Eddie!" Cerise's voice rose in volume. "What happened, where are you? My God, are you in the hospital?"

"No," Eddie gave a quick laugh. He wanted to tell her where he was but realized he didn't really know. "I'm at—the station. I must've fallen asleep."

There was a long silence at the other end of the phone.

"That was my first thought, Edward."

She's calling me Edward, he thought. *I am in serious trouble.*

"That's why I sent Luis to look for you. He said you weren't in the bunk rooms at the precinct."

Busted.

"I fell asleep in the locker room," Eddie tried to sound like it was all a silly misunderstanding. "Went down to change and lay down on a bench to rest my eyes and off I went."

"I see." Cerise's tone suggested the only thing she saw was Eddie rotating on a spit over a very tall fire.

"Really, honey." Eddie hoped he sounded less pathetic in his wife's ear than he did in his own.

"I have been up all night worried about you, Edward Joseph Berman," Cerise chided.

She was using his middle name. That was even worse.

Cerise went on. "I was sure that you were shot and lying in some ditch, bleeding to death. Now you call me up to tell me, 'Oh, honey, I fell asleep in the locker room.' That is the most ridiculous excuse I have ever heard, and if you think that I am so stupid as to believe it, then you have a damn low opinion of me."

"Cerise, baby," Eddie soothed.

"Go to hell," she shrilled as she slammed down the phone.

Eddie looked at his phone, then returned it to his suit pocket. "For all I know, that's where I was." He shook his head. "I guarantee it's where I'll be when I get home."

Eddie put on his shirt, his holster and weapon, and checked to make sure that his jacket covered the bulge. Finally, he grabbed his staff and left with one last look, wondering how Marlowe found a place to live in New York City with such a great bathroom.

In the hall, he had no idea which direction to go. He couldn't recall which way he'd come in the dimly lit vestibule.

"Lost?" a voice came from behind him.

Eddie leapt around quickly, his staff raised. A tall man stood behind him, and with lightning speed grabbed Eddie's upraised arm.

The man held Eddie's staff in place. "Let's not have any accidents, shall we? I've been changed into far too many things for one lifetime."

The man wore a pleasant look on his face. He possessed fine features and was as handsome as a Greek statue and almost as pale. His hair was short and black as a raven, and his eyes appeared to glow.

"I...I..." Eddie stammered, dumbfounded.

"I'll show you the way downstairs." The man gently released Eddie's arm. "Marlowe is waiting."

"Who are you?" Eddie asked as he followed the man down the hall.

The man stopped, turned. "Oh, forgive me, bad manners." He extended his hand with a fluidity of movement. "Kraft, Daniel Kraft. I'm one of Marlowe's guests—you might even say I work for him."

"You aren't sure?"

The man sighed and gave Eddie a sad smile as they began to walk again. "I'm afraid I can't say exactly how I fit into Marlowe's world. He gives me a room here, helps me when I need it, and I get information unavailable to him."

"The guy's a wizard. What doesn't he know?" Eddie said, and found it odd he couldn't take his eyes off the good-looking man.

"There are dark forces that oppose what he does," Kraft mused solemnly. "He cannot be associated with them, but it is not my place to instruct you. Marlowe will tell you what you need to know."

They reached the top of a staircase with light marble steps circling several times in a downward spiral toward a brighter first floor. The entire center tube was wrapped with black painted wrought iron. The thin bars ran from the floor to the ceiling, with alternating decorative rods between each support. These shorter rods were shaped with fleur-de-lis and pointed tops and bottoms, and ran in a diagonal design that complemented the twisting stairs. Above him, Eddie could see a pulley mechanism in the ceiling with steel cables which ran to a tubular elevator *inside* the center of the staircase. It was a magnificent artifice, but Eddie suspected the elevator was too ancient to actually work.

"How long is this stairway?" Eddie leaned over the edge to peer down.

"Several floors." Kraft stayed in the shadows and avoided the edge. "The daylight doesn't penetrate this level."

"Why?" Eddie said.

Again Kraft flashed him that sad smile, as if something terribly ironic passed through his mind.

"Something else that Marlowe will tell you," Kraft explained as his eyes caught the dim light in a most unusual way. "I understand you have much to learn."

Eddie's gaze returned to the stairway. "And every minute it's like I know less."

"I might suggest a good place to start. You're a police officer, is that right?"

"Homicide."

"Difficult line of work. Are you accomplished at it?"

Eddie nodded. "I'm a lieutenant."

"If you've risen that high, you have the stamina for what you are undertaking now."

"So what's your advice?" Eddie inquired.

"Trust your instincts." Kraft shook Eddie's hand. "Nice meeting you, lieutenant."

He turned and headed away down the passageway where he faded into the shadowy corridor.

FIFTEEN

As Eddie descended the stairs, he considered what Kraft had told him. It was sound advice.

When he was a rookie, he always second-guessed himself. He only became good at the job when he went with his gut and trusted his instincts. That was how he made lieutenant.

He went down the last step and looked at the ceiling that towered above his head like a dome. The rest of the room sparkled from floors of polished marble and walls painted taupe. The woodwork was the same as upstairs, except as sunlight streamed in, the wood appeared more warm and inviting.

"Eddie!" a voice called out, and he turned to see Marlowe, fully dressed and with his walking stick. He wore a green velvet jacket with a robin's egg blue shirt, and carried a large book in a heavy leather binding. "Would you join me in the breakfast room?"

Eddie gave a nod, then closed his eyes and thought of the staff's other form. As soon as he did, he could feel it become lighter and smaller. He opened his eyes to see the black card in his hand, which he then slipped into his wallet as he approached Marlowe.

"Very good, Eddie," Marlowe beamed. "You didn't need me to walk you through the process. It is good that you learn quickly. Come."

They walked into another room, not as grand as the first, but still impressive. Another vaulted ceiling rose up impossibly high. There were two fireplaces, one at either end of the room, beautiful tapestries over the marble floors, and a mixture of fine furniture: overstuffed chairs, comfortable sofas, and small tables. Everything looked old and valuable, yet in perfect condition.

"What is this, a meeting hall?"

"Sometimes, Eddie, but it's actually my living room," Marlowe led Eddie through a side door. They perambulated into a large sun porch. It had windows on three sides with a view of a small garden and a brick wall. There was a beautifully hand-carved wooden table with ten chairs around it. At one end, on a linen tablecloth, were several silver chafing dishes.

Marlowe picked up a china plate from a stack, handed it to Eddie, and opened the first chafing dish, which exposed scrambled eggs.

"I've eaten, please help yourself." Marlowe sat at the table and opened a large, dusty book.

Eddie began to serve himself. "This isn't what I expected."

"I'm sorry?"

"I thought after last night, you'd have the dishes floating and coffee appearing in my cup—things like that."

"Such things are commonplace in this house," Marlowe considered. "I thought it would be...grounding...to have breakfast the way you are used to."

Eddie glanced around the room. The floors here were polished oak and the ceiling was twelve feet high. "I'll tell you, Marlowe, this is a lot fancier breakfast than at my house. Your breakfast table wouldn't fit in my dining room."

"Ah!" Marlowe looked up as if he noticed the room for the first time. "Yes, I suppose the townhouse is a bit ostentatious."

Eddie opened the next chafing dish and took some bacon. He was hungry and couldn't quite recall when he last ate.

Marlowe turned a page in the book, which sent dust rising from it.

Eddie put his plate down at the table and held up a gleaming silver teapot. "Is this coffee?"

"Hmm?" Marlowe said. "Oh, yes, help yourself. As I recall, you take your coffee with cream—not milk—and no sugar."

"How do you know that?" Eddie poured the brown liquid into a cup on a saucer.

Marlowe turned another page. "Since you were summoned, I have observed you in my crystal."

"Great, and I thought my momma was nosy."

"I assure you," Marlowe stressed, as he sipped his own coffee, "I did not watch you too…intimately."

"Having anyone watch me is disconcerting."

Eddie began to eat as Marlowe continued to scan the book.

"I met Daniel." Eddie stabbed a forkful of egg. "Weird guy."

That made Marlowe smile. "Weird is all perspective. Daniel acts as an arbitrator between myself and many other beings."

"He didn't want to come downstairs."

"That is astute. You see, the sunlight would be very bad for him."

Eddie frowned, "Why?"

Marlowe turned another page. "Didn't he tell you? Daniel is a vampire."

Eddie almost spat out his coffee. He fought to swallow it and fell into a coughing fit. Marlowe peered over the book in concern.

"A vampire?" Eddie gurgled in a raspy voice. "You work with a vampire?"

"Actually, *he* works with *me*. It is a difficult position for Daniel. There is bad blood between vampires and wizards."

"Bad blood?"

"Perhaps a poor choice of words," Marlowe retorted. "There are many factions among supernatural beings. In the past there has been open warfare between groups. The wizards wish to improve the world and lead mankind to higher consciousness. Others wish to dominate mortals and the world."

"So, the vampires would more likely be in league with a bad guy like Abraxas."

Marlowe nodded solemnly. "They would enjoy the release of destruction, anarchy, and evil. It would allow them free rein of their darker lusts."

"So why does Daniel work with you?"

"Many years ago, I had the opportunity to save his life. A favor he has returned more than once. He goes places I would not be welcome and brings me insights I would never hear. However, I deal with the undead quite a bit. Among my skills, I am a necromancer."

"A what?"

"Necromancer. I conjure spirits of the dead."

"I thought you were an herbalist," Eddie quizzed.

"That too," Marlowe replied. "Anytime someone needs help with hauntings, spirit possession, that sort of thing, I'm usually called in."

"So, we're kind of in the same line of work."

Marlowe brightened at this statement. "Why yes, Eddie. We both are involved in cases that deal with the dead. You, on a physical level, and myself on a spiritual one."

"It's a wonder we haven't met before."

Marlowe shrugged innocently and turned another page.

"So, you guys have your specialties?" Eddie challenged.

"There are many fields of endeavor open to us. I have expanded mine over the years. I once was adept at divination— seeing the future."

"But not now?"

"It was difficult for me. I was forced to live backwards and remember what was yet to happen."

"I don't quite follow that."

"That was my problem as well. Frisha is wonderful at prophecy, absolutely first-rate."

"Maybe we should ask her to find Abraxas?"

"I asked her here this very morning for that purpose." Marlowe suddenly stabbed the aged book with his index finger. "Aha!"

"What is it?"

"The question you asked earlier. Another way for the demonic forces to gain power. I don't know why I didn't remember—"

"Nobody's perfect," Eddie said, as he chewed on his bacon.

Marlowe shook his head. "There is no excuse. I have grown lax, too comfortable in my old age."

"So what is it?"

"Hmm? Oh, yes." Marlowe gazed down at the book. "The other way for an entity to gain power in the physical world is through the use of a talisman."

"A what-a-man?" Eddie sipped his coffee.

"A talisman," Marlowe explained. "It is a religious or ritualistic symbol imbued with spiritual energies."

"Like a lucky rabbit's foot or a cross?"

"Yes, good, Eddie," Marlowe acknowledged. "Only there are some talismans, very old, very ancient, in which a being leaves a portion of its essence."

"Why would it do that?" Eddie asked as he finished his eggs.

"To create a pathway to this physical plane and to leave some of its own essence to strengthen it."

"Like a battery?" Eddie guessed.

Marlowe gave a laugh and looked at Eddie with amazement.

"What? Have I got food hanging off my face?"

"No," Marlowe chuckled. "It is you, Eddie. You have gone through a most unusual experience, more than most mortals will ever know. Then this morning I tell you that you must help stop a demon. Instead of going insane or running off, you sit with me and translate ancient lore into its modern equivalent. You are quite unexpected!"

Eddie shrugged. "Look, Marlowe. I'm a cop, a detective. My job is to take what witnesses tell me and interpret it so I can use it. I don't know anything about this wizard stuff."

Marlowe shut the book and pushed it away from him. "This might be the right time for you to start finding out." Marlowe picked up his coffee cup and asked, "What is this made of?"

Eddie frowned. "Uh...china, porcelain...I guess."

"Good! That is on the broad, physical level. But, if we put this under an electron microscope, what would it be made of?"

Eddie thought for a moment. "Molecules?"

"Very good— and what are molecules made of?"

"Atoms?"

"Excellent. Now, Eddie, I am sure you were taught that atoms are made of even smaller particles?"

"Sure." Eddie glanced up at the ceiling as he tried to recall. "Protons, neutrons, croutons…something like that."

"Close enough." Marlowe smiled. "Now, are you familiar with research into quarks?"

Eddie scratched his head. "Guess I'm behind in my reading."

"I'll keep it in layman's terms. Scientists found that test results on subatomic particles were influenced by the desire of the researchers. If someone observed this tiny, invisible particle and wanted it to turn left, it would be influenced by that desire."

"Where are you going with this?"

"Those scientists discovered a secret those who walk the path have known for millennia. All things are made from the same substance: in modern terms, atoms. And this substance can be affected by the *intent* of the observer."

Marlowe held the cup above the table and opened his hand. Eddie cringed, expecting it to fall to the heavy wooden table. However, it remained suspended in the air.

It didn't hover or spin, but merely hung perfectly still as if it rested on an invisible shelf.

Eddie's mouth fell open.

"How?" was all he could think to say.

"Simple." Marlowe leaned back in his chair.

"But you're defying gravity."

"There are things that defy gravity all the time," Marlowe said. "The air floating about us, and lighter than air gases. These are made from atoms, like the cup, are they not?"

"Well, yeah, sure, but they're, I don't know, lighter or thinner." Eddie found he was unable to take his eyes off the cup residing in midair.

"I did not change gravity, Eddie. I altered the cup so it was no longer affected the same way. It is the cup that changed, not gravity."

"How?"

"Through my *will* and my *intent*, the building blocks of existence." Marlowe reached up to take the cup by its handle and return it to the table. "Now you try."

Eddie frowned, and carefully picked up his own cup. He drained the coffee in one gulp. "No point wasting it."

"You must *know* you can do it, Eddie. Don't just *try* to do it or *think* you can. Know it and want it! Desire is an important part of intent," Marlowe expounded.

Eddie looked doubtful, then his jaw set and he nodded. "You got it!"

Eddie held the cup only an inch or two from the table. Marlowe gave him a look, and Eddie held it up higher.

"Good. Now look at the cup— become aware of it, not just with your eyes or hand, but with your mind."

Eddie stared at the cup, and the flowered design on the white porcelain grew brighter.

"Whoa!" Eddie marveled.

"Did the colors become more intense?" Marlowe asked, his attention focused only on Eddie.

"Yes." Eddie stared at the shimmering hues on the cup.

"Now, feel the cup, feel it disconnect from what pulls it down. Feel it grow lighter."

"I feel it," Eddie whispered.

Eddie tentatively removed his hand, one finger at a time. As he removed the last one, the cup dipped a little, but held its position in midair.

"Wow!" A huge smile broke on his face.

"Well done!"

"I don't believe it!" Eddie said, and as soon as the words were out of his mouth, the cup fell to the tabletop and smashed into pieces.

Eddie leapt back in surprise, which knocked his chair over. He fell backward and braced for an impact—which didn't occur.

Eddie found the chair had stopped a few inches above the floor. Marlowe was still in his seat, but his walking stick was raised. He made a simple gesture, and Eddie's chair returned to its upright position, with Eddie in it.

Eddie looked at Marlowe in shock, as the older man lowered his cane. "You see, it is a useful skill."

"Yeah." Eddie felt a stupid grin break out on his face. "I'm sorry about your—"

The words stopped as he looked to the spot where the cup fell, only to find it sat undamaged on its saucer.

"It, ah…the cup…it, ah…" Eddie struggled.

"I merely put it back together again, Eddie, atom by atom," Marlowe expounded.

"Man," Eddie said, as he picked up the cup and turned it in his hand. "You ever patent that and Krazy Glue will be out of business."

"Do you know what you did wrong, Edward?"

"Uh—well, I thought I…that is, I think I…uh…" Eddie gave a shrug and added, "No."

"You said words that a wizard must never use. You said you didn't believe it!"

"Well, yeah, but that's just an expression."

"Not to a wizard, Eddie," Marlowe speculated, his face very serious. "Our word is our bond, and can be used against us by others. We are very careful in what we say. When you claimed to not believe it, you negated your influence. Belief is another necessary part of intent."

"Okay, I won't do *that* again," Eddie said.

"Nevertheless, you made a good start. Now, if we begin right now, then by this afternoon—"

"Wait a minute." Eddie glanced at his watch. "This has been very informative, but I've got to get to work."

"Work?" Marlowe repeated, at a loss.

"Yeah, work. I'm a detective, working on a murder, remember?"

"Oh, of course," Marlowe went on. "But there is so little time, and you have so much to learn."

Eddie rose, "I also have a mortgage, taxes to pay, and a family to support."

Marlowe also stood up and gently grabbed Eddie's arm. "Eddie, money is no longer an issue for you. If you need me to give you some—"

"Hey, I don't take charity." Eddie shook Marlowe's hand loose.

"That's not what I meant." Marlowe's cheeks flushed with embarrassment. "It's just that money is the easiest thing to manifest."

"It's more than just money. I earned my job, and I'm damn good at it."

"Of course you are, Eddie," Marlowe assured in a calming voice.

There came a loud rapping on the door.

Instantly, Bob, the small green glob, rolled through the air into the room. He looked much paler in the sunlight and was almost transparent.

The makeshift face appeared out of the green ball, and the mouth opened up to announce, "Bankrock at door."

"Very well," Marlowe said, a bit annoyed. "Please let him in, Bob."

"Who is Bankrock?"

"Bankrock. He is— well, I guess the best way to describe him is that he is our CMO."

"CMO?"

"Yes," Marlowe explained. "Chief Magickal Officer. He helps to regulate the use of our abilities and keep us hidden from the mortal world. I asked him here this morning."

"Ah, the newest member," Bankrock announced as he entered from the foyer. He slipped his leather binder under his arm, adjusted his spectacles, and held out his hand. "Bankrock. Glad to meet you, Mr. Riftstone."

Eddie took the man's limp hand. "I'm Berman, Eddie Berman."

"Oh?" Bankrock looked surprised. "I assumed you would take the name of your master."

Eddie dropped the man's hand and felt his collar grow warm. "My what?"

"He who held your staff before you." Bankrock gulped, unnerved by the look in Eddie's eye. "It is a common tradition. Drusilicus took the name Greywacke in honor of his master."

"I don't got no 'master,'" Eddie countered as his temper flared.

Bankrock stood aghast. "I-I meant no disrespect."

"And where'd you get your stupid names, anyway? Riftstone, Bankrock. What are you guys, the damn Flintstones?"

"Well, I never!" Bankrock huffed and made a note on his pad.

Marlowe put himself between the two men. "Please, Bankrock, I asked you here for a specific purpose. Why don't we all sit and I shall explain."

"I'm goin' to work." Eddie turned toward the door.

"Eddie, please, if you can give me just a few minutes more, I'll explain my plan."

Eddie glared at Marlowe.

"Please?" Marlowe repeated.

"Yeah, sure." Eddie peeked at his watch. He did still have time.

"Trefoil and I have created a strategy to dispatch the demon," Marlowe affirmed.

"I was not informed of this," Bankrock sniffed.

"That is why I asked you here this morning. Trefoil was concerned about how Riftstone was killed."

"Considering the nature of the murder…" Bankrock began.

"No, the question we have is how did the demon catch a prophet unawares? Trefoil and I resolved that Abraxas must have disrupted Riftstone's prophetic powers, hence causing the magickal disturbance you detected, Bankrock."

"A level nine disturbance," Bankrock considered. "That *could* affect a seer."

"We felt that we needed to go on the offensive. We need to track the demon down during the daytime while he is resting. With Trefoil's and my own abilities combined, we should easily cast him out."

"So what do you need me to hang around for?" Eddie interjected. "I don't know anything about casting out demons."

"We believe your presence would assure our success, Eddie."

"How are you going to find the demon?" Bankrock said.

"With Frisha's help," Marlowe explained, a smile curved on his lips.

"Ah," Bankrock considered. "Provided the magickal disturbance hasn't affected her as well."

"That's why I wanted you along, Bankrock. Your own prophetic ability is limited, but it could be just what we need. What's more, by attacking the monster as a group of five, we might convince the demon that the Five came together."

"Lemme get this straight," Eddie cautioned. "You're gonna try to bluff a demon?"

"Yes." Bankrock nodded his head slowly. "This proposal might have some merit."

"Look, I would only be in the way," Eddie protested.

Marlowe sighed. "I know you are inexperienced, but if you were there to provide us—what do you call it—background?"

"You mean 'backup,'" Eddie corrected.

"Yes! I believe it would assure our victory!"

There was a knock at the door.

"Our final guest!" Marlowe yelped. "Eddie, if you could spare just a few hours, we could end this today. You can solve the crime, as well as help us dispense justice."

Marlowe walked to the front door and pulled it open, just as Frisha, in mismatched garments, fell into the foyer.

Marlowe knelt to her. "Are you all right, Frisha?"

"'Tis terrible, terrible," she gasped. She held up a hand and waved them away as she huffed and puffed like a bison of some variety.

"What is it?" Marlowe took her hand.

"Is she hurt?" Bankrock rushed over.

"Not…me," she wheezed, "*Trefoil.*"

SIXTEEN

Eddie and Marlowe shot a look to each other. Eddie was surprised that he saw fear in the older man's face.

"He was supposed to meet us this morning," Marlowe revealed. "What has happened?"

"Everybody calm down." Eddie helped Frisha to her feet and led her to one of the nearby overstuffed, ornate chairs. "Tell us about it."

"I saw…the whole thing," Frisha panted as she tried to get her breath back.

"You were a witness?" Eddie asked.

Marlowe touched Eddie's arm. "Not necessarily, Eddie. What did you see, Frisha?"

"T'were Trefoil in the park, last night," she clasped her hands to her eyes. "Oh, 'tis terrible."

"By himself?" Marlowe worried.

"Was that part of your plan?" Eddie challenged.

"No, we had decided to hunt the creature down in daylight," Marlowe said.

"There was no record of an event last night…" Bankrock stated as he leafed through the pages on his pad.

"Yes!" Frisha croaked. "I mean, no, I mean…I don't know. He wert attacked, and I know not if he be alive or dead. The vision left me fore I could tell."

"Eddie, would you mind getting her a cup of coffee, please?" Marlowe requested, as he patted her hand.

"Extra cream and sugar," Frisha added as Eddie ran into the breakfast room. He quickly poured and brought out a cup of the amber liquid balanced on a gleaming white saucer.

"Thou art a love." Frisha slurped at the cup in a most unladylike fashion.

"So, let me get this straight. You saw Trefoil…in a vision?" Eddie prompted to get the old woman back on track.

"Yes. T'wert staring in me crystal, and there t'was Trefoil, fine as you please."

"In your crystal?" Eddie repeated.

"She is a prophetess," Bankrock explained, "of rather great renown."

"So I've been told," Eddie concurred.

"Thou art a dear to say that." Frisha licked her lips. "He t'was in the park, and all at once there wert someone with him, laughing."

She gave a deep, menacing, masculine chuckle.

"Then, Trefoil, he leapt out of the way, as a blast of fire slashed through the air and lit a bush aflame, right t'where he'd been standing!"

Marlowe pulled another of the sizable chairs over with one hand, as if it weighed nothing, and sat across from Frisha.

Bankrock leaned closer.

"The street lamp went out o'er his head and he lifted his staff to the ready."

Frisha rose from her seat theatrically and held up her wooden spoon to demonstrate. "So, our dear, brave Trefoil calls out, 'Show yourself!' Just like that!" Frisha collapsed back into the chair. "He's so brave, and now he be gone. All is lost!"

She began to wail with a terrible croaking sound.

"Frisha, please!" Marlowe sympathized, attempting to calm her. "You must tell us what happened!"

"Yes," Bankrock found his voice. "We must know every detail!"

She extracted the world's dirtiest handkerchief from one of her pockets and blew her nose with a noise like a congested elephant.

"O' course, I'm sorry, Marlowe, I get so afeard," she fretted.

"Go on, dear lady," Marlowe encouraged her. Eddie pulled out his own notebook and began to take notes.

"I saw him hold up his hands and make a protective bubble of blue light— you know blue is his staff's color—"

"I know, Frisha, please," Marlowe urged.

"So, he's standing there," —Frisha replaced the filthy rag up her sleeve, like a lady at a medieval pageant— "and nothing happens. He just peered up at the trees. And then, I saw it! A serpent, so small and quick as to be unnoticed slid down the trees, fine as you like, and wiggles sideways towards him."

"A snake?" Eddie repeated, still writing. "What kind of snake?"

"Very small and red," Frisha said. "Trefoil watches the trees, he sees not the snake, so I yell out, 'Look out!'"

"Did he hear you?" Bankrock inquired.

"No, 'twas no time," Frisha whined, her eyes wet with tears. "Quick as a wink this snake bites him on the leg!" She snapped her fingers for effect. "Then that voice calls out, 'You've lost your edge, wizard!'"

She spoke in a mock deep voice, which sounded very male and demonic.

"So Trefoil yells out, 'Face me, monster,' but his leg is already beginning to swell. I sees him raise his staff to purge the poison, and he sends white light into the wound."

Eddie turned to Marlowe "Is that normal? I mean, for you guys?"

"Absolutely," Bankrock interjected. "Standard practice to cleanse any poison, especially from a metaphysical creature."

"But, he din't!" Frisha said, as she became upset again. "The light traveled into the wound, then Trefoil jiggled and quaked as a man having a fit. Then the deep voice calls out, 'You weren't much of a challenge.' Trefoil falls to the ground—and it looked like he was in…in…"

"What, Frisha?" Marlowe begged.

Her voice lowered to a whisper. "As if he fell into the Dark Sleep."

Marlowe collapsed into his chair heavily, a look of panic on his face. "The Dark Sleep," he repeated in a solemn undertone.

Bankrock, who'd gone so pale he was almost the color of Bob, mouthed the words, but no sound issued from his lips.

Eddie frowned. "What is it, what's the Dark Sleep?"

Marlowe blinked and tried to focus.

Bankrock spoke in a tight, quiet voice, "A place between life and death, and once there it takes more than the power of a single wizard to bring you back."

"Aye," Frisha blubbered, "and some do not come back at all."

"This explains why I was not aware of this attack," Bankrock said. "It was poison, not the use of magick."

Eddie took the woman by the shoulders and turned her to him. "Frisha, can you tell us where Trefoil is?"

"I cannot," Frisha said. "As soon as I saw what happened, I fell to a swoon. I only awoke a few minutes ago and ran right here."

"Are you sure you're all right?" Marlowe said.

"I know not." Frisha shook her head. "I think this vision did something to me. My second sight 'tis all confused." She slipped to the edge of the chair and grabbed Marlowe's knees. "Am I bewitched?"

"I warned you of this," Bankrock snapped at Marlowe and adjusted his glasses. "The level nine magickal disturbance from Riftstone's murder is creating shock waves that will affect other prophets."

"Don't panic, Frisha," Marlowe encouraged. "We're safe in the daylight. We must find Trefoil."

"Aye." Frisha gave an unenthusiastic nod. "As long as you're there to protect me, Marlowe."

"Yes, good lady. Now, have you eaten?"

"I'm too distraught to eat," Frisha lamented. "But if ye have breakfast laid out, I suppose, to keep me strength up…"

"Please help yourself," Marlowe comforted as she rose. "It's all in there, I'll join you in a moment."

"You're too kind, Marlowe," Frisha lumbered into the breakfast room.

"Marlowe!" Bankrock turned on the older man. "This is unacceptable!"

"I beg your pardon?"

"You are coven master, the bearer of the staff of Spirit, *and* the leader of the Five. Do something!"

"I intend to," Marlowe vowed in a calm but stern voice. "I cannot understand why Trefoil went to confront the demon last night on his own! It is utter madness."

"When word of this gets out there will be panic throughout the coven," Bankrock surmised. "Some may accept that Riftstone was killed, but now Trefoil? No one is safe!"

"We must think of ways to help our situation." Marlowe rubbed his forehead with one hand. "Running about like beheaded chickens is not the solution."

"But the danger—" Bankrock started.

"We must find Trefoil." Marlowe grabbed Bankrock's arm. "Can you do that?"

"What is he, a bloodhound?" Eddie asked.

Bankrock glared at Eddie, his eyes still a bit wild. "With effort, I can locate any wizard within the coven. It is one of my talents." He took out a small crystal ball from his tweed jacket pocket. "I only hope my faculties haven't been affected as well."

"How can I help?" Eddie suggested.

"Ah!" Marlowe considered. "Perhaps it would be best if you did return to your duties."

"How about this," Eddie said. "I'll check with the precinct, to see if there is any reports about Trefoil or any homeless guy in the park."

"Mayhaps the police can help," Bankrock said hopefully. "But of course, do not tell them what you know."

"Right," Eddie agreed. "Like, I would go to my captain and tell him that the homeless guy was murdered by a demon, who attacked another guy when he turned himself into a snake. That way he can put me in a nice padded cell."

"You see the problem we face, Eddie." Marlowe pulled Eddie away from Bankrock and toward the front door. "It is difficult to know the truth and still live among mortals."

Eddie stared at him, unable to think of anything to say.

Marlowe went on. "You need to know one other thing. Abraxas attacked Riftstone and Trefoil because they were two of the Five."

"Yeah, I get that," Eddie said, as they reached the door.

Marlowe's eyes narrowed. "Now that you carry the Staff of Fire, he will seek to kill you as well."

SEVENTEEN

A police station is always hectic. Phones ring, witnesses are interviewed, collared criminals demand their rights, and voices yell above the din. However, for the trained cop, the sounds become a background canvas on which their work is painted.

Eddie Berman walked into chaos which would overwhelm the average man, and barely noticed it. His world had undergone a complete shift in the last thirty-six hours. What he believed was real had been forcibly altered.

It was a huge surprise to Eddie when he walked out of Marlowe's front door to find himself coming out of an impressive brownstone on the corner of 85th Street and Central Park West. The four-story brick edifice was built with a huge turret that jutted from the facade like a fairy-tale tower. However, like the box where Frisha resided, Marlowe's house was much larger on the inside than what was possible based on the outside.

Eddie immediately got his bearings and walked the block to the 86th Street transverse road. His mind drifted to a question beyond his first lesson in magic and the attack on Trefoil: what would he tell his wife? This was followed by the equally close second: what would he tell his partner?

Eddie never lied to either of them before. But what other choice did he have? He could barely believe what he'd seen. How could his partner or spouse accept such things secondhand? His daddy had an expression for times like these: "When shit flies, it hits everything."

Eddie was suddenly choked up by a wish that he could sit down with his old man and talk. He would be the only one who would listen to Eddie's tale and actually give him advice he could use. Or would this situation be even too much for Lawrence Berman?

He missed his daddy so much some days.

Walking up the stairs to the detectives' room, Eddie saw Luis behind his desk writing in his own small notebook.

Luis didn't even look up as Eddie sat at his desk across from him.

"You gonna tell me about it, or what?" Luis snapped, his eyes focused on the movement of his pencil.

"Tell you about what?" Eddie replied, aware that his response was completely lame.

"You say you can't meet with me, you gotta go alone, your wife calls me because you're not home, and now you stroll in like nothin's happened." Luis raised his head. "You wanna talk?"

"There isn't much to say," Eddie declared. "Last night turned out to be a dead-end. In fact, every part of this case goes nowhere. I think you were right. List it as unsolved and file it."

Luis sat back in his chair, his eyes never leaving Eddie's. But the expression softened, shifted from anger to a befuddled astonishment.

"Let me get this straight," Luis replied. "Eddie Berman is telling me to give up on a case? What happened to not wanting to settle?"

"It happens," Eddie griped. "No leads, no witnesses, weird forensics. Maybe we have to let it go."

Eddie lowered his head and picked up the nearest folder on his desk and began to peruse it. There was a sudden "SLAM" as Luis threw his entire caseload on Eddie's desk.

"Okay, partner," Luis's voice was quiet but intense. "What's going on?"

Eddie sat up, still startled. "Nothing's going on!"

"Well, my bullshit detector has gone into the red zone!" Vasquez forced himself to keep his voice low. He glanced around the room to make sure that they were not being watched by any of the other detectives. "You don't go home, you lie to your wife. What you got? Some chippy on the side?"

Eddie's face flushed. "Absolutely not! You think that's what this is about?"

"I don't know what it's about, 'cause you won't tell me." Luis leaned closer to Eddie. "But when a man starts lying, that's the first place to start. If I'm wrong, why don't you straighten me out?"

Eddie exhaled with force and stared at his partner. Here was a man who once took a bullet meant for him.

"Luis, I…it's just…" Eddie's mind raced to try to give his partner something that was true. "I'm not having an affair."

"Good thing, because I would be the first one to kick your sorry ass," Luis threatened.

"But things—*strange* things—are happening because of this case," Eddie explained.

"Oh, yeah?" Luis said, a bit placated. "Like that homeless lady yesterday?"

"Yeah." Eddie sighed. "I think maybe you were right. This case is a no-win. Let's pass it on to the Feds and let Wilcox botch it instead of us."

"You *want* to give a case to that son-of-a-bitch?"

"It can't be solved."

Luis sat back in his chair, his eyebrows heavy with suspicion. "You gonna tell me where you were last night?"

Eddie blew air out again. "It's a long story."

Luis looked past Eddie and said in a low voice, "Well, you'd better make it short, because here comes someone else who wants to know."

Eddie turned to see Cerise as she strode straight toward them. Her jaw jutted with determination and Eddie could see circles under her eyes from lack of sleep, even with her dark skin. She'd obviously been crying.

Damn, Eddie thought, *I can't lie to her. I'll tell her the truth even if she thinks I'm crazy.*

She approached Eddie slowly, like a female praying mantis preparing to spring and consume her mate alive.

Then, a most peculiar event happened at the same moment. Hank, the evidence clerk, entered the room. He was reading a file and didn't even notice the oncoming freight train that was Cerise Berman. He walked right past her to Eddie's desk.

"Hey, Lew," Hank said, "you need to sign here, even though you didn't take that evidence yesterday."

Eddie looked at the paper open in the man's hand as his wife drew closer.

"You must've been worn out yesterday." Hank smiled. "I got here around five AM, and you were sacked out in the locker room."

Eddie turned his head so fast it almost gave him whiplash. "What?"

Cerise stopped dead and listened intently.

"Yeah," Hank went on, oblivious to Eddie's wife. "I got here and there you were sleeping like a baby. Didn't have the heart to wake you. Bet your neck'll be stiff today. Sign here."

Hank pointed at a line as Eddie stood open-mouthed. As if in a dream, he pulled out his pen and signed his name.

"You *saw* me?" Eddie marveled.

"Yeah. What happened? You and your old lady have a fight?" Hank chortled, his back still to Cerise who stood as shocked as her husband.

"No, I was just, you know, tired." Eddie wondered how on earth this happened.

"Don't make it a habit," Hank stated as he closed the folder. "Captain frowns on cops sacking out in the station, unless you are in a bunk room and you signed up for it. I don't want to report you, Lew."

"Thanks, Hank, I, uh, appreciate that," Eddie stammered.

Hank shrugged, turned, and walked past Cerise. Her face had undergone a surprising transformation. Gone was the tight mouth and angry glare.

Eddie carefully approached her. "Hey, baby."

"Oh, Eddie, I'm sorry. I was coming here to yell at you, and you were so tired—" She fell against his shoulder and hugged him fiercely. "I'm so stupid sometimes!"

"Is that where you ended up, Eddie?" Luis rose from his desk and drew closer to the couple. "Jeez, I didn't think to look down there."

Eddie smiled. A miracle had just taken place.

"I made a spectacle of myself." Cerise pulled a tissue from her purse to blot her nose and eyes. "And, Luis, I bothered you last night—"

"It was no problem, Cerise," Luis comforted. "We both worry about this guy."

"But I thought—I mean—" Cerise stammered. "Oh, Eddie, I thought you were with another woman."

Eddie held his wife at arm's length. "Baby, I would never, ever —"

"I feel like a fool. I'll go to work. Will you be home for dinner?"

Eddie nodded emphatically, overjoyed that this problem solved itself without any action on his part.

"Lieutenant Berman?" said a short, bearded man.

Eddie turned toward the familiar voice, and found Marlowe as he stood nearby. He now wore a conservative dark suit with a multicolored tie so bright it practically lit the room. But, if one possessed the ability to transform clothing at will, one might change clothes a lot.

"Yes," Eddie found himself at a loss as to the correct way to react.

"I may have located that witness you asked me about," Marlowe said. "We spoke last night? Did you get home all right? I was concerned, you looked tired."

"Oh." Eddie gave a quick look to Cerise. "Yeah."

"I'll let you get to work, Eddie." Cerise pulled away.

"I hope you don't mind, officer," Marlowe went on, "but those people you asked about are only available tonight. Do you still wish to question them? Or have you changed your mind?"

"No, no, I need to speak to them," Eddie affirmed and put his head near his wife's ear. "I'll be late tonight."

"That's fine," she whispered back. "Just please come home. And take good care of my big, black man."

Eddie smiled and with a nod to Luis, Cerise left.

"I thought you didn't get anywhere with the case." Luis folded his arms as he carefully observed Eddie and Marlowe.

"I'm afraid I wasn't much help," Marlowe admitted, "but the lieutenant was very thorough. He asked to meet with several people—possible witnesses."

Luis looked at Eddie with one eyebrow raised.

Luis is not buying this, Eddie thought, then too enthusiastically he declared loudly, "At least we can try!"

"Sure," Luis agreed, suspicion still in his eyes. "I could tag along, Eddie, help you question the witnesses."

Marlowe glanced at Eddie. "That's a kind gesture, sergeant. But some of them are elderly. I think two policemen might intimidate them."

Eddie tried to look thoughtful. "I think you're right, Mister —"

"Marlowe."

"That's right." Eddie snapped his fingers as if the memory just returned. "Luis, it's probably better if I talk to them. You know, kid gloves."

Luis nodded, his mouth a tight line.

"Now, about that homeless gentleman you asked about," Marlowe continued, and Eddie could see that something was wrong.

"Yes?"

"I'm afraid he's in the hospital," Marlowe explained. "I know you're busy, but—"

"I should talk to him, if he's conscious," Eddie instructed. "Luis, can you hold down the fort?"

"Yes sir, *lieutenant,*" Luis responded and looked as if he'd like to punch Eddie.

With a nod, Eddie followed Marlowe as the older man walked along with his cane.

Luis watched them leave and considered that the entire incident was just a little too convenient. He also wondered how the older man had known he was a sergeant.

EIGHTEEN

Eddie drove his car with Marlowe in the passenger seat as they rode south down Park Avenue on the way to Bellevue, New York's premier hospital. Neither had spoken since they got in the car.

"So how the hell did all that happen?" Eddie ventured.

"I beg your pardon?" Marlowe responded.

"Hank showed up just in time to settle things with my wife. How could he remember me in the locker room? That was just some lame-ass excuse I came up with."

Marlowe nodded. "I was aware of your—how did you put it —'lame-ass excuse.'"

"But that doesn't explain—"

"I was on my way to see you and I became aware of your wife parking her car," Marlowe explained. "Since I had observed you from afar last night, I recognized her. So, all I did was touch the mind of your evidence clerk and gave him an overwhelming desire to have you sign a paper."

"But all that stuff about seeing me—"

"Memory is a peculiar thing, especially to the untrained mind. It's misty and open to reinterpretation. I merely planted a situation within his mind."

Eddie exhaled. "So, he remembers something that never happened."

Marlowe shrugged. "Well, he *did* go down to the locker room this morning. He has seen you there on occasion. But, the specific recollection, I *placed* there. It is a useful skill, Eddie. When a supernatural event occurs and there are witnesses, it is sometimes necessary to alter memories."

Eddie looked out the windshield and smiled. "And that's how your coven stays secret."

"Exactly."

"Well, you saved my bacon."

"You not going home last night was my fault. It is only right that I resolve the situation."

"So, Trefoil is in the hospital?"

Marlowe's face went grim. "Yes. Bankrock was able to locate him. I also spoke to a witness to his attack."

"A witness? Why didn't you bring him to the station? I could've questioned him."

"That would not have been a good choice," Marlowe insisted. "He was a member of SCAN."

"SCAN?"

"The Squirrel Combined Action Network. A friend of mine, Quiptail, told me. Trefoil was indeed attacked exactly as Frisha divined."

The car was silent.

"Quiptail?" Eddie repeated flatly. "He's a squirrel?"

"That's right."

"And he was a witness?"

"He does get around," Marlowe suggested. "Very little goes on in the park that the squirrels don't see."

"You talk to squirrels."

"An extra language is always a boon, Eddie."

"Since I can't do follow-up with your witness, how is Trefoil?" Eddie said.

"He survived." Marlowe's face grew hard. "But he is in a state of catalepsy."

"That's the Dark Sleep thing, right?"

"Yes."

"Will he come out of it?"

Marlowe nodded. "That's why I came for you, Eddie."

"What can I do?"

"Wizards must combine their powers to rouse one in such a state. Perhaps you and I together—"

"Marlowe, I just did my first lesson this morning, and blew it pretty bad. You want me to try when it's a matter of life and death?"

Marlowe sighed. "I am afraid that you must learn through trial by fire, Eddie. Abraxas has, in seventy-two hours, attacked and defeated two expert wizards."

"That worries you?"

"More than that, I assure you." Marlowe stroked his beard. "Not since the ancient days, when he had temples and worshippers by the score, did he demonstrate such power. I told Bankrock to research the histories to find out as much as possible. There has to be something we overlooked." He faced the windshield with his jaw set. "But first, we must divine a way to get to Trefoil."

"That I can handle," Eddie said. He pulled out his cell phone and spoke a name as he drove.

"Who are you calling?" Marlowe asked.

"The cavalry."

Marlowe frowned. "I fail to see how horseback warriors could help."

They pulled into Bellevue's parking lot on First Avenue. Eddie's badge helped a great deal to get past the security checkpoint and into the special lot reserved for police and emergency vehicles.

They made their way to the main lobby where they were directed to the charity wing, the place many of the city's indigent were given healthcare.

As they walked through the hallways, it was obvious where the facility changed into the wing designed for the poor. The walls grew dirtier, the faces more glum, and a feeling of overwork was almost a scent in the air.

There were many people who sat on benches or stood about the large unkempt waiting room, as they waited to hear of loved ones. There was also a clinic section for people to be treated for minor injuries, or to receive needed inoculations.

Eddie approached the receptionist, a meaty nurse who looked like she'd seen it all, done it all, and then kicked its ass for bothering her. He showed his shield.

"That don't mean much here, buddy," she said with a cursory glance at the badge. "Whaddayaneed?"

"You had a John Doe brought in this morning?" Eddie said. "Black guy, curly gray beard?"

She nodded, grabbed a file, and gave it a quick perusal. "At least he didn't stink like half of 'em."

"Thank you, Miss Alcott." Marlowe smiled at her.

She blinked for a moment. "How did you…" she started to say, then decided he merely read her name tag.

"Has he been treated?" Eddie asked.

Her expression hardened as she returned her eyes to Eddie. She checked the folder. "Haven't gotten the blood work back, and you may have noticed, we're pretty busy here. Got him hooked up to an IV and monitors, and he's stable. That's about all we can do."

"We need to see him." Eddie reached for the folder.

She batted his hand away. "Officer, this is a hospital. You ain't seeing nobody unless you got a doctor with you."

"Got here as fast as I could, Eddie," came a voice behind them.

Eddie turned to see Doctor Beverly Warren walk up to the reception desk, a Bellevue ID around her neck.

Miss Alcott's expression softened. "Doctor Warren, I didn't know you were scheduled for today."

"I'm not, but I will take Lieutenant Berman up to see the patient," she spoke without any anger or malice, and simply put her hand out for the folder.

Instantly cowed, Miss Alcott handed it over.

Beverly turned and strode off, with Eddie fast on her heels. Marlowe gave Miss Alcott a wink as he turned away, and she felt herself flush like a schoolgirl.

She touched her lapel, found she wasn't wearing her name tag and wondered how the white-haired man had known her name.

Eddie caught up to Beverly. "On the phone you said you could help. I didn't know you worked here."

"I volunteer here, Eddie." She threw her chestnut hair back. "The charity ward needs doctors, and I need to treat patients that are not corpses. It makes me better at my job."

"How?"

She exhaled deeply, almost a sigh. "I need to remember that the dead aren't just bodies, but real people that once laughed and spoke and were loved." She opened the file. "Well, I got you in, what's your interest?"

"He's a witness in the case of the dismembered homeless guy."

She looked at the report as they walked. "Another John Doe? Have we got a perp who targets the homeless?"

Eddie stepped in front of her, and she stopped. "I don't know, but if so, it's *my* case, there's no 'we' here."

Her mouth grew hard. "Oh, Eddie, you're so masculine when you become territorial," Beverly said, her expression not shifting. "You want my help, or do you just want to stuff it up your ass?"

"Of course, your help would be most useful, Doctor Warren," Marlowe said, which made Beverly turn to face him.

"Pardon me," she replied and looked back and forth to the two men. "Who are you?"

"Marlowe. I'm a friend of the John Doe, who by the way, is named Trey."

"Charmed, I'm sure," she deadpanned. "So the civilian gets an in on the case but I'm interfering." She thrust the file at Eddie and turned to storm away. "Good luck, lieutenant."

"Doctor…Beverly, please, I'm sorry." Eddie rushed to her to gently touch her arm. "I *do* need your help. I've just had a rough night. I'm sorry."

She looked back at him and crossed her arms adamantly. "Sorry?"

"Very, very, sorry," Eddie repeated, then added, "I'm a jerk."

Beverly visibly relaxed. She cocked a finger at Eddie's face. "Okay, groveling accepted, but watch your mouth. I don't leave my morgue to run all over the city because some hotshot cop phones me."

"You're right, and I appreciate it."

"Now, good lady, can you tell us what room he is in?" Marlowe asked.

"Cute." Beverly eyed Marlowe. "You're the real gentleman. He doesn't have a room; he's in the Intensive Care ward."

"Intensive Care?" Eddie considered. "That's not good."

She retrieved the file from Eddie and looked at it again. "He's stable, but he's comatose. They need to keep track of his vitals in case he takes a turn for the worse."

She led them down a hallway and into a large room, more long than wide, lined with beds on both sides. Many beds were empty, but a few were occupied with patients hooked up to various kinds of machinery. They walked to the end of the row where Trefoil lay.

His skin bore a grayish hue, his lips were dry, and his eyes carried dark circles underneath.

Marlowe whispered to Eddie, "Keep Doctor Warren busy for a moment or two."

Eddie took Beverly to the other side of the room, with a gentle arm pull and a nod of his head.

"What's the prognosis?" Eddie whispered, trying to give the impression that he didn't want Marlowe to overhear.

"Well, according to this," Beverly spoke quietly, "some jogger found him, took him for dead, and called 911. The police and paramedics arrived and found a heartbeat. Brought him here." She rifled through the papers. "The resident who did the prelim assumed he was probably suffering from a combination of drugs and alcohol—"

She stopped dead. Her eyes scanned one line over and over.

"What?" Eddie questioned.

She looked up at Eddie in a way that scared him. "You holding back on me, Berman?"

"No," Eddie blurted, surprised.

"You read this report?"

"No, for crying out loud—" Eddie was cognizant that his voice was too loud. He went on, quietly. "What is it?"

"According to this, he has gold teeth. And they don't appear to be crowns. The initial theory is that they're dental implants."

Eddie tried to act nonchalant and failed miserably.

"Is this guy like the other one?" Beverly stepped toward the inert patient. "That can't be a coincidence."

"Indeed it is not, Doctor Warren," Marlowe affirmed. Beverly looked over to Marlowe, who held his walking stick and moved it in a small circle. Her expression grew relaxed, and she stared through Marlowe without blinking.

"Beverly?" Eddie spoke, aware that she was no longer cognizant of the world around her. He passed a hand before her eyes but she didn't blink. "What did you do?"

"Nothing that will harm her," Marlowe said. "What does she know Eddie?"

"She did the autopsy on Riftstone."

Marlowe's eyebrows lifted. "I'm sure she found many curious things."

"You bet your staff. He was too healthy for an old guy, and his teeth, some of them were gold."

Marlowe nodded. "Not an uncommon manifestation."

"What causes that?"

Marlowe shrugged "There are theories, but to be honest, we are not sure. Some believe that due to the amount of mystical energy that passes through our bodies, our teeth change into a more conductive material."

Eddie looked at Beverly. "You can't leave her like this."

"True," Marlowe considered, "but I think she can help. We need the blood report." Marlowe took the folder from her stiff hands and glanced at it.

"Can't we just wave our sticks, you know, Ala-ka—"

Marlowe quickly placed two fingers to Eddie's mouth to stop him speaking. "Don't. You dare not use any 'magic' words you learned in your mortal life." Marlowe took his hand away.

"Why not?"

"Because you might change someone into something, or worse. You have great power now, remember that."

"Great, you give me a loaded weapon, and I don't know how to use it."

"Quaint way of putting it, but it sums up the situation." Marlowe focused on the paperwork. "Now, we cannot manifest a counter spell on Trefoil unless we know what type of poison was used."

"Poison?"

Marlowe nodded, then rolled back the sheet covering Trefoil's inert frame and pointed to two tiny marks on his leg.

"Are those what I think they are?" Eddie said.

"Snakebite."

"And Abraxas *was* that snake?"

"The poison must have been designed to react to a counter spell. If I knew what it was, it would help."

"Seems like this Abraxas dude is one clever son-of-a-bitch."

"Well put, Eddie." Marlowe closed the folder and handed it to him. "It's not here." He turned his attention to the unmoving Doctor Warren. "We'll need her to get that report."

"Can't you just, y'know, wave your stick and have it appear?"

"Please, Eddie, don't tell me my job," Marlowe sniped, annoyed with his student. He held his cane in front of Beverly and waved it in a counterclockwise motion.

"What are you doing?" Eddie whispered.

"Remember that I said memory is easy to influence? I'm just making her forget that she read that line about the teeth."

"Don't do too much."

"A wizard is like a physician. 'Do no harm' is our first objective."

"You guys got that from doctors?"

"Actually, Eddie, they got that from us. Most advances in medicine were due to intervention by one who walks the path."

Beverly blinked once and was abruptly animated again.

"What was I saying?" she asked.

"You were talking about the resident physician believing that my friend's state was due to a combination of drugs and alcohol," Marlowe said without a moment of hesitation.

"That's right," she looked at her hands, a bit surprised that the file was no longer in them.

"You told us you wanted to get a hold of the blood work report," Eddie picked up on Marlowe's cue. "That would be a big help, Beverly."

She nodded. "That can be arranged. They took his blood hours ago. I'll go and lean on them."

"You're the best." Eddie broke into a grin.

"Remember that the next time I talk to you about one of *our* cases."

"I am properly chastised," Eddie acknowledged, as Beverly grabbed the file and left the room.

Eddie slumped against Trefoil's bed. "Jeez! I thought you had to lie a lot to be a cop!"

"We are not lying, Eddie, we are putting things in ways that fit a mortal's view of reality."

"So I'm not a mortal anymore?"

"No, Eddie, you're not," Marlowe advised. "And they cannot know of the battles we fight or the things we face."

"Why?"

Marlowe sat on the other side of the bed and gazed down at the still Trefoil. "Look at your society and your idea of celebrity. If people knew there were divine masters all around them, they would want to make them famous. Or worse, try to put them on a television show to demonstrate their abilities."

"What's wrong with that? I mean, we got that guy who bends spoons, and that other guy who talks to dead people."

"Both charlatans, I assure you." Marlowe's focus shifted to the top of his cane.

"Really? I suppose you would know, but how come?"

"Because the last thing a true wizard wants is his own television show. When you can have anything, your needs become smaller."

"Yeah?" Eddie frowned. "You got some perks. Your big house? It's pretty fancy."

Marlowe sighed. "Yes, it is, but not by my choice. As coven master, I often act as an ambassador. But, like Frisha, I could easily be content living in a cardboard box."

They both rose as Beverly entered the room.

She held up a paper "Okay, it's getting weird again."

"How do you mean?" Eddie hoped he sounded helpful.

"Although it looks like a snakebite, from his blood work, it appears that he was injected with an unusual combination of herbs and strange animal byproducts. The tox guy thinks one of them is the urine of a large cat—like a tiger."

Marlowe nodded. "Well done! Though it was probably a black panther."

Eddie held out his hand for the report and Beverly handed him the paper. "It's pretty technical— Hey!" she added as Eddie handed the paper to Marlowe. "I thought he was here to help his friend."

"He is," Eddie agreed, "but he happens to be an expert on unusual herbs and poisons."

"Oh, really?" Beverly asked with suspicion.

"Why yes," Marlowe skimmed the chemical breakdown. "Sort of a lifelong hobby."

"So what do you think the herbs are, oh expert?" Beverly folded her arms to strike an "impress me" stance.

"A combination of several exotic ones, belladonna to begin with, and the mammal hemoglobin you detected is bat's blood." Marlowe returned the sheet to Beverly. "Thank you."

Beverly gaped at the paper, then to Eddie. "Is he for real?"

"Oh, yes," Eddie effused, "the real deal."

"You would come in handy on the tox we got off the dismembered guy. He ingested some pretty weird stuff," Beverly said.

"I'd be happy to." Marlowe made another quick circle with his stick.

Beverly stared at him for the briefest of moments, and then told them, "Well, I gotta go." She headed for the door. "You let me know anything you find out, Eddie."

"Thanks, Beverly," Eddie called as she walked out the door. He then leaned to Marlowe and whispered, "I saw that."

"What?"

"You put the whammy on her, to get her to leave."

"I did not put a 'whammy' on her. I merely reminded her of a pressing engagement. We need a few minutes alone with Trefoil."

"Can the pair of us wake him?"

"After looking at the potion ingredients, that will be insufficient. We must get him to my house."

"Great, so we wave our sticks and *poof!* Off we go!"

Marlowe sighed. "Eddie, teleportation is an ability held by a master wizard—"

"Then let's go." Eddie stood straighter and closed his eyes. "Beam me up, Scotty."

Marlowe shook Eddie's shoulder to rouse him. "In a city as crowded as this, there are far too many dangers. The slightest miscalculation could be disastrous."

"How do you mean?"

"Materializing inside a solid wall? Or worse, inside another person or an animal? I'll put it in a context you'll understand. Did you see the movie *The Fly*?"

Eddie thought for a moment. "Yuck."

"Indeed."

"What are our other options? It's not like we can just walk out of here with him on a gurney."

Marlowe stood for a moment and considered this as he rubbed his beard with his free left hand. "Actually, Edward, that is a good idea!"

"Look, Marlowe, so far I know you can float cups, travel the world by walking into the woods, and other stuff. But old Nurse Bulldog at that front desk is not going to let you stroll out of here with Trefoil."

"Yes, she will, Eddie. If she sees what looks acceptable to her. It is time I introduced you to the power of illusion."

"Illusion?"

Marlowe nodded with a twinkle in his eye. "It requires deceit. But the deception is merely a visual one, and we do not tell untruths with our lips. It is a case of the 'eye of the beholder.'"

"I have no clue what you are talking about, old man," Eddie replied, frustrated.

"It shall all be clear. But, you must follow my directions *exactly*, do you ken?"

"I ken, I ken. What do I do?"

"First, you must get the car…"

Nineteen

Five minutes later, Eddie waved to the security man as he drove out of the lot. Following Marlowe's instructions, he pulled the car into the driveway marked "EMERGENCY: AMBULANCES ONLY." Marlowe hadn't totally explained everything, only that Eddie must park the unmarked police car close to an ambulance.

"What the hell does he think this will do?" Eddie said to himself, as he pulled the car behind a row of three emergency vehicles. He got out of the car and watched the doors that led to the Emergency Room. He glanced at his suit and found it wasn't a suit anymore but a set of green hospital scrubs.

Marlowe had suggested that money was the easiest thing to manifest. To Eddie, it seemed that what was manifested most was abrupt changes of clothing.

He looked at what he wore again, and his suit was back and yet at the same time it wasn't. He turned to peer at the car, and instead found a large ambulance in its place, with "SAINT MARLOWES HOSPITAL" emblazoned on the sides.

Eddie gave a yelp of surprise and walked back to examine it. There was indeed an ambulance in place of his NYPD vehicle. Eddie rubbed his eyes.

He uncovered them to find his unmarked police car sat where it belonged. This caused him to blink, and in that nictitate, it again was replaced by the ambulance.

He peered about to observe if anyone else noticed. There were a few people coming and going, but they didn't discern anything out of the ordinary.

They see what they expect to see, Eddie thought.

He casually reached out to the ambulance and found his hand passed through the outside of it.

He leapt back, closed his eyes, and felt for the vehicle. He touched the back fender, and felt along the trunk of the car, the metal against his hand, the sun warming it. His car was indeed there.

He backed away and opened his eyes.

A siren went off a few short feet from him, and Eddie turned to see a large ambulance coming straight toward him.

With reflexes that saved him on more than one occasion, Eddie leapt out of the way, the speeding conveyance missing him with room to spare.

Eddie stood next to his vehicle and breathed heavily. It still projected the SAINT MARLOWES HOSPITAL conveyance to anyone who noticed.

The newly arrived real ambulance was busily discharging its patient. From the corner of his eye, Eddie saw a gurney slowly coming out of the Emergency Room doors. It was being pushed by a young and handsome doctor in a clean, white coat, a stethoscope hung from his neck. Eddie realized this doctor gave the appearance of someone cast for a television show. In fact, the man was reminiscent of every handsome doctor he'd ever seen on any soap opera.

But the patient in the gurney was Trefoil.

Trusting his instincts, he rubbed his eyes.

He opened them and Eddie saw Trefoil was not on a gurney at all, but hovered in the air.

For a moment he wanted to laugh, because it reminded him of an old trick one of the neighborhood kids used to do. A kid would lie down with his feet sticking out from under a bed sheet and start to rise up in the air. Of course, this was accomplished with a pair of legs made from scrap wood with shoes at the end. The kid held the wood in his arms, as if he were laying straight out, and the long sheet covered his real legs to give the appearance he floated in the air.

But Trefoil was not walking with fake legs. He floated. The young, handsome doctor was actually Marlowe, who walked behind his friend with one hand on the back of his head.

Eddie glanced down as his own green scrubs which seemed to fade in and out with each step, and walked toward Marlowe. As he approached, his outfit changed completely to hospital garb, and Marlowe was once again the handsome young doctor. The only thing constant was Trefoil, oblivious to the illusions around him— or anything else.

The two men drew close to the parked car and Eddie stopped, not sure what to do.

"Hit your head," Marlowe's voice emanated from the handsome doctor's mouth.

"What?" Eddie was convinced he'd heard him wrong.

"*Hit your head,*" the young, beardless, ruggedly handsome face repeated, and then added, "with the flat of your hand."

Eddie lightly smacked his hand against the side of his head.

The ambulance was gone, and Eddie's car sat where he parked it. Just as he absorbed this, the image of the larger vehicle returned.

"Where do we load him in?" Eddie asked.

"Open the rear seat door. I'll take care of the rest," the handsome doctor replied with a winning smile.

Eddie struck the side of his head, saw the back door handle, reached out and grabbed it. As he pulled it open, he saw the large, rear door of the projected ambulance open and the young doctor touched something on the gurney to fold it up and push it in the back.

He smacked his head again and saw the truth. Marlowe waved his stick and the floating Trefoil lowered into the back seat of the car.

The doctor got in the vehicle, which to the world still appeared as an ambulance.

Eddie quickly walked around to the driver's side and slapped his head again to grasp the door handle, open the door, and get in.

Inside the car, everything was as Eddie remembered it. He was relieved to see Marlowe beside him, and Trefoil lay on the back seat.

"Don't worry, it's safe to drive. The illusion is only *outside* the vehicle."

"Man, that was…" Eddie hesitated and took a large lungful of air. "That was—"

"Drive, Eddie, time is passing, and I don't want to maintain the illusion any longer than I have to."

"Oh! Right, right." Eddie started the car, pulled it around the circular roadway, and out the way he'd come.

Two blocks away, Marlowe visibly relaxed. "Very well, now all anyone sees is the car."

"Are we taking him to your place?"

"I *do* have more than enough room."

Eddie nodded. "No doubt about that. You could move my entire precinct into your house."

Negotiating the midtown traffic as well as one could manage, Marlowe and Eddie arrived at the 85th Street house and were able to get Trefoil up the stairs and stoop, held between them like a friend who imbibed too much. Once inside, they ceased all attempts at stealth and Marlowe levitated the man to the elevator in the center of the spiral stairs. The elevator was small, and the three men were crammed in together.

"Is this thing safe?" Eddie asked, as the tubular contrivance lifted and shook.

"Perfectly." Marlowe seemed unperturbed by the rattle of chains and the unsteady ride.

On the high second floor, Marlowe carefully lifted Trefoil from the elevator car and levitated him into one of the many bedrooms.

At Marlowe's behest, Eddie brought out his staff and held it aloft as Marlowe chanted strange words. A beam of red light shot forth from Eddie's staff, combined with white light from Marlowe's, and rained down as pink sparkles on Trefoil's still form. The unconscious man began to breathe deeper and more fully. His face regained a little color. He now resembled someone merely asleep, instead of near death.

"Can we bring him out of it?" Eddie wondered when Marlowe stopped vocalizing and the glow faded from their raised staffs.

"The pair of us do not have enough power," Marlowe said. "But we helped."

Eddie nodded. "That's good. I like Trey." He glanced at his wristwatch. "Is that the time? I gotta get back to work."

"Eddie, I am concerned. We should practice."

"I have to report in," Eddie said with a shrug. "I will come here after work for an hour or two."

"I would prefer you remain here tonight."

Eddie slowly turned to face Marlowe, as his wooden staff shrank down to a credit card and was replaced in his wallet.

"Look, I can't. I have a wife, a family, and a sick momma. They need me."

"So does the world, Eddie," Marlowe said. "In a few days the summer solstice will come. It is a day of great power. If the staves of the Five can come together on the longest day of the year, our combined might will break the power of the Great Evil."

"You are already one down without Trefoil," Eddie warned.

Marlowe looked over at his friend's inert form. "Yes, but once the other two join us, we should be able to rouse him."

"Even so, you really expect me to be ready by then?"

"You see why we must begin at once!" Marlowe implored. "You must train! Eddie. Only great souls are summoned. Those who were called left their old lives behind."

Eddie shook his head. "I'm no great soul, I'm just a cop. I'm not interested in starting a religion or anything."

Marlowe sighed. "Sometimes, wizards teach spiritual insights after gaining their staffs. However, most of the great masters found being religious leaders too great a burden."

"A burden?"

"Yes, a spiritual master points the way. However, a religion is designed to control its members and teach a dogma, which leads to holy wars and other such foolishness. Those of us who walk the path now know this, which is why we live in secrecy."

"What about you?" Eddie asked. "The writing on the ambulance said Saint Marlowe."

"Ah, yes." Marlowe stroked his beard. "Not as bad as that. I created myth and legend of a different sort, but it ended badly. I had an apprentice who deceived me and used my powers against me. I decided never again to take on the risk of another apprentice."

"Until me."

"I couldn't refuse," Marlowe mused. "Drusilicus left me no choice."

"I'm glad you took me on." Eddie gave the older man a smile. "You're good."

"You appear to be a very adept student, Eddie. If you are going to your police duties, could I ask you to do some…what is it called in your line of work…legwork?"

"You want me to follow-up a clue?"

"Precisely. There is an occult store in Greenwich Village. Bankrock told me the other day that there might be suspicious activity there. As a police officer, you could look into it with more authority than I could."

"What's it about?"

"Bankrock suggested there were odd energy readings that may involve a talisman."

"Oh yeah, that tally-thing…"

"Yes. Since I now know that a talisman could have been connected with Abraxas's release, I think anything involving talismans, even minor incidents, should be examined."

Eddie nodded. "I don't know anything about talismans, but I know how to ask questions. What's the place called?"

"Magickal Cherub; it's on the corner of Eighth Street and Avenue B."

Eddie's eyes grew wide.

"What is it?" Marlowe asked.

"My partner mentioned that place just the other day."

"Hmm. Interesting. But, if you can find out anything, that would be useful. Later we will practice and you will stay here at the townhouse—"

"I told you, I can't, Marlowe. I swear I'll give you a few hours each night."

"Can you take vacation time?"

"I might, but damn if Cerise would want to kill me."

"Why?"

Eddie looked at his feet. "I've been promising her since we got married that I'd take her to Aruba."

"And have you?"

Eddie rubbed the back of his neck. "Something always comes up."

"I see." Marlowe's face took on a decisive visage. "Well then, if you cannot come here, I shall go with you."

"Say, what?"

"I shall accompany you to your home," Marlowe announced. "It is the only way you will be safe. I doubt Abraxas will attack two of the Five together. I can watch over you and yours."

"You want to stay at my house? What about Trefoil?"

"There is naught I can do for him until the others arrive. I will have Frisha watch over him."

"She doesn't seem all that stable. What about your, uh, vampire friend?"

"Daniel is on a special mission that cannot be disturbed. But there are spells that protect the townhouse. If anything should happen, Daniel will sense it and return. He is quite a fighter!"

"Tooth and nail, I would imagine," Eddie quipped.

"Was that a joke?"

"Never mind! What do I tell my wife?"

"Tell her I am a witness that needs protecting. Really, Eddie, I solved your problem this morning! I would think you'd be more adept at lying to your own wife!"

"I don't make it a habit!" Eddie asserted defensively. "I'll think of something."

"Well and good, apprentice!" Marlowe smiled.

"Yeah, yeah," Eddie muttered glumly, "just don't start calling me 'boy'!"

For a moment, Marlowe turned beet red, and Eddie had to admit he felt satisfaction seeing him flustered for a change.

"Why…why, Eddie…I would never…I mean, really!" Marlowe stammered.

"I know, pops," Eddie found he was unable to enjoy his victory. "You really are a good guy. You just presume a lot."

"I fear for you, Eddie. Far worse, I fear for us all."

"You and me both."

TWENTY

Outside the townhouse, Eddie pulled out his phone to call Luis. But to tell him what? That he was going to another place without him?

Eddie quickly moved his unmarked car back to the lot, as he decided the subway would be the faster way to go.

Downtown Manhattan had a section known as Alphabet City. It ran south of 14th Street all the way down to the Bowery, with cross streets of Avenue A, B, and so on. There, in a dirty building near the corner of Eighth Street and Avenue B, Eddie stepped through the doorway of a small retail business. The lettering painted on the dirty glass of the display window read "Magickal Cherub."

"Who's there?" a voice demanded, as Eddie's entrance jiggled a bell connected to the door.

"Hello? Where are you?" Eddie called out.

The small store was crammed almost to bursting with dusty shelves filled with books and strange paraphernalia. Every square inch of counter space was covered with bottles of scented oils, incense, small cardboard boxes with labels that announced *Spell Kit*, and everything from strange knives with twisted blades to a human skeleton standing forlornly in the corner.

The store smelled of a combination of incense and oils, which covered a trace odor of old marijuana.

All of the aromas gave Eddie a headache.

"Can I help you?"

Eddie turned to see an older woman behind a makeshift counter. She wore heavy make-up on her wrinkled face, and her hair was an odd reddish-purple color that could not be found in nature. Eddie was not quite sure of the shape of her body between her loose garment and the many chains she wore around her neck.

"Yes," Eddie said, "I'm interested in talismans."

The older woman's face brightened.

"Ahhhh!" she cooed. "We have the largest selection in New York."

"What exactly are they good for?"

"A beginner!" she smiled. "Talismans can do many things: attract love, influence people, bring you riches or power. Of course, our spell kits can do the same and are very reasonably priced—"

"I'm only interested in talismans," Eddie replied firmly.

"Ah! Well, you are in luck," she leaned forward to speak in a lowered voice. "We have our very own enchanter!"

"A what?"

"An enchanter. He makes talismans, knows them and their uses. I believe he is in today."

"You're not sure?" Eddie said.

She waved her hand, which was adorned with many different cheap rings. "He has done so well with his spells, he doesn't need to work here. He only comes in to continue his research and look through our latest stock."

"Research? What kind of research?"

"He is always looking for new ways to use them." She looked down the narrow aisles of the store. "I saw him earlier. If he's here, he'll be at the back counter."

She pointed toward the rear of the store.

"Thanks," Eddie strolled through the cramped aisles and glanced at the books. Some of the titles read: *The True Story of Witches; 1,000 Spells for Everyday Use; Magick by Night.*

Eddie stopped at a small opening between display cases filled with round medallions on chains. Each metal circle was covered with symbols and writing unlike any he'd ever seen.

He leaned into the opening and asked, "Anyone here?"

"Yeah, what?" A young man looked up from a desk in the corner. There was a book open in his lap which he quickly closed and carried with him to the open space.

He was dressed all in black with numerous body piercings, which showed shiny metal around his eyebrows, ears, nose, and even his lower lip. His tee-shirt displayed the name of a rock band in such odd lettering as to be unreadable. His long hair was unnaturally black and slick as if oiled.

He put the book on top of a small stack of similar tomes.

"Can I help you?" he spoke in a flat, bored voice.

"Yes," Eddie responded. "I'm interested in a talisman."

"Which one?"

"Huh?"

The young man gestured at the metallic circles all around them. "These are all talismans. Many of them are pentacles from the *Greater Key of Solomon the King*, if you put any faith in that."

"And you don't?"

He shrugged. "I started with the *Key*, but I've moved on. Way too limiting."

"Lady up front said you know your stuff," Eddie said.

He gave a small smile. "Probably one of the few people she ever hired that isn't a burnt-out Satanist."

"I'm Eddie."

"I imagine you are. They call me Caleb."

"They?"

"You know. The world," he sneered.

Eddie bent close to one of the items in the display case. "These look kinda cheap. What are they made from, steel?"

The young man made a noise that was halfway between a snort and a laugh. "Steel? You're new at this, aren't you?"

"How do you know that?"

"No amulets are made of steel, and only one dedicated to Mars are made with iron. Steel stops the magic. These are made from pewter, and the quality is all right for something that costs ten bucks."

"But you don't think much of them."

"A talisman can be made from almost anything. They activate forces within the human psyche. To be truly effective, a talisman should be made of precious metal: silver, gold, platinum. It increases the power of the charm, and the practitioner's power level as well."

"I understand the best ones are very old."

"Yes, but those cost." Caleb eyed Eddie from head to toe. "I might be able to set you up with something. What kind of spell are you trying to cast? Not love, I'm sure."

"How come?"

"Wedding ring on the finger." He pulled a loose strand of black hair away from his eye. "And from the looks of it, it's been there a while."

"Observant."

The young man shrugged. "I have an eye for jewelry. It reveals secrets, at least to me." He turned to a display case. "So, what are you interested in? The usual? Money, fame, power?"

"How about something to unleash a demon?" Eddie watched Caleb's face for a reaction. He didn't even raise an eyebrow.

This is one cool customer, Eddie thought. *Street-smart, too. He can probably smell I'm a cop.*

"Now, that's an interesting choice," Caleb said, his eyes narrowed a little. "But a tall order for a beginner."

He reached behind the counter, and Eddie felt a defensive urge to go for the service weapon in his shoulder holster.

"I do, however, have something you might be interested in," Caleb said with a smug look as he brought his hand out holding a bright, shiny medal that hung from a chain. "This one is real silver, and as you mentioned, very old."

He spun the chain and the silver disk sparkled in the light.

"Now, how about you tell me why you're asking about demons?" Caleb spoke casually, as if in friendly conversation.

Eddie felt an overwhelming desire to tell the young man everything, about Abraxas and Marlowe and the weirdest two days of his entire life.

Suddenly, he felt a warmth against his chest, as if something was growing hot in his wallet.

The card, my staff, Eddie thought, *it's trying to protect me.*

Eddie blinked and looked away from the spinning silver disk to meet Caleb's eyes.

"No reason, I've just heard a lot about demons," Eddie said, as a smile played his lips. "Thought it would be a fun place to start."

Eddie noticed the pale young man grow paler. He'd managed to surprise him at last.

"So, what are you playing at," Eddie demanded, "waving this thing at me?"

"I thought you might like it." Caleb instantly restored his composure. "But this is pricey. I couldn't let it go for less than five thousand."

"For that? What does it do, produce money?" Eddie reached out for it.

Caleb pulled the medallion out of reach. "No, it gives one influence over weaker minds. It's from the late Renaissance, and I use it as a basis for my own designs." He turned to look at the disk and flipped it over to examine it.

Eddie glanced at the artifact in Caleb's hand. "Craftsmanship looks good."

"It might have an error," Caleb said, focused on the medallion. "The slightest imperfection invalidates the charm. Look, since you're just starting out, you might want to get *Talismans through the Ages*."

"What's that?"

"A book, right here," he pointed vaguely at the tome he had carried over, which lay next to him. "Once you know what magicks you want to work, come back, and I'll set you up. I could design something for you. That would be a little cheaper."

"Thanks, you've been a big help."

Caleb stared down at the silver medal in his hand and ignored Eddie. With a shrug, Eddie grabbed the book from in front of Caleb, returned to the woman up front, and paid her.

"So glad we could help you on your spiritual journey," she said, giving a smile that showed lipstick on one of her upper teeth. "Do come again."

Eddie walked out, and Caleb moved to the front of the store, the silver medallion in his hand.

The woman began to speak, "Now there's a type we don't normally get here."

Caleb held the talisman by its chain in front of the old woman's eyes, which immediately glazed over.

"Shut up."

She stared at the glittering disk.

"It works fine," Caleb murmured and turned his head toward the door that Eddie just walked through. "Why didn't it affect him?"

Caleb considered this as he made the old woman forget he interrupted her, or that he took twenty dollars out of the register.

Caleb didn't need the money. He just enjoyed doing little things like that.

TWENTY-ONE

Riding the subway uptown gave Eddie a chance to delve into the thick book. It was a slow read, as the writer seemed enamored of his own elucidation.

Eddie soon gave up on the opening chapter which put forth the author's theory behind the use of talismans. Instead, he moved to the back of the book, which had drawings and photos of hundreds of various talismans from around the world.

Eddie soon learned that talismans were made from almost anything: there were little figures carved out of ivory from Africa, with strange symbols added; there were tiger skin bracelets from India, with coins each showing pictographs of the ancient deities; there was a Mayan earring carved out of stone covered with unique designs.

He closed the book and put it back in the paper bag, overwhelmed. If a talisman empowered Abraxas as Marlowe suggested, it could be almost anything and hidden almost anywhere.

He decided if he talked to Marlowe, maybe they could narrow it down to only a few dozen possibilities. After all, he'd said that Abraxas had 365 personas. He couldn't be every god in all the historic pantheons.

He got off at 79th Street, looked up at the Metropolitan Museum of Art, and something touched his memory. There had been a robbery there of something ancient. He cracked the book to the heading "Mayan Artifacts" and saw numerous small figurines, rings, and amulets carved from stone, and samples of pottery. He shut the book and decided he needed to do some follow-up on that robbery.

Eddie entered the precinct and marched up the stairs to the second floor.

I feel like a juggler with too many spheres, Eddie thought, *and not enough hands.*

He found Luis at his desk studying a file.

"We got the coroner's report from Doctor Warren." Luis didn't look up as Eddie approached.

"That's good." Eddie felt unexpectedly awkward with his partner. "Look, about this case…I mean the way I keep running off without you…"

Luis looked up, a cold gleam in his eyes. He shrugged with forced nonchalance. "Hey, you're the lieutenant. If you don't want to work with your partner, who is only a sergeant, you don't have to."

Ouch, Eddie thought.

"Luis, I'm real sorry to keep things from you," Eddie said. "It's just this case has gotten so…so…"

Luis put the report down and faced Eddie. "Look, in the past we've chased our own tails in cases that looked like we wouldn't ever get a suspect, let alone a conviction. But I felt I was part of the team. Suddenly, you wanna play 'Lone Ranger,' and I don't feel like being Tonto."

"I…I…" Eddie attempted.

"I don't know if it is your *madre* being sick, or seeing that head, or, I don't know, sunspots. But you've changed, man. You're leaving me out of the loop, and I'm mad as hell about it."

Eddie raised his head, and he could see it in his partner's eyes. There was anger, but more than that. Luis was hurt and confused. Everything he held dear—his partnership with Eddie, the fact that they were equals—had been taken from him and it wounded him.

Eddie ran his hand through his short curly hair that felt like steel-wool against his palm. "I don't mean to shut you out, Luis. But, you're right, this case has put me in a weird place. I've been trying to chase down leads, but they just keep getting stranger."

"Like what?" Luis's expression was grim.

Eddie dropped the large book on the table with a thud.

"Talismans?" Luis glanced at the cover. "What does that have to do with murder?"

"Maybe nothing." Eddie thought fast to edit what he had learned. "But now I'll give you my crazy theory."

Luis crossed his large arms over his chest. "I'm listening."

"I think this murder has to do with the occult."

Luis's brow knit in thought. "I'm not following you."

"The physical evidence—an attacker with huge hands with claws, cloven hoof prints—what does that sound like?"

Luis shrugged. "Like someone raised the devil?"

Eddie snapped his fingers. "Yes, but what if they just *wanted* us to think so? I mean, maybe some guy on stilts, or hanging from ropes so they didn't leave footprints—"

"This doesn't explain why you've been out on your own."

"I wanted to do some research. I needed to back this theory up with some evidence."

Luis shook his head. "The captain will never buy it."

"I guess it sounds crazy."

"No, it *is* crazy."

"Well, I've got an idea how we can check." Eddie picked up the book, returned it to its paper sack, and put it in his desk drawer. "Do you know anything about the Mayans?"

"Yeah, they're all dead," Luis replied with an annoyed look. "Maybe you wanna find out who killed *them*?"

"That's not what I'm getting at. Wasn't there an exhibit of South American artifacts at the Metropolitan Museum of Art?"

"Right, the one that had stuff stolen, and we weren't in on the investigation," Luis moped.

"Can you get a list of what was taken?"

Luis considered it. "I know someone in robbery who could find out."

"And we may have a serial killer."

"Whadda ya mean?" Luis asked.

"There's been a second attack on a homeless guy. We've seen him around, black guy with gray hair and a beard named Trey. He always wears army camouflage, carries a broomstick."

"Was he the guy you went to see?"

"Yes. He's in Bellevue in a coma."

"But not torn apart? Why do you think he was attacked by the same perp?"

Know it, Eddie thought, *but I can't tell you how.*

"He was found in the park, mistaken for dead. I think we should treat it like it's the same perp using a different technique. We should go question the homeless again and try to—"

"Oh geez." Luis slapped his forehead. "I forgot to tell you. That crazy woman from the cardboard box showed up looking for you."

"What?" Eddie burst out. "You mean, Frisha?"

"Yep, brought her big-ass spoon with her and everything. I got her stashed in interview room two—you know, the one with the best ventilation."

"How long has she been here?" Eddie decided she wouldn't show up at a police station if it wasn't important.

"A couple of minutes before you got here. Doesn't stink as bad as in her box, but whew!" Luis pinched his nose for emphasis. "She insisted that she talk to you. *Only* you."

Eddie nodded. "Maybe she saw something." He moved toward the far end of the room.

"You want me to observe through the one-way glass?" Luis offered.

It felt right, the two of them side by side, a team once again. Eddie hated to ruin the moment. "I don't want to spook her."

Luis nodded and turned back toward the desk. For once it appeared that he wasn't taking it personally. "I'll make that call about the artifacts."

Eddie went to the door of interview room two and entered. Frisha was taken aback for a moment, as if she didn't expect him.

Old girl's slipping, Eddie thought. *I shouldn't be able to sneak up on a clairvoyant.*

He was surprised to find that there was no foul smell like at the box. In fact, the air was perfectly clear, and the room only carried the scent of old cigarettes that lingered in all the interview rooms.

"Frisha, can I get you anything?" Eddie began.

"No, thy coffee is lousy, and I doubt ye'll get me a drink." Frisha gave Eddie one of her toothless grins. "Though if you checked the desk of Detective Dominic, you'd find a half-empty bottle of bourbon. Come in and sit by an old woman."

Eddie scanned the office, and certain that no one observed them, he entered the room and sat across the table from Frisha.

"I cast off the odor," Frisha said as way of introduction. "I do not need it for thee."

"Beg pardon?" Eddie was not sure what she was talking about.

"'Tis part of the disguise," she muttered conspiratorially. "Makes the mortals shy back from us. Keeps 'em from getting too close."

"So you just…whip it up?"

"'Tis an easy bit of trickery."

"How can I help you, Frisha?"

She reached out and grabbed his arm with her leathery fingers. "There be danger, danger for thee."

"Abraxas?"

She nodded vigorously. "I have seen, and what I have seen… 'tis terrible."

"Frisha, just tell me what's wrong. And skip the Oldspeak."

"Aye, I mean, yes, Fred." Frisha released his arm.

"Not Fred—Ed. Eddie Berman."

She sat back in the chair and raised her fingers to her face, then picked up her spoon. "I'm sorry, Ed. Do ye wish the long and short of it?"

"Please."

"Very well." She shook her spoon at him for emphasis. "The Great Evil is going to try to kill ye through one of many possible ways, some of them most creative." Frisha looked at Eddie, dismayed. "I'm afeerd."

"What do you mean, 'many possible ways?' I thought you could see the future."

"'Tis the trouble. I see him killing ye as a tiny serpent, by biting your leg. Then the next moment, he is a terrible huge bird, ripping your heart straight out of your chest with his beak. Oh, 'tis a mess," Frisha said as tears appeared in her eyes.

"What are these, visions?"

"Aye," Frisha whispered solemnly.

"Can't you do better? Tell me where and when he's going to attack?"

"Nay, I canna, Ed. And 'tis pissing me off."

Eddie grinned at her choice of words.

"One minute thou art being assaulted in Central Park, then the next in a dark cavern—"

"This really isn't any help, Frisha."

"I know, I know. Don't you see? The Great Evil has bent the fabric of time to the point that I cannot tell which future is the true one. The totality of possibilities fall upon each other. 'Tis bad, Ed, very bad. It means tha' the Great Evil could win!"

"Win? Don't you think the Five can stop him?"

"Nay, and if the Great Evil is victorious, it can only lead to one thing."

"What's that?"

"Armageddon, the end of the world," she croaked. "Then all the denizens of Hell shall be released upon mankind. I'm terrible afeerd."

"Don't panic, Frisha." Eddie tried to think of the best way to handle the situation. "First things first. While it's still daylight, go to Marlowe's townhouse. He'll know what to do."

"It's *you* I'm afeerd for, Ed. That's why I came. Give thy staff to another, one trained in the arts who can fight the beast. If ye are lost, then the Five can no longer stand."

"I promise I'll go right to Marlowe's when I get off work. There's nothing to worry about." Eddie wondered why his words felt so hollow.

"Be on thy guard! And think on what I say. 'Tis no shame to surrender thy staff."

"I will, Frisha." Eddie rose from his chair. "Now, go to the townhouse. You can see Trey."

She gasped. "Trefoil is there as well?"

"Yes, Marlowe and I brought him out of the hospital."

"And I knew it not!" Frisha exclaimed. "Ay! This is terrible. I have lost me divination!"

She fell into a heap on the chair, covered her head, and began to moan. Loudly, of course.

"Frisha, Frisha!" Eddie shouted to be heard over the racket she produced, and came around the table to grab the woman by the arms. "Listen to me!"

She ceased caterwauling.

"Did you ever think that Abraxas might be sending you false visions? Could he somehow have gotten into whatever you use—I don't know...Psychic Friends Love Line...and messed up the wiring?"

She considered this for a moment.

"I suppose such a thing be possible, Ed." A grateful smile appeared on her lips. "See! Thou art wise. It was truly a blessing that I came to thee."

"Now, go to Marlowe, talk to him. If something is out of whack, he'll want to know. Besides, he's a big fan of yours."

"Many's the time I've been a help to him."

"Good, good. You talk to him and I'm sure you'll figure this out."

"That's what I'll do then!" Frisha rose.

"That's great," Eddie escorted her heavyset figure around the table.

"Give an old lady a hug." She encircled Eddie with her arms before he could squirm away and planted a wet kiss upon his cheek as Eddie grimaced.

"You're a good man, Fred. And I'll work with Marlowe to clear me visions. I need to see clearly, so thou canst be warned."

"I appreciate that, Frisha." Eddie snaked out of her embrace.

She strolled from the interview room, and Eddie followed her. As he passed, he saw a man leaned over Luis's desk. His back was to Eddie, but he was almost the same height as Luis, though thinner and more graceful. He wore a beautifully cut gray suit, and his hair long.

Frisha went down the stairs, her spoon raised, and Eddie waved to her as she took one last look back.

"Lieutenant?" a familiar voice called to him, and Eddie turned.

The man who had spoken to Luis was now facing him. He possessed pinched features and Eddie tried to place him.

"Yes," Eddie said, "Mister…"

"Greywacke," the man intoned. "Please call me Dru. We met last night. You were asking about the man who was murdered?"

"Ah yes!" Eddie realized it was Drusilicus, the one who stepped forward from the circle to object to his joining.

Eddie was surprised that the man looked totally different, and resembled a successful attorney or stockbroker in his well-cut suit and power tie. Apparently, he didn't share Marlowe's penchant for outlandish neckwear, and in fact projected such a conservative image that it was hard to accept that he was part of the secret coven.

"I see I am not your first visitor." Drusilicus raised an eyebrow toward the stairs down which Frisha had just departed. "May I have a word with you, lieutenant?"

Eddie exchanged a look with Luis, who through gestures indicated that he had a low opinion of the man.

"Sure, c'mon." Eddie led him to the same interview room he'd recently vacated.

"What did our lady Frisha wish?" Drusilicus coaxed as they entered and Eddie closed the door.

"I'm sure you can ask her yourself."

Drusilicus gave a deep chuckle that seemed well-practiced. "I doubt I will be visiting her cardboard box, and I must admit, she seldom comes down to my part of Fifth Avenue."

"Where? Near Central Park?"

"No, I live a few blocks from where Fifth Avenue ends at Washington Square. Number twenty."

Eddie whistled. "Nice neighborhood." It was the most expensive real estate in the entire city.

"Not as ostentatious as our friend Marlowe, but I live well." Drusilicus grinned. "May I smoke here?"

"It won't be the first time someone has lit up in this room."

With the slightest of nods, Drusilicus reached into the air and a cigarette appeared at the tip of his long, slender fingers. He touched it to his lips and inhaled deeply, then blew out the smoke.

"I'm not impressed. There are magicians who can do that with just skill."

Drusilicus looked at the burning cylinder in his hand. "Yes, I'm sure. I often do this at parties to entertain young ladies. They all think it is manipulation." He took another long, slow drag then exhaled smoke slowly. "But you and I know differently, don't we, lieutenant?"

"I'm a busy man, Mister—was that Greywacke? Like the arch?"

"The arch was named for my mentor, one of the truly great prophets." Drusilicus puffed nonchalantly on the cigarette. "In fact, the old boy was involved in the creation of the park."

Eddie folded his arms. "Thank you for the history lesson. Now, is there something I can help you with?"

"Perhaps I can help *you*." Drusilicus touched the cigarette to the dirty ashtray. "Now that we are not in a place of high passions, we can look at the situation with clear daylight in our eyes."

Eddie looked at the ashtray, but the cigarette was gone.

"You have been summoned, which I will grant is quite an honor." Drusilicus leaned back in his chair. "But let me ask you, as a policeman, do you want a partner who is highly decorated or good at his job?"

"One doesn't necessarily preclude the other."

"Well put. I am sure you know men in law enforcement who have received acclaim, but you consider to be inferior, do you not?"

The image of Wilcox flashed through Eddie's mind. "I do, what of it?"

"Word has come to me that Trefoil was attacked last night. This should make you aware of the danger. I am here today because I believe you to be a man of honor. Considering your calling, you are someone who is willing to put the needs of others above his own."

"I believe in justice, if that's what you mean." Eddie sensed that Drusilicus was as slippery as any politician.

"Good! And I am sure you have faced times where you felt out of your element, or in over your head?"

"Yes, but I found experts who could help me." Eddie didn't like this bend in the conversation.

"I am such an expert." Drusilicus rose from his chair and opened his arms. "Lieutenant, since the unfortunate demise of Riftstone and your summoning, I am sure things have occurred that you are not pleased about."

"It's been different."

"Yes, and Marlowe—he means well. But, he can be blind to anything beyond his own perception." Drusilicus returned to his seat and issued a perfectly modulated sigh as he sat. "It is what happens to those that have been around as long as he. They forget what it is like to be mortal. They go within themselves, and shut out the world."

"Like Riftstone?"

"Exactly!" A smile flashed to Drusilicus' lips. "You *are* perceptive, lieutenant."

"So how can we help Marlowe?" Eddie wanted to avoid being complemented to death. *Saccharin poisoning,* he thought.

"May I speak plain?"

"Please do."

"Marlowe cannot see how totally unprepared you are! I do not say this to offend you, but as a plea to save the lives of others. Marlowe himself is in very great danger, but he cannot discern the wisest course of action."

"But you can." Eddie sat on the edge of the table, watching Drusilicus as if he was a snake. Eddie assumed the role of the careful mongoose.

"Let me tell you my idea, and you can see it makes sense. After all, you are a man of the world, as am I. You understand the risks."

"And your plan is…?"

Drusilicus leaned forward. "Pass your staff to me and, in exchange, I shall give you mine. You will still have powers, which you can learn to master slowly, as your schedule allows."

"This way, you'll carry the Staff of Fire, and be one of the Five."

"Yes, or if you prefer—I realize how much this must have confused your life—I have an apprentice who could take my staff, and you could be relieved of the burden entirely. Think of it! You'll be free of these distractions. I can even alter your memories, so the entire experience will be as nothing but a dream."

Eddie thought of the last two days and how his life had become utterly insane. He'd lied to his wife and his partner. This would only be the start of the lies if he was to work with Marlowe. Deceit would become a way of life.

"I don't know." Eddie felt himself waver. *Summoned or not, wouldn't somebody who had a clue be a better choice?*

Drusilicus stood and drew closer to Eddie.

"I understand you have a sick mother, do you not?"

"Yeah, how did you know that?" Eddie challenged. *Where was this going?*

"I have my sources," Drusilicus whispered. "Perhaps a wizard —a *trained* wizard—can help where mortal doctors cannot."

He leaned back as Eddie contemplated the words. "I have made healing my specialty. Of course, it drains me a great deal, but if you were willing to make sacrifices for me, I, in turn, would be willing to make sacrifices for you."

Eddie frowned and silently watched Drusilicus as he returned to his chair and leaned back in it.

"That is my offer, lieutenant. It would solve your troubles, and it would give us a fighting chance against the Great Evil."

Eddie nodded, but his father's voice spoke up in the back of his mind. *He's slippery, son. But, he's just another stuck-up white dude who doesn't want you in his country club.*

Eddie inhaled. "That's a very tempting offer, Mr. Greywacke. Let me consider it."

"Of course, lieutenant," Drusilicus effused with a smile on his lips. "I'll check back with you tomorrow then, shall I?"

"That should be fine."

"Good afternoon, then." Drusilicus moved to the door. "By the way, may I ask you to keep our little discussion between the two of us? You know how excitable Marlowe can be."

"Of course," Eddie replied as they exited the conference room.

"I'm sure you'll make the right choice." Drusilicus continued to the stairs and descended out of view.

Luis stood up and moved to stand behind his partner. "Who was that creep?"

"Another self-important New Yorker," Eddie snorted as he shook his head.

"Like we don't deal with enough of those."

"Did you get anywhere with Robbery Division?"

Luis nodded. "They are e-mailing me pictures of the two missing items. Doesn't sound very helpful."

"How come?"

"Because it isn't anything like in your book. No statues or earrings. All that was taken was two pots."

"Pots?"

"Well, vases or somethin'. Real old clay ones. And here is the funny part. They were in a back room, being prepared to be x-rayed."

"X-rayed? Why?"

"They were sealed up, and the researchers wanted to find out what was inside without breaking them. So, the pair were stolen the night before they were going to do the tests."

"Another strange turn of events." Eddie sat down at his desk and booted up his computer. "Are we okay?"

"Right as rain," Luis said, then sat at his desk and was quickly engrossed in his own machine.

TWENTY-TWO

Marlowe pulled back the hood of his heavy cloak to reveal his face in the flickering candlelight. "We shall try again."

Eddie stepped on the small platform in the center of the room. He was also wearing a cloak, a crimson one with full sleeves and a hood that covered the back of his head and left his face in shadows.

They stood in the huge, open cavern of Marlowe's basement. It had a twenty-foot ceiling, dark-gray walls, and was illuminated by candles in tall stanchions that lined the room.

"Go!" Marlowe said.

Eddie struck his staff against the floor. Lines of fire shot up to form a pentagram with him at the center. However, Eddie felt none of the flames' heat, and they neither burned his wooden rod nor his tall leather boots.

"Here it comes!" Marlowe warned as a green light extended from the top of his staff. The beam took shape and changed into a huge, green dragon. It was covered in thousands of iridescent scales that glimmered in the candlelight. The creature stood just outside Eddie's circle, the huge, yellow cat-eyes watched him as it raised sharp talons.

Eddie's brow was furrowed in concentration, a flaming, red light shot from his staff, and the creature fell back a step.

It raised its head and flames shot from its mouth. Eddie held his staff aloft and the blaze divided in two, to pass on either side of him.

The large, green creature blinked twice in surprise, then, with a roar, leapt at Eddie. Its mouth opened to show a huge maw filled with pointed teeth. Eddie held up his staff and screamed, as the creature dissolved into mist all around him.

"No, no, no!" Marlowe said. "Eddie you must stay focused."

"We've been at this for three hours." Eddie coughed and waved his hand to dissipate the burning design. He sat down on the raised platform.

"I know, but we've only scratched the surface!" Marlowe implored.

"Aren't there some magic words you can teach me?" Eddie said.

"Many, but they are complicated, and if you say them wrong you could do more damage than good. It is more useful that you learn to focus your *will* and *intent*. They are the building blocks of all magick. You have learned the basics that allow you to control fire. That is a good sign."

"Why was that part less difficult?" Eddie asked. "Is it because this staff is the one that represents fire?"

Marlowe nodded. "Your element is fire, so your staff has the ability to control it in all its guises."

"Now, Trefoil's staff is water. He can, what, make it rain?"

"No. However, if it is raining, he can manipulate the drops as they fall. He can make water rise from a lake and throw it at an adversary."

"Good to know." Eddie turned the pole in his hand. "Any fire, huh?"

"You may use any flame to your benefit, as tiny as a candle, or as huge as a forest fire," Marlowe said. "Shall we continue?"

"Man, I'm all in. Have a heart, it's ten o'clock."

Marlowe's jaw grew firm. "Then let us once more practice the shielding spell."

Eddie glared at him, tired and disgusted.

"It could save your life," Marlowe added as he tried to hide his own annoyance.

Eddie nodded and rose. Marlowe held up his staff, and white light sprang from the top. Eddie raised his stave, and a ball of red light encircled him, which deflected Marlowe's beam.

"Good! It's not taking you as long to prepare."

"We've done it about a hundred times," Eddie whined. "I hope I'm starting to get it."

"Yes," Marlowe said, the light fading on the top of his staff. "But you must do it a hundred more times, until it is second-nature."

"Whatever. Look, you and I have got to get out to New Jersey." Eddie waved the staff in the air and his cloak dissolved around him, and the cloth rewove itself into his suit.

"Nicely done." A smile pulled at the corners of Marlowe's mouth. "You have made a fair start, after all. I know! If we don't sleep! I have a spell that will—"

"Marlowe please! I am exhausted and I have no intention of giving up sleeping with my wife." Eddie checked his pockets and pulled out his wallet. He transformed the staff into the credit card and slipped it in. "I am willing to make sacrifices, but I have slept with that woman for fifteen years, except for when I was in the hospital and these last two nights. I have no intention of missing another night." He pulled out his phone.

"I am all for marital harmony, but, Eddie, this is your first day of training, and you have learned only the most basic defenses. You cannot protect yourself against even a—"

"Damn," Eddie complained, "my cell phone screen is backwards." He held it out to Marlowe, who tapped it lightly with his stick. The phone glowed.

Eddie glanced at the screen. "All fixed, thanks. Marlowe, if you want my brain to absorb this stuff, I need down time."

"Of course, Eddie. I forget that you do not have the stamina of one who has walked the path as long as I."

"So, let's get going. I have to set you up on the sofa."

"I could make myself invisible. Your family won't even know I'm there."

"Why didn't you suggest this earlier?"

Marlowe shrugged. "It's not my first choice. It clogs up my sinuses."

There was a resonant knock on the commodious basement door.

"Yes?" Marlowe grumbled, annoyed at the disturbance.

Bob, wearing his preferred face with a large nose and lips, passed effortlessly through the heavy door.

"What is it, Bob?" Marlowe sat on the platform next to Eddie.

"Message," Bob quavered.

"Bob, I told you we were not to be disturbed!"

"Special delivery…" Bob attempted tentatively.

"Oh, bother." Marlowe glared at his floating house ghost. "Thank you, Bob, that will be all."

Greatly relieved, Bob dove for the door and passed through it to safety.

"He has better manners than this morning," Eddie noted.

"You giving him an ectoplasmic hot foot improved his disposition." Marlowe gave Eddie a smile.

"Glad to help." Eddie rose. "Let's get going."

"I have to take this delivery."

"Guess you can't have Bob sign for UPS." Eddie smirked.

"Hmm, I think it would be best if you went to the far end of the room, close to the wall."

"What's up?" Eddie said.

"The delivery, of course." He leapt onto the platform and waved his staff. A circle appeared in the center, glowed, and issued a thick, low-hanging fog. It slowly rose up and began to bubble and boil.

Marlowe stepped back as the rising section of wood began to shimmer and change, until it took on the appearance of a cauldron. The simmering liquid exuded a greenish-yellow glow that made Marlowe's face appear jaundiced.

"Who calls upon the Wizard Marlowe!" he yelled into the simmering ooze.

The cauldron began to vent steam like an old locomotive, with a rasping hiss that echoed through the huge room.

Suddenly the mist began to coalesce, and a shape uplifted from the center. A face appeared, with a twisted mouth and pointed ears. Horns sat on the skull-like head, and a naked chest came forth. The demonic apparition ascended above the cauldron, but its legs—if it had any—remained hidden.

Despite the lavish entrance, the creature itself was not that impressive. It was only slightly larger than an average man, and it was thin, with matchstick arms and a bony face. With its yellowish skin tone, it resembled nothing more than an anorexic view of Hell, where the evil hordes were far too hungry to torture the denizens very thoroughly.

"I have a message from the *Onmyōji*," the bulimic demon uttered in a weak voice.

"Ah good." Marlowe breathed a sigh. "What be his word? Speak ye plain."

"He wert deeply saddened by the loss of our companion." The effort to speak appeared to be almost too much trouble. "He shall come to thy city soon. Expect him and arrange lodging."

"*Speak ye true?*" Marlowe boomed.

"Aye, master," the demon responded, and waved his hand as if this response was too large an effort.

"Well, indeed. Return to he that sent thee, and tell him I have heard and shall do as he bids."

The creature nodded its weary head, then stood unmoving, the lower part of its body still resting in the greenish ooze.

Marlowe blinked and glanced at Eddie, who shrugged.

"Is there anything else?" Marlowe finally asked the creature.

"No tip?" the demon responded, as if to even ask was the height of rudeness on Marlowe's part.

Marlowe exhaled heavily and reached into the pocket of his cloak, extracted a large, shimmering gold coin the size of a silver dollar, and tossed it to the half-formed demon.

The creature caught the coin and his face opened into a broad grin. "Nothing but the best at this house," he purred and threw the coin into his mouth, as if it was a foil-wrapped chocolate.

It chewed, making a horrible grinding sound, but the metallic meal seemed to strengthen the emaciated fiend, who slid back into the mist. The fog itself was sucked back into the cauldron as if by a vacuum. With the merest wave of his staff, the huge pot deliquesced into the platform, and all traces of it were gone.

"Is that a normal way to communicate?" Eddie asked as Marlowe's cloak transformed into a fashionably cut velvet jacket.

"It's an ancient technique, fallen into disuse these days." Marlowe looked back at the wooden dais as his staff transmuted into a walking stick. "Most of us use mirrors; it's faster."

"So why did he go to all that trouble?" Eddie said, as they walked to the massive door.

"Mirrors are not completely secure. They can help with communication, transportation, even transubstantiation—"

"Transub-what?"

"We'll get to that when we have more time. It is possible for powerful beings to listen in on mirror conversations."

"Like hackers on the internet?"

"What?" Marlowe questioned, confused by the concept.

"Never mind, go on."

"Ah! Besides that, there are certain mirrors that can trap a wizard's power. It was wise for Ahbay to have a care."

"He's one of the Five?"

"He carries the Staff of Earth." A smile curled on his lips. "Bit of a dirty sort."

"Was that a joke?" Eddie said as they ascended the marble staircase up to the living room from the subterranean training room. "Did you, old wizard-guru guy, make a joke? I'm impressed."

"We have only one other of the Five to locate."

Eddie stopped at the top of the stairs. "Wait a sec. You don't know where they are?"

"I am capable of many things, Edward, but I am neither omniscient nor omnipotent."

"That's good, I don't need the pressure of trying to be those things."

They passed through a much less impressive door and entered the living room where Frisha sat on a sofa and yammered at

Daniel Kraft. She was no longer in her homeless disguise, but instead wore a silky cloak. Her hair was clean, brushed and styled, and she looked as if she was wearing make-up.

"Fred," she bleated, and rose to run over and hug Eddie.

"Eddie."

"Of course, I meant Ed." Frisha turned to her seated companion. "Daniel, did I tell thee how he advised me to come here?"

"Repeatedly." Daniel sighed.

Eddie noticed that the tall, good-looking vampire seemed outwardly unruffled, but his hair was a tad unkempt, and the shadow of a rather nasty bruise was under one eye.

"May I speak to you, Marlowe?" Daniel requested, grateful for the interruption as Eddie wrestled free from Frisha's embrace.

Marlowe gave a backward look to Eddie. "We must be off."

"It will only take a moment." Daniel fell into pace with them.

"Come back soon, Daniel," Frisha cooed. "I'll tell you the romance I had during the Bubonic Plague."

"I cannot wait, my dear," Daniel replied with a dazzling smile. "However, I have to go out for a few hours."

"Very well," Frisha sighed, disappointed.

"I'll return as soon as I can," Daniel said, then strolled with the others into the entrance hall.

"How's it going with Frisha?" Eddie asked.

"I may have to kill her," Daniel mused straight-faced.

Eddie's smile faded.

"I'm joking." His expression was unchanged. "I don't hunt humans, only animals. Considering the old girl's been a hermit for so long, she's certainly making up for the lack of conversation."

"That's not unusual," Marlowe pointed out. "Be gentle, Daniel. She is quite vulnerable right now."

"I have indulged her," Daniel defended. "However, I believe my time would be better spent if I was following up on your request."

"Request?" Eddie repeated.

Marlowe nodded. "You're probably right, Daniel. Do you think any of your contacts can be of any help?"

"So far, they have not been forthcoming." Daniel touched the bruise under his eye. "Only time will tell."

"Where you gonna check?" Eddie challenged. "I mean, the guy's a demon. It's not like you can find his hangout or anything."

"If the demon has manifested in this dimensional plane," Marlowe corrected, "he must be 'hanging out' somewhere."

"I'll continue as you asked, Marlowe," Daniel vowed.

"Very well," Marlowe agreed. "Also keep your ear to the ground. I still cannot explain how he's become so emboldened, or how he came up with the poison used on Trefoil."

"What do you mean?" Eddie queried.

"You were there when I was told of the ingredients," Marlowe explained. "Abraxas has many powers, but I doubt he knows how to create such a mixture. I believe he had no problem injecting it with his fangs while in snake form. But, where did he get the potion to begin with?"

"I will report to you in the morning," Daniel assured. "Meet me upstairs away from the sun."

"I imagine sunburn would be a big problem." Eddie smirked.

"Oh, hilarious." Daniel was unamused. "As if I haven't heard *that* one in the last two score or so. What's next? You going to advise me that if I go out to have a 'bite,' I should avoid the 'stake'? What are you, Detective Henny Youngman?"

"Henny Youngman's dead," Eddie remarked.

"So am I," Daniel responded.

"Just trying to lighten the mood," Eddie explained with a shrug.

"Now, now, gentlemen," Marlowe took charge, "we need to be patient with each other. We are all under a great deal of strain." Marlowe opened the front door and they stepped onto the ornate front stoop. "Daniel, Eddie isn't aware that you've heard every vampire joke ever written."

"I guess they all suck," Eddie chuckled. He covered his mouth and doubled over with laughter.

"How nice," Daniel sneered at Eddie in disgust. "Small wonder vampires hate wizards. I'm off."

With that, he leapt into the air and was gone. Eddie's laughter caught in his throat and he raised his head to try to find Daniel.

"I thought you said you can't teleport in the city," Eddie blurted.

"He didn't teleport." Marlowe pointed at the night sky. "There he goes now."

Eddie saw a small creature as it flapped its wings and disappeared into the darkness of the park.

"Was that a…a…" Eddie stammered.

"A bat, yes."

"Vampires can really do that?"

"Yes, Eddie, they really can," Marlowe advised, as they reached the bottom of the steps and turned toward Central Park.

"Isn't it dangerous?" Eddie glanced up and down the street. "I mean, what if someone saw him?"

"Daniel has remarkable senses. If there was anyone nearby, he would've sensed them. Then again, he does like to be… flamboyant."

"I'll say. Are we going to pick up my car?"

"That would be tiresome, Eddie. It is much more expeditious to enter that grove of trees."

"But where will we end up? I mean, I live in Teaneck, not Sherwood Forest."

"Nonsense, Eddie." Marlowe stepped on the concrete path lit only by a street lamp. "There is a park only two blocks from your house."

"How did you learn that? That crystal ball of yours?"

"Actually, I looked at a map."

"Don't we need a lot of trees?" Eddie pulled out his special credit card.

"There will be enough for our needs." Marlowe's walking stick grew into a staff at the same time Eddie's revealed its true form as well.

They entered the thicket and disappeared.

They didn't see the small, dark-red lizard scurry off a rock and sniff at the ground where Marlowe and Eddie passed. It licked its lips and observed the place where they vanished with a smile that would look more appropriate on an alligator.

"Interesting," it said in a voice too deep for such a small creature.

The quiet night was broken by a screech. An owl flew out of the night sky, its mouth open and its sharp talons aimed for the tiny lizard.

A burst of flame shot from the reptile's mouth and engulfed the bird in mid-flight. There was a horrible, garbled screech, and the acrid smell of burned feathers. The charred strigiform fell to the earth with a thud, still smoldering.

"Ah, dinner," the lizard smirked, and despite its diminutive size, consumed the smoking remains in one large bite.

TWENTY-THREE

"Well, here we are," Eddie announced, as he unlocked the back door and let Marlowe into the kitchen. "Be it ever so humble…"

"It's nice, Eddie." Marlowe looked around at the simple but neat room and the small nook with a table and four chairs. "You have a breakfast room…uh…area."

"Not nearly as fancy as your digs, Marlowe."

Marlowe sighed. "Yes, but it is draining to have such a large house, so much to take care of. As I grow older, I long for the days when I wandered with nothing more than a pack on my back."

Eddie gazed at Marlowe and tried to see the man in that light. "I guess you were a real 'hippy' in your youth."

"My youth was long before hippies, Eddie. In fact, long before the twentieth century."

Eddie paused and knew his next question would be telling. "Just how old are you?"

"Eddie?" Cerise swept into the room. She was wearing a dark-pink, silky bathrobe, which covered a flimsy negligee completely. She always wore very little to bed, due to the fact that she was always too warm. This was unique for Eddie, as most women he'd known always complained of being cold. But it was one more thing he loved about her, an internal thermostat that necessitated a penchant for scanty bedtime apparel.

She put her hand to the top of her robe, making sure it was completely closed, as her eyes moved to the figure by the door.

"Who's this?" she asked.

"Huh?" Eddie said, too captivated by his wife to think rationally. Had he only been away from her for a night? It felt like a week, and he wanted to embrace her. More than that, he wanted to seduce her.

"We have a guest?" Cerise said and touched his arm with her free hand to startle him back to awareness. But he could also see a twinkle of delight in her eye that beckoned him in their secret language of love as if to say, "You still want me after all this time?"

"How do you do." Marlowe removed his hat. "I'm Marlowe."

Cerise glanced at Eddie questioningly.

"I need him to stay." Eddie tried to think fast. "His friend was attacked in the park. I thought it would be safer if he was under police protection."

Cerise's face lost the look of amusement that had danced upon it, and dismay whirled in to take its place.

"You thought—?" Cerise muttered. "Mr. Marlowe, would you please excuse us?"

"Certainly. And it's not 'mister,' just Marlowe."

Cerise pulled Eddie out of the kitchen and into the dining room.

"What were you thinking?" her voice low but intense. "You show up at this hour with a guest, and you don't call to warn me?"

"I was interviewing him," Eddie lied, "and it was a spur-of-the-moment decision. We'll put him up on the sofa, it's no big deal."

"It's no big deal!" her voice rose.

"Sh!"

"It *is* a big deal. Edward Berman, I don't know what's gotten into you lately, but you are not thinking of your family."

Eddie exhaled deeply. "I'm sorry, baby, but so much is happening. And this case, it might be a serial killer."

Who has his sights on me now, Eddie thought.

"Oh, well then, it's fine." Cerise sighed, not placated. "You get your friend or witness or whatever…he…is set up. I'll get the sheets."

"Thanks for understanding, baby." Eddie touched her arm and looked deeply into her eyes.

"I don't understand much of what you are doing, Eddie." She took his head in her hands and gave him a peck on his cheek. "But I *am* grateful you're home."

Eddie felt a small smile slip onto his face.

Cerise stuck her head into the kitchen. "Welcome to our home, Mr. Marlowe. Eddie will show you where you are sleeping."

"You're too kind, Mrs. Berman. I am quite certain this is an imposition."

"Not at all." Cerise left the kitchen by the back stairs.

Eddie walked back into the kitchen and drew close to Marlowe. "Hey, you didn't *hex* her or anything, did you?"

"Hex her? I don't really *do* hexes, Eddie."

"No, I mean to calm her down. I thought my ass was going to be in a sling."

Marlowe shook his head. "No hexes, spells, or even a minor bit of illusion, Eddie. Whatever she experienced was real."

In a few short minutes, Eddie unfolded the sofa bed and covered it with sheets. Marlowe excused himself and went into the bathroom, coming out wearing an elaborate set of pajamas and bathrobe. Eddie was glad Cerise wasn't there to observe that the man with no luggage ended up in a completely different outfit.

Leaving Marlowe downstairs, Eddie went up to his room and undressed. He removed his shoulder harness, separated the magazine from his handgun and put it into the small combination lockbox bolted to the floor under his bed. Cerise had lit two candles on their dresser, the signal that they would make love.

As he finished undressing, Cerise got out of bed and embraced her husband. She removed her robe, followed quickly by her negligee. She stood dark and proud in the dim light. Her body owned a few stretch marks, and her breasts sagged a little from her childbearing, but she was magnificent.

He kissed her.

"I *did* miss you," she whispered.

"Oh man, I missed you so much, baby." He kissed down her neck to her shoulder.

"So, I think I know what really happened last night," Cerise whispered, a wicked, brilliantly white smile grew on her face in contrast to her ebony skin.

Eddie froze. *Busted.*

"What?" He kissed her again, as his hand moved to cup her left breast.

She pushed him to arm's length and met his eyes. "You were upset about Momma, went out, and got drunk. That's why you fell asleep in the locker room."

Eddie tried to grasp this idea and push away the memories of the stone circle.

"I just want you to know, I understand," Cerise confided. "A man sometimes needs to do such things."

"Well, I—" Eddie started to say, but decided it would be better if he just shut up.

"And you being a policeman and all, you couldn't drive home drunk. So you slept in the locker room, and made up this whole story of how tired you were. Eddie, I understand, but please call me next time."

"Thanks, baby." Eddie decided that agreement would be the fastest way to his goal, which now was more carnal than intellectual. "I promise I'll call from now on."

She pushed him onto the bed, and with nimble fingers, pulled his undershorts off.

She knelt over him and kissed him. "I want you to know, I'm here for you, sugar."

"I love you, Cerise," Eddie said, and took her face between his hands, glad he could say something that he knew to be true.

"I love my big, black man," she said. "Now, you owe me for not coming home last night."

"How do you want me to pay?" Eddie asked, feeling her hand moving downward.

"I'll take what I'm owed," she said as she kissed him. "Oooh, love me, daddy." She lifted herself up and onto him, and in one slick move, pulled him into her body.

Their lovemaking was fast and intense. They both sensed each other's need, wild like animals, as opposed to soft caresses. They indulged each other, their bodies shifting positions and places— him on top, now her. They wrestled and tumbled, and flesh met flesh as a yawning chasm opened under them and they were swept away in a torrent of joined, gasped pleasures.

Spent, they held each other tightly, until their bodies relaxed and fell into another abyss—the quiet cave of sleep.

Eddie drifted off, sated and content.

There was a noise.

Eddie sat up in bed.

The candles were burned out and gutted.

He looked over at the clock by the bed, discerned the red numerals, which seemed to float in the lightless room.

1:30.

He had fallen asleep for about two hours. What woke him?

Carefully, he got up. He didn't want to disturb Cerise, who was turned on her side. He made his way to the hall to use the bathroom.

He used the commode and because of years of spousal training, put the lid down. He rubbed his face as he headed for the bedroom.

There was a sound downstairs.

It was the same noise that woke him.

Eddie froze, reached for his shoulder holster, which, of course, wasn't there. This surprised him for a moment, until it occurred to him that he didn't wear his gun to bed. Soundlessly, he made his way to the top of the stairs and peeked down.

Marlowe sat on the sofa bed and Eddie could feel himself relax.

And yet, something was not right.

Marlowe sat like a statue of the Buddha—if the Buddha wore plaid pajamas—cross-legged and straight-backed. And Eddie also noticed that large candles burned in two very tall candleholders.

Eddie had no idea where they had come from. Then again, anyone who could produce an entire wardrobe from thin air should be able to conjure a couple of candlesticks.

Between his folded legs was a small pot that was filled with something that glowed a sickly green.

Marlowe had his eyes closed and chanted in that weird language the coven had used in the stone circle.

Eddie kept to the shadows and leaned against the wall. Marlowe was lost in concentration.

Marlowe's cantillation, though quiet, reached a crescendo, and the bearded man lowered his head, grabbed his cane, and made passes with it over the small, glowing cauldron. Mist began to pour forth. It was as thick as a cloud, and flashes of green luminescence permeated it like distant lightning. The vapor rose up above his head and began to coalesce. A shape became more coherent, and a figure emerged from the smoke. A face appeared, then the chest and arms of a young man.

He was green and translucent and reminded Eddie of the troublesome Bob. Yet, he could make out a profile and strands of the figure's hair, making this manifestation appear more human than the ever-shifting Bob.

He seemed far too young to have died, and Eddie searched the misty phantom for any signs of violent death: a slashed throat or a bullet wound.

He couldn't see anything from where he stood.

Marlowe began to speak, very quietly, and Eddie leaned a little closer to try to hear his words. It was an exercise in futility, as he only caught a few "thee's" and "thou's."

Marlowe was using Oldspeak.

The ephemeral figure moved his lips in response, but Eddie didn't hear any sound. Marlowe nodded, as if he understood the spirit, then answered. They were having a conversation, with only Marlowe's side being vocalized.

However, the look on Marlowe's face suggested that he was deeply troubled by what he was being told. The more the apparition spoke, the more distraught his mentor became.

Eddie remembered what Marlowe had told him that one of his fields of expertise was communicating with the dead. Here in his own living room, Marlowe had conjured a ghost.

But, *whose* ghost? And why did the old man need to speak to him now?

Then all at once, the specter's head shot up, as if he was pulled by invisible wires, and its color changed as if lit with an inner red light, the color of blood.

The translucent shape burst into flames, and a strange, hot breeze passed through the room. The candles went out and one of the candlesticks toppled over.

The mist that composed the spirit body dissipated.

Marlowe grabbed his cane, which grew into its true form in his hand. He grabbed the small cauldron and leapt up from the couch with his staff aloft.

Silence.

Marlowe looked around, his eyes wide.

He's scared, Eddie thought, *really scared.*

The old man crumpled against Eddie's lounge chair and sat heavily on the arm.

Eddie quietly came down the stairs.

Marlowe rose to his full height, his staff at the ready.

"It's me!" Eddie said in a hoarse whisper. "I'm unarmed."

"You saw?" Marlowe said, and returned to the chair arm.

"Yes. What was that? And why were you doing it in my house?"

Marlowe shook his head. "There was no danger. My research with Bankrock led me to a new idea. I conjured a spirit. One who is now cursed."

"So what did he tell you?"

"He explained how Abraxas breached the barriers into this world. I know why the demon has gained so much power, and how he knew enough of potions to poison Trefoil."

"So tell me, how'd he do it?"

Marlowe's eyes grew dark. "A wizard is helping him."

TWENTY-FOUR

Mr. Yamasuto left the café named *"Rain"* on West 82nd Street and into the cool spring night. He was warm enough, though he wore only a three-piece suit. The fabric was a beautiful gray wool, and his trousers were perfectly pressed. The tie matched his handkerchief as a flawless final touch to his ensemble.

The bistro was the first floor of a restored brownstone, and its eclectic menu was designed for high-class, well-to-do patrons such as himself.

"Get a cab for you, sir?" a doorman in a short black coat with many shiny buttons said from one of the buildings as he walked down 81st Street.

"No, I am fine," Yamasuto said. His voice carried an accent, but his diction was perfect. "My driver is meeting me." He looked across the street at the American Museum of Natural History. From where he stood on the north side of the street, he could see the entrance of the Planetarium, with its huge windows and colorful planets glowing yellow and red under dark-blue lights.

He continued toward the shadowy park beyond the safety of the street lights.

"Sir?" another doorman said as he passed. The man had observed the exchange with the doorman up the street. "The park —it's late—are you sure you'll be all right?"

"I have been in New York many times," Yamasuto remarked dismissively.

He strode purposefully through Hunter Gate and into Central Park, his hand clutched around the small jade statue in his pocket.

He carried himself with the confidence of a king. As he carried this artifact, he did indeed have nothing to fear.

Haiku Yamasuto enjoyed the café and dined there on occasion, when, as part of his duties, he wasn't called to one of the many other fine restaurants the city offered. Such was the life of a representative of the Japanese delegation to the United Nations.

It was a position that carried much honor and respect, as well as many perks that he did not have in his native Japan. He had risen up the ranks over the years, until now he was the major policy representative for his homeland, and had a dozen people under him.

The downside was that he was forced to attend so many of the laborious meetings at the UN building on First Avenue and 49th Street. That could be tolerated for the benefits.

He now held in his hand the greatest boon his illustrious position had ever given him.

Over the years, he took advantage of his diplomatic immunity and freedom from searches by United States Customs to bring over many beautiful treasures of his cultural heritage. He'd sold ancient statues of Shinto "*kami*" or "little gods" to a select group of collectors who made sure to keep their source a secret. Through such sales, Yamasuto had amassed a tidy fortune. His "retirement fund," as he preferred to call it.

He found his latest acquisition only a month ago. While visiting Kyushu Island, he made a stop in the Miyazaki Prefecture. This lovely area was considered the location where Japanese mythology began. There was a considerable concentration of ancient sites, as well as Shinto and Buddhist shrines.

It was the perfect location to find collectibles of the sort Yamasuto's buyers would pay dearly for.

He visited an old man, an acquaintance, in his simple home. The elderly gentleman beckoned him into a small room with the enthusiasm of one much younger.

"I have come across a rare find, Mr. Yamasuto," the old man said, his teeth mostly gone, as he sat on a mat and uncovered a small bag.

Yamasuto bowed respectfully. "I am honored you would share it with me."

The old man returned the bow and pulled a piece of leather from the bag. He gently unrolled it. The moment the small statue glinted in the sunlight, Yamasuto was more than pleased.

He was stunned.

The energy around the object made it seem alive. He took it into his hand, and the jade, instead of being cold, was warm to the touch.

He looked at the six-inch-high figure. Its carved face and body were hellish in design. The face was human and wore a small, noble crown, but also a grin suggesting horrible pleasures. Down the body it became more demonic, and the feet that peeked out from the carved robes were the talons of a monster.

"It appears to be an *Oni*," Yamasuto said, referring to the evil beings from Buddhist stories. He turned the figurine in his hand. "Wait. It is not."

"You are wise, Mr. Yamasuto," the old man said, a gleam in his eye. "It is far too old. It predates the arrival of the teaching of the Buddha to our shores."

"Can it be?" Yamasuto looked at the figure, his eyes widening. He paused, almost afraid to say the name. Finally, he whispered, "Amatsu Mikaboshi?"

There was a silence in the room, as if time itself stopped.

"You know the ancient legends." The old man smiled and nodded.

It was true. Haiku Yamasuto was an expert in Shinto mythology. Not that he accepted the belief in anything larger than himself, but he was knowledgeable about the artifacts he sought.

It was the only way to be sure not to be cheated. Of course, he cheated his own government and the National Museum with his smuggling. But, he would be shocked if anyone suggested that the additions to his retirement fund could be considered common thievery.

Yamasuto smiled and looked down at the tiny statue of the Shinto God of Evil. It would fetch a handsome price in America.

The old man requested a tidy, but reasonable, sum. Yamasuto nodded and retrieved the necessary funds from a money belt he wore for such transactions.

In America, he contacted several buyers, and even heard from one he did not know.

He would not do business with strangers. And this one spoke oddly over the phone in a muffled tone. He offered a great deal of money, yet Yamasuto declined.

He'd made the deal with one of the richest and most silent of his buyers. He only needed to perambulate across to Fifth Avenue to meet him. The peculiar energy around the artifact would easily sell it, better than any of the fanciful history he could recite.

He smiled to himself again. Not a bad life for a man whose parents spelled his name with the *kanji* for "poem." He'd always been a small child, and only an average student, but he'd succeeded well beyond his peers.

Walking past the Delacourte Theater, he paused for a moment at the statue of "The Tempest." Modern sculpture was not to his taste, but this artwork of an old man and his daughter, his cloak blown by the wind, seemed almost to move. What was it about this so-called wizard that caught the eye?

A flash of light appeared within the theater. That was odd. Yamasuto recalled there was no performance of the New York Shakespeare Company this night. He'd let his mind wander, not a wise thing to do.

He did not fear for his safety. He'd brought his small pistol fitted with a silencer; illegal, but if an attacker presented himself, Yamasuto could dispatch him quietly, then move on without having to deal with the police and their many questions.

Yamasuto continued on the path and discerned Belvedere Castle to his right just beyond Turtle Pond in the moonlight. He stopped and turned to see a figure follow him from the theater.

Yamasuto's eyes grew wide.

The approaching man was obviously Asian, but he wore long hair and was dressed in a *kimono* and *haori*, with pleated *hakama* pants. His outfit was finished with an *Obi* sash around his waist and wooden sandals.

What disturbed him was the fact that the man resembled the face on the statue in his pocket. Even to the detail of having a small crown about his head.

As he drew nearer, Yamasuto noticed the entire outfit was in red with only a few black Japanese letters woven into the silk. Unusual for a man to wear. But even more peculiar was the fact that at his waist he wore a *Katana*, the classic sword of the feudal warrior.

Now Yamasuto became alarmed.

In his youth, his grandmother told him stories of avenging deities who assumed human form, as well as other shapes, to punish thieves and scoundrels. Even as a child, he'd believed such tales to offer little beyond a simple morality lesson.

But here was a figure who walked in an American park, swathed in garments of a bygone era. He carried a sword, and Yamasuto was nervous that there might be talons where his feet should be.

"Haiku Yamasuto," the figure said as it drew near.

Yamasuto started, his eyes pulled up from watching the man's feet. He became cold inside.

It knew his name.

"Who are you?" Yamasuto demanded in his native tongue. He gently reached into his jacket and touched the gun. It waited there for him, in the excellent holster that would dump it into his hand with one simple gesture.

The figure smiled and held out his hand. "I believe you have something of mine."

Yamasuto stood stock-still for a moment, then his face broke into a smile, and he began to laugh.

The red-garbed man stood before him unmoving.

"Well played," Yamasuto suggested, the smile tight on his face. "You pulled me into your fantasy for a moment. I must say, I admire your sense of the theatrical."

Someone knew of his recent acquisition, probably from his worthless assistant, Akio. Now they wanted to steal his prize.

"You'll excuse me, I have business to attend to." Yamasuto slowly brought out the pistol. He held it in front of him and circled the man, making sure to remain outside the reach of the sword.

He hoped the man was alone.

"Yes, I am alone," the strange man said in Japanese. "I need no help to take what is mine from a lowly thief."

Somehow this man could hear his thoughts.

Yamasuto continued to back away, his eyes on his opponent, who didn't make a move toward him, just stood there with that evil grin on his face.

He transferred the pistol to his left hand and reached with his right into his pocket to grasp the jade statue.

It was as hot as fire.

He pulled his hand from his pocket with a yelp of pain.

"Warm, is it not?" The strange man's mouth parted to show two rows of pointed teeth. "I am glad you decided not to make this easy."

Yamasuto held the pistol in both hands and backed farther away, but the red figure only lowered his head to his chest. Yamasuto tried to decide the best course of action. Shoot him? Be done with it? No, let him return to whoever sent him with failure upon his shoulders.

The man raised his head, in the midst of a terrible transformation. Still clothed in the red and black garments, the face was now red, with black marks on it and short horns stabbing out of his forehead.

Yamasuto paused for a moment, certain it must be a mask, but the creature opened his mouth.

And it continued to open.

It was impossibly huge, opening up half the monster's head. And Yamasuto could see that the pointed teeth were too enormous to fit a human mouth. An evil tongue the size of a grown snake rose from the mouth.

There was no doubt who this was.

Yamasuto gave a grunt of fear and turned to flee as fast as he could run. His right hand grabbed the statue through the fabric of his suit, and he could still feel the horrid heat of it and imagined if he pulled it out, it would not be the green of jade, but fiery red like heated iron.

Yamasuto heard footsteps follow him and increased his pace, afraid that the awful demon-thing was right behind him. He ran down the path and toward an archway, passing the small sign that read "Greywacke Arch." He passed under it and straight toward the lights surrounding the Metropolitan Museum of Art.

The sound of running feet stopped.

This so shocked him that he pulled up short. He carefully stuck his head out of the tunnel and looked around.

His foe was gone.

He saw no one. He lifted the pistol and scanned the path behind him, but there was no one nearby.

Yamasuto knew he was close to Fifth Avenue. He turned, and with the Museum on his left, walked toward the busy rush of traffic. He never realized how desolate this part of the park was late at night.

He was breathing hard, but he straightened his hair with his hand and pulled his jacket tight, keeping the gun in his hand but out of sight. Up ahead on his left was an empty playground with a statue of three bears, which children often climbed.

He would get to the buyer, make his transaction, and then take a cab to the safety of his diplomatic residence. He turned to peer over his shoulder. Assured he wasn't being followed, he returned his gaze ahead.

A figure, cloaked and hooded, stood before him.

"Cheating me, Mr. Yamasuto?" a familiar voice grated from the inky blackness of the hood. "I offered you more money, yet you sell the sygil to Mr. Cuccolo. I am sorely disappointed."

Yamasuto stepped back. "You!" he said, recognizing the voice from the phone. He raised the pistol and said, "I'll kill you!"

"I doubt it," the voice in the hood said.

The red and black demon stepped into view from behind the hooded figure.

Yamasuto yelled in surprise. The horrible face frightened him as it drew closer, the unblinking yellow eyes focused on him.

"I see you know my friend, Amatsu Mikaboshi, the 'star of the heaven,'" the cloaked person said.

"I think not," Yamasuto replied, as he tried to regain his courage. He lifted the gun and fired point-blank at the silk-clad demon.

There was a soft THUP as the pistol recoiled reassuringly in his hand.

The creature stood unaffected. His demonic face broke into the huge, oversized grin.

"Missed me," it spoke in perfect Japanese, and took the sword in one of its red, claw-like hands. There was a quick "swish" in the air.

The front half of Yamasuto's gun fell to the ground, a pristine line separated the two pieces as if severed by a laser.

Yamasuto's jaw fell open as he tried to find his breath. *That's not possible,* he thought.

Yamasuto's fingers felt cold, and he looked down to find his thumb also missing. The cut was so quick and sharp he hadn't even perceived it.

The remains of the gun fell from his maimed hand, and Yamasuto went down on his knees and bundled his hand in his suit jacket. He pulled the statue from his pocket with his uninjured right hand. It was still burning hot, so he dropped it to the grass next to the two parts of the pistol.

"Take it!" Yamasuto whimpered.

It lay there and glowed with a glaring, red light.

"Ah, how nice," the demon said, but stepped away from it. Instead, the cloaked figure reached down and picked it up, then gave a bow of respect.

"Thank you for the next piece of our puzzle," the hooded creature croaked. "You have been most kind."

Yamasuto felt he might go into shock. This couldn't be happening—such things were not possible. He bowed to the figure, thought of his grandmother and the scary stories she'd told. Why didn't he pay closer attention?

The cloaked figure began to walk away. However, the thing in the kimono stared at Yamasuto. It held up the sword, which wore a small, crimson spot of blood from Yamasuto's thumb.

The impossible tongue came out of the maw and licked the end of the sword, savoring the flavor.

"I should tell you that it really makes no difference," the cloaked being said as he strode away. "He is going to kill you anyway."

The demon in red and black leapt toward Yamasuto. There was another "swish," and Yamasuto felt hot blood on his cheek.

He looked to the ground to see his own ear lying there. Horror filled his heart, and he raised his head to meet the awful yellow eyes of the monster.

The demon smiled again.

"Now it starts to be fun," it said, and raised the blade.

Yamasuto began to scream.

TWENTY-FIVE

Eddie got out of bed in a great mood. His world felt centered again. He could clearly recall making love to Cerise the night before, wild and passionate, like their honeymoon.

Not bad after fifteen years and two kids.

But Eddie was vaguely aware of an odd dream of a ghost in his living room, a strange fortunetelling lady, and a stick that changed into a credit card.

He turned off the clock radio alarm, though it wouldn't go off for another half-hour. He gazed at his wife's supine form.

God, how he loved her.

He would wake her with kisses, right after he started coffee.

He walked downstairs and smelled the most wonderful odor coming from his kitchen. His mother must have gotten up early and decided to cook. Was it Saturday or Sunday? No, only Friday; this was unusual.

He walked into the kitchen to find a griddle on the stove as coffee brewed, bacon sizzled, sausages browned, and flapjacks baked.

"Wow!" Eddie said, a silly grin on his face.

"Glad you like it." Marlowe came into the kitchen from the laundry room. He wore a simple white shirt and pants, with a black apron covering his clothes.

Eddie fell backward into a kitchen chair.

"Whoa!" Marlowe said. "Easy, Eddie."

"You! You're real."

"Was there some doubt?" Marlowe asked, surprised.

Eddie shook his head. "I woke up convinced you were just a crazy dream."

"Then I guess you don't want breakfast," Marlowe replied with a twinkle in his eye.

"Okay, you're a dream that cooks." Eddie went to the counter and poured a cup of coffee. "We don't eat like this on weekdays."

"Least I could do, Eddie," Marlowe said, his face growing serious. "After waking you up in the night."

Eddie frowned. "That's right. The ghost in my living room. That was real, too?"

"Quite." Marlowe went back to cooking. "I was trying to raise the spirit of Greywacke."

"Isn't that the name of the guy from the coven? He visited me at the precinct."

"I speak of his mentor, Greywacke the First. He trained the man you met. For me, he was an old friend."

"What did you want him for?"

"He was a great prophet. I thought if I could touch his mind, he might send me a vision. Then, I could get some insight into what will happen."

"Any luck?"

"When a wizard moves beyond this plane, it is rare that his essence can be reached by those still here."

"So that means no?"

"Correct. However, I did locate another spirit who proved very useful. Do you recall any of what I told you last night?"

"You said a wizard was helping Abraxas…is that right? I don't remember much after that."

"You were exhausted, Eddie, and there was no point in going any further. I used a sleep spell and put you back to bed. That's why your memory feels a little hazy; it's a side effect."

"But is it true?"

Marlowe didn't meet Eddie's eyes, but his brow was troubled. "I must do more research. As it is written, 'good news can wait and bad news won't go away.'"

"Is that a quote from one of your great wizard philosophers?"

Marlowe looked up at the ceiling. "No, I believe it was *Fiddler on the Roof*. Best thing you could do is take a shower and get dressed."

"But what about…" Eddie's voice faded as he realized Marlowe had the kitchen well under control.

Eddie added half-n-half to a cup of coffee and took it upstairs. He started the shower and got under the hard spray, which helped his muscles unwind and put his brain on alert.

He stepped out and wiped his body with a towel. The last thing he did was rub the mirror to remove the layer of mist so he could shave.

Watching him was Drusilicus.

"Lieutenant!" the man in the mirror said. "I've been trying to reach you."

Eddie let out a little shriek and clutched the towel to his exposed lower half.

"What are you…" Eddie bellowed, then with a quick look to his bedroom door lowered his voice to a harsh whisper, "…doing here?"

Drusilicus smiled in an attempt to be friendly, but it came across as a smirk. "I wanted to know your decision. Really, lieutenant, if you are going to walk the path of the wise, you have to get used to our way of communicating."

"Sh!" Eddie demanded. "Keep your voice down, my wife is in the next room."

Drusilicus nodded and went on in a quieter tone. "Haven't told the little woman? My word, lieutenant, one of the most important events of your life, and you haven't shared it with her. Tsk…tsk…"

"I can handle my wife." Eddie was a bit cross. "Now as for you—"

"Eddie?" came Cerise's semi-coherent voice from the next room. "Who are you talking to?"

"Aw Jeez!" Eddie gasped. Then he raised his voice. "No one, baby. I'm just singing."

Eddie broke into an off-key rendition of the first thing he could think of. Unfortunately, it was the seventies hit "Boogie Fever."

"I've got the boogie fever!" Eddie bellowed off-key. "I want to boogie down."

"Well, stop singing and clear out," Cerise said at the door, "I've got to pee."

"Right away." Eddie turned to the mirror and sang in a near whisper, "Get out of my mirror! I'll call you later."

Drusilicus glared at Eddie as if he were a lunatic. "If that's the quality of your singing, I'm happy to leave. Contact me. I need to know. Things are—"

"I'll call you ba-aa-aa-ack," Eddie sang, and cut him off while still using the "Boogie Fever" melody. "Now will you get lost?"

With a disgusted shake of his head, the mirror glazed over, momentarily transformed into pure silver, then once again reflected Eddie and his bathroom.

Eddie opened the door to Cerise's befuddled stare. "Eddie, have you lost your mind?"

"I'm a morning person. I like to sing!"

"Fifteen years and this is the first time."

Thinking fast, Eddie kissed her. "Well after last night—"

"Let me go, didn't you get enough? I *really* have to pee. Come on, get out!" Cerise shoved him out the door.

Eddie leaned against the closed door and exhaled heavily with relief. He paused, afraid there might be a shriek from his wife because someone else showed up in the mirror. But all was quiet.

"Man," he said aloud as he started to dress. "Marketing phone calls at dinner and spam on the computer are bad enough. Now, I got people peeking in my damn bathroom."

He dressed in underwear, shirt and pants, then used the combination to retrieve his weapon, which he checked carefully before he put it in its holster. After donning a jacket, he shoved cell phone, wallet, and keys into pockets.

He made his way down to the kitchen to find the breakfast table set with dishes, silverware, and napkins. Eddie's mother already sat and served herself from a huge plate of pancakes.

"Momma," Eddie spoke, pained at the realization of how little he'd seen her over the last few days. "Should you be up?"

She gazed up at her son, her glasses making her eyes look huge on her small body. "I can still get around, Edward. And I'm having me some breakfast. I could smell it from my room."

She popped a piece of the cooked batter into her mouth as if as punctuation. "And these flapjacks are good—almost as good as mine!"

Marlowe brought bacon from the stove and smiled appreciatively. "You are too kind, madam," he said, and put down the platter, took her hand in his oven mitt and kissed it, as if she was a highborn lady at an afternoon tea.

"Oh, stop, you old flatterer," Eleanor giggled, and brought one hand to her heart in a charmed gesture. But Eddie saw that she lit up with pleasure.

Marlowe returned to the stove, as Eddie sat in shock. Marlowe was romancing his *mother*, for God's sake.

"I like your friend," Eleanor told him. "You bring him back any time you want." She dipped the flapjack in a small stream of caramel-colored, thick liquid, and put it in her mouth with an "mmmm" of pleasure. "I don't know where he got this syrup. I never tasted anything like it."

Eddie looked at the small brown bottle on the table. It was a glass container, shaped as if it held the name-brand kind of syrup he was used to. But it bore no label. Eddie picked it up and sniffed at it.

The aroma of maple touched his nose, but there was more. It reminded him of apple orchards, warm nights, and exotic flowers.

He threw several pancakes on his plate, poured some of the syrup over them, cut off a small piece, and placed it suspiciously on his tongue.

The feeling it produced—he couldn't call it merely a taste—it was like a warm shower that traveled up his spine. The syrup was delicious, but more than that, it was a feast for his spirit. He felt lighter, freer, happier.

"Do you like it, Eddie?" Marlowe carried over a plate with scrambled eggs.

"It's unbelievable," Eddie said with astonishment.

Marlowe's eyes shifted to Eddie's mother. Eddie got the message and quickly added, "But, the pancakes aren't as good as my momma's."

From the corner of his eye, Eddie could see her puff up with pride.

"That's why I needed my special syrup," Marlowe explained. "It makes up for my lacking as a chef."

"This is a *fine* breakfast, Mister Marlowe," Eleanor piped up. "You should be right proud of it."

"Thank you, dear lady," Marlowe said. "And please, just call me Marlowe. No 'mister.'"

"What smells good?" Douglas, the younger boy, said as he came down the stairs with his brother. The noise of their combined feet heralded their arrival like a herd of elephants.

"Breakfast? A real breakfast? On a weekday!" William said as they entered the kitchen.

They both stopped when they saw Marlowe at the stove.

"Dad," William announced, "we got some white dude in our kitchen."

"We *have* some white dude in our kitchen," Eddie corrected. "This is Mister Marlowe, and he's the one responsible for the food. He's staying with us for a couple days."

"We part of the witness-protection program?" Douglas smiled at the thought. "I'm down wid that."

"You are not down with anything, young man," Cerise said, as she exited the back stairs and confronted them, her African accent pronounced. "I won't have that ghetto talk in my house."

"Yes, ma'am," Doug and William nodded in unison.

"Now sit and eat," Cerise ordered and turned on the charm for Marlowe. "Thank you for the fine meal, Marlowe."

"The least I can do to repay your hospitality," Marlowe replied.

"Now here is a man who speaks beautifully," Cerise said. "You boys could learn a thing or two from him."

Neither Douglas nor William listened, both lost in the rapture of the remarkable syrup.

"Take human bites," Eddie addressed William.

"Have some eggs, Eddie." Marlowe served him from a frying pan. "While you still can."

"What do you mean—" Eddie started to say.

The ring of Eddie's cell phone stopped him mid-sentence. Eddie glanced at his watch. It wasn't even seven AM.

"Oh dear." Marlowe looked at Eddie's jacket pocket. "You'd better get that."

Suspiciously, Eddie pulled out the phone and put it to his ear. "Hello?"

"Lieutenant Berman? It's Captain Jacobs."

Eddie sat up straighter. "Yes, captain."

The younger Bermans were in breakfast rapture and lost in the tunnel-vision of youth, but Cerise, the wife of a cop, and Eleanor, the widow of another, stopped eating and looked at Eddie. There was tension in the air.

"I'm sorry to call so early," Jacobs apologized.

"I was up, sir."

Jacobs went on, "I'm afraid we have a situation. There's been another murder in the park."

"Another homeless man, sir?" Eddie asked.

Marlowe put cooking utensils in the dishwasher and casually removed the apron as all the adults watched Eddie.

"Not this time. The murder was a similar MO but the victim was a big-shot Japanese diplomat from the UN."

Eddie hissed out the breath he didn't know he'd held. "How?"

"Sliced to pieces with a sword. I believe it's connected, lieutenant."

"I wouldn't be surprised, sir."

"Get to the scene, ASAP," Jacobs commanded. "Seventy-Ninth Street just west of Fifth Avenue. The playground on the side of the museum."

"I'm on it, sir."

"And, Eddie, I don't have to tell you that this ratchets up your case to a totally different level. We have got to get answers, and fast. I've already been contacted by the mayor's office."

"I will do my best, sir."

"I'm sure of that, lieutenant," Jacobs asserted. "Now, get to the scene."

"Yes, sir." Eddie hung up the phone.

"You'd better finish your eggs, Eddie," Marlowe said. "I think you'll have a long day ahead of you."

Their eyes met.

He knew, Eddie thought. *He knew this was going to happen.*

Eddie pictured the spirit in his living room the previous night. Was that how Marlowe knew what was coming?

Eddie grabbed his plate and shoveled in several mouthfuls of eggs, and followed it with a huge gulp of coffee.

"I have to go," Eddie said and kissed his wife.

"But, Eddie—" Cerise implored.

"You boys work hard today. And I want you home early," Eddie told his sons.

"All right, Dad!" William agreed.

"Go get 'em, Dad!" Douglas chimed in.

"Eddie—" Cerise repeated.

He bent and kissed his mother on the cheek, and she reached up and patted his face.

"Got to go, Momma." Eddie rose from the table and nodded to Marlowe, who put on his jacket. The two men headed for the front door.

"But, Eddie," Cerise blurted, "where's your car?"

Eddie stopped and turned slowly.

"M-my car?" Eddie regarded Marlowe for help.

"You remember, Eddie?" Marlowe explained, nonplussed. "We took *my* car last night, and you suggested I park two blocks away."

"Yeah, that's right," Eddie told Cerise, relieved. "We just have to walk a couple of blocks."

"But, Eddie," Cerise said, "why didn't you park in the driveway?"

"Uh, yeah, well, Marlowe, tell my wife why we didn't park in the driveway."

"You said it would be safer."

"Right, right. That's it, baby. You know, protect the witness and that…" Eddie was stumped for a moment. "Stuff."

Eddie looked wildly to Marlowe and wanted to get out before he was forced to tell another lie, sure that his untruthfulness was as transparent as glass.

Cerise impulsively grabbed Eddie in a hug.

"Take good care of my big, black man," she whispered in his ear.

Eddie couldn't help but smile. "Just going to work, baby. Same as any other day."

"I know." Cerise held fast, then released him. "And I worry, like every other day."

Marlowe was at the door and the two men walked out of the house and into the brightening sunlight.

They started up the block.

"Since we're alone," Eddie said, "are you going to tell me about the wizard working for Abraxas, or do I have to take you to the station and interrogate you?"

"Ever hear of a warlock, Eddie?" Marlowe said as they walked.

"Yeah, I once watched *'Bewitched'* on TV."

Marlowe gave an involuntary shudder. "You have my condolences. However, in our community—"

"Or coven," Eddie added.

"Yes. A warlock is a wizard who has strayed from the path of the wise and aligned himself with evil forces."

In jest, Eddie covered his mouth with his hands, breathed heavily and deepened his voice. "Come to the dark side, Luke."

Marlowe stopped and stared at Eddie as if he'd lost his mind. "What on earth are you doing?"

Eddie dropped his hands. "Nothing. I forget you're not always aware of cultural references."

Marlowe began to walk again.

"I now know why the attacks occurred in Central Park. Unknown to me…well to us all, it appears there was a talisman of great power hidden there. The reason Abraxas went on the attack was to keep the wizards out. Central Park is a place of great power. You can feel it."

"It's unspoiled, that makes people feel good, so what?"

Marlowe stopped in his footsteps. "You have just stated one of the legendary inaccuracies."

"Huh?"

"It is not unspoiled. It was completely man-made. The rolling hills, the wide vistas? All planned. And wizards were involved in every part of its creation, especially Greywacke."

Marlowe continued to walk. Eddie ran ahead, turned around, and walked backward, facing the older man as he spoke.

"You mean your old friend, Greywacke the First?" Eddie said.

"Yes, he was more than a prophet, he was a visionary. The arches in the park are named for famed and renowned wizards:

Willowdell, Dalehead, Greyshot. One hundred and fifty years ago, Greywacke worked with the men who designed the park. It was created to be a focal point for the mystical energy in New York."

"From what I've seen so far, that would be a lot," Eddie kept up with the older man.

"Exactly, Eddie. Until last night I did not see the connection."

"What is it?"

"There is someone I need to interrogate. Will you help me?"

"Great, something I know how to do. What's your theory?"

"The attacks occurred in Central Park because a very old talisman was hidden there, unknown to all of us." Marlowe shifted his cane into the long staff. "Think of it, Eddie. A potent charm hidden in a place of great power, where it built up energy year after year."

"Is that what makes Abraxas so strong?" Eddie queried as he pulled out his special card and changed it.

"It might make him unstoppable," Marlowe confessed, as they stepped into the woods and disappeared.

TWENTY-SIX

Luis Vasquez left the Bronx ten minutes after he received his own call from the captain. It took him forty minutes to get from his house to the 22nd Precinct using back routes. It then took him an additional ten minutes to quickly walk his lumbering body to the murder site.

He was surprised to find his partner at the scene.

"Hey, Eddie!" Luis said, out of breath from his stroll through the park.

"Morning, Luis." Eddie sat on his haunches and stared fixedly at some broken metal and what appeared to be a thumb. He didn't raise his head. "There's a cup of coffee for you over there," he indicated a bench with a slight nod. "Might be cold by now."

"Thanks." Luis walked over to a tree where two cups of coffee sat. One was empty, and the other was prepared just the way Luis liked it, and was indeed cold.

Luis sipped it anyway.

"So," Luis returned to where Eddie was hunkered down, "you get called hours ago?"

"Something like that." Eddie examined the twisted metal with his gloved hands. "I've been here a while."

"How did you get here from Jersey so fast?"

Eddie glanced up at his large partner. He couldn't very well tell him that he materialized only a few hundred feet away in a patch of trees.

"Missed rush hour, I guess," Eddie lied and returned his eyes to the ground.

Luis took another sip and felt his bullshit detector go off again. He looked over at the statue of the bears. The shiny brass creatures were spattered with dry crimson streaks. It was as if the bears had come to life and eaten the victim.

"What does this look like to you?" Eddie asked.

Luis' attention shifted to Eddie's hands.

"Looks like a thumb, lieutenant," Luis said.

"Brilliant, sergeant, I meant this." Eddie held up one of the metal pieces in his gloved hand. Luis bent close.

"Looks like a pistol grip and a trigger guard from a gun," Luis ventured.

"How about if I add this?" Eddie said, placing the other metal fragment in place.

"It's a handgun, all right." Luis gave an appreciative whistle. "With a silencer! That's no Saturday Night Special."

"Serial number's been erased, and I have a feeling it is stolen."

"How did it end up in pieces?" Luis asked.

"It was cut." To illustrate his point, Eddie folded the upper section on an imaginary hinge and brought the other piece up, then back into place.

Luis sipped his cold coffee. After a long pause he finally spoke. "How do you cut a gun?"

"I don't know." Eddie returned the pieces to the ground. "Forensics says the victim was sliced up with a sword."

"A sword?" Luis grunted, and took another look at all the blood and body parts flung about. "Are you kidding? You think the perp used a *sword* to cut that gun in half?"

"It's a possibility," Eddie suggested.

"You can't *slice* a gun."

Eddie felt a desperate urge to tell Luis that what he thought was possible had undergone a major shift in the last three days.

"Well, it *is* cut." Eddie sighed. "And I would very much like to know how."

"Maybe the perp did it before he came here. Y'know, used a high powered electric saw or something, and then brought the pieces to leave here—"

"To throw us off?"

Luis shrugged. "It's like you were saying yesterday. Maybe whoever is committing these murders wants to make it look like they have supernatural powers. He made it *look* like he cut a gun in two."

Eddie nodded and stood. "If you're right, we need containment."

Eddie walked to a group of forensic operatives going over the hacked pieces of the corpse, followed by Luis. "We need to talk to whoever is in charge."

Forensic officers were not full police agents, and didn't have the same ranks. But every unit had a senior agent who ran the show. In this case, it was a short, thin, white guy named Irving Feldman.

After introductions, Eddie got right to the point. "I want the forensic evidence to go through Beverly Warren."

"The assistant medical examiner?" Feldman questioned, his eyes growing wide behind his glasses. "Detective—"

"Lieutenant," Eddie replied.

"Very well, lieutenant, that's not how we do things…"

At that exact moment, Captain Jacobs arrived.

It would have been hard to miss him, surrounded by a bevy of reporters who yelled questions as he walked. Only when he entered the cordoned off area was he able to disengage them.

He approached the three men.

"Lieutenant, sergeant, Feldman," Jacobs said with a nod to each as he approached.

"Captain," Eddie and Luis said in unison.

"Captain," Feldman said as he drew near. "I'm glad you're here. *Lieutenant* Berman has requested that all my data go through the medical examiner's office."

Jacobs glanced over to Eddie. "Lieutenant?"

"Not just the medical examiner's office. I specifically want it to go to Doctor Warren."

"Why?" Jacobs fired back.

"Containment, sir," Eddie stressed. "Without going into detail, there is unusual evidence in this case. If any information found its way to the media, there could be a lot of nasty speculation. I trust Beverly, and I can work with her. What's more, I know she'll work with us."

"I must protest," Feldman whined. "The crime scene unit has a history of—"

Jacobs lifted his hand in one quick motion that cut the man off. "Sounds good, lieutenant. I am aware that there are sometimes more facts in the paper than *we* release." He faced Irving and added, "Please act on the lieutenant's request."

Feldman looked properly cowed. "Very well, sir."

Jacobs approached the raised platform that supported the statue, awash with caked blood, crusty and brown on the gray sidewalk.

"All this blood," Jacobs said. "Looks like the perp tried to redecorate the park."

"The body parts were spread all over the playground," Eddie pointed out. "I just found a thumb and another man located what he believes was his...uh...organ."

"You mean...?" Jacobs turned his head a little toward Eddie.

"Yes," Eddie said.

"*Madre de Dios*," Luis muttered.

"You were right sir, similar MO," Eddie concluded. "Captain, when you called me, you knew who he was. How did we get the ID?"

"According to the officer on the scene, his wallet was lying right on top of the torso, open to his UN identification card."

"The perp wanted us to know who he was," Eddie considered.

"It's more than that, lieutenant," Jacobs snapped. "The perp wants to rub our noses in it."

"He's on a power trip and wants to show us who's in charge," Luis said, his jaw hard.

Sounds like our boy Abraxas, Eddie thought.

"Everything on this goes only through *my* office," Jacobs demanded. "You find out anything, I hear it first, no matter how insignificant."

Eddie and Luis nodded.

"The homeless guy may have been practice," Jacobs went on. "I want you to find out everything you can about the victim. I want to know where he lived, where he ate, and especially, what he was doing in my park in the middle of the night."

"Yes, sir," Eddie replied.

"You gentlemen are working this weekend. Let your families know."

Eddie made a low grunt of acquiescence.

"Get me answers. The mayor wants to bring in the FBI and the Urban Crime Task Force."

"This is our turf," Luis asserted, defensively.

"The homeless man getting hacked up didn't attract a lot of media," Jacobs cautioned. "That's changed now. This is a front-page crime. The press will be hounding us for answers and they will complain the longer they have to wait for results. Also, Manhattan North Homicide and the Urban Crime Task Force will want to get into the limelight."

"We'll do the best we can, sir," Eddie promised.

"Then get me answers, the sooner the better," Jacobs sighed. "Now I must go obfuscate the ladies and gentlemen of the press."

TWENTY-SEVEN

Friday morning was spent in a whirlwind of interviews. Eddie and Luis went to the UN building on First Avenue and 49th Street. Security required them to surrender their weapons and go through several guarded areas with an escort until they arrived at the offices of the Japanese delegation.

They met with several diplomats who behaved agreeably, but divulged little. Most of them spoke fluent English, and it was obvious that several wished to fill the position vacated by the deceased.

Eddie and Luis, as they got nowhere, retrieved their weapons, and went off to the delegate's residence. There they found a female servant who claimed in broken English that she was the cook and maid. They also located Yamasuto's personal assistant, an anxious young man named Akio.

They asked a couple of questions, but Akio offered little information. Instead he peered around the room nervously.

Cop instinct has a powerful effect on men whose lives depend on its whispers. Although the young man answered questions in brief sentences, both Eddie and Luis could sense that there was an encyclopedia underneath each one. Akio was unhappy about the things he knew.

As Luis sat and took notes, Eddie pulled out his cell phone and quickly called Captain Jacobs. He wanted to bring the assistant to the station and *really* interview him. He wanted to work on him with Luis in the good cop/bad cop roles that would break down his resistance.

Jacobs was concerned about the assistant's diplomatic immunity and coaxed Eddie to get as much as he could in the safe environment of the residence.

In plain English, bureaucratic bullshit won.

Disappointed, Eddie put on a good front and returned to his partner.

Upon his return to the comfortable sitting room, the young man broke down, and began to speak with moderate weeping. Eddie felt the crying jag may have been induced for effect, but Akio confessed that his superior smuggled artifacts from Japan to sell in America.

It took a while to calm him, but they were finally able to coax him to go into detail.

Eddie began to get a clearer picture of Yamasuto. Akio was afraid that whoever killed his employer would come after him, because he'd seen the small figurine that was supposed to be delivered to the buyer the previous night.

They took time and got Akio to describe the figure in detail. They even asked him to draw what he'd seen. Akio surprised them by demonstrating the talent of a gifted artist. He drew a very detailed reproduction of the statuette with nothing more than a piece of typing paper and a pencil.

"Do you have any idea who the buyer was?" Luis asked, continuing the role of the gruff bad cop.

Akio nodded and opened up a small date book. In it were notes written in Japanese.

"Does this have all of Mr. Yamasuto's transactions?"

Akio nodded. "Yes, in code."

Luis looked over his shoulder. "Looks more like chicken scratch."

"It is Japanese, but unreadable if you do not know the key."

"And you do?" Eddie said.

"I have been with Mr. Yamasuto for five years," Akio said. "He was a good employer and I wish to help catch his killer."

"Who was the appointment last night?" Eddie said.

"If I read it correctly, I believe that it was a person named Cuccolo," Akio said.

Luis and Eddie exchanged a glance.

"Alfonso Cuccolo?" Luis queried.

"I do not know. There is only the one name," Akio answered.

Quickly, Eddie called the precinct and requested a uniformed officer to watch the diplomatic residence.

"Let us know if you can name any other buyer in the last six months," Eddie said, and gave the young man a business card while they bolted for the door.

Eddie and Luis drove back to the "22" and parked the car.

"I need to walk, come on," Eddie said, as they got out of the car. Luis followed. It was a sunny day, not too hot, and the fresh, clean air made the world feel alive. But Eddie was oblivious. His body walked through the beauty of the Great Lawn, but his mind was elsewhere.

"Can you believe," Eddie pondered, "that all of this was created?"

"Say what?"

"None of this was originally here. Not the ball fields, not Turtle Pond, not even the hills. It was all built. Did you know that?"

Luis shrugged. "Never occurred to me."

They wandered farther along the path, and Eddie looked up at the tall stone obelisk that rose above the trees. He felt attracted to it somehow.

"Cuccolo," Eddie muttered.

"Do you think Akio knows who he is?"

"Why else would he be scared?" Eddie admitted. "Alfonso Cuccolo, operator with the Avecchio crime family."

"Not good, Eddie," Luis divulged. "He's got the FBI all over him, and more lawyers than I got kids."

"I'll call the captain, and you call to see how soon Beverly will have info for us."

Luis nodded, and as if they were gunslingers in an old western movie, they both whipped out their cell phones, dialed, and spoke. Though right next to each other, they stood worlds apart.

"Cuccolo?" Captain Jacob responded to Eddie, "The Feds won't let us near him—"

"I'm only one person," Beverly decried. "Do you have any idea how many cases I have down here? How dare you put me in charge of forensics without *asking* me!"

Eddie and Luis wheedled, cajoled, and begged their individual associates to give them what they needed.

"All right, you can *talk* to Cuccolo. Just talk," Jacobs proclaimed. "Only to see if he knows Yamasuto, nothing more."

"I can have something for you by three o'clock, maybe two," Beverly grumbled. "You guys owe me big time for this one."

As if they planned it, both men managed to end their calls at the same time. They returned the implements of the modern road-warrior to their pockets, and smiled at each other, just as they exited the park and set foot on the pavement of Central Park West.

"We can talk to Cuccolo," Eddie said.

Luis nodded. "Beverly can see us after two."

Eddie checked his watch. It was noon.

"I've got to meet someone. Why don't we meet at two, talk to Beverly, then go have a chat with Alfonso?"

"You doing something about the case, or are you seeing your chippy?"

"Would you stop with the 'chippy' stuff?" Eddie said and felt hot around the collar. "For all I know, you killed Yamasuto to keep an eye on me."

"Swords aren't my style. Now, if he'd been beaten to death with a tire iron…" Luis suggested. His eyes suddenly fixed on an approaching man. "Hold up."

Eddie turned to see Jason Wilcox draw near, flanked not only by his shadow, Sam, but another man as well. This new man, a little over thirty with a receding hairline, was tall, but more thin and lithe than Wilcox.

"Well, Berman and Vasquez, the bumbling detectives," Wilcox mocked. "I'm on my way to *your* crime scene. Second time this week."

"That's good, Wilcox, they should have the blood cleaned up by now," Eddie confirmed. "So you won't get a tummy ache."

"Says the man who loses control of bodily functions over a severed head." Wilcox gave a wink to Sam and the new man. The older man lit another cigarette and guffawed appreciatively. The other man merely smiled.

"You want something, Wilcox, or do you just like to annoy people who actually work?" Luis chided.

"City Hall wants this case solved, as does Homeland Security. And now, yours truly is *officially* on the case. In fact, I've been given some extra men." Wilcox pointed in the direction of the third agent. "This is Phil Conners."

"The musician?" Luis asked.

"He's Collins, different job," Conners said with a well-practiced delivery. He must have responded to that question a hundred times.

"I've been assigned a dozen men," Wilcox bragged.

"Before you get caught up in your crowing, Wilcox," Eddie speculated. "Don't forget it's *our* case."

"Berman," Wilcox leaned close. "If there isn't some serious movement by the end of the weekend, everybody except the marines will be involved. The advantage the FBI has—"

"Hey, man," Luis badgered, "you keepin' information from the NYPD?"

Wilcox opened his hands in a gesture of subservience. "What could you mean, sergeant? I'm under a different jurisdiction. I *have* to keep things from you. It's my job."

"Thanks for the 'heads up,'" Eddie grumbled. "Let's go, Luis."

"I want copies of your reports by this afternoon." Wilcox handed Eddie a business card. "Fax 'em, e-mail 'em, or hand-deliver them to Federal Plaza. I trust you know where it is?"

"Wall Street area, right?" Luis jeered. "As far from the action as possible."

"You'll get your reports, Wilcox," Eddie assured. "You'll have to wait until we get the physical evidence from the ME."

"Before five o'clock, Berman," Wilcox demanded. "No matter what your opinion of me or the Bureau, you hold me up and I'll slap you down."

"Good to see you reverting to your regular style," Eddie pointed out. "You were almost polite for a minute. C'mon, Luis."

Eddie turned and Luis gave one dirty look toward Wilcox, and walked off.

With a nod to Sam and Conners, Wilcox continued in the direction of the East Side.

"Sir," Conners asked as they walked, "is it wise to create animosity with the NYPD?"

"It's fine, Conners," Wilcox surmised. "You need to let them know where they stand. Those two are trouble."

As Eddie and Luis stood on Central Park West watching them go, Luis said under his breath, "Next time we see him, I want to punch him, just once."

"Remember what your mother said about the neighborhood bully. Just *ignore* him," Eddie instructed.

"My *madre* never tol' me that."

"So, what did you do about bullies?"

Luis shrugged. "I beat the hell out of them."

TWENTY-EIGHT

Eddie walked with Luis back to the "22" where he made copies of Akio's drawing and picked up *Talismans through the Ages* from his desk drawer. He slipped a copy between the pages of the book, and with it under his arm, Eddie left the precinct and soon climbed the stairs of Marlowe's townhouse.

In answer to his knock, the door was opened by Frisha, still dressed in her flowing robes, although she looked disheveled.

"Frisha, how are you? Visions any clearer?"

She brought a hand to her head. "More confused than e'er. I'm tryin' to wait 'till I can see things plain."

"Maybe that's best," Eddie suggested.

"There is something...that's tryin' to come to light..." her voice faded at the end.

"What?" Eddie asked.

"I don't know, keeps changing," Frisha rubbed her forehead. "Oooh, I need to mix a potion—"

Eddie decided she'd imbibed a few too many potions the night before. He wandered through the huge entrance hall and entered the large living room.

Marlowe sat in a wing-backed chair before one of the empty fireplaces. Eddie was surprised at how *old* he looked. "Is it Trefoil?"

Marlowe shook his head, and Eddie exhaled with relief. Marlowe then gestured to a chair next to him.

They sat in silence for a moment as Marlowe watched the barren fireplace, as if logs kindled in the expanse.

"I am an old fool," Marlowe finally spoke.

"I don't think so." Eddie pulled out the copy of the sketch of the statuette. "This look familiar to you?"

Marlowe looked at it but registered no surprise.

"Amatsu Mikaboshi, the Shinto God of Evil," Marlowe's eyes rested on the drawing. "Do you know the mythology?"

Eddie whipped out his notebook and was scribbling the name down. "Uh no, I was planning to look it up. I got a book."

Marlowe glanced at the book cover. "Don't bother, it won't be in there. You'll find very little about him anywhere. Amatsu Mikaboshi was considered such a monster that most of his deeds were stricken from the holy writings."

"Do tell," Eddie said.

"Do you know how he was finally removed from a reign of terror in Ancient Japan?" his eyes returned to the fireplace. He went on, not waiting for a reply. "He was cast out by five wise men, great in learning and odd to look upon."

"An early version of the Five?" Eddie said, more of a statement than a question.

Marlowe nodded. "Different people, yes. It was long before my time. In every culture throughout the world, Abraxas has sought dominance using different names, different forms, and each time he is tracked down and cast out by the Five."

"And this time as well!" Eddie hoped he sounded surer than he felt. "We just have to get Trey on his feet—"

"This time is different, as I told you last night, there is a Warlock in our midst, who is helping the Great Evil. That statue is an ancient talisman of great power, and the victim was manipulated into bringing it into Central Park."

"What are you talking about?"

A gong resounded three loud tones, which echoed through the hall.

"I contacted someone we must speak to." Marlowe eyes went to the doorway. Eddie rose from his chair. He could faintly hear echo voices of Frisha and others. He glanced at Marlowe who raised an eyebrow and waited.

Through the doorway walked Drusilicus with his gray-black hair loose, and in what looked to be a thousand-dollar suit. By his side walked a young man dressed in black, who glanced about the room in awe.

Eddie recognized the young man immediately. "Hey! You're the kid from 'Magickal Cherub.' What is he doing here?"

The young man turned to Drusilicus and pointed at Eddie. "What is *he* doing here?"

Drusilicus gave them both a withering look.

Marlowe rose from his chair. "You know him, Eddie?"

"He sold me that book, and tried to pull something with an amulet—"

"Oh yeah?" the young man spat, his eyes aflame. "He's a cop!"

Drusilicus held up his hand, and the young man quieted. "When spoken to—"

"But, he's a—"

"We are fully aware of Lieutenant Berman's position in the police force," Drusilicus interrupted. "I told you that we were meeting wizards today and I spoke the truth."

"He's a cop *and* a wizard?" Caleb puzzled.

"Yes, now hush."

The young man hung his head like a naughty dog.

"Marlowe and Lieutenant Berman, forgive the outburst." Drusilicus smiled wanly. He gestured to the young man, who still watched his feet. "This is my apprentice, Caleb."

Caleb gave a polite bow. "I live to serve and learn at your feet."

"Thank you for coming on such short notice, Drusilicus," Marlowe said.

"Yes, and I must admit, I admire your courage, Marlowe." Drusilicus closed the distance between himself and the two men. "And you, lieutenant, it takes a truly wise man to know when he is out of his depth."

"Say what?" Eddie replied.

Drusilicus grasped Eddie's hand warmly. "Tut, tut, lieutenant. I am sure your decision to pass the Staff of Fire to an experienced wizard was difficult, but it is best to know one's limitations. And, Marlowe, no apology is necessary."

"Drusilicus!" Marlowe bellowed. "I called you here to speak to you about your apprentice."

"Ah." Drusilicus glanced back to Caleb. "Of course, you are concerned about who will receive my staff. I want to assure you that despite his inability to hold his tongue, Caleb is quite—"

Eddie looked at Marlowe. The older man grew very red in the face and appeared as if any moment he was going to explode.

"It is not Caleb I wish to speak of!" Marlowe shouted. "Tell me of Alex."

"Alex?" Eddie repeated.

"Alex?" Drusilicus was stunned by the older man's reaction. "He moved beyond this level of existence."

"Yes, Drusilicus, I know he's dead."

"What does that have to do with the lieutenant relinquishing his staff?" Drusilicus' expression grew hard.

"Nothing!" Marlowe snapped. "Now, sit down!"

Two large chairs rose up across the room and flew over and behind Drusilicus and Caleb. They sat as they watched Marlowe, suspiciously.

"You have more than one apprentice, the Divine only knows why!" Marlowe accused.

"It is my right!" Drusilicus argued.

"By Zoroaster, you mislead them. A true wizard only takes on an apprentice when he is ready to leave this plane, as Greywacke the First did with you. But, on the other hand, you take on students, with no intention of giving them a staff."

Drusilicus reddened and leaned closer. "It is wise to train an apprentice. Only then can he be ready if a staff becomes available."

"Which seldom happens," Marlowe corrected.

"Who are you to judge me?" Drusilicus puffed his chest out. "It is well known that your apprentice almost destroyed you."

"Oh, enough of ancient history!" Marlowe smacked his walking stick against the marble floor. "You do it for your own vanity, giving this world a foolish young man who knows too much of our ways, but not enough to help anyone."

Drusilicus arose and stared at Marlowe with blazing eyes. "If you wish to complain about my practices we can bring it before the coven!"

"Very well," Marlowe shot back. "I wonder how the coven will react when I tell them your apprentices unleashed the monster we now face!"

They stood silent.

"Time out." Eddie held his hands in the traditional "T" formation. "What are you talking about, Marlowe?"

The old man shifted his glance to Caleb, who sat very still.

"*You* know," Marlowe focused on Caleb. "There is no need to deny it. Last night I raised Alex's spirit. He told me of the last moments of his life."

Caleb's lips grew tight. "It wasn't my fault."

Drusilicus frowned. "You never spoke of this to me."

"You might think I had something to do with it," Caleb fretted.

"But you were there," Marlowe charged. "Perhaps at the bidding of your master?"

Drusilicus jumped from his chair. "Do you accuse me of releasing Abraxas upon this world?" He glanced sidelong at Eddie. "And in front of this...this..."

"I'd be careful if I were you, buddy," Eddie warned as he rose from his seat.

"...this *Newling!*" Drusilicus shouted.

Eddie was surprised at the unfamiliar word. "What did you call me?"

"It means you're a beginner," Caleb jeered.

"Oh!" Eddie was almost disappointed. He wanted it to be an insult, or at least a racial slur, so he could clock Drusilicus.

Marlowe went on. "You are here with the lieutenant because he is both a wizard and the police officer assigned to the murder of Riftstone. Last night, another was killed by the demon."

"Another wizard?" Drusilicus' face grew pale.

"No, a mortal. However, I believe the secret of Abraxas' newfound power rests within your apprentice's memory. If we relive it, it will help us to take the appropriate action."

"Oh no." Caleb rose from his chair. "I don't want him getting in my head—"

Sit down!" Drusilicus barked and Caleb returned to his seat. "You have no right to complain. You never told me you witnessed

Alex's death." He returned his focus to Marlowe. "If I allow this, you must limit your probing only to that night. Do you know the date?"

"May first," Marlowe declared.

"So mote it be," Drusilicus replied solemnly.

Caleb shook his head. "Master—"

"Silence," Drusilicus intoned in a quiet, but firm voice.

"Wait a minute," Eddie asked. "What are you going to do?"

"*We* are going to share a memory with Caleb," Marlowe explained. "See all he saw and be aware of everything as he experienced it."

"Really?" Eddie whispered to Marlowe. "We can do that?"

"Yes," Drusilicus interjected. "But it must be done carefully."

"What happens if you're not careful?" Eddie inquired.

"Brain damage," Drusilicus remarked simply.

Caleb grew very pale.

"I am well practiced." Marlowe changed the cane by his side into his staff. "You three pull close and join hands."

"Master, I do not wish—" Caleb beseeched in a low voice.

"You *will* cooperate," Drusilicus snapped.

Eddie, Drusilicus, and Caleb pulled their chairs close and joined hands, as Marlowe stood behind Caleb, and placed his free hand on the young man's head.

"Wait!" Caleb reached under his shirt to pull off several silver disks that hung from chains around his neck. He placed them on the floor as Marlowe raised an eyebrow.

"The boy carries many talismans," Marlowe declared with suspicion.

"It is not an unusual way to practice and learn," Drusilicus expounded, though he seemed a bit surprised by the number himself.

The three men joined hands again, and Marlowe returned his hand to Caleb's head.

"Close your eyes, and relax," Marlowe instructed. "Allow your mind to go back."

Eddie sat with his eyes closed, and felt weightless. The room fell away around him. All at once, he found himself in Central Park on a beautiful day, in the late afternoon, the sun casting long shadows all about.

Eddie looked over and saw Marlowe, Drusilicus, and Caleb standing next to him. A few feet away stood another Caleb. Eddie did a double-take at the doppelgänger.

"How the hell?" Eddie muttered.

"We experience Caleb's memory in the role of observers, Eddie," Marlowe explained. "It allows us to perceive all he deported, without invading his mind."

"Why not?" Eddie asked.

"If we shared his memory *through* his eyes, we might influence those memories. As I've told you, remembrances are simple to manipulate. This way we shall not alter his."

"Man!" Caleb peered about. "Master, I've never done this."

"We did not yet reach this level in your training," Drusilicus elucidated.

"So, where are we?" Eddie put forward.

"Summit Rock," Marlowe disclosed. "One of the places of power within the park."

"Yes," Drusilicus added, "and it appears to be close to twilight."

Eddie turned to see a group of young people clad in unusual clothing, who carried a twelve-foot wooden pole five inches in diameter, which was gaily decorated with ribbons.

The women wore dresses from a bygone era, with hanging sleeves, bodices, and skirts that covered their legs. The men were likewise fancifully outfitted, wearing tights and loose Renaissance shirts with caps and cloaks.

A woman led the procession, clad in a deep-green velvet dress, which contrasted the auburn fire of her hair.

"Who are they?" Eddie pointed to the revelers.

"He really doesn't know anything, does he?" Caleb scoffed.

Marlowe turned to Eddie. "On May first, there is a holiday, a very old one, known as Beltane. Those who keep it light a bonfire and put up a Maypole."

"A Maypole?" Eddie considered this. "That's from a holiday? I thought kids did that."

"They do, but it is based on an ancient rite, just like the Yule log or a Christmas tree."

"A Christmas tree?" Eddie repeated.

"It has a basis in ancient pagan rituals."

"I'm on the move." Caleb watched his double rise from the stone bench and walk off.

"Let us go," Marlowe directed, and the group followed.

A woman walked toward Eddie and he tried to avoid her, but couldn't get out of her way.

She passed right through him.

"What the…" Eddie touched himself to make sure he was there.

Marlowe moved next to Eddie. "This is only a memory. Nothing here is real. No one can see us and we cannot intervene."

"A memory?" Eddie gulped. "Then how come I can hear the people talking, and the noise of cars?"

"We experience all my apprentice remembers," Drusilicus asserted.

They strolled a few hundred feet north of Summit Rock to a fenced-off area. The Caleb who lived the events glanced about and snuck through an unseen opening in the fence.

"I can't fit through there," Eddie indicated.

"No need." Drusilicus, ghostlike, walked right through the fence.

The others went through as well, Eddie last. He checked himself on the other side to make sure that he was untouched by his egress.

The real-time Caleb hid near a bush, as they looked down on a young man who sifted through the dirt. He was dressed in jeans and heavy shirt, covered with a layer of dust. He sported a Van Dyke beard and mustache and several rings passed through his earlobes.

Sod was removed from the lawn, and several rectangular pits were excavated in patterns suggesting walls and remnants of long-ago habitats.

"That is Alex." Drusilicus pointed at the young man.

A supervisor, dressed in jeans and a flannel shirt that sported its own layer of dust, came over. "We're done. The sun is going down."

Alex looked up. "Just a few minutes more, Charles? I'll be careful."

"This is an archaeological dig site." Charles sighed. "We have to secure the area, replace the tarpaulin, to make sure our findings aren't contaminated!"

"I know the drill," Alex said. "Please? I'll clean up everything myself."

"What's the big deal?" Charles grumbled.

"I feel lucky. If I find something of significance it could help with our funding."

Charles sighed again. "Okay, but if you do find something good, leave it so we can photograph it in its original position."

Alex nodded and gave Charles a quick smile. He continued to dig as the other man put tools into a small shed, and pulled out a large tarpaulin, which he placed on the ground near Alex.

The Caleb in the scene remained hidden.

"Good night," Charles said with a wave, and was off without a look back.

"Night!" Alex watched the man leave.

Caleb rose and crept over to Alex. "I was afraid that fool would never leave."

Alex looked up and spoke in a whisper. "Careful, he might hear you."

"If we get lucky, you don't need to work this crummy job after tonight," Caleb murmured.

"It would be easier if you worked here, too," Alex argued.

"I influenced them to hire you, I did my part." Caleb double-checked to make sure they were alone. "I've also helped you dig after hours."

"Occasionally," Alex whined.

"You want me to get a shovel?"

"Give me a minute." Alex took a small trowel and pulled the dirt away from a spot he'd avoided while Charles stood near. He scraped and dug, finally dropped the tool and clawed at the soil with his bare hands.

Alex pulled back his hands as if he'd been dealt an electric shock. "It *is* here."

"Like you were told?" Caleb expressed with excitement.

Alex nodded, pulled a leather glove from his pocket, put it on, and carefully brushed away the dirt to reveal a thin chain.

Caleb hunkered down on his haunches and pointed at the revealed chain. "That's gold, and look, each link is made by hand."

Gently, Alex pulled. The buried line of gold began to expose like a hidden ground snake, burrowed deeply in its secret pit.

The chain caught.

Breathing hard with excitement, Alex gave an additional yank and a round metal disk slipped loose from the earth.

A giggle of joy escaped from both Alex and Caleb, as they stood with their prize held high in Alex's gloved hand.

Caleb extracted a paintbrush from Alex's kit and delicately wiped the caked loam from the medallion.

Slowly, a figure was exposed. The creature bore the head of a rooster, chest and arms of a man, with legs that were snakes. This mythical creature held a whip in one of the outstretched hands and a round shield in the other.

"That's it!" Caleb announced. "The Amulet of Abracadabra!"

"I can feel the power, even through my glove," Alex exulted. "It's warm in my hand."

"So, who told you to look here?"

"Sorry, bud." Alex looked quickly left and right. "I'm sworn to secrecy." Alex carefully put the amulet in his pants pocket.

"What are you doing?" Caleb questioned.

"We can't do anything here," Alex explained. "Let's clean up and take it to my apartment. I have an enchanted circle."

"So do I! Why not my place?" Caleb insisted. "Hey, you need me, I'm the one who knows the release spell."

"I could look it up!" Alex put his tools and the leather gloves into a small basket.

"You don't have the resources I do," Caleb wheedled. "Look, if it is as powerful as you said, we can share it."

Alex replaced his basket in the shed. "That was the plan, dummy."

"Watch it, lame-oh."

As Eddie, Marlowe, Drusilicus, and Caleb watched, the two young men laid the tarpaulin out over the dig. The thick, plastic sheet locked down to stakes planted in the ground with heavy hasps that ran through metal eyes.

Eddie spoke to Marlowe. "What is that amulet about?"

"The Amulet of Abracadabra is a powerful talisman. It was lost for over a hundred and seventy-five years," Marlowe told him. "Somehow, someone brought it to this country and buried it in the park."

Eddie said, "But who told these guys where to find it?"

"It was not I," Drusilicus speculated. "Last anyone heard of the damn thing, it was in one of the Caribbean Islands."

Twilight deepened and night descended as Caleb and Alex finished their work, locked the shed and the gate, and began to walk south.

"What's that light in the distance?" Alex pointed.

"There are pagans on Summit Rock, lighting the Beltane Fire," Caleb told him.

"How perfect is that?" Alex said. "Let's go watch."

"I thought you wanted to—"

"Best time would be midnight, right?" Alex interrupted, as they walked up the winding path. "Let's see what rituals the wannabes are doing."

As they drew closer, they could hear singing, and a large bonfire blazed on the rocky incline.

A pole was fitted into one of the large stones near the top of the hill. A group of festively dressed figures held ribbons and scampered about the wooden totem.

The woman in green ascended the flagstone steps to the top of the hill and approached the fire. She held up her hands. The others stopped dancing and faced her.

The group of the visible and invisible stayed in the shadows near the edge of the hill that descended to Central Park West.

"Blessed be," she spoke and the others replied the same. "We are here this Beltane night to give thanks to the god and goddess and call them to our…our…"

She stopped speaking, her mouth open, and her eyes glazed over. Murmurs of concern went through the small crowd, as she stood unblinking.

"Did you do that?" Alex turned to Caleb.

"Not me," smirked Caleb. "But it looks like it might get interesting."

Her mouth moved slowly, like a fish taken from water. Then her face underwent a transformation, which the firelight seemed to emphasize.

It was a shocking change. The woman no longer looked lovely; in fact, she resembled a hideous hag.

"Alsi ku nushi…" she began in a strange, deep and powerful voice.

Alex and Caleb looked at each other.

"Isn't that—" Alex said.

"She's calling upon the gods of the night, asking them to do her bidding," Caleb explained with a frown.

Alex leapt up.

"What?"

"Ah!" Alex yelled as he pulled the heavy fabric of his pants away from the skin of his leg.

"What is the matter with you?" Caleb demanded in a hoarse whisper.

Muttering, "Hot, hot," Alex slid behind the bench and down the grassy side of the hill that faced the dark street. He shucked off his pants and fell to the mossy grass.

Alex got to his knees, turned his pants over and shook them. The golden medal and chain dropped out, yet it glowed brilliant red, as if just pulled from a forge.

Caleb peeked up the crest of the hill to see that the woman still spoke in the deep, hoarse voice. Eddie watched completely puzzled. "What's going on?"

"It is a spell," Marlowe explained. "She just said, 'It is finished,' the part of the conjuration designed to complete an enchantment."

The woman visibly relaxed, shook her head, and returned to normal.

The invisible witnesses and Alex gazed down at the amulet on the ground. It no longer glowed. He carefully reached down to pick it up.

"It's okay," he hissed to Caleb.

"I see you found it," a deep voice intoned.

Alex, both Calebs, Eddie, Marlowe, and Drusilicus all looked at the bottom of the hill next to the stone wall that surrounded the park. There stood a creature that was at least ten feet tall. Even in the shadows, its body was a dark red, strong and muscled, like a bodybuilder. But the feet were red snakes writhing with black eyes scanning and tongues darting. There was a fierce red whip in one of the huge hands, and the face…was not a face at all.

It was a rooster.

Not a cartoon rooster, or the blank face of a domesticated hen, but the fierce stare of a fighting cock.

"Abraxas!" Marlowe whispered. "That is one of his many forms."

"Man," Eddie decided, "he is one ugly dude."

"Good of you to assist in my release," the creature said. It moved its head side to side like a bird of prey, the eyes going quickly from object to object. The beak moved in time to the words, as if to talk was a normal occupation for a bird.

"I…uh…" Alex stammered, then looked at the amulet, which bore the same configuration. He held it up and offered it to the monster.

In the background, they could hear the revelers sing at the top of the hill. Some foolish tune about the turn of the seasons, and praise to the goddess of the earth.

The creature moved toward him. Not so much walked as slithered, the snake legs wriggling as their beady eyes watched Alex intently. One taloned hand casually reached and plucked the talisman from the boy's open hand.

The bird head stared at it, and an expression of pleasure—you couldn't call it a smile—crossed the cockerel's face.

"You must forgive me. I am weak, or I would do this right," the beak moved to enunciate each word. "Rip you to pieces, slice you up, something like that. I need a sacrifice, boy, nothing personal. I'm sure you understand."

In a panic, Alex rose unsteadily to his feet, turned, and ran back up the hill, completely forgetting he wore no pants. He sprinted to the clearing where the peaceful pagans sat around the huge fire and chanted their bland song.

However, Alex ran far too fast and possessed no control over his legs.

He ran onto the concrete pathway as fast as his legs could carry him. The group leapt to their feet, and the red-haired woman turned to him. Seeing him pantless, she yelled, "Put your clothes on! That's not what we are about."

That was all Alex heard, or would ever hear again.

With a scream, Alex ran past the circle and leapt onto the huge bonfire.

TWENTY-NINE

They were back in the living room, each in their chairs, as Marlowe removed his hand from Caleb's head.

Woozily, the boy opened his eyes.

"What happened?" Eddie queried, surprised that they were back in the living room.

"We have seen all we need to know of that incident," Marlowe explained.

Caleb nodded, still a bit unfocused. "When I went back, the demon and the talisman were gone."

"Drusilicus," Marlowe accused, "you neglected to tell any of the coven that your apprentices sought such a dangerous talisman!"

"I didn't know!" Drusilicus responded, anger burning just below the surface. "Alex was headstrong, but I expected more from this one." He gave a nod toward Caleb. "Who told them where to look? Even a wizard would have a hard time finding it."

"How about an enchanter?" Eddie suggested.

All heads turned to Eddie.

"The lady at 'Magickal Cherub' said that Caleb was an enchanter."

Drusilicus and Marlowe turned to Caleb.

The young man reached for the collection of talismans he'd worn that rested on the floor.

Marlowe's staff slammed down and pinned Caleb's hand in place.

"Ow!" Caleb gasped.

"I would advise, young man," Marlowe threatened, "that you not touch those. There are three wizards here, and any of us could destroy thee with but a thought."

Sweat appeared on Caleb's forehead.

"I...I..." Caleb stammered, obviously in pain, "I merely wished to show that these are protective charms."

Marlowe lifted his staff and the young man pulled his hand back and caressed it with the other.

Eddie reached down and slid the amulets toward himself, out of Caleb's reach as Drusilicus looked at his apprentice with annoyance.

"What is worse, Abraxas has attained another powerful charm, the *Kami* of Amatsu Mikaboshi." Marlowe picked up the drawing Eddie brought to hold it out for Drusilicus.

Drusilicus' eyes narrowed, and he leaned back in his chair. "If he has two empowered talismans of his ancient forms, that could be very dangerous indeed."

"Hold on, Marlowe." Eddie turned to the older man. "If a warlock or enchanter is helping him, what do they get out of the deal?"

"Once the power of a talisman is unleashed, a wizard can tap into that energy, increasing his own abilities exponentially." Marlowe glared intently at Caleb.

Eddie, however, looked pointedly at Drusilicus. "I think I know a wizard who seeks more power."

"You dare!" Drusilicus came to his feet in one swift move. Although Eddie did not know where it came from, he saw a staff appear in Drusilicus' hand.

Eddie felt a rush of adrenaline and leapt up as well. He fumbled for his wallet. He wanted his staff—*needed* his staff.

He was shocked when he felt it jump by itself into his hand and expanded as it did. By the time he was fully to his feet, he held his own wood rod tightly. He shot a look to Marlowe, who also stood at the ready, a full-sized staff in his hand as well.

Caleb grabbed the arms of his chair in panic.

"Back down, Drusilicus Greywacke," Marlowe ordered, his voice calm but firm.

"This Newling is no concern to me," Drusilicus responded, his features contorted in a terrible scowl.

"This Newling is going to kick your lily-white ass all the way back down to fashionable Fifth Avenue if you don't put your damn stick down." Eddie aimed the top of his staff at Drusilicus' head.

Drusilicus looked from one man to the other, then dropped into his chair. He lowered his staff and released it so it clattered to the floor by his feet. "I see no reason for me to be insulted in this way."

Eddie and Marlowe sat as well and placed their own staffs on the marble floor.

"Perhaps we should discuss this calmly," Marlowe proposed.

"Very well," Drusilicus agreed, and Eddie could almost see him shift gears into "politician" mode. "Are you certain that a warlock is in league with the Great Evil?"

"You saw in the memory. That woman became possessed and recited the spell of release," Marlowe recounted.

Drusilicus shrugged. "Perhaps she was possessed by Abraxas?"

"He doesn't have the ability to manifest his own release. Someone else put the conjuration on her lips. Alex was thrown into that fire by one with the power to make him do so."

"Is that something wizards do?" Eddie frowned. "Take people over, make them move where and how they want?"

"Possession is possible in many ways," Marlowe stated. "A spirit can inhabit and take dominion over an individual. However, a wizard can make a person do his will, like a puppet."

"It is disapproved of," Drusilicus pointed out.

"Sometimes it is necessary," Marlowe surmised. "To move a small child out of the way of a bus, to stop someone from jumping off a bridge. Such skills are *only* to be used to save a life."

Drusilicus shook his head. "But to use someone to release a demon or kill themselves…"

Eddie looked at Caleb, who had been silent since the confrontation with Drusilicus. "Your apprentice tried to influence me, by waving an amulet at me yesterday."

Caleb grew crimson. "He was asking about demons." His eyes narrowed. "And I knew he was a cop."

"You have a talisman that gives you such power?" Marlowe pointed at the charms at Eddie's feet. "Eddie, hand me those."

"Sure." Eddie picked up the shiny medallions, and handed them to Marlowe. Caleb watched Marlowe as he studied them.

"Could Caleb do the possession thing?" Eddie asked.

"Hey!" Caleb whined.

"Apprentices train in controlled ways." Marlowe examined the talismans one by one. "They study spells and rituals, but use them only in a limited capacity. They can't actually manifest until they are bequeathed a staff."

Eddie nodded. "I think Caleb is doing things way beyond the theoretical."

Drusilicus looked at his apprentice. "Speak, fool."

Caleb glared at Drusilicus and then spoke sullenly. "I may have found techniques that work for me."

Marlowe held a medallion aloft. "Is this a first pentacle of the sun?"

"Might be," Caleb muttered glumly.

"This talisman is designed to make any obey." Marlowe turned the large coin-shaped medallion in his hand. "By Zoroaster! This is very powerful. Was this designed by Inscope?"

"Who?" Eddie said.

"A great wizard who specialized in talismans," Drusilicus explained and turned to Caleb. "Where did you get that?"

"Around," Caleb sulked. "I talk to people, go on the Internet."

"So there *are* ways to do things without a staff," Eddie concluded.

"There are many ways to walk the path of the wise." Marlowe continued his examination of the talismans. "That is why there are Tarot cards, Ouija boards, and many divinatory techniques."

"None of which has anywhere near the power of a staff," Drusilicus said with disdain.

"Except for these talismans Abraxas is collecting," Eddie put forth.

Marlowe lay the coins in his lap. "Those are powerful on a level we cannot understand because they contain part of his demonic essence."

"But why here, and why now?" Drusilicus asked.

"My question is, what could this kid do with talismans that powerful?" Eddie turned again to Caleb. "I may be the new guy, but seeing the kinds of miracles you guys perform, I understand how tempting it would be for someone to want it."

Marlowe held out the talismans to Caleb, but kept two. "These are indeed for protection, spiritual purity, and opening the mind to higher consciousness."

"Thank you," Caleb mumbled and didn't look up.

"This one is to control others." Marlowe held up one, then indicated the other. "And this is to open any lock. I shall hold onto them. They are very old and I sense much power in them. They are not appropriate for an apprentice. You should only use talismans you make yourself."

A flash of anger passed over Caleb's face. "I work hard and study to improve my skills. I wish to be worthy of a staff and to be knowledgeable when I receive it."

"I shall warn thee only once. Do not overstep thy place." Marlowe's eyes narrowed. He turned to Drusilicus and relaxed. "Stay for tea, Drusilicus."

"And listen to Frisha go on about what she can and cannot see, and who did what to her and when? I think not, Marlowe." Drusilicus grimaced. "Besides, I believe Caleb and I must discuss the rules of being my pupil."

Caleb rose, his head lowered and a frightened look in his eyes.

"Ahbay and Eugenia will be here tonight," Marlowe announced.

"Let them put up with Frisha. Or your pet paranormal parasite, Bob, or that vampire you keep…" Drusilicus went on, his patience gone.

"Can I at least ask you to look in on Trefoil?" Marlowe inquired. "Your healing abilities…"

Drusilicus sighed theatrically and bent to pick up his staff. "You said that the Five will be united tonight. Your combined energy should bring him around." He then gave Eddie a look that spoke volumes. "If all of you know how."

"I'm learning," Eddie affirmed.

"I advise you to learn quickly, lieutenant."

He doesn't like me or Marlowe, Eddie thought. *He expects to be treated like royalty and we just treat him like anyone else.*

"We'll let ourselves out." Drusilicus turned toward the door. His staff shrank and disappeared into his pocket as he went. Caleb followed him without a word.

"We have to keep an eye on that kid," Eddie murmured to break the silence.

"Indeed we must." Marlowe looked at the two talismans he held.

"So, Dru can really heal people?"

"Yes," Marlowe agreed, "he is actually quite adept at it."

"He offered to heal my momma."

Marlowe looked surprised. "Really?"

"All I had to do was exchange my staff for his."

Marlowe blinked. "So he tempted you with the only thing you truly want."

"Marlowe, is there any way that I...I mean, how hard would it be to cure my momma?"

Marlowe inhaled sharply. "Such things are possible, Eddie, but they must be done with caution. All mortals die, as eventually all wizards do as well. If you spare your mother this end, it would only lead to another. It is the way of things. You'd only have her a few more years at best."

"Even that would be a great gift." Eddie found he could not meet Marlowe's eyes.

A pained look went over Marlowe's face. "You should ask *her,* Eddie."

"Ask her?"

"Perhaps she wishes to move on, to make her peace."

Eddie stood still and tried to absorb the impact of Marlowe's words. "Yeah," he murmured, and checked his watch. "I've got to meet my partner."

"Be here before dark, Eddie, for all our sakes."

THIRTY

"I wish you guys would give me more time," Doctor Warren stormed. "I'm not a magician."

"What?" Eddie said, startled.

"Just an expression, lieutenant. Boy, are you jumpy."

"Tell me about it," Luis muttered.

The ride downtown with Luis had been chilly. Once again, Eddie was not forthcoming regarding where he spent their time apart. He might have tried to win his large partner over, but the concept that his mother *wanted* to die overwhelmed him, and his mind returned to it again and again.

They reached the morgue to talk to Doctor Warren about the second dismembered body in the park in one week.

"On the good side, nothing unusual on Mr. Yamasuto. No gold teeth, strange herbs, or unusually healthy organs. He looked like a middle-aged man in the prime of life."

"Anything on the pistol?" Eddie asked.

"You are a strange one, lieutenant. Yesterday you tell me it's not *our* case, and today, you have your captain put me in charge." Beverly lowered her clipboard. "Did I mention the fact that you should *ask* me? I have more than I can handle, and now CSU is pissed."

"Sorry, and yes, since we arrived, you've told me repeatedly," Eddie grumbled, his lips tight.

"I wish you'd just make up your mind." Concern showed on her face. "Are you all right? This isn't the witty repartee I'm used to, Berman."

"He ain't himself, doc." Luis glared at Eddie.

Beverly shrugged her shoulders and carelessly threw her hair back. Her eyes returned to the clipboard.

"So, you want to know about the gun?" she inquired.

"Yeah, was it his? Did he fire it?"

"Yes, to both." Beverly flipped a page. "The pistol was indeed fired, and there was gunpowder residue on Mr. Yamasuto's left hand…once it was located."

"Our diplomat went down fightin'," Luis observed.

"From my tests, there were only a few attempts at self-defense. No skin under his fingernails, no blood except his own. But, the weapon is very interesting. A Springfield Nine Millimeter Subcompact XD. Small, but packs a good kick."

"What the well-heeled diplomat carries this year," Luis quipped.

Beverly went on, "With work, I was able to bring up the serial number, which does not trace to any of the police databases. He added a silencer. Compact, very efficient."

"Very illegal," Eddie added.

"That's more like the LT I know and love." Beverly gave him a smirk. "And you're right. I don't know where Mr. Yamasuto got his weapon."

"But to me, it screams organized crime," Luis declared. "A throwaway piece designed for a hit."

Eddie nodded. "I have a feeling that if Mr. Yamasuto succeeded in killing his assailant, he wouldn't have waited around for New York's Finest to ask a lot of embarrassing questions."

"A fine, upstanding visitor," Luis sneered.

"So, are you ready for it to start getting weird again?" Beverly reviewed several pages on her clipboard.

"Does it have to?" Luis pleaded.

"Yes," Beverly went on. "The preliminary forensics, based on particles left on the body parts and the pistol, show that they were both cut with a finely honed sword."

"You *cannot* cut through a gun with a sword!" Luis bellowed, ready to stamp his large foot in frustration.

"I just report the evidence." Beverly shrugged. "How did you know this would get bizarre, Berman?"

"I beg your pardon?"

"You got me involved, just like with your witness in the hospital. By the way, right after I left, John Doe was taken off in an ambulance to a hospital no one ever heard of. Know anything about that, Eddie?"

Eddie flushed. "Maybe he had relatives?"

"Lieutenant, I don't know what is going on, but I would appreciate an explanation." Beverly stared at him intently.

"Yeah, me too," Luis demanded. "This entire case keeps going nutsy on us."

Eddie could see he needed to say something, and the best choice would be the truth.

"Okay, these murders are unusual, but what I've been tellin' Luis is that someone is leaving evidence designed to look weird." Eddie began to pace to help himself think. "Someone wants us to be thrown by all the strangeness and give up. There has to be something concrete we can take to the brass. Beverly, you are the only person who can find it."

Eddie could sense both of them relax. He sounded like his old self, and needed to keep them headed in the direction of pursuing evidence, while he handled the supernatural part of the case with Marlowe.

"I don't know what else I can find, Eddie," Beverly admitted. "Even with a whole team working on the evidence from both murder sites, we don't have a clue to the perp."

"Any footprints?" Luis said.

"From where the victim was sliced and diced, we found tracks from a pair of Japanese shoes."

"In Chinatown they sell those by the hundreds," Luis griped.

"Not these. The soles were unique. They left a rectangular impression, with Japanese characters in the design. Due to the clarity of the indentations, I deduced they were not rubber or even leather, but hand-carved wood."

She pulled out a computer printout. There was a pair of shoes lifted off the ground on top of wooden blocks.

"Are those shoes," Luis asked, "or stilts?"

"With the sword and wooden soles, it suggests a Japanese historical garment," Beverly theorized. "But the footprints, they show up where the victim lost the gun and his finger. Again, no in or out, just there. So, the perp floated into the park, killed him, and then slithered off."

"Slithered?" Eddie repeated.

"Oh, yeah, didn't I mention that?" Beverly checked her clipboard yet again. "The only other tracks found were left by a snake that crawled through the blood."

"What kind of snake?" Eddie insisted.

"Still don't know," Beverly countered. "But like our homeless man, it was one that moved sideways."

"You think a snake slashed up the Japanese guy?" Luis snickered.

"Hard to use a sword without arms," Beverly considered. "But it did make an appearance at *both* crime scenes."

"Let me ponder that a minute," Eddie said, an idea clear in his mind. "I gotta use the can, excuse me."

Eddie turned and walked off. Luis and Beverly shrugged to each other as he left.

"He's flippin' out," Luis complained.

"What's his problem?"

"His momma's sick, dying."

"That's rough." Beverly frowned and looked after Eddie.

"This case is messing with his mind. I mean, it's like he's hiding something."

"Why don't you find out, Vasquez?"

"How do I do that, Doc? He won't open up to me."

She returned his gaze with an expression suggesting that he missed the obvious. "You're a detective, right?"

"What do you mean?"

Beverly gave a gentle punch to his shoulder. "Follow him, big guy. You know, like a detective?"

Luis grunted. "They only do that in books."

Meanwhile, Eddie entered the morgue bathroom and locked the door. It was a single-user model with only one toilet, which stood in plain sight inside the white-tiled room.

But that wasn't why he was there.

He moved to the sink and the mirror above it. The silvery surface reflected his careworn face.

Eddie tried to remember what happened with Drusilicus earlier that day, when in the heat of the moment his staff jumped into his hand.

Eddie held out his hand, closed his eyes, and concentrated.

Nothing happened.

It was more than the concept of having it, he thought, *it was the wanting.*

Eddie wanted his staff. He imagined it fondly, like a lost-love that he needed desperately.

Wood slapped into his palm, and he felt the object growing. He opened his eyes to find the wooden rod solidly in his palm.

He *did* it.

He held the staff aloft, stared at the mirror, and spoke clearly, "Marlowe."

Nothing happened.

Eddie frantically tried to remember what he'd done the first time he contacted the wizard. Once again, it was *wanting* that made it work.

Eddie stood up straighter, faced the mirror and said louder, "*Marlowe!*"

There was the tiniest flash of light, from where Eddie couldn't be sure. The mirror's surface began to look as if it was changing from solid to liquid; melting.

Eddie gasped. It was beautiful.

Ripples appeared in the center, like a lake with a pebble dropped in it.

He heard a voice that sounded far away. "This is Marlowe."

"Marlowe, it's Eddie. Hey, this is great—"

"I'm sorry I can't answer you at this time, but I've stepped away from my mirror…"

"What the hell?" Eddie blurted.

"Please leave your name and the best time to reach you after the gong and I'll get back to you in another space and time."

"He has a damn answering machine on his mirror!" Eddie gave the floor a good "whack" with his staff in annoyance.

There was a loud gong that not only reverberated in the too small room, it made the ripples in the glass go jagged.

"Marlowe!" Eddie yelled. "It's Eddie. Answer your damn mirror. I need to get in touch with Daniel. It's very important I talk to Daniel about—"

The glass suddenly went blank, and Eddie found himself staring at a flat black square that looked like it absorbed all light. Then, the darkness cleared and Eddie recognized the bathroom he'd used at Marlowe's townhouse. But there was no one there, only a blank wall.

"H-hello?"

"Lieutenant," a voice answered primly. "Is it really necessary to shout?"

Eddie squinted his eyes but could see nothing. "Who is this?"

"It's Daniel Kraft. You yelled my name," the voice replied huffily.

"I can't see you!" Eddie rose up on tiptoe to look down and then crouched to look up, to see if he could find Daniel hidden on the other side of the glass.

"Lieutenant," the voice jeered. "I'm a vampire? I cast no reflection in the glass."

"Oh, yeah, of course, that makes sense." Eddie stared at the blank space and forced a smile. "Did I wake you?"

"Why no, who would sleep during the day?" annoyance crept into his voice. "Except maybe a vampire!"

"Yeah, well, sorry," Eddie explained. "I really need your help."

"I can't tell you how happy that makes me, lieutenant. I have an appointment to crawl into my coffin until sundown, call me then." The image of the bathroom began to waver.

"No, no, Daniel, please, hear me out."

The mirror stopped fluctuating, and the tile work became very clear.

"All right," the disembodied voice sighed. "What is it?"

"I've got a clue, but I can't follow it up. How good are you at tracking?"

"Good," he admitted, and began to sound interested. "My eyesight, hearing, and sense of smell are far above human. Why?"

"Abrax—"

"Don't say his name," Daniel interrupted. Then his voice lowered to a whisper. "This isn't a secure reflection."

Eddie tried to absorb this concept, but to speak to a blank wall was difficult enough for him, so he went on. "The person… we're pursuing…committed another murder last night."

"I heard about it. In the park."

"The only tracks leaving the scene were of a snake slithering sideways. It could be our…friend."

"He left tracks?" the voice responded, impressed.

"Right. And I remember something Marlowe told me that if he is in this plane of existence, he can change form, but he has to be somewhere and disguised as *something*."

"As soon as the sun sets, I'll look into it," Daniel stated decisively. "Good thinking…for a Newling."

Eddie felt a smile on his face. "Thanks, Daniel. Nice seeing you…ah…not seeing you…well, nice talking."

"Fare thee well, lieutenant."

The mirror silvered over and once again reflected Eddie's face. He put his staff away and left the bathroom to find his partner skulking outside the door.

"You all right, Eddie?"

"Fine." Eddie's face grew hot. Had Luis overheard him? "Where's Beverly?"

"Back to work. She said she'll send us reports as soon as she gets more information."

Eddie nodded. "Let's go talk with Alfonso Cuccolo. See if he knew our Mr. Yamasuto."

Luis nodded and they headed for the elevator.

Vasquez was not sure if following Doc Warren's advice was a good choice. Then, he'd heard Eddie in the bathroom as he carried on two sides of a conversation. He couldn't hear the words clearly, but it was about the case. He knew it couldn't have been a cell call, or he would only have heard Eddie's end of the conversation. His partner must have made both voices. Maybe Eddie really was losing his mind. So, if he *did* follow his partner and friend, it was for his own good.

Wasn't it?

THIRTY-ONE

Alfonso Cuccolo could always be easily found, his practices were more predictable than the Pope's.

Years of surveillance by the FBI, the Major Crimes Unit, the Organized Crime Task Force, as well as recently by the Urban Crime Task Force, made him a creature of habit.

He was partaking of an afternoon latté at his favorite dive on Mulberry Street, in the colorful section of downtown New York known as Little Italy. It was a short collection of streets with Italian restaurants, bistros, and stores. Two blocks to the south was Canal Street, the center of Chinatown, which every year expanded farther north into the Italian district.

Most of the Italians had moved to other parts of the city. They no longer needed to band together in one section as new immigrants. All that was left of "the neighborhood" was a small assembly of businesses, a tiny reminder of the old days.

It didn't matter. Cuccolo was comfortable here. He wasn't a gangster like on television; he was the real thing, and he wanted to stay in NYC.

At the restauranté, he could give orders to his lieutenants, and receive orders from his superiors without phones, notes, or anything that might be traced. He did it the old-fashioned way—direct human contact.

Eddie and Luis arrived and showed their detective shields to a rather burly gentleman who stood by the door to the private upstairs room and asked for the mob boss.

After only a minute of waiting, they were brought into Cuccolo's presence. He was tall, good-looking, well-dressed, and moved with the lithe grace of a professional dancer. He wore his gray hair long and pulled away from his face in a ponytail.

"Gentlemen." Cuccolo rose while the detectives were shown in. There were six other men in the room, all of them looking like extras from *The Godfather*, with gold chains and expensive suits.

Cuccolo turned to a man. "Give the detectives chairs."

"We'll stand, if it's all right with you, Mr. Cuccolo," Eddie said.

Cuccolo held up his hands in a move that on anyone else would look pretentious and sat down.

"Can I offer you gentlemen a cappuccino, maybe a cannoli?" Cuccolo turned his glance to Luis. "You look like a man who enjoys a good cannoli."

Cuccolo said this with a tone that could be meant to mock the large man, or not; it was hard to be sure.

"Mr. Cuccolo, we need to ask you if you are familiar with a diplomat named Haiku Yamasuto?" He held out the autopsy photo Luis had received from Beverly.

His face betrayed no expression. "I like that. You don't beat around the bush, right to the point." He took the photo and looked at it. "You're in the wrong neighborhood, officer. Go downtown a few blocks and you'll find a hundred guys who look just like this."

This made the other men in the room snicker.

"Perhaps you know something about this." Eddie held out the drawing made by Akio of the statuette.

Cuccolo's eyes widened; not much, just the smallest fraction. "Nice piece. I'm more familiar with Native American antiquities." He handed the drawing and photo back to Eddie.

"Can you tell us your whereabouts last night between eleven PM and one AM?" Eddie said.

"Ask the FBI. I was home. My wife and I live uptown just off Fifth Avenue."

"Near the Metropolitan Museum of Art?"

"As a matter of fact, yeah."

"Which is where this man was found murdered." Eddie flashed the photo again.

"Really?" Cuccolo said with a shrug. "What a coincidence."

Eddie nodded. This was going to be no help. Cuccolo spent the majority of his life deceiving law enforcement. Did he really expect the gangster to be forthcoming?

Then, in a flash, Eddie realized he wasn't stuck like a regular cop.

He was a wizard.

"Mr. Cuccolo, may I give you my card?" Eddie carefully kept his hands in plain sight as he slowly reached for his wallet. "In case you recall anything."

The men near Cuccolo watched at the ready, just in case Eddie was some crazy cop who might pull his gun. Eddie knew they all had weapons and probably knew places they could dump bodies, if the need arose.

Eddie pulled out his wallet and extracted, not his regular white business card, but the black wood-grain credit card.

Luis frowned, not sure what his partner was up to.

Eddie held the card out, and as Cuccolo's fingers grasped it, casually said, "If you know anything that might help, I'd really appreciate it."

Cuccolo looked like he'd been struck with a heavy object. He snapped his head back, and his eyes underwent a change. Yet, he still held his end of the card.

"Detective," he finally said, "I cannot suggest that I would be anywhere near the site of such a terrible crime. To say such a thing would mean that I could fool a bunch of federal agents whose job it is to know my whereabouts."

"I understand, Mr. Cuccolo," Eddie agreed.

"But, I have been known to collect antiques, especially ancient religious symbols."

"A harmless enough hobby." Eddie smiled.

"I have heard rumors of the availability of an ancient Shinto talisman rather like the one you showed me," Cuccolo went on, his face relaxed, but his hand still tight on the black card. "As I understood it, several people were interested in purchasing it."

"These are just rumors?"

"Well, the odd thing was one specific buyer contacted me, interested in both the Shinto and a rare Native American artifact in my possession."

"But you didn't wish to do business with this buyer?" Eddie suggested.

"Too pushy. If I were involved…and I'm not saying I was…"

"Of course."

Cuccolo tapped the photo that Eddie held with his free hand. "I would have offered your guy here, whatever he wanted to keep his piece from that buyer."

Luis' mouth fell open, as well as the six men in the room. None of them could understand why Cuccolo was telling Eddie so much.

Eddie spoke in a concerned tone. "I should point out that whoever did this to Mr. Yamasuto might attempt to get your artifact as well."

A sudden look of surprise came over Cuccolo's face, and he shook his head, as if he woke from a nap, and his hand retracted from the card. Eddie could tell that the magic that made him forthcoming was being pushed aside by the gangster's own secretive nature.

"Of course, these are all just rumors, officer." Cuccolo instantly regained the calm look on his face.

"Thank you, Mr. Cuccolo, you've been most helpful." Eddie returned the black card back to his wallet and extracted a standard white one with his contact numbers.

"If you hear any more rumors, it might be an idea to call me. My cell number is there," Eddie offered.

Cuccolo frowned as if he tried to understand what just happened. He finally took the card from Eddie. "Yeah, sure."

Eddie turned and walked down the stairs as Luis shambled behind him.

"Don't that beat all," Luis wondered. "He practically tol' you he was the buyer. How did you get him to do that?"

Eddie shrugged. "My winning personality."

THIRTY-TWO

It wasn't until they got back to the precinct and Eddie finished his preliminary report on the Yamasuto murder that he tried to reach Marlowe again.

He decided that if someone caught him in the locker room as he yelled into a mirror, it might bring to reality his repeated fantasy of a padded cell.

Instead, he took out his cell phone and dialed, '212-18', then pushed the 'SEND' button, all the time holding his special credit card.

"Marlowe," said the voice over the line.

"It's Eddie."

"Eddie! Good to hear from you. When will you get here?"

Eddie looked over to see that Luis was busy at the coffee machine. "As soon as I can. I may have a break. I think whoever is working with Abraxas is trying to get his hands on another talisman."

"Really? Do you know where this one originated?"

"I think it's Native American. But, I don't know if Abraxas or his warlock can get it."

"Why not?"

"It's owned by a criminal named Alfonso Cuccolo. Not only does he have a small army of his own protection, but the FBI watches him like a hawk."

"A wizard would have no trouble stealing it."

"Which is not a good thing."

"Your grasp of the situation is astounding, Eddie."

There was a pause as Eddie thought about this. "Now, you're just messing with me, right?"

"Me?"

"I wanted to let you know, I got him to tell more than he wanted—"

"You cast a truth spell?"

"I guess. That was what I was trying for," Eddie glanced at Luis who was now going through the remains of a box of donuts.

Marlowe mused, "I begin to see a pattern in the events, the artifacts, and the murders."

"Glad to hear it."

"I must do more research, get new ideas, perhaps consult Bankrock. Please come here as soon as you can," Marlowe advised. "Perhaps we can conceive a way to protect your Mr. Cuccolo."

"We won't be the only ones with an eye on him," Eddie stated grimly. "I'll be there soon."

He ended the phone call as Luis sauntered back to his desk, munching on a glazed donut.

"Hey," Eddie said, as Luis sat.

Luis raised the remaining half of a pastry in a salute.

"I'm done with my report," Eddie acknowledged. "How is yours going?"

"Goin'," Luis said, and he began to work on the computer keyboard in his personal style, which consisted of moving one finger around as he hit an occasional letter. Fortunately, this mode of typing did not interfere with his eating.

"I want to get out and go over the scene again," Eddie suggested. "Then call it a day."

Luis didn't look up, and his face didn't register even a hint of suspicion. "Good idea. We got to work the weekend anyway; you might as well have a night with the family."

Inwardly, Eddie sighed with relief. "Great! Well, bright and early tomorrow, then."

"You got it, partner." Luis clicked away and chewed his donut.

Eddie rose and put on his jacket, checked his tie, and headed for the door and out into the early evening.

Eddie inhaled deeply as he walked up the sidewalk while cars rushed by him. The spring air cleared his head. It was June in New York, and the air was scrubbed clean.

The sun had descended behind the top of the trees, and the day moved toward sunset, still at least a half an hour away.

He crossed Central Park West and walked up the stairs to Marlowe's townhouse. He knocked on the door and was let in by Frisha.

Unknown to Eddie, as he had wandered outdoors, Luis casually shut down his computer and moved to the window to watch as Eddie turned up the transverse road.

Luis quickly got downstairs, a pair of binoculars in his hand. He watched as Eddie crossed Central Park West, walked up the steps, and knocked. A woman let him in, and Luis tried to remember where he'd seen her before.

Once Eddie was inside, Luis casually strolled across the traverse road and into the police parking lot. He drove his car as close to the townhouse as he could. Luis knew that parking spots opened up on the street as the commuters left for home.

It took him only ten minutes, his third time around the block, to locate a space and park. The site was perfect, perpendicular to the building, and gave him a view of the front door. He was annoyed that he couldn't look inside the building, but there were closed curtains on all four floors.

He focused his binoculars on the front door and found it odd that there wasn't a big mailbox with apartment's names and numbers. He wondered if the building could possibly have only one tenant.

He put the seat back and watched the building. Forty-five minutes or so passed, and Luis checked the door repeatedly.

As the shadows thickened, he saw two figures walk out of the park. One was a thin Asian man, neatly dressed, accompanied by a woman about five-foot-ten.

They seemed oblivious to the world around them and gave the appearance of two close friends who hadn't seen each other in years. The man was dressed in a suit, except the coat was long, rather like the ones worn at old-fashioned weddings, and a bright vest with Asian symbols on it. The woman was attractive with long, gray-black hair, and dressed in a maroon jacket and long skirt with a black blouse.

The strange thing about them was that they carried two large poles with them.

Luis sat up with as much stealth as he possessed and watched the two carefully.

They indeed carried sticks—not the ones mountain climbers used, but like Moses in that old movie *The Ten Commandments*.

They crossed the street, and Luis sank as low in the car as his large frame allowed.

When he peeked up again, he instantly located the couple as they stopped at the bottom of a set of stairs.

They no longer held the sticks.

The man now carried a cane with a hook on the end, and the woman was putting a large wooden clip through her bounty of hair, and pulled it back as she did.

Luis narrowed his eyes.

Did he just see that?

To add to the mystery, they ascended the steps to the very townhouse Eddie was in!

Luis lifted his binoculars to watch them as the man knocked on the door with his cane. The same familiar woman opened the door and gave each one a hug.

The woman at the door was heavy, dressed in a flowing robe covered with moons and stars than emanated a glow of their own.

Something in Luis' mind went "click." It was the crazy lady who lived in the box!

Questions ran through his head. What was she doing here? What was Eddie doing here? Who were these new people?

He still had no idea what was going on, but he made a vow to himself that he wouldn't leave until he found out.

THIRTY-THREE

"No, no," Marlowe chided. "That will not work!"

Eddie rose up slowly from the floor, his cloak smoldering and his face marked by soot.

"How could I know that fireball you sent would turn and come back at me?" Eddie was aware that smoke issued from his mouth as he spoke. "I thought fire couldn't hurt me."

"You're not hurt, only singed." Marlowe, with his thumb and forefinger, tweaked out a small flame on Eddie's shoulder. "And in a battle you must stay focused. None of your abilities just happen; they must be activated by—"

"I know, I know," Eddie sniped. "By will and intent."

"Good!" Marlowe praised. "Some of my teaching is sinking in. But you must be able to act from instinct. I am sure you trained with your pistol by firing it again and again."

"I still go to the range at least once a month."

"There you are—"

Three loud gongs rang, and Bob materialized through the door.

"Front door!" Bob tumbled excitedly in the air. "'Genia here!"

"Ah!" Marlowe said. "Our guests have finally arrived. Bob, you must wait upstairs. We cannot be disturbed."

"Awww!" Bob said, his lower lip drooping halfway to the floor in abject misery. "Want to see 'Genia."

"You will, Bob," Marlowe assured, as the small spirit sadly flew up and through the high ceiling.

Marlowe turned to Eddie. "It is time to meet the rest of the Five." With a small wave of his staff his clothes shifted to modern dress with another outlandish tie.

Eddie followed and made his own small circle in the air, which transformed his robes into his suit. Unfortunately, it was burned in all the places his cloak had been.

"Uh, Marlowe," Eddie pleaded, as he looked over the damage.

"Oh! This will not do at all." Marlowe made a quick wave of his staff, and Eddie's clothes were immediately repaired and his face cleaned.

They walked up the stairs into the grand entrance hall, where two people stood with Frisha. Marlowe moved forward to embrace the pair: an average-height Asian gentleman and a tall woman with dark hair.

"It's like old times, I'll tell ye plain," Frisha effused and wiped a tear from her eye. "To see ye all together like this."

"Yes, with a new member in our distinguished group," Marlowe reported. "This is Eddie Berman, who bears the Staff of Fire."

"More likely our *extinguished* group," the Asian man said with a slight accent, as he leaned on a fairly plain walking stick with a hook. His hair was white and the lines in his face were deeper than Marlowe's. He wore a long black jacket with a red silk vest embroidered with Japanese symbols in the cloth. The cut coupled with his straight back and sturdy shoulders made him seem appropriately attired.

"This gentleman is Ahbay Ōbaru," Marlowe put forward.

"The name I currently choose," Ahbay explained and gave a short bow toward Eddie. "How do you do, young man?"

"Good to meet you." Eddie returned the bow.

"And this lady is Eugenia Philalethes."

"Perhaps you've had a chance to read my books?" Eugenia spoke with an upper-class British accent. Her face was striking, thin, and possessed of marvelous cheekbones. In her youth she could have easily turned heads.

"I don't know," Eddie replied, "I mostly read murder mysteries."

"I mean in your studies," Eugenia said graciously. "*The Marrow of Alchemy* mayhaps? Or *Lumen De Lumine*?"

Marlowe stepped forward. "Eddie is still practicing the basics. But I intend to include your writings as part of his ongoing education."

"Good, good." Eugenia broke into a wide smile. She looked Eddie up and down as one might examine a prize horse. She then gave Marlowe an approving nod. "I like him, Marlowe."

"I understand you were summoned," Ahbay said and hooked his cane over his arm, as Marlowe led them into the large living room.

"That's what happened." Eddie had no wish to go into detail about the severed head of their former compatriot.

"What a surprise for you," Eugenia beamed. "You must feel like Alice gone down the rabbit hole. I am sure your life has been topsy-turvy ever since."

"It's been a challenge," Eddie agreed.

"One can only imagine!" Ahbay chuckled.

Eddie smiled grimly as they sat down. The chairs were in a small circle, as in the morning meeting with Drusilicus.

As the group sat, Eddie was affected by just how *unimpressive* the other three were. They appeared so ordinary that it was inconceivable that this group would be asked to fight a demon.

Marlowe turned to the breakfast room and called out, "Tea!"

He returned his gaze to the company, as a tea cart rolled out of the breakfast room, and without the need of an operator to propel it, made its way to the group as they made small talk.

Eddie watched it, dumbfounded. On the metal tray sat two silver teapots with a sugar bowl and creamer. There were also two tiered round trays, each with three large plates at different levels. One was filled with small sandwiches and the other with elegant little pastries.

"It is good to see you once again, Marlowe," Ahbay said.

"I'm sorry it is under such circumstances." Marlowe shook his head.

"We were indeed unhappy to hear of Abraxas' return," Eugenia sympathized. "And in New York City of all places!"

"*Hie,*" Ahbay agreed. "Once again, we are called to lock him away."

The tea cart cart rolled up to Eugenia.

"Ah, ladies first? Such gentlemen." Eugenia turned to the trolley. "Tea, please!"

The moment the words left her lips, the larger polished teapot rose into thin air and began to tip. A cup flew onto a saucer and maneuvered directly under the brown liquid as it poured. The cup hovered, unaffected by the extra weight of the tea.

"Cream and sugar, if you would." Eugenia surveyed the trays of food, and then pointed at various treats. As she pointed, the chosen ones flew onto a plate, which then sailed lightly to her lap. The plate was followed by her tea, which had been prepared exactly to her liking.

Marlowe meanwhile spoke to his companions. "Do not take this lightly, my friends. Riftstone was lost from underestimating our foe."

The trolley stopped next to Ahbay.

"Coffee, black," Ahbay commanded, then turned to the others. "It is a treat, as I most often drink tea." His attention returned to the trolley as it prepared his request. "I shall have a small assortment, *kudasai*." Then he turned to Marlowe. "Really, Marlowe, we have fought Abraxas several times. He is at best an inconvenience."

"True," Eugenia agreed. "The last time we tracked him down —do you remember—in that bunker in Berlin? It was merely the pair of us, Marlowe, but we quickly dispatched him."

"It is different this time," Marlowe warned. "He is more powerful, more dangerous."

As Marlowe spoke, Eddie was focused on the floating teapot and unable to control his curiosity. "Are you doing that?"

Ahbay and Eugenia chuckled quietly.

Marlowe looked at Eddie, a bit annoyed at the interruption. "No, Eddie. I enchanted the trolley and the tea set."

"You enchanted it?" Eddie questioned. "Isn't that what you do with a talisman?"

"My dear man," Eugenia interjected, "an enchantment is any spell that uses an inanimate object."

"Excuse our laughter, we meant no disrespect," Ahbay explained. "The technique is quite simple. To us, such sights are common."

The cart now traveled over to Eddie, who realized he hadn't eaten anything since breakfast.

"It's a bit unnerving, if you're not used to it." Eddie eyed the cart with suspicion. "What do I do?"

"Tell it what you want, Eddie," Marlowe suggested. "Be clear and precise, and keep a picture in your mind as to how you like your beverage."

"Coffee!" Eddie announced, a bit too loudly. "Cream, no sugar."

The smaller teapot and the teacup obeyed, which made Eddie break into a grin. "Don't that beat all?"

Marlowe nodded encouragingly. "Would you like some sandwiches, Eddie?"

"Yeah, yeah." Eddie relaxed as the teacup flew into his hand. "I'll take a small assortment…uh…please."

The food began leaping off the trays onto a plate.

"You see, Eddie," Marlowe declared, "by enchanting an object, it can provide a service whenever we need it."

"Oh, yes," Eugenia said, as Eddie's plate flew to him and the cart moved on to Marlowe. "And you were quite right, that is how talismans possess their power. Energy is stored within them for an ongoing use and grows stronger with the passage of time."

"Yes, that is what we are up against with Abraxas, which is why he is so dangerous," Marlowe advised. "An ancient talisman was used to return him to this plane of existence. Since then, he has stolen another sigil that contained a portion of his own essence."

"Oh dear." A troubled look passed over Eugenia's face.

"Ah!" Ahbay took a bite from a sandwich. "I might suggest you overestimate his abilities, old friend."

"It would be wise to be on guard," Marlowe implored. "But I should not tell you more until Trefoil can join us."

There was a silence that hung in the air, as if the statement was more like: if Trefoil *could* join them.

"Well, now." Eugenia looked at Eddie. "If you wish to cast an enchantment, the tasks must always be simple and repetitive, if you enchant an object to do anything too complicated…well, it can lead to trouble."

"I recall a chess set I had," Ahbay smiled. "I attempted to instill within it far too many moves. Pieces flung themselves at me each time I entered the room."

"I think I got it. An enchantment is like a computer," Eddie considered. "You program it, but it can't exceed its programing."

The three people stared at him in stunned silence, as the tea trolley, which knew its master's preferences, poured tea and put together a plateful of hors d'oeuvres without even a verbal command from Marlowe.

"You…you…" Eugenia stammered, "know how to *use* a computer?"

"Sure." Eddie sipped his coffee. He felt a little uncomfortable as everyone gaped at him. "I mean, I have one at the precinct and a laptop I use at home. I used to have a desktop, but I gave that to my kids for their schoolwork."

"You have taught your *kodomo* how to use it?" Ahbay gasped, a look of wonder on his face.

"C-Could you show us?" Eugenia asked shyly.

"Well, sure." Eddie looked at the anxious faces around the room as the realization passed through him like an electrical current. "You mean…none of you…know how to use a computer?"

"They are infernal things," Ahbay said, his voice rising. "Built by demons to drive us mad!"

"Really, Ahbay," Eugenia soothed. "Don't get yourself all worked up—"

"Of course!" Ahbay said. Color rose in his cheeks and he seemed embarrassed for his outburst. "However, they do not make sense, and this thing—this Internet—it is most difficult."

Marlowe calmly sipped his tea. "It appears, Eddie, that there are things you can teach us."

"Hey, computers aren't that hard," Eddie insisted, "and you really need to know how to use one these days—"

A musical theme emanated from Eddie's jacket pocket. He retrieved his cell phone, stood, and stepped away from the others. "Berman."

"Lieutenant, this is Alfonso Cuccolo."

"What can I do for you, Mr. Cuccolo?" Eddie tried to control the surprise in his voice.

"I have been contacted by that buyer. The one who was interested in that Native American artifact in my possession?"

"You think he's connected with Mr. Yamasuto?"

"It was the same guy who called me before."

"The one that was 'too pushy'?"

"Yeah. And get this, he wants to meet me in Central Park." There was a pause. "Eleven o'clock, alone."

"Really?" Eddie checked his watch. A few short hours away.

"I have given consideration to the suggestion you made earlier that this buyer may wish to do me harm. And I, for one, would prefer to make it clear that I had nothing to do with Yamasuto."

"I see that." Eddie fought to feel sympathy for a hood like Cuccolo.

"My men will be there. And I shall be a visible enough target that even the Feds should be able to follow. Perhaps you wish to be in on this meeting?"

"And help protect you?"

"I'm a citizen, why shouldn't I be protected?" Cuccolo's voice dripped with contempt. "However, if I find the need to defend myself, you must be aware that I might need to shoot the bastard…with a legal firearm, of course. You got that?"

"I understand. NYPD might overlook weapons charges, if it's a licensed firearm and you own a carry permit." Eddie hoped the captain wouldn't give him hell that he'd agreed to this.

There was a pause followed by a chuckle.

"I like you, lieutenant. I don't know why, but you come across as a straight shooter. The buyer told me to meet him at the carousel. You know where that is?"

"Yeah. And whatever you do, don't bring the item into the park with you," Eddie warned.

"You're tellin' me?" Cuccolo replied. "It's stayin' safe under lock and key. See you later."

Eddie returned his phone to his pocket.

"What was that about?" Marlowe said.

"Another talisman."

"Oh my!" Eugenia sipped her tea. "Who has it?"

"A man named Cuccolo. He collects Native American artifacts. He's also a hood."

"A hood?" Ahbay frowned. "He wears a cloak?"

"A *kusemono*," Marlowe explained in Japanese.

"Ah!" Ahbay nodded. "A gangster."

"He has set up a meeting. Our warlock wants to buy his artifact," Eddie went on. "How come Abraxas is after these different talismans?"

Marlowe rose. "Abraxas transversed the dimensional barriers with the use of the Amulet of Abracadabra, an ancient Persian artifact. Last night, he slaughtered a man to purloin a Shinto statuette."

"What was the figure?" Ahbay leaned forward in his chair.

"Amatsu Mikaboshi," Marlowe said simply.

"The Shinto God of Evil. I was the last warrior to face him. He came to me disguised as a sorcerer. We had a battle with *katana* before I removed him from this plane."

"Anything you can tell us from your fight?" Eddie hoped.

Ahbay shrugged. "He is excellent with a blade."

"So, you believe he is collecting talismans from different traditions?" Eugenia queried.

"Not just different traditions," Marlowe said. "I believe each one holds an extraordinary portion of his own essence."

"Yeah," Eddie interjected. "Cuccolo was asked to bring his *to* the park."

"It is one of the strongest places of power in all the world," Eugenia surmised.

"The releasing amulet lay long hidden there," Marlowe cautioned. "Any talisman would gain energy in Central Park. This Cuccolo fellow should not bring the charm."

"He told me he's going to the meeting with nothing more than a gun," Eddie confirmed.

"Small help against the Great Evil," Eugenia said.

"Unless we show up." Eddie looked around the room at the trio.

Ahbay politely took tiny bites from a small sandwich. "Marlowe, let us restore Trefoil and then hunt down Abraxas. Even if he has gained power, he cannot stand against us all."

"I must agree with Ahbay," Eugenia reckoned. "With Trefoil, we will be the Five united once again."

"Then we cast him out and be done with it," Ahbay stated forcefully.

"We are not getting any younger, after all," Eugenia noted breezily.

Eddie looked from Eugenia to Ahbay. "You ain't that old. I mean Ahbay, you're about sixty-five and Miss…what was your last name, again?"

"Philalethes," Eugenia obliged.

"You can't be more than fifty," Eddie guessed.

"I was born in 1491."

"Say what?" Eddie said.

Ahbay's smile grew. "And I was born, by your calendar, in 921."

Eugenia smiled as well. "He just likes to mention that because he looks so good."

"Be that as it may, madam, you are still a beauty," Ahbay complemented with a slight bow.

"Especially for my age." Eugenia added drolly.

"Let me get this straight," Eddie said to Eugenia. "You're over five hundred years old?"

"Yes," Eugenia said, "and I am young compared to Marlowe. He is over—"

"Please, Eugenia." Marlowe sipped his coffee. "I will tell of my history when it becomes necessary."

Eddie stared around the room at them, his mouth suddenly dry. "You people live forever?"

"Not forever, Eddie," Marlowe corrected, "but a very long time. You will as well."

"What!" Eddie exclaimed.

"He is quite correct," Ahbay offered. "When you accepted your staff, you became a new creature. You will age much slower."

"And he is the first who can use a computer!" Eugenia put her teacup on her lap and clapped her hands with glee.

"Wait a minute! You're tellin' me I'll live for hundreds of years?" An enormous grin spread across Eddie's face.

Marlowe spoke quietly. "Yes, Eddie. But it comes at a terrible price."

Eddie's smile faded. "I don't have to give up...y'know...sex or anything?"

"The price is this, Eddie," Marlowe went on. "You are left to bury everyone you ever cared for. Friends, spouses, children, grandchildren. By the time you have great-great-grandchildren, no one really knows who you are, or feels any connection to you. Many wizards fake their own deaths, assume new identities, and move on."

He took a contemplative sip from his cup. "It can be heartbreaking to look at a young woman and see the face of a wife long gone. After centuries, the pain of loss becomes a heavy burden to bear. We become less and less attached to others and seek a solitary life."

The room was silent, except for the clink of teacups, and the noise of coffee and tea being imbibed.

Eddie looked at Eugenia, whose eyes reflected brightly with tears. Even Ahbay seemed lost in remembrance. He considered it for a moment and saw himself unchanged, while his wife grew old and passed away.

Every day Eddie faced the possibility of his own demise and could live with that. But, the idea of a continued existence without Cerise made the world a darker and colder place.

"We have work to do, my friends," Marlowe reminded solemnly. "The final member of our assembly lies upstairs lost to this world. Our combined power shall rouse him."

"Then we should begin." Ahbay set aside his cup and empty plate.

"My dear Marlowe," Eugenia recommended, "shouldn't we wait until the witching hour?"

"Nay, we must do it while the powers of light are stronger. After midnight, the dark forces will abound."

"Even in your home, guarded by its many spells and protections?" Ahbay asked.

"Even here," Marlowe said.

"Let's do this." Eddie reached to his plate to pop one of the small sandwiches in his mouth. An expression of total disgust swept over his face. He spoke with his mouth full. "What wath that?"

"I believe that you just had a watercress sandwich," Eugenia clarified.

"It'th not poithonouth, ith it?" Eddie muttered.

"No, it won't hurt you."

Eddie grimaced, chewed, swallowed, and grabbed his teacup to drink the final swig of coffee.

"It *is* an acquired taste," Eugenia added brightly.

"Yeah," Eddie scowled, "guess so." He stared at the tea trolley. "Coffee!"

The pot floated over to him and refilled his cup, followed in quick succession by the creamer that poured a good-sized dollop.

Eddie took a careful sip and left his plate of remaining foodstuffs.

"I've got to get me one of these," Eddie gazed longingly at the trolley. "They'd love it at the precinct."

THIRTY-FOUR

The four of them walked up the long staircase to the second level. The wrought iron lining the center elevator shaft looked both beautiful and menacing.

Eddie huffed and puffed with each step by the time they neared the top. However, the other three did not breathe hard from the exertion at all. They looked fresh and relaxed as if climbing a thousand steps was part of their daily workout.

Ahbay smiled as Eddie dragged himself the last few steps. "Do not worry, your body will grow stronger each day you carry the staff."

"But...but..." Eddie gasped, "How do you—"

"It takes time, Eddie," Marlowe interjected. "You have been mortal too long. You still believe that your physical body rules your spirit, when it truly is the other way around."

"I'll...be glad...when I...understand...what you just said," Eddie wheezed and leaned against the handrail that ran the length of the open hall. His mouth was full of mucus from the exertion, and he wished there was a place he could spit.

"I suppose we could've taken the elevator," Eugenia offered.

"I use it so seldom." Marlowe shrugged.

"Next time, I'm using it." Eddie pulled himself along the handrail. The dark wood felt sleek under his hand, until it met something that moved.

Eddie straightened up and stared at his hand, just in time to see a green, glowing creature rise up between his fingers, making a horrid screech as it went.

Eddie yelled and took several steps back, to be saved from a fall down the stairs by Marlowe and Ahbay's strong arms.

"*Bob!*" Eddie shrieked. "If you weren't dead, I'd kill you!"

The small wraith somersaulted in midair and chuckled with glee at Eddie's reaction, its unformed face twisted in a huge grin.

"Bob!" Eugenia beamed fondly.

The spirit stopped spinning, and with a quick bark of glee, flew to Eugenia and nuzzled her face like a puppy.

"You're still with Marlowe after all this time!" Eugenia cuddled the green glob.

"Don't let him lick you," Eddie warned.

"He has no tongue," Marlowe said.

"He could manifest one, could he not?" Ahbay pointed out.

Eugenia laughed and gently pushed the affectionate Bob away.

"'Genia here!" Bob gurgled.

"Not now, Bob," Eugenia lovingly pinched his spectral cheek. "I promise we'll play later."

"Okay!" Bob rose up and vanished through the ceiling.

"What's he got against me?" Eddie complained.

"You're the first person he's been able to scare in a hundred years, Eddie," Marlowe insisted. "He'll calm down when the novelty wears off."

"Within a decade, I am sure," Ahbay proposed.

"What?" Eddie gawked.

"He jests with you," Eugenia encouraged. "Bob will grow to like you. He's just literally a free spirit."

"I got a jail cell I'd love to stick him in," Eddie muttered.

Led by Marlowe, the group walked down the hall and through an open door into one of the large bedrooms. Candles burned on an ancient dresser, and there stood a four-poster bed, which cradled the inert form of Trefoil. On the covers next to him lay his staff.

"It doesn't look like he's breathing." Eddie frowned as they drew close.

"He is quite alive," Marlowe said.

"How can you be sure?"

"We can feel it." Eugenia took Eddie's hand.

"We must begin, Marlowe," Ahbay urged.

Ahbay moved ahead of the others, and his cane shifted into a full-sized staff, as did Marlowe's. Eugenia held out her hand, and the wooden clip leapt from her hair and shifted to its true form. Eddie recalled the desire for his staff, and this time, saw it vault from his pocket and become solid wood in his grasp.

Each made a pass with their staves and their clothes transformed. Eugenia's became a bright-yellow tunic in a medieval British style, similar to Marlowe's white robes. Ahbay's robes were a traditional Japanese *kimono* and *haori* in bright green silk and beautiful *shishu* embroidery.

Marlowe passed his hand over Trefoil, and his clothing became the blue African-style robe Eddie had observed at the initiation ceremony.

Eddie gave his staff a wave and his red robes and tall boots appeared, much to his delight.

The four of them assembled around the bed, one at each of the corners, next to the upright wooden supports of the four-poster.

Marlowe lifted his staff and spoke. "We come here this day to aid our companion."

The room seemed to grow darker around them.

Marlowe went on. "We carry the elements of the ancients. We call back a member of our sacred quintet, or should we fail, we release his spirit."

If we fail, Eddie realized, *Trefoil is dead.*

Marlowe chanted, "Isa ya! We call upon the powers of the ancient elements, the power of the first of the wise who walked the earth. We call upon Air!"

A breeze filled the room, gentle and loving, and rippled through Eugenia's hair. Her staff began to glow with a bright yellow light at its tip.

"Isa ya!" she said quietly. "The power that gives us the sweet breath of life, and brings the wind that fills the mariners' sail, answers. Air is with thee."

Marlowe gave a nod and turned his head to Ahbay. "We call upon Earth."

The breeze faded at once and a smell filled the room. It was the ripe scent of growing things, warm days and clear nights, just before harvest time.

"Isa ya!" Ahbay announced, the tip of his staff glowed with a green light. "The mother of us all, that brings us food from her bounty, from whose dust we were made and to whom we must return, answers. Earth is with thee!"

Marlowe gave a nod and faced Eddie.

Here it comes, Eddie thought. *I hope I can do this.*

"We call upon Fire," Marlowe said, and Eddie heard a hesitancy like a whispered "I hope" in his voice.

"Isa ya!" Eddie forced himself not to look at Marlowe or his staff, afraid it might not light up. "The heat of the sun and the warmth of the hearth, answers."

Eddie was pleased with the reply. It was as if the words just popped into his head. He glanced sidelong at his staff, where instead of a light, a small flame danced on its tip.

He returned his gaze to Marlowe.

"Fire is with thee," Eddie gushed, impressed that he succeeded. He looked around the room and noted that it appeared brighter, warmer than it had been.

"We call upon Water," Marlowe announced. The staff next to Trefoil on the bed shivered a bit and the tip began to glow a brilliant blue. "Isa ya! The power of the mighty ocean, the streams from which we drink, answers. Water is with us," Marlowe held his own staff aloft and said loudly. "We call upon Spirit."

His staff glowed with a pure, clear, white light, like the night Eddie stood before the coven.

"Isa ya! The power to bind the elements, to animate the flesh, and to bring miracles into this world, answers. Spirit is with us," Marlowe said, and looked down at the figure as it lay in the bed. "We call to thee, Trefoil. Our combined power shall heal your body and return you to us. So mote it be!"

The staff next to Trefoil on the bed began to glow brighter, and a blue aura began to surround his body.

"So mote it be!" Eugenia declared as a beam of yellow light shot forth from the top of her staff. joining the blue aura, coloring it to an aquamarine.

"So mote it be!" Ahbay proclaimed as emerald light joined the irradiation around Trefoil and it shifted to a yellow-green.

"So mote it be!" Eddie focused his attention on Trefoil, *wanted* to help him. A brilliant scarlet light came forth which bathed his supine form in deep violet.

"So mote it be!" Marlowe professed, and a white light flickered on his staff to be united with the others, making the glow a regal shade of purple. It was a purple worn by kings and more royal than any blue could ever be.

Trefoil's body began to rise from the bed, only about an inch or two, but suspended in beams of light.

There was a flash like distant lightning in the room, and Eddie started, as if struck with a cattle prod.

"What was that!" Eddie shouted. He found he needed to yell to overcome a terrible, ugly buzz in his ears, like a thousand large and awful insects lined the walls and floors of the room.

"Something is wrong!" Eugenia said, as there was another flash, much closer this time. Eddie's body twisted and arched, and he could see the others were affected the same.

"We must stop!" Ahbay cried out. "Marlowe, release us!"

"I cannot!" Marlowe roared, as there was another flash of lightning, all around them this time. A crash of thunder and wind howled about them. Eddie grabbed the bedpost as rain pelted him combined with the awful energy of the lightning, making him twitch and bounce like a rag doll. He wanted desperately to let go of his staff, to withdraw the energy going to Trefoil, but his hand no longer obeyed him, nor did his staff.

"Our power is being pulled…twisted…" Marlowe cried out over the noise of the storm that now, impossibly, was *inside* the room. "Withdraw, withdraw!"

"I cannot!" Ahbay shrieked.

Eddie knew this was bad. He could hear the panic in the others' voices, as the thunderstorm fulminated all around them. His mind flashed back to a night only a few short months ago.

He and Luis served at Manhattan North Homicide, good at their jobs with a solid success rate. Until they were assigned to a "joint effort" between the NYPD and the FBI Urban Crime Task Force to track down a drug dealer named Viper, who had brutally murdered a witness.

It was their first meeting with agent Wilcox, who made it clear he was in charge from the beginning and wanted to be the one to bring Viper in.

It was all right, until Luis received an anonymous tip where they could find Viper. Eddie didn't tell Wilcox, his captain, or anyone else. He and Luis decided to follow-up on the tip on their own.

It had been on a rainy night, when Eddie and Luis drove to the back lot of a Harlem Elementary School where a small groundskeeper's brick house sat. It was a remnant of a bygone era, when wealthy landowners made up a large segment of the uptown neighborhood.

They pulled their unmarked car in, and Eddie was on edge before they'd even parked. The rain poured down from the heavens in a steady stream, and there were distant flashes of lightning.

"Okay, Luis, let's take a look, but if we see anything at all, we call for backup," Eddie told his partner.

"Let's find out if he's even here," Luis said as they exited the car. While they still had the doors open, they simultaneously heard the click of multiple guns being cocked. The two detectives crouched down just as a firestorm of bullets began to burst around them.

He and Luis dove behind a metal dumpster, drew their weapons, and returned fire.

"It's a friggin' trap!" Luis screamed.

"How did he know we were coming?" Eddie could hear the fear in his own voice.

"I don' know!" Luis shouted. "But he pops us and it improves his standing. He'll be the baddest mofo in Harlem."

"Until the next one comes along." Eddie groaned. "Cover me." He got up and as quickly as he could, dove for the car as shots rang out. Eddie could barely see the barrel flashes in the heavy downpour.

As the wind whipped him, he felt the terror, raw and angry inside him. He was convinced he was going to die, right here, right now.

Then a voice spoke to him, a memory of his father.

"The first thing a cop must do is not panic," Lawrence Berman said as clearly as when he'd been alive. "Look at the situation, clear and calm, follow your instincts, and then take action! If not, you are nothing but a sitting duck."

Eddie took a deep breath and focused on a window where he'd thought there'd been the flash of a handgun.

He fired at it and shattered the glass. Then, he hit the ground, rolled, and instead of staying in the relative safety of the police car, ran straight for the building.

From the corner of his eye, he saw two figures rise up from behind garbage cans.

Without a thought, as if they traveled in slow motion, Eddie fired twice at the twin silhouettes. Slowly, they each fell, and Eddie kept running toward the building.

He saw two faces in the empty window frame. He immediately recognized Viper from his mug shot. He just stood there, surprised at this development, and next to him was a younger man with a very large gun.

A Magnum 45.

Viper's mouth moved and Eddie could hear him say, "Shoot him, shoot him!"

Eddie pointed and fired at the younger man without even taking time to aim, and the young man's head burst open with a red spray as the body fell back.

Viper raised his own pistol. It was laughably small, nothing more than a .22.

Eddie ran harder. He planned to leap through the window, feet first, to stop Viper with the sheer audacity of his attack.

Only a large shape moved out of the shadows, got between Viper and Eddie as the shot rang out.

It was so loud and so close, it sounded like a bomb went off. At that moment, Luis's huge body was in front of Eddie, and it fell back, back, against him. He was knocked over, as his partner pushed him down to the ground. Eddie's head hit the pavement and he saw stars.

The world shimmered in and out of focus.

He couldn't see with Luis on top of him. He knew his partner had been hit, but how bad? Was he dead? He tried to move but was pinned.

He could see a small slice of pavement, and the rain beat down, bounced and leapt as it struck the asphalt in a steady rhythm. A pair of shoes appeared in his line of vision.

Snakeskin boots.

Viper.

If Luis isn't dead, he will be soon, Eddie thought, *and so will I.*

"You crazy asshole," a voice hissed, mixed with respect and awe. "You killed my posse and then ran right at me. Damn."

Eddie could hear the *rat-a-tat* of the water strike the top of the nearby police car, and not another sound. He lay there on the cold, wet pavement and waited for the explosion that would end his life.

"Next time," the voice said. And with that, the shoes turned and walked away. The click-clack of the heels receded as another peal of thunder crashed.

He let go of his pinned gun, and with all his remaining strength rolled his partner partway off him, grabbed the cell phone from his pocket, and pushed 911.

Later that night, Eddie lay in a hospital bed as Luis was wheeled in from surgery, wounded but alive.

"You got lucky. Small caliber," the doctor said. "Another quarter of an inch, and the bullet would have severed his spine."

While Eddie and Luis were in the hospital, Viper was caught by Wilcox, who made headlines as "the valiant FBI agent who caught the cop-shooter".

It gave the NYPD a black eye. Their commander, Captain Seville, immediately reassigned Eddie and Luis to the Twenty-Second Precinct for their failure to share information or call for backup before they entered a scene.

Eddie often thought back to that voice that came to him in his moment of need when his courage failed. Was it really his father or just a memory?

He realized what the voice pushed him to do. Not to panic, to let the cold part of his brain take over and take action.

Eddie needed to do that now, and hoped it ended better.

He pulled himself close to the bedpost, wrapped his left arm around it as the room shook under his feet.

Wind smashed his face, as well as another wave of heavy rain. He took his left hand, which still obeyed him, and grabbed his right fingers.

With a grunt, and no help from his inoperative hand, he pried a finger loose from the glowing wooden pole. His index finger came away and Eddie moved down the row. As his pinkie released, the staff fell away and clattered to the floor.

It was like a switch was thrown.

The wind, rain, thunder, and lightning ceased instantly, and Marlowe, Eugenia, and Ahbay collapsed, as if the only thing that held them up was the wind. Trefoil dropped the short distance to the bed, a puff of smoke rising up at his midsection. The room was plunged into total darkness.

"Lights!" Marlowe shouted hoarsely.

The candles sparked to life, as Marlowe stood, wet, bedraggled, and wild-eyed, his staff at the ready.

"What happened?" Eugenia pulled herself up by her own staff, her hair wet and stringy, her tunic soaked.

"How could anything attack here in your home?" asked Ahbay, his hair askew and fear in his eyes.

Marlowe surveyed the room. "Something evil got into the house..."

"Look!" Eugenia pointed at the bed. Eddie turned his head to follow where she indicated.

Trefoil sat up and blinked his eyes.

"Trefoil?" Ahbay said, amazed. "You are awake."

"Damn straight." Trefoil looked around the room and wiped water off his face with his hand. "I take a short nap, and everything goes to hell."

THIRTY-FIVE

Ahbay lent a hand as Eddie helped Trefoil out of the bed. Wet and bedraggled, the other four escorted him to the creaky elevator, which they all took down to the first floor.

They all moved, wet and shivering, in a state of shock to the breakfast room.

As often as he could, Trefoil would release his grip on Eddie's arm and walk unsteadily but determined as he leaned heavily on his staff.

As they sat at the breakfast table, the others hid their staffs away.

"Let's have some eats, Marlowe," Trefoil said. "I'm hungry."

"I can imagine," Marlowe replied dully. "You have been unconscious for two days, old friend."

"That s'plains it." Trefoil seemed totally unaffected by the recent events in the bedroom. Then again, he'd been unconscious until the danger was past.

Marlowe rose and walked out to the tea trolley, just as Frisha ran into the room, followed by Bankrock.

The thin man wore a different tweed coat and appeared disheveled, his hair awry, his tie missing, his spectacles dirty. It was as if he'd shifted his clothes with as much inexperience as Eddie.

Bankrock stopped to stare at the others with their sopping clothes and windblown hair, then he uttered a soft, "Oh my!"

Frisha, on the other hand, was completely unaware, and with a great cry of relief, hugged Trefoil to her large bosom. Her flowing cloak practically hid him in its voluminous folds.

"Easy, Frisha, I didn't survive the Dark Sleep to be smothered by you," Trefoil griped.

"Thought thou wert dead," Frisha wailed. "Thought thy soul moved on to the next plane."

"It will, if you don't let go, woman." Trefoil pushed the enveloping cloak from his face.

"Forgi'e me, forgi'e me." Frisha relaxed her grip on Trefoil and collapsed into a chair. "It's just to see you like that, and knowing there t'were naught I could do!"

She pulled a large, stained rag from her cloak and blew her nose in it.

Bankrock cleared his throat and stepped forward. "Good evening, Eugenia, Ahbay." He gave Eddie a withering look. "*Mister* Berman. Glad to see you back with us, Trefoil."

"Good to be here," Trefoil acknowledged wearily.

"I am sorry to intrude, but there was a powerful magickal event. I was, uh…surprised…when I found this townhouse was the source."

"It has been quite a night," Ahbay said, a look of shock still on his face. He ran his hand through his wet hair, then gave a small wave of his cane and his robe transformed back into his suit, which was totally dry, and his hair tidied itself back into position.

Eddie stood, waved his staff, and his clothes shifted to his suit, which was mostly dry. He moved to Trefoil and asked, "Do you remember the attack?" He pulled his notebook from his pocket and opened it to find it dripping wet and unusable.

"It's all pretty misty for me," Trefoil grunted, as Marlowe returned to the room through a side door, a cup of tea in his hands. "I was being attacked from above, then something bit me."

"A snake?" Eddie suggested.

"I guess so. Tooth marks on my leg. I tried to heal them—"

"That's what put you into the Dark Sleep." Marlowe set the tea in front of Trefoil. "The venom was designed to use your powers against you. Here, drink, it shall restore thee."

"Marlowe, my readings were very strange," Bankrock advised. "However, I detected an event that registered a six-point-oh-two. I am going to require a statement from all witnesses present."

"Not now, Bankrock," Marlowe considered the man testily.

Bankrock raised himself up to his full height, which wasn't much. "There are directives to be followed! Directives that you voted on—"

"Could that venom explain what just happened?" Eddie queried. "Our energy reacted to it?"

"I know the mixture used." Marlowe shook his head. "Our combined power should have cleansed Trefoil of it instantly."

"You think it was something else?" Eddie proposed.

"Yes," Marlowe said. "I believe this was an attempt to steal the power of the Five."

The others stared in silence.

"Another talisman?" Eddie asked.

Marlowe rose and moved closer to Trefoil. "Do you carry any charms?"

"Nope." Trefoil sipped his tea. "You can examine me if you want."

"I suppose we should all eat." Marlowe clapped his hands.

From the doorway, a different, larger trolley with three chafing dishes rolled out. It was followed by another cart, which held a large salad bowl brimming with succulent greens, a stack of plates, and silverware wrapped in napkins.

The two carts rolled quickly in and took positions not far from their table.

"I understand your desire to be a good host," Bankrock commented. "But if there has been an attempt to steal any wizard's power, you need to file a 'Supernatural Misappropriation Form C.'"

"In due time, Bankrock." Marlowe waved his cane in front of Trefoil. "Please help yourselves."

"Thank you, Marlowe," Ahbay said. "However, this experience, has taken my appetite."

Frisha, however, rose up and began to fill two plates.

Eugenia sat with a languid look on her face, then all at once, noticed her wet clothes. "Is there a bathroom? I wish to freshen up."

Marlowe gestured to a nearby door for Eugenia, who toddled off. He then turned back to continue his examination of Trefoil.

"To have such a thing happen inside the Coven Master's residence. It is most troubling…" Ahbay pondered as he sat in his chair and stared into space.

"That's exactly my point." Bankrock's fingers felt for his tie, and not finding one, he touched a cat's eye finger ring to his shirt, and one appeared.

Marlowe finished with Trefoil, lowered his cane, and sat down.

"I was hopin' for a haircut and a shave, while you were at it," Trefoil quipped.

"Sorry, my friend." Marlowe leaned back and closed his eyes.

"Anything there?" Eddie questioned.

"Nothing from Trefoil." Marlowe opened his eyes. "And yet… there is…something."

"Aye, Marlowe." Frisha put a plate of food in front of Trefoil. "I can see nary a thing, let me tell you. Do thee know what 'tis like to be a prophetess and naught get one clear vision? I'd say you don't."

"I am having trouble as well." Bankrock removed a small crystal ball from his pocket. "At first, I had trouble getting an exact location of the event that just occurred. Once I found it was this house, I assumed the magickal energies were involved in helping Trefoil…"

Marlowe began to wave his stick again. "It isn't that! There is something that disrupts my power. Do any of you feel drained?"

Ahbay nodded and Eddie shrugged.

"Ah! Now thou knowst what I've been goin' through," Frisha blurted. "Not to mention that the bed you've given me makes me back ache. I'll tell you, 'tis terrible. But, ye wish to speak of things that do not concern a simple wizard as meself, I'll keep a watch at the door."

Frisha left the room, her plate of food balanced in one hand.

"If it was a talisman," Marlowe confessed, "I cannot locate it."

"What talisman could possibly do that? I know of none." Bankrock shook his head.

"Could it be the Great Evil?" Ahbay said. "Has he found a way to attack us here?"

"You were correct, Marlowe." Eugenia stepped into the room, dry and coifed. "Things are indeed different."

"Eugenia!" Trefoil stabbed his food with a fork. "You look good!"

"How come we just dried ourselves, and you needed a bathroom?" Eddie said.

"Obviously." Eugenia forced a smile. "I didn't stay in such good shape for five hundred years without the aid of a mirror."

"Now we are assembled, the Five is whole again," Marlowe said, and looked at Trefoil. "Much has happened in the last few days."

"Do tell!" Trefoil said as he ate.

"First, let me tell you of what we are certain. Our foe is indeed Abraxas, released to this earth through the Amulet of Abracadabra. This release was accomplished through the aid of two foolish apprentices, with the help of a warlock."

Bankrock stood up straight. "A warlock! Why wasn't I informed of this immediately!"

"We only found out this morning," Marlowe said.

Bankrock turned pale. "If there is a warlock operating outside the control of the coven, he must be stopped."

"A warlock doesn't explain what happened upstairs," Eugenia insisted, and turned to Eddie. "We are all thankful for your quick actions, Edward."

"You keep talkin' 'bout that. What happened?" Trefoil finished the last bite of his victuals.

"When we combined our powers, a force took over," Ahbay reported. "We could not move, yet Eddie pulled his staff free, broke the circle, and released us."

Eddie smiled shyly. "Being a cop, you learn to stay cool in an emergency."

Trefoil did not look pleased. "Didn't anyone tell you how dangerous it is to break a circle in the middle of a spell?"

"His ignorance saved us," Marlowe said. "The rest of us knew the danger and took no action. Eddie freed us. If not, we all could have ended up in the Dark Sleep."

"Even so," Bankrock lectured. "Trefoil is correct. If Eddie had gone through basic training, he would know—"

"Well, he didn't," Trefoil argued. "And that demon will use his inexperience against him, against us all."

Eddie sat up straight. "Sounds to me like he used your *experience* against you. He poisoned you, and then something happened so all of us were affected. If a warlock is working with him, he knows how you guys operate. The only way you can beat Abraxas is to act in ways he won't expect. We have to think outside the box."

Trefoil rose. Ahbay stood to help him, but Trefoil waived him away. "Listen to this, wet behind the ears and lecturing us! Look, Newling, each of us has defeated demons before, and you ain't done shit."

"I see no reason to curse," Bankrock clucked.

Trefoil glanced at the little man, then returned his gaze to Eddie. "I'm tired, and I want to sleep. Normal sleep." He held his staff, walked to the door, and turned to add one point. "Eddie, if you took on Abraxas tonight, you don't know enough to even slow him down."

He walked out of the room, as the others looked embarrassed by his outburst.

"He is tired," Ahbay explained. "And he was defeated while you were not. That must—how do you say—stick in his craw."

Eddie nodded and glanced at his watch. "Yeah, but right now, we have to go to that meeting. We've got four of the Five. I hope that's enough."

"We cannot confront the demon this night," Ahbay stated.

"I thought that was the plan," Eddie insisted.

The others glanced guiltily at each other and would not meet his eyes.

"What is it?" Eddie held out his hands. "Come on, you said we were going to hunt down the demon tonight. Let's do it!"

"We are all weakened from what transpired upstairs," Marlowe said. "Each of us has lost some of our power." He looked at Eugenia and Ahbay. "What say you?"

Ahbay and Eugenia nodded in agreement.

"Trefoil is too infirm to meet such a challenge," Marlowe worried. "It would be foolishness itself to go up against the Great Evil."

"It is even worse to face him at a time and place of his own choosing," Eugenia pleaded. "This could be a trap!"

"She has a point," Marlowe agreed. "The warlock may have influenced this Cuccolo fellow to contact you."

"We have to take that chance," Eddie exclaimed.

"I disagree," Bankrock said. "I have brought research Marlowe requested. Our best course of action would be to read through it and form a long-term plan."

"None of the plans you guys came up with have worked so far," Eddie answered. "Look at you! Super-powered wizards, and you don't have a clue! Cuccolo won't stand a chance."

"If he doesn't bring the talisman," Marlowe said. "Perhaps the demon will not reveal himself."

"Or he'll get really pissed and kill Cuccolo for the hell of it," Eddie seethed.

"Eddie," Marlowe explained, "the blood sacrifice is to release the potency of each talisman."

Eddie turned to Marlowe, his eyes aflame. "So that's why the murders? He needs to kill each time he gets one of these baubles?"

"That's not the point. The demon could seek to make one of us the next sacrifice." Marlowe glanced to Eugenia and Ahbay.

"I take that risk every day. It doesn't change 'cause the bad guys get badder." Eddie set his jaw. "You guys are just scared."

Marlowe and the others stared at the floor.

"Wow, the first time it doesn't go your way, you run and hide." Eddie shook his head, rose, and moved for the door. "Well, I'm gonna face him down."

"Eddie, no." Marlowe stood to block his egress. "I beg you, do not do this."

"I have to."

"I told you of my apprentice." Marlowe's face became a deep crimson. "When things went horribly wrong, I warned him that his choices would bring a terrible fate, as it did. I do not want your choices to destroy you, Eddie."

Eddie stared into the old man's eyes. He could see the concern and the fear. "Protect and serve. It's the only reason I joined you guys."

He walked from the room and the front door banged closed a moment later.

"He certainly doesn't lack courage." Eugenia sighed.

"He could be killed," Ahbay added.

"He could get us all killed!" Marlowe muttered. "And then who remains to fight?"

THIRTY-SIX

Luis found it hard to keep his eyes open as he sat in his parked car in the late spring air. Eddie had gone into the townhouse hours ago, and after the strange man and woman went in, little had occurred.

Luis noticed some strange coruscation in an upper window at one point, like someone taking flash photographs, and the curtains fluttered and bucked as if from a breeze. But, the movement had not been enough to give him a glimpse of the interior, even with his binoculars. Strangely enough, droplets of water appeared on the glass, as if a storm occurred *inside* the house.

Luis sat back in his seat and thought it would soon be time for a cup of coffee and a restroom break.

His cell phone rang.

"Vasquez."

"Luis, when are you comin' hoooome?" whined Maria in his ear.

"Maria, I'm on stakeout. I tol' you I was workin' a case tonight."

"Luis, you promised to take me out for dinner two weeks ago. I've been cooped up in this house with *your* children…"

As Luis recalled, she had been a healthy participant in the act of creating their six kids, but he also knew it would be foolish to mention that at this particular moment.

"I know, baby, I know. But a big shot got himself murdered, and we all got to work overtime. You know I can't talk about it, 'specially not over the phone."

"I don' see you no more! And what do I tell the kids? They want their papa. You know how the boys get when you're not around."

Luis, in spite of himself, felt a lump in his throat. He missed the children, too. His four-year-old, Rosita, was one of those dream children everyone wishes for. No matter how bad his mood when he got home, she would climb into his lap, give him a hug, and his cares would vanish.

He also missed the rambunctious boys: Manuel, who was ten, Roberto, eight, and Julio, six. Each was a handful, but they looked up to him worshipfully as if he was an ancient god arrived from Mount Olympus. They loved their mother, but he was the one who kept them in line.

Luis was familiar with how quickly their attitudes became snotty and their chores slovenly if he wasn't there to remind them how men should behave.

Lastly, the littlest girls, Bonita, two and-a-half, who he called Bonnie, and Cerista, about to be one, named in honor of his partner's wife.

Six children, all under the age of eleven. He and Maria would have a blessed event every two years or so, which made the priest of their local church in the Bronx claim that they were good Catholics.

Luis didn't mind. He came from a large family and adored each child, but he knew how it could overwhelm Maria. Always one child in diapers, usually one on the breast, and all of the falls and hurts and arguments, while he spent his days finding killers in the city's dark underbelly.

Luis knew that despite their mutual hot tempers, they each saw the other as an oasis from their difficult jobs. Hers, bringing life into the world, and his, finding justice for those who'd lost theirs.

This week was rough. He'd been home late every night, and Eddie going off the deep end was an unnecessary burden.

"Call Cerise," Luis suggested. "Maybe she can come by. You know she's always happy to help out."

"She's takin' care of Eddie's *madre*, Luis. I need *you*. I miss you," Maria said, then her voice fell to a conspiratorial whisper. "I *want* you."

Luis felt a stirring in his loins. They had both been so busy in the last few weeks that they didn't have a chance to be intimate. Luis suddenly felt this self-imposed stakeout was a waste of time, and he was ready to go home to the loving arms of his wife. They would probably argue first, which was Maria's favorite foreplay, usually followed by an energetic bout in the bedroom.

Then in the morning, he could hug his children and kiss them all before coming back to work.

Luis saw the door of the townhouse open and Eddie walked out.

"Jeez!" Luis said, his wife's entreaties forgotten. "Gotta go!"

He pushed the 'END' button on his phone before Maria could protest. His eyes never left Eddie as he descended the steps and turned toward Central Park.

Luis slid his bulky body down in the car, safe in the shadows. Eddie was far too focused to notice him.

Eddie headed downtown. Luis got out of the car and took a backward look to the townhouse to make sure no one else came out. Then, he followed his partner down the shadowy sidewalk lit only by the occasional street lamp.

Unaware of being followed, Eddie turned into the park in the direction of the carousel. He reflected on the fact that as a boy, his father brought him there on his infrequent days off.

"New York is not only the greatest city in the world," his father had told him, "it's the greatest place to be a kid."

The carousel lay housed in an eight-sided brick building with a copper roof not far from the Central Park Zoo. The sides of the octagon were decorated with bricks in rows of red and yellow, which matched the Playmates Arch, a walkway under the East Drive. It originally housed a small, hand-driven merry-go-round. During a major renovation in 1907 when electric lampposts were put in, a larger carousel from Coney Island was installed.

When Eddie rode the wooden horses in the 1980s, they had grown seedy and the entire structure was in disrepair.

In the 1990s, the Central Park Zoo underwent a major transformation, as did the carousel, which was recognized for the craftsmanship of its fanciful hand-carved menagerie and brass-tube calliope.

The entire carousel was lovingly taken apart by experts who restored the scratched paint and broken lights. Through private funds, it was brought back and maintained at its original splendor.

During the day, it was awash with the laughter of children and families. At night, overhead garage doors on four sides were rolled down and locked solidly in place, which transformed it into another unnoticed brick outbuilding.

However, this night, with the moon waxing and almost full, it shimmered like an apparition.

It's like a house built by fairies, Eddie thought.

He was a bit fed up the way his mind kept turning toward the supernatural. A few days ago, he didn't think of the metaphysical at all, and certainly not of fairies. It probably wouldn't be long before he'd meet one.

After all, he'd met a vampire.

He stayed in the shadows and moved silently behind a large boulder held in position by metal staves that flanked the carousel's west side. He looked around to see the best place to attack—or retreat, if that was necessary.

There wasn't a lot of cover at the front of the carousel, and nothing but open fields with bushes to the south. On its north face, a grove of trees banked a protective fence to the 65th Street transverse road and shielded parkgoers from a sickening fall onto that roadway.

Eddie didn't like this location.

If Abraxas was being helped by a warlock, they could strike and then use the grove of trees to flee anywhere on the entire planet.

Eddie sat behind the stationary boulder and tried to get into a position where he could observe the front of the carousel as well as the trees.

Unknown to Eddie, and as silent as an army tank in low gear, Luis Vasquez crept, or rather crunched, his way to his own hiding place: a large tree. He pulled out his binoculars to observe Eddie.

Time passed, slowly.

Eddie was growing bored when he saw a quick movement in the dark.

Close to him; too close.

Eddie ducked down, quietly and smoothly pulling his service weapon from its shoulder holster.

Something leapt to the top of the rock, and Eddie, as his heart raced, lifted his gun, his jaw clamped tight.

Over his head, on its hind legs, a large gray squirrel stood and looked down at him.

"Jesus," Eddie whispered. "You scared the hell out of me."

He holstered his weapon. The furry creature stayed stock-still and watched him. After a moment, it made a chittering noise.

"Get lost," Eddie murmured hoarsely, surprised that the rodent made noises. "I'm busy. Scat."

The small creature cocked his head and looked at Eddie with is beady eyes. It chittered, then added clicking sounds.

"You want to blow my cover?" Eddie said. "I don't speak squirrel. No *habla* squirrel. Go!"

The squirrel stomped one of its back legs in annoyance, and as suddenly as he appeared, leapt off the top of the rock and vanished into the dark.

"Great," Eddie muttered. "I even got the squirrels pissed at me."

Then another movement caught Eddie's eye. He saw a man in a dark suit duck behind an impressive bush about one hundred feet away. A moment later, another man, wearing black, moved into another clump of bushes opposite the first arrival. This man was wearing a turtleneck and had a bulletproof vest, a belt with his weapon and accoutrements and a head covering that only showed his eyes.

Even dressed in that way, Eddie knew him at once: Wilcox.

The way he moved was unmistakable, and his gear looked like it came out of an FBI catalogue.

Cuccolo's men were there, hidden from the buyer. The FBI was there, hidden from the gangsters.

Here was Eddie, concealed from them all.

He'd always done things by the book. How did he end up in this situation? If something went wrong, more people could be killed by crossfire than by Abraxas.

Nearby, Luis watched the new arrivals through his binoculars, trying to figure out what was going on.

Eddie saw a figure stroll down the concrete path from the orange and yellow Playmate Arch in the moonlight.

Cuccolo.

He was wearing a light-gray suit and a red silk shirt, easy to spot. He had his hands in the pockets of his coat and behaved like a man without a care in the world.

Eddie noticed he didn't carry anything. He'd agreed not to bring the talisman, but there were bulges in his jacket that suggested something in his pockets. Perhaps the gun he had mentioned?

Cuccolo strutted to the shuttered carousel, checked his watch, surveyed the open field opposite, and sat at one of the many black, steel-mesh tables bolted to the ground. He didn't look anxious, but being out there in the open probably was tough on his nerves.

Eddie glanced over at the dark shapes hidden in the trees.

Cuccolo pulled out a cigarette and lit it. Waiting was something he seldom did.

There was the sound of movement in the underbrush.

Cuccolo turned left and right, his hand going into his jacket.

"Hello?" Cuccolo said.

Something short and squat crawled out of the woods next to the transverse road.

Eddie stared at the shadowy figure. At first he thought it was the annoying squirrel, but then decided it was far too large. It moved in an odd way, *waddled* in that peculiar undulating movement of a ferret.

The shape lumbered into a better view in the moonlight. It was a large rodent with a flat tail.

A beaver!

As it drew closer to Cuccolo, Eddie could see it was the largest beaver he could imagine. It was the size of a large dog, and it was a shiny crimson, as if drenched in blood.

Eddie stared at it. *Could that be Abraxas?*

Cuccolo stood and stepped back. The creature was undergoing a metamorphosis as it slunk forward, its tail growing smaller and its legs longer until it resembled a dog-like creature.

Cuccolo pulled out his pistol.

The thing on the ground rose up on its back legs and held up its front paws in a posture of supplication.

"You wouldn't want to shoot me, would you?" the thing said, the muzzle moving as it spoke. "Not when we have a deal?"

Eddie heard the makeshift monster speak in a deep, grating voice that sent goose bumps down his back.

"Oh Jeez," Cuccolo said, and licked his lips. "Are you...Lox?"

The thing before him bowed like an actor who has been recognized. "I am indeed, servant of Malsum."

Cuccolo lowered the handgun, as he stared at the odd red animal. It took a tentative step forward and began to change again. It grew taller, the back straightened, and the hair on its head grew long, filled out, and became a thousand feathers falling from a large headdress.

It was now at least ten feet tall, and naked except for a loincloth, moccasins, and a magnificent war bonnet, which tumbled down his back to his knees. The man's skin was the same shade of red as the animal, and he raised a hand in greeting.

Eddie wondered why Cuccolo's men didn't shoot at this giant Native American that towered over their boss.

"Malsum! You are *Malsum*! Oh God, it's all true!" Cuccolo moaned, stepped back, and glanced to the left and right for help.

"Give me what is mine!" the giant boomed, as it held out his hand.

Cuccolo was too stunned to raise the pistol. With his free hand, he reached slowly for the pocket of his jacket.

Eddie knew that if the demon got a hold of another talisman, a blood sacrifice would soon follow.

"Police!" Eddie yelled, and whipped out his gun and shield as he ran toward them.

Both Cuccolo and the giant turned to Eddie with equally stunned expressions.

"Cuccolo, step away!" Eddie yelled, his shield held high in one hand, and his service weapon in the other.

Eddie's sudden appearance made Cuccolo regain some of his self-control. He raised his own pistol.

"So," the giant chuckled. "We meet face to face, Newling."

Eddie slipped his shield into his pocket and grabbed the gun in both hands to assume a shooter's stance. "Hands in the air."

"Your command of the language is succinct," the figure making the last word sound like it was something that tasted bad.

In one quick move, the huge red-skinned man grabbed Cuccolo's arm and forced the gun he held skyward just as Cuccolo fired. Then he lifted Cuccolo and held him in front of his massive body as a shield.

From Luis's point of view it was an entirely different event. He'd seen Cuccolo talk to empty space, and then Eddie ran up with his gun drawn. Now, he saw Cuccolo gyrate, raise his arm, fire a shot, as he was lifted off the ground to hang suspended in midair.

Luis pulled the binoculars from his eyes, blinked twice, and stared up at the front of the carousel. There stood Eddie, as Alfonso Cuccolo floated in the air as if he'd joined a traveling magic show.

Luis leapt up and pulled out his own gun and ran toward Eddie. He had no idea what was going on, but his place was at his partner's side.

From where Eddie stood, the Indian reached into Cuccolo's pocket and extracted a small box. Even in the moonlight, Eddie could see it was carved and encrusted with topaz and silver.

"Oh crap," Eddie muttered, then yelled, "I told you not to bring that!"

"Many thanks," the creature announced to Cuccolo. "But I am not done with you yet."

He put the man under one of his massive arms, turned, and walked off. Eddie fired right at the huge feathered headdress. Not a feather moved, but the bullet ricocheted off the brick facing of the carousel building.

Eddie's mouth fell open.

Bullets don't hurt it! he thought.

Suddenly, people were rushing in from all sides. Men in black SWAT outfits with infrared goggles, and at least six of Cuccolo's henchmen. They all raised their weapons and did nothing but stare in disbelief as Cuccolo was carried off toward the grove of trees between the carousel and the 65th Street transverse road.

Eddie cursed, holstered his weapon, and ran after them. As he went he willed the staff into his hand. The small black card flew into his palm.

Luis was on his way down the hill toward the south end of the carousel, but Eddie rushed after Cuccolo on the north side.

As Eddie entered the small grove, the staff expanded in his hand, and he pursued the giant, who dodged and weaved through the trees with practiced ease. He ran over a stone hill and down behind the Ballfield Cafe, past a trash dumpster and a chained gate for the transverse road.

"Help me, Berman!" Cuccolo yelled, as he fought to pull himself free of the monster's grasp. It mounted another hill and climbed as if the gangster weighed no more than a rag doll.

Eddie lifted his staff and passionately yelled the first thing that came to his mind.

"Stop in the name of the law!"

In retrospect, it was a silly thing to say, a clichéd phrase from a thousand television shows.

But the effect was instant.

A brilliant red light shot from the end of his staff, whipped at his foe with a crackle of displaced air, and struck his intended target in the head.

The giant reeled, stumbled, and roared in anger.

"Yesss," Eddie hissed, a smile on his lips. "You ain't so bad, Abraxas."

The giant faced him, then a strange smirk appeared on his lips. He was on top of the hill and looked down at Eddie. He held up Cuccolo, reached as high as he could, and placed him up on the branch of a large tree, fifteen feet off the ground. Cuccolo clung to the tree for dear life.

The behemoth reached to his belt and pulled out a tomahawk the size of a fire ax. It appeared to be made from wood with a flint blade held by leather straps. But like the body, loincloth, and headdress, it was a deep, leathery red.

He raised the ancient weapon, as Eddie held up his staff and yelled, "*Isa ya!*"

Another beam of red light slashed through the air and struck Abraxas and knocked him back. He fell onto its huge rear end.

Eddie shouted, "I thought you were powerful, Abraxas. You ain't nothin'!"

"You think not, Newling?" the creature said, and rose to its feet. "I killed he who bore your staff, and I shall destroy you as well!"

He turned and ran again through the woods toward the West Side. Eddie took a deep breath and pursued.

Alfonso Cuccolo maneuvered himself on the branch and called down, "Berman, what about me?" to Eddie's retreating form.

"Aw jeez," Cuccolo said, and laid his head against the trunk. Whatever that thing was that grabbed him, it looked like two ancient myths of the Algonquin tribe. First Lox, a clever creature that changed from beaver to wolverine, and Malsum, the God of Evil.

As he considered this, he looked down at the branch his feet rested on. There was his carved box of wood and turquoise.

He carefully bent down and picked it up.

"What the hell?" Cuccolo said, and tried to think why the giant Indian would leave his prize after going to all the trouble to take it. It made no sense.

It began to grow warm in his hand.

"Whoa," Cuccolo said, as the box shimmered.

Something slipped around his neck, and before Cuccolo could react, it pulled tight against his throat and cut off his vocalization.

A voice croaked in his ear. "How nice of you to show up with so many friends. I told you to come alone."

He turned his head as much as he could and saw a face concealed by a large hood.

A gloved hand came from a sleeve and snatched the box from him. It now glowed brighter.

"Thank you for this. My large companion left it so I could activate the charm. And you are going to help," the figure said. "Unfortunately, not while you're alive."

The hooded man kicked Cuccolo's legs out from under him.

With the rope around his throat, Cuccolo fell a good ten feet. The noose pulled taut, and with a snap, broke his neck.

Cuccolo hung suspended a few feet above the ground, dead.

The cloaked figure chanted several words and held the box up, as it glowed brilliant sapphire, then climbed down the tree to take what was needed.

THIRTY-SEVEN

"I got him on the run!" Eddie whispered to himself, his face scratched by unseen branches. The giant led him out of the grove and onto a lawn.

Eddie glanced around quickly, reassured that he was still in Central Park and hadn't transported halfway across the globe while among the trees. As best as he could tell, Abraxas didn't have the ability to use the woods to shift location.

He does have limits, Eddie thought.

Now out in the open, Eddie held up his staff and shot another beam of fiery light at his quarry.

The nimble giant ducked and weaved, and the blast missed him. He crossed over West Drive and onto an empty bridle path.

Eddie followed as the Indian turned and ducked into a huge tunnel. Eddie stopped.

Why did he go in there? his cop instinct screamed. *There must be a reason.*

"I'm not going to let him get away," Eddie said aloud, and began to run after the red-skinned colossus.

Meanwhile, Luis was far behind him circumventing the grove. He saw Eddie run from the trees and lift a stick he was carrying and wondered where the heck Eddie had gotten that. Then there was a flash, like distant lightning before a storm.

Luis watched Eddie stand still for a moment. Luis waved his arms and tried to call out, but he was too winded to do so. His large frame wasn't designed for long runs.

Eddie approached the tunnel with his staff held tightly in both hands. The light inside blinked once and then went out, which plunged the man-made cavern into utter blackness.

Eddie stopped at the aperture. Every instinct told him it was a trap.

He looked at his staff and closed his eyes. He needed a light. There was a flash, and a ball of red light the size of a baseball appeared above his stick. It quivered, flared like a miniature sun, as if a number of tiny nuclear explosions created the illumination.

He waved the staff once, and the ball of light came loose and moved into the tunnel, as it followed Eddie's will.

The tunnel appeared empty.

He stepped in cautiously, his staff at the ready, as he looked from side to side for unexpected movement.

Can Abraxas turn invisible? Eddie considered. *If so, it would explain how he got the jump on Riftstone.*

A few hundred feet away, Luis clambered over the small hill as Eddie entered the tunnel. Luis still couldn't call out. His breath passed through his lungs with the sound of a large motor and his heart smacked against his chest as if it sought escape. Luis reached the tunnel and grabbed the stone wall to steady himself.

Eddie leapt around to face Luis, his stick aloft.

Luis panted and held up his hands in a pose of surrender.

"Luis!" Eddie gasped, stunned. "What are you doing here?"

Luis wanted to say, "Following you!" but instead he panted harder and tried to swallow, as if he'd just completed the New York City Marathon.

"How much have you seen?" Eddie stepped toward his partner.

As Eddie moved closer, Luis raised his head to see a giant figure appear out of the shadows.

It was at least ten feet tall, with blood-red skin and horns that looked like a large bull's rising from its head. It walked on hoofed feet, the bottom half of its body covered with a thick pelt, as crimson as the rest.

It was a demon, more real and frightening than any tales his Sunday school teacher regaled him with as a boy in the basement of St. Joseph's in the Bronx. Taloned hands rose and reached for Eddie.

Luis' jaw dropped open and his eyes bulged. He wanted to point, to yell, to let Eddie know, but shock paralyzed him.

Eddie saw the panic in his partner's eyes and turned.

The demon reached for him.

"*Isa ya!*" Eddie yelled, and a fiery blast flew from his staff and engulfed the demon's head with strange ruby flames. It was as if he'd been soaked with lighter fluid and set ablaze.

"Holy crap," Luis wheezed.

"Got him!" Eddie said, teeth clenched.

The flames burned brightly, but a low chuckle began to emerge from the monster. Eddie suddenly noticed that although his head was on fire, Abraxas' body didn't flail about in pain or even discomfort.

The demon only raised one hand and snapped his fingers. The flames ceased, to reveal a huge, evil grin on the monster's face.

"Oh boy," Luis gasped.

"I have toyed with you, lured you here!" it bellowed. "I am too powerful to be stopped by a Newling!"

He lunged forward, grabbed Eddie by the shoulders with his huge hands, and picked him up.

Eddie yelled in shock and pain, as he felt the demon's talons dig into his skin.

A blur of motion slashed past Eddie as a figure leapt on top of the creature's outstretched arms and onto its shoulders.

It was a man, but no human could leap so high or move so fast. It jumped to the creature's back, as if to seek a hellish piggyback ride, and sank oversized fangs into the creature's neck.

"It's Daniel!" Eddie cried out.

"*Madre de Dios!*" Luis fell back a step.

The demon howled in outrage and pain, but with his hands on Eddie he couldn't knock Daniel off. Abraxas threw his head right and left in an attempt to dislodge the sharp teeth.

Eddie twisted his head and yelled, "Luis, get out of here."

Luis took a few more steps out of the tunnel.

Eddie still held his staff, and with a glance to it, he gazed at the demon.

I want to stop him, I need to stop him, he thought, and put as much emotion as he could behind the thought.

He extended his staff and yelled, "*Get thee behind me!*"

Fiery light slammed from his staff with a recoil that made both of Eddie's arms quake. There was a scarlet burst of light, like a bomb going off.

The demon's arms sprang open and Eddie fell the few feet to the ground. Daniel was struck free from the monster's flesh and also fell off. Eddie noticed that Daniel's teeth had grown overlarge and extended almost to his chin.

The demon fell down to one knee and shook his huge head. Then, with a roar, it rose up toward Eddie again.

A brilliant white light came from behind Abraxas and encircled him.

At the other end of the tunnel stood Marlowe, his staff crackling with energy. Next to him were Ahbay and Eugenia. Without even a gesture, their staffs shot forth their green and yellow lights to engulf the demon, who grunted with pain as each new beam struck him.

Eddie lifted his staff and added his own scarlet energy to the magick glow.

"You may attack one lone wizard!" Marlowe shouted. "But four of the Five shall cast thee out!"

"No," the demon croaked. "You are all weak, while I am more powerful than you have e'er known."

Abraxas glanced from person to person, his large eyes reflecting the energy that surrounded him.

"The End Time is nigh! Soon, all will be in alignment. When the time is right I shall possess the power of the fifth talisman. Then, I shall conquer this world and you will pay for this indignity!" He turned to Eddie, eyes clouded. "You most of all!"

And the monster was gone.

There was no puff of smoke, or fading away like mist. The huge demon was there one moment, empty air the next. The enchanted circle merely dissipated.

Eddie was so stunned he couldn't move. Daniel Kraft came out of the shadows next to him.

"Look to the ground, all of you!" Marlowe yelled. "He could be anything, a snake or even a bug. Eyes sharp!"

Eddie, Marlowe, and Daniel bent forward and looked through the gravel for anything that moved or jumped. However, Ahbay and Eugenia stood like statues.

"Our power was not enough to bind him." Eugenia's voice sounded far away.

Eddie saw a quick movement near his feet.

"Here!" Daniel pointed and dove to the ground. Eddie shifted his ball of light and illuminated where Daniel was pointing.

"He's gone," Daniel said, keeping his eyes on the ground. There was a metal grate dug into the earth, with openings too small for a man, but a perfect fit for a snake.

Eddie leaned heavily on his staff. He was suddenly exhausted.

Marlowe went down on his knees and stared at the drainage cover. "An escape route. He planned this attack, and even his egress if he should fail!"

Eugenia spoke again, still with that ethereal tone. "Our power should have locked him in place and form."

"Okay, who's gonna tell me what's goin' on?"

All five of them turned to see Luis Vasquez as he loomed over them, his hands folded across his chest in a posture of defiance.

Marlowe took one step forward, waved his stick in a small semicircle, and Luis froze in place, a blank look in his eyes.

"What are you doing?" Eddie demanded.

"He witnessed the battle. We must make him forget," Marlowe explained.

Daniel, Ahbay, and Eugenia murmured in agreement.

"No you don't." Eddie slapped Marlowe's staff away. "This is my partner. You don't do hocus-pocus on my partner."

"Eddie," Marlowe said calmly, "we cannot allow one who does not walk the path to know that demons truly exist."

"He is right." Ahbay moved closer, free of his own temporary paralysis. "It is too great a burden."

"They're wight, Eddie," Daniel lisped. "He'll be much happier if he never knowth the entire epithode happened." He had trouble enunciating, because his teeth were still well beyond his lower lip. As Eddie watched, they grew smaller, but it was a slow process.

"Eddie," Marlowe cautioned, "only an apprentice may know a wizard's true nature."

Eddie looked at Luis, still frozen in place. Would he truly be better off not knowing?

Suddenly, a figure was next to Eddie, and he whirled around with his staff raised.

Drusilicus, wearing a cloak with the hood down jumped back, his hands raised. "Easy."

"What are *you* doing here?" Eddie asked.

"I was following my apprentice, Caleb," Drusilicus said, almost as an apology.

"Where is Caleb?" Eddie asked.

"I seem to have lost him," Drusilicus said, not happy to admit he'd made a mistake. "I was distracted by the commotion and all those witnesses."

"Witnesses?" Marlowe fretted. "There are others here?"

"Jeez," Eddie slapped his head. "The FBI and a half-dozen Mafia goons. I left Cuccolo to tell them all about it!"

"People, people," a voice shouted from behind Marlowe, Eugenia, and Ahbay. "We have a situation."

It was Bankrock, who rubbed his cat's eye ring and transformed it into his staff as he drew closer.

"C'mon, man," Eddie exhaled. "Did we call a convention?"

"I thought you should know," Bankrock clarified. "There are many men with guns at the Ballpark Cafe and they are on their way here."

Eddie turned to Marlowe. "You guys gotta split."

"Split what?" Ahbay asked.

"Leave, go to Marlowe's," Eddie insisted. "Last thing I need is you being interviewed. With what the FBI saw tonight—"

"They saw little," Bankrock admitted.

"What're you talkin' about?" Eddie burst out. "Abraxas was a ten-foot-tall Indian! You think they missed that?"

"Mister Berman, I assure you, they probably didn't see it," Bankrock explained.

"He's right, Eddie," Marlowe commented. "Mortals do not possess the Seeing."

"The what?"

"They simply cannot see supernatural beings."

"He was a giant Indian in loincloth and headdress!" Eddie blurted. "Cuccolo saw that, and my partner saw the demon."

"Abraxas *can* reveal himself," Marlowe expounded.

Bankrock cleared his throat and raised a finger. "That is why mortals *do* occasionally experience supernatural events. However, the others watching, they did not see Abraxas at all."

"But they did see you," Ahbay pointed out. "They will have many questions."

"Fine." Eddie shook his head. "All of you go back to the townhouse. I'll deal with the Feds."

"If you think that's best, Eddie." Marlowe turned to go. "Come, my friends."

Eugenia stood as stock-still as Luis. Finally, Ahbay gently took her arm and guided her toward Central Park West.

"Wait!" Eddie ventured after them. "What made you guys change your minds?"

"Actually, it was Quiptail," Marlowe answered.

"Quip—what?"

"Quiptail. He came and told us you were in grave danger."

"Is that the squirrel you were talking about?" Eddie frowned.

"Exactly," Marlowe agreed. "He made a most passionate plea for you."

"You mean you could understand him?" Eddie said. "He just made a bunch of clicking noises to me."

"I am fluent in Squirrel," Marlowe went on. "Also Lion, Bat, Canary—"

"Great, I ask and you say no, but a damn squirrel can talk you into it." Eddie gave a look to his petrified partner. "How do I unfreeze Luis?"

"I'm sorry, but he witnessed Abraxas in demon form," Bankrock retorted. "Under decree fifteen-oh-four, he must be made to forget any and all—"

"I'm askin' him if he wants to remember or not," Eddie said. "Maybe it's better if he doesn't, like Fangs said—"

"Fangs?" Daniel huffed. "I *have* a name."

"Yeah, yeah," Eddie dismissed. "I'll ask my partner if he can handle knowing the truth. If he can't, I'll bring him to you for a little forget-me-now spell."

"Marlowe," Bankrock protested, "did you inform him that only an apprentice may know our true nature—"

"Fine!" Eddie stormed. "He's my apprentice."

"Oh good," Drusilicus interjected, "just what we need, another untrained practitioner!"

"Well *your* apprentice is trained enough to fool your flabby ass," Eddie pointed at Drusilicus. "I want to talk to Caleb again, and sooner rather than later."

"You can't just make him your apprentice," Bankrock's voice raised as if he were about to have a tiff.

"I've picked. Now, go!"

"To wake him, you only need to rotate your staff in front of him one half-turn clockwise, Eddie," Marlowe instructed. "And *want* him to come out of it."

Eddie nodded. He now understood that intention and desire really did make the magick work. When his life was in danger, he activated the staff's true power through his *want* and *need*.

"You guys put your heads together. Come up with a guaranteed plan to get rid of this demon. Go!"

Daniel spun around quickly, and with a blur of motion, a bat flew off. Marlowe, Ahbay, Bankrock, and Drusilicus started to leave. Marlowe carefully turned Eugenia and guided her away.

The overhead light in the tunnel blinked back on.

Eddie looked at Luis. He was so still he could've been a statue. Eddie held up his staff and moved it a half-circle to the right as he said, "Come on, partner, wake up."

Luis blinked his eyes and his hand went to his face as Eddie returned his staff to its card form. Luis raised his head and looked around, alarmed as memory returned.

"Where is the demon?' he looked left to right.

"Gone, it's gone," Eddie said in a soothing tone, his hands open and extended.

"Those other people?" Luis asked. "The guy with the teeth?"

"Gone as well. Look, Luis, we have to talk. Things probably look pretty strange to you."

"Strange? You wanna talk strange? How did Cuccolo float in the air?"

"Float in the—" Eddie's mouth fell open.

"Yeah, you run up there with your gun drawn and he lifts off the ground and floats off into the woods."

"You didn't see the Indian?"

"What Indian?" Luis frowned.

"But you saw the demon?"

"You're damn straight I saw the demon," Luis said, "and I wanna know what's going on!"

"And I'm goin' to tell you. As best as I can."

"I'm listening."

"Anything I tell you, you have to keep a secret."

Luis looked hurt. "Man, I took a bullet for you, and you don't trust me?"

"This isn't about trust…it's all crazy…but it will explain things. But I have one question, and you have to answer me honestly."

"Shoot."

"Do you want to know the truth? Because, if not, I have a friend that can make you forget everything you just saw."

"I thought we were partners." Luis once again folded his arms over his massive chest.

"We *are,* but it means—"

"I don't care what it means. If it's happening to you, I go through it, too."

Eddie grabbed Luis' arm. "I'm lucky to have you for a friend, Luis."

"'Bout time you knew it."

"*Freeze!*" a voice shouted. "*Hands in the air!*"

Luis and Eddie raised their hands.

"We're NYPD," Luis said, almost calmly. "I got my badge in my—"

"I know who the hell you are," the man said, as he strode out of the darkness. He carried an automatic rifle, and his free hand pulled off a black hood.

Wilcox.

Eddie lowered his hands. "Jesus, Wilcox, you scared the shit out of us."

Wilcox gestured toward Eddie with the rifle. "Keep 'em up, Berman."

Eddie raised his hands as Wilcox pulled out his walkie-talkie.

"I've got them, near the 65th Street arch. Send backup."

"What are you doing, Wilcox?" Luis complained.

"I should've figured you'd be close by, Vasquez," Wilcox glanced over as other black-clothed figures came toward them. "Too bad you didn't know better."

"What is this about?" Eddie asked.

"Edward Berman and Luis Vasquez, by the authority of the Federal Bureau of Investigation, I am placing both of you under arrest." Wilcox pulled a pair of handcuffs out of a leather case on his belt.

"For what?" Luis demanded.

"For the murder of Alfonso Cuccolo." Wilcox turned Eddie around to slap the cuffs on his wrists. "We just found him hanged from a tree, with his hand cut off."

THIRTY-EIGHT

Downtown at Federal Plaza, Eddie sat in an interrogation room, alone. He'd been left there after the third round of questions, this one lasting an hour-and-a-half. At least the third time he was cross-examined by someone other than Wilcox.

The story was mostly truthful from Eddie's point of view.

Yes, he'd received a call from Cuccolo, and they could check his cellphone records.

Yes, he'd been in the park at the crime boss's request.

Yes, he gone out and yelled "NYPD" because he believed Cuccolo to be in danger.

Yes, Cuccolo appeared to rise into the air, but Eddie was sure it was a trick of the light, and that he was actually standing on one of the black-iron mesh tables that littered the area. One could make that mistake in the darkness. Cuccolo ran into the woods. Eddie followed, still concerned for his safety, but soon lost him.

Yes, he ran into his partner nearby.

No, he didn't strangle Cuccolo, or cut off his hand. Until Agent Wilcox arrested him, he didn't even know Cuccolo was dead.

No, he didn't have Cuccolo's missing hand or know where it was.

And on and on. He told the story as clearly as he could, with the assumption the FBI agents didn't see the giant dressed like a display from the world's largest cigar store.

Eddie claimed to be astounded by the act of levitation as much as anyone else. But, at least he offered a plausible explanation.

It was now five AM Saturday morning and Eddie had not been allowed to make a phone call.

The Feds didn't have to let him.

His personal belongings, including his shield and gun, were taken from him, and he sat in his rumpled suit, without even a cup of coffee since his arrival.

He assumed that Luis would tell the same story and not divulge the demon attack in the tunnel. They didn't get a chance to get their stories straight, but he trusted his partner.

Hell, he didn't even know what Luis was *doing* there.

The door opened and Wilcox walked in, followed by Agent Phil Conners. Both seemed not to be tired, despite the hour.

"Captain Jacobs is here, and so is your lawyer from the PBA," Conners announced, a stern expression on his face.

Wilcox put his fists on the table and leaned toward Eddie, his manner almost friendly. "Now, lieutenant, before I let your guests in, I want to know if you are withholding any information—"

"I told you all I know," Eddie said.

"I understand." Wilcox's eyes never left Eddie's. "But you see my problem. Cuccolo went into that grove of trees and so did you. The next thing I know, he's dead."

"Perhaps one of his own men killed him. I understand he had bodyguards nearby—"

"They were all under surveillance. You must have seen *something*, Berman," Wilcox demanded.

"I want to call my wife," Eddie stated. "She'll be worried."

"She'll be more worried when your ass is sitting in federal lockup, Berman," Wilcox answered calmly. "You've just blown a three-year federal investigation this office was conducting on Cuccolo."

"As I've stated before," Eddie pointed out. "What possible motive do I have for offing Cuccolo?"

"Uh, sir?" Conners said. "The captain and lawyer are waiting."

Wilcox stood up straight and backed away from Eddie. "Good point, Conners. We'll let his captain see how his mighty lieutenant has fallen." He headed for the door, but looked over his shoulder at Eddie. "You get booted out of the Central Park Precinct, Berman, and they'll have no place left to put you."

The agents withdrew, and Captain Jacobs entered followed by a heavy-lidded young man with an unruly shock of brown hair and a briefcase.

Eddie rose.

"Sit, lieutenant. I've brought Mr. Antés, your PBA attorney."

"Sir, can I please call my wife?" Eddie pleaded. "I've been here all night."

Jacobs pulled out his cell phone and gave it to Eddie, who pushed in the number and waited for his home phone to ring.

It was picked up on the first ring.

"H-Hello," Cerise said.

"Baby, it's me."

There was a deep exhale of breath on the other end of the phone. "You must stop doing this to me, Eddie."

"'Fraid I didn't have a choice. I've been arrested."

There was an equally sharp intake of air.

"Where's Luis?"

"He's been arrested too."

"Oh my sweet Lord," Cerise said.

"Baby, it's all a big mistake. I've got to get it cleared up, but I don't know when I'll be home."

"Do you need me to come in and get you?"

"No, baby, but call Maria for Luis, she'll be worried. Then get some sleep."

"No chance of that."

"Try. Make excuses to the kids. I'll call you when I'm out of here."

"Take care."

He closed the phone and returned it to Jacobs.

"I'll leave you with the lawyer, Eddie." Jacobs rose from the table.

"Captain, you can stay. I have nothing to hide," Eddie said.

And once again, Eddie went through the carefully edited rendition of the previous evening's events. He concluded with the arrest and the ride down to Federal Plaza in handcuffs.

The two men both listened, though what was keeping the tired young lawyer awake was beyond Eddie.

As he finished, his captain crossed his arms sternly. "You had no business meeting Cuccolo without checking with me, lieutenant."

"You're right, sir," Eddie admitted. "I made a judgment call, and it was the wrong one. But I didn't kill Cuccolo, and I didn't see who did."

At least that was true. Eddie had followed Abraxas and fought him. Someone else hid in those woods.

The warlock.

And Cuccolo had that talisman on him, even after Eddie told him not to bring it. And now the warlock had it, as well as the blood sacrifice to activate it.

The whole thing made his head ache.

"Wrong place at the wrong time, lieutenant. I have to take your shield and weapon. You are suspended until further notice."

"Captain, it was a logical part of the investigation," Eddie defended. "Cuccolo was my only connection to Yamasuto."

"And now he's dead and the Feds are screaming," Jacobs snapped. "Look, Eddie, I have to take action. You and Vasquez are suspended, and I'm turning these homicides over to Manhattan North Homicide and the Urban Crime Task Force."

Eddie stared at the floor to keep his temper in check.

Jacobs went on. "Look at it this way, Eddie, now it's their problem and you get some time off."

"I've filled out the paperwork for your release, lieutenant," Antés finally entered the conversation. "At least you're not stuck in a holding cell until tomorrow."

He held forth a short stack of papers and pointed to places for Eddie to sign.

Then, business done, they left the room, and Eddie sat alone for another half-hour until Agent Conners came in to tell him he could collect his personal effects at the front desk.

There, for the first time since their arrest, he found Luis.

"Hey," Eddie said, as a large envelope was passed to him.

"Hey yourself," Luis mumbled sullenly.

"I told Cerise to call Maria."

"She hears I've been suspended, she gonna blow a gasket."

"I don't see why they suspended you. I was the one who followed Cuccolo—"

"I'm your partner, remember? They want to charge me as an accessory."

They stood without speaking as they replaced their belongings in their pockets. Then they walked out of the building and headed north into the unlit morning.

"Do you think we can get a cab?" Luis asked.

"What were you doing in the park last night?"

"I was following you."

"Following me?"

"Yeah," Luis said. "You've been acting strange. Now I know why."

Eddie exhaled.

"Who were those people?"

"My group. They're kind of…training me."

"Training you for what?"

Eddie stopped and faced his large partner. "To be something more than human."

Luis stared at him for a long moment, then turned and began to walk again. Eddie followed.

"Like that guy with the fangs?"

"No, I don't bite people in the neck."

"Then what?"

They walked on in silence while Eddie tried to get his mind around everything and put it in a way that would make sense. "You saw that demon?"

"Sure did. Uglier than my mother-in-law."

"But not meaner?"

"No one's meaner than my mother-in-law."

"I have to be able to defeat that thing," Eddie stated matter-of-factly.

"What are you training with? A bazooka?"

"That stick I was holding."

"That's it? What are you supposed to be? Robin Hood?"

"The stick is special. It's magic."

Luis came to an abrupt stop again, and stared at Eddie. "You mean that?"

"Yes. The stick, it was the cane of the decapitated homeless guy. Turns out he wasn't homeless. He was a wizard."

"So who killed him?"

"The big-ass demon."

Luis nodded. "That stuff Beverly found, giant hands, strong enough to pull off the limbs. Now, it fits."

"I've been living with the crazy stuff since I touched that cane."

"Why didn't you tell me?" Luis' tired eyes were intense.

"I could barely believe it myself. How could I burden you with it?"

"Because, I'm your partner." Luis turned away from him and looked at the tall buildings. This part of the city was totally empty at this hour. Even the traffic for the Brooklyn Bridge was sparse. "You tell Cerise?"

"I was not to tell anyone. I'm not supposed to tell you."

"So why did you?"

"You saw Abraxas."

"Whatsis?"

"The demon," Eddie said. "Then my mentor—"

"You have a mentor?"

"The old guy with the beard."

"Oh?" Luis began to walk again. "He *has* been hanging out with you a lot."

"He said he was going to make you forget you'd seen it."

"He can do that?"

"Yes. And I-I couldn't let them. I said I wanted to tell you the truth. Then it would be your decision."

"Why? Didn't he think I could handle it?"

Now it was Eddie's turn to stop short. "I'm living it, and I can't handle it. Luis, I'm stuck in a damn fairy tale. Add the fact that if I screw up, this demon could bring about the end of the world."

"Really?" Luis smiled.

"What are you grinning about?"

"I'm hanging with a celebrity."

Eddie shook his head in disgust. "Glad you're impressed."

"Let's get a cab." Luis lifted his arm as one drove up.

A few short minutes later, they were dropped off outside Marlowe's townhouse.

As they paid and got out, Luis started to talk again. "So all those other guys, they're what?"

"Wizards. Except for the guy with the fangs."

"He's a vampire?"

"Now you've got it."

"Happy freakin' Halloween," Luis said, as they reached the top of the steps and Eddie knocked.

Frisha appeared at the door and peeked out.

"Who is it?" she whispered.

"It's Eddie and..." Eddie gave a glance to Luis. "My apprentice."

"When did I become your apprentice?"

"Work with me, Luis," Eddie whispered.

The door opened and Frisha came out and took Eddie in her arms. "We were much worried about thee. Come in."

They stepped into the majestic entrance hall, and Luis' mouth fell open as he stared at the high ceilings, the marble floor, and the huge spiral staircase wrapping around the wrought iron elevator shaft.

"*Madre de Dios*!" Luis exclaimed. "How did…I mean…it's bigger inside than outside."

"Fourth dimensional physics." Eddie was too tired to explain that he didn't know how it worked either.

Frisha was at his arm and led him toward the stairs. "Everyone else has gone to bed, but I sat dozing near the door, in case ye came. I was tol' there are rooms for both of ye."

Eddie nodded. "I'm glad. We're pretty tired."

Frisha brightened. "Do not march up all yonder stairs, Fred. Take the elevator; 'tis much easier and faster."

"Thanks, Frisha," Eddie said, as the older woman returned to her spot near the door.

Luis asked, "Ain't that the lady from the park?"

"Yes."

"She's a wizard, too?"

"A prophetess."

"Why'd she call you Fred?"

"Long story."

Luis was staring at the huge staircase. "Look at all those steps!"

"Don't worry, we'll use the elevator."

"Thank God!"

As Eddie led them, Luis examined the decorative iron cage and found the gate, which perfectly blended into the rest of the structure. Eddie opened it, and a light went on automatically in the cylindrical box suspended in the shaft.

"You sure this thing is safe?" Luis glared at the open cage.

"This elevator shaft is as stable as a concrete tube, Luis," Eddie remarked. "Five of us rode in it the other day."

Luis stared at the top of the iron rails that went up the center shaft of stairs. "The top of this fence looks like spears."

Eddie stepped easily through the gate and Luis, with a combination of turning and ducking, barely got on. Eddie pushed the button marked "2" and the car rattled and slowly began to rise.

"So your 'mentor' lives here?"

"He owns the building."

Luis shrugged. "Who says you can't find a place in Manhattan?"

"He's got some cool things." Eddie was warmed by the idea that he could talk freely. "He has this tea set that serves you by itself. You tell it what you want, and the coffee pot and cup float in the air and pour themselves."

"That's pretty cool," Luis agreed with a nod.

The elevator shuddered and came to a stop.

"That didn't sound good," Eddie worried.

"Maybe I'm too heavy."

They looked out through the gaps in the ironwork. They were about three quarters of the way up, but not at the top.

"How do we help it along?"

"I think I can," Eddie gestured and his staff flew into his hand.

"Wow!" Luis said. "That is awe—"

He didn't finish the word, as with one violent shake, the elevator came loose and plummeted toward the ground.

THIRTY-NINE

Eddie and Luis were thrown to the walls as the box around them fell.

Eddie raised his staff and tried to focus. He was exhausted and bone-weary, but suddenly had a rush of adrenaline.

He forced himself to remember the feeling when he'd floated the tea cup at the breakfast table. This was the same thing, just on a larger scale.

And he needed to do it fast.

"*Stop!*" Eddie yelled, his staff high in his hand.

Instead of their descent being gently slowed, he found himself being thrown to the floor by the sudden cessation of movement, and for a moment he thought they'd hit the ground.

As Luis fell down on top of him, the air in his lungs whooshed out under the weight of his large partner.

"Up!" Eddie gasped, his hand still firm on his staff.

Luis' bulk was suddenly no longer resting on him and Eddie felt himself rise off the floor and into the air.

They were like astronauts in zero-gravity. He wasn't quite sure what was up and what was down.

Above him, Luis began to laugh like a big child. "Oh, man, if my kids could see this!"

Eddie focused his mind on the second floor and the elevator getting to it. He could sense the lift move, but wasn't sure which direction. He didn't want to try to undo what he'd done for fear that they might fall and he wouldn't be able to stop them a second time.

He glanced out through the wrought iron bars and tried to establish up from down. He could see the first floor, and the elevator indeed rose, but with a slow, dreamlike quality.

Eddie tried to push past Luis, and the two of them spun in the air, making Eddie feel nauseous. He concentrated on the second floor and on the gate opening. His staff glowed fiery red. A moment passed, then the elevator stopped and the protective fence moved aside to expose the second floor hallway.

Which was upside-down.

Eddie panicked for a moment, and then decided he must be the one turned the wrong way. He grabbed for the doorway and pulled himself through.

It was like swimming underwater, except he could breathe. His entire body was buoyant, supported by the air currents like a balloon.

Eddie kicked his feet to push his way into the hall.

"Luis, come on!" Eddie braced his feet against the wall to reach into the elevator for his partner.

Luis grabbed his hand and Eddie pulled him free. Then he kicked off the wall and waved the staff in a counterclockwise direction.

He and Luis dropped to the floor.

The elevator noisily fell down the shaft. With a resounding crash, it landed somewhere far below in the basement.

Eddie crawled to the open gate and looked down as a cloud of dust rose up.

"*Madre de Dios*," Luis whispered.

"Sweet Lord," Eddie intoned.

"By Zoroaster!"

Eddie rolled over to see that Marlowe stood over them. He was dressed in a red bathrobe that was trimmed in burgundy velvet and was covered with flower patterns woven into the design. He wore a matching old-fashioned stocking cap, whose top hung down on the right side of his head.

"Are you all right, Eddie?" Marlowe's face reflected concern.

"I'm fine," Eddie responded.

"Someone's been messin' with your elevator, man," Luis pointed out.

"Ah," Marlowe's eyebrows went up. "Sergeant Vasquez, isn't it?"

"Yes," Eddie said, "my apprentice."

"I see." Marlowe offered his hand to help Eddie up. Eddie took it, got up, and the two men pulled Luis to his feet with some difficulty.

"I'm no prophet, but I have a feeling that elevator was booby-trapped." Eddie brushed off his rumpled suit with his hands. "Who could've done it?"

"I'm as shocked as you, Eddie," Marlowe brooded. "We came here straight from the park as you requested."

"Including Drusilicus and Bankrock?" Eddie asked.

"Yes." Marlowe closed his eyes and sighed. "Bankrock felt an overwhelming need to tell us how many regulations you broke tonight with the use of your abilities in public. Then he spent another half-hour fretting that we don't have a plan to stop Abraxas."

"Do Ahbay and Eugenia understand now how dangerous he is?" Eddie said. "I know I got my eyes opened."

"We must face the truth. We have never gone up against the demon at his full power."

Eddie stared into the older man's eyes. "Marlowe, that's a tough thing to accept. I mean, you guys took him on for what, centuries?"

"Yes," Marlowe worried. "And now, we must find a new way to defeat him."

"Well, add to that the fact that there is no doubt that a warlock is working with Abraxas."

"Why?" Marlowe asked.

"While I chased the demon, someone murdered Alfonso Cuccolo and cut off his hand."

"Really?" Marlowe considered this carefully. "His hand. How extraordinary. Tell me everything you know and leave out no detail, large or small."

With a glance at Luis, Eddie retold the story: the beaver that became a wolverine that became an Indian chieftain. He was surprised that his tired mind could recall the events in great detail, and even the names that Cuccolo called out, "Lox" and "Malsum."

The whole time they stood in the hall, Marlowe listened, running his fingers through his beard with one hand, as his other rested on his cane.

Eddie finished by describing the intricately carved wooden box inlaid with turquoise and silver. Marlowe's eyes flashed as Eddie completed his version of the events.

"I have to agree with you, Eddie. You were led off by the Great Evil so that this man could be killed in a very specific way. A blood sacrifice to activate the talisman's power."

"Which leads me to a rather nasty conclusion, Marlowe," Eddie announced. "Abraxas has committed four murders, each killed in a different way: burned in fire, ripped apart, sliced with a sword, and hung."

Marlowe looked at the ceiling in thought. "Four blood sacrifices. Yet we only knew of three talismans."

"Exactly, and last night Abraxas said that when he unleashes the power of the fifth talisman he'll conquer the world."

Marlowe's eyes shifted to Eddie, and he said in a hoarse whisper, "You believe he currently possesses the fourth talisman?"

"He killed Riftstone, but Trefoil he only put in a coma. If blood is needed to activate the talismans—"

"By Zoroaster!" Marlowe barked. "He could have the fourth talisman and be using it!"

"These talismans and sacrifices have all taken place *in* Central Park," Eddie said.

"That is true."

"There's got to be a reason," Eddie affirmed. "I think I might have it. Luis and I found out that Mayan artifacts were stolen from the Metropolitan Museum of Art."

"Right, right," Luis spoke up. "And in spite of all the alarms and things, the thief snuck in and out without being seen or caught on video."

"What were these artifacts?" Marlowe said.

"A couple of sealed earthenware pots," Luis said. "They were supposed to be X-rayed the next day, to find out what was inside."

"Can you get me a photograph of the vessels?" Marlowe asked. "If there were markings on the outside—"

"Marlowe, we both have to get some sleep."

"Of course, you must rest." Marlowe nodded in agreement. "I have slept enough. I must to work."

"So what did Cuccolo have that Abraxas wanted?" Eddie wondered.

"I believe it was one of the four boxes of Glooskap."

"I missed that. Who is he?" Luis asked.

"A Native American deity. According to legend, he gave four exceptional boxes to four mortals. If the Great Evil has one, then we have more to fear."

"What's the problem?" Luis shrugged. "He might sell it on eBay?"

"No." Marlowe's expression was stony. "The talisman grants to the bearer the thing he desires most."

Eddie nodded. "And what 'big, red, and bad' desires most is all of us dead."

FORTY

Eddie woke in the guest room he'd used on his last stay. Someone spoke gently in his ear.

"Eddie? Play with me?"

Eddie leapt up with a start and called out, "Lights."

Candles burst into brilliant fire at his command, and he saw that Bob hovered above the bed. He'd grown stick arms with three fingered hands which tightly held a box of checkers.

A hopeful look moved across Bob's suggestion of a face. Eddie lay back in the bed and tried to slow his breathing.

"I can't play now, Bob." Eddie found for once he wasn't angry at the small ghost. In fact, the creature's gentle wake-up to play was almost endearing.

Almost.

He checked his watch: just past noon.

"I gotta wake up Luis," Eddie said.

Bob's unmatched pair of eyes lit up with excitement.

"Me wake! Me wake!" he tumbled over and over.

For the briefest moment, Eddie considered Bob waking his partner with the same technique the blob of ectoplasm used on him previously.

"No, Bob, you'd better let me do it," Eddie finally decided.

"Awww!" Bob said, disheartened; that is, if he possessed a heart or any other internal organs.

"I'll play whatever game you want next time I'm here."

"Promise?" Bob said, his attitude elated.

"I promise."

"Okay, Edddieee!" Bob cried gleefully and put the box on a table, then disappeared through the wall.

"What did I get myself into?" Eddie got out of bed.

He was dressed in a pair of pajamas, transformed from his suit. He grabbed his staff, which had been in the bed next to him.

He made his way down the hall to the bathroom. There, he showered and shaved, again delighted by the fact that the exact grooming products he wanted were available on a shelf.

Eddie placed his pajamas on the wooden hanger, which rested on the towel rack, and with a wave of his staff altered them back to their original form. The transformation went well, except when he opened his cell phone, it now used Chinese characters.

He sighed and walked down the hall. On the front of each door he noticed a subtle accessory he'd overlooked: a small brass plate with lettering etched on it.

The one for his door was blank, but when he touched the doorknob his name inscribed itself into the metal, as if an invisible hand engraved it.

He continued down the hall to the next door, and looked at the little plate. In fancy lettering, there were the words:

Luis Vasquez

Eddie knocked on the door.

A mutter came from within. Eddie opened the door and said, "Lights" as the candles burst into flame.

"Jeez!" Luis sat up in bed and rubbed his face. He wore a pair of boxer shorts and a muscle-style undershirt.

"Come on, we have to get moving," Eddie told him.

"Why, we got no jobs." Luis covered his face with a pillow and lay back down.

Eddie stood still for a moment. Luis was right, they were suspended. He could go home in time to help make dinner. Even more important, he could spend time with his mother.

While he did, the demonic bastard and whoever helped him would be closer to the completion of their plans.

Eddie set his jaw. "Because, I've got to train, and you are my freakin' apprentice."

"You got a better term for me? You make it sound like I go out for coffee."

"I'll see what I can do. Bathroom is down the hall. Breakfast is downstairs."

"Yeah, and I shouldn't use the elevator."

"Can you find your way?"

Luis shrugged. "I think so."

"Also, watch out. There is a small green ghost—"

"A what?"

"A ghost, named Bob—"

"Bob?"

"Yeah, well he likes to scare people."

Luis sat up in bed. "Isn't that what ghosts do?"

"Well, yeah, but he won't hurt you. He just likes to surprise. He got me in the shower the other day."

"Great." Luis wiped his hand one more time over his face. "There'd better be coffee when I get down there."

"You want me to call Maria?"

"I'm a big boy. You call Cerise, I'll call Maria. Head downstairs. Considering just how many stairs there are, I'll be down by two in the afternoon."

Eddie nodded, walked out, and started the trek downward to the first floor.

He pulled out his cell as he walked and called home. He believed he got the right number, even in Chinese.

"Hello!" Cerise answered, a hopeful tone to her voice.

"Hi, baby," Eddie said.

"You sound better, sugar." Cerise's voice was tired but under control. "You're not in jail, are you?"

"No, I'm not. But Luis and I were so wiped we stayed here in the city."

"Where did you go?"

"That guy I brought out, Marlowe? He's got a place and put us up."

"When are you coming home?"

"I'll be home tonight, I promise."

"I'm counting on you, Eddie. I *really* need you home by seven-thirty?"

There was something in the back of Eddie's mind, but he couldn't recall it. "No problem, baby, I'll be there."

"Tell me what happened."

Eddie quickly gave her the edited explanation as he trudged down the steps. The entire time, Cerise listened patiently.

"So, I'm suspended until further notice."

Cerise sighed. "At least you're not in jail."

"Someone knew I would be there, Cerise. Someone set me up so I would be suspected for the murder. Luis and I are going to nose around, see if we get any leads."

"Is that wise, sugar? You go near an official investigation while suspended and they have grounds for dismissal."

"It'll be okay, baby. I'm definitely traveling *only* in unofficial circles."

"Just come home tonight, sugar, please? Seven-thirty."

Eddie smiled. "I adore you, baby."

"We'll get through this. Seven-thirty, don't forget."

He hung up just as he reached the bottom step and walked to the breakfast room.

Marlowe sat with a coffee cup, reading a large and dusty leather-bound book that appeared ancient. Spread out on the table were several very old books in various conditions: four scrolls, one of which looked as if it might fall apart then and there, and a stone carved tablet with what looked like hieroglyphics.

The open book was written in strange characters that didn't look like any language. The symbols were shaped like small triangles with little tails hanging from different locations.

"What's all this?" Eddie asked.

"Research Bankrock found," Marlowe answered, as casually as if he was riffling through the morning newspaper. "This writing is Cuneiform, the language of ancient Babylon."

"Silly me." Eddie went to the chafing dishes, which once again held fresh, hot food. He helped himself to bacon and eggs. "What is the book about? Good plot, exciting characters?"

"All of these are prophecies of the End Times," Marlowe gestured at the scrolls and stone tablet. "All cultures have their stories, but Babylonians were the most fascinated by the destruction of the world."

"Big partygoers, huh?"

"Actually, the festival of Eaoster was quite a celebration. Went on for days, lots of costumes and drunkenness."

"And now we celebrate it as Easter?"

"The name was passed down, but it was more like Mardi Gras or Carnivalé. That would be the closest modern equivalent."

"Anything in your reading material to help us?"

"This is an interesting correlation." Marlowe's hands gingerly turned the book's pages as if they were quite delicate. "The information herein was written 2,500 years ago, by a prophet named Abednego during the reign of the Babylonian king, Belshazzar, the son of Nebuchadnezzar. The book I'm holding was hand copied from the original scrolls more than five hundred years ago."

"Great. But, is there anything to help us in the here and now?" Eddie faced the coffee set and said, "Coffee, light no sugar."

The cup and saucer leapt at his words, as though eager to have someone to serve. The coffee pot poured, the creamer pirouetted and added its contribution, and the china with the finished mixture floated into Eddie's hand.

"Considering this prophet didn't even know there was a land across the sea that would be one day called America, it is quite… poignant."

Eddie sat across from Marlowe. "In what way?"

"The author speaks of a distant future, and a place where a great oasis is in the middle of a man-made desert—"

"That could be Central Park."

"He claims it to be a place of great power. Then, here," Marlowe turned the page, "he writes of a time when a Great Evil will rise, casting aside the fetters that bind it."

"Sounds like our guy." Eddie chewed on the delicious bacon.

"Here it says, 'And it shall gain great power from five potent charms.'"

"We know he's got at least three, right?"

"Abednego also mentions those who carry a dark power. This allows the Great Evil to bring down on mankind the final destruction."

"Points to our warlock," Eddie said. "Last night, I was set up by someone. You've got to ask yourself, who knew I would be there?"

"Those of us here, of course. But, I cannot believe that Eugenia or Ahbay have anything to do with the Great Evil."

"What about Daniel? I mean, he showed up in the nick of time. How did he know where to be?"

"He was on a mission for me in the park, but he told me you asked him to track a snake?"

"That's right!" Eddie slapped his forehead as memory returned. "The only tracks away from two of the murders were of a snake. I was thinking that Abraxas left the scene of each murder as a snake."

"Daniel said it was very slow going, but following a broken path he happened to be led to that tunnel just as the demon attacked you."

"I don't want to complain about someone saving my life, but the timing is suspicious. What about the others? I mean, besides Eugenia and Ahbay, Drusilicus showed up with Bankrock, and Dru said Caleb was lurking nearby."

"A large list of suspects." Marlowe frowned.

"Marlowe, I *know* it wasn't me who set that trap, and I don't think it was you."

"Thanks for the vote of confidence," Marlowe sniffed.

"You're the one who said it had to be a powerful wizard to make Alex throw himself into that fire. I gotta ask, who is more powerful than one of the Five?"

Marlowe blanched a bit, looked to his book, and began to turn pages frantically.

"What did I say?" Eddie asked.

"A passage I read, I just scanned it, but now that you—" Marlowe found the correct page and reread it. "Here it is."

"Can you translate?"

Marlowe studied the odd script. "It says that one of the elements upon which the world is created has fallen to an angry heart."

"Well, that's clear as mud. Care to translate your translation?"

"One of the elements could be one of the Five. We each carry a representation of the five elements. One who has fallen to an angry heart, that could be someone with a vendetta."

"So, this prophesy suggests that it *might* be one of the Five?"

"I don't know, Eddie. Although we do not spend much time together, these are my friends, I have known them for centuries, and fought by their sides." Marlowe's eyes were suddenly quite sad.

"I have to look at everyone as part of the investigation. I also need to question the people who were here about that elevator…"

"I examined it, Eddie. The supporting cables were damaged by magical means. It's a good thing you were at the ready."

"I got lucky." Eddie looked at the other books and scrolls. "What else did you find?"

"Have you heard of the Hebrew name for Hell, Eddie—Genhinnom?" Marlowe lifted one of the scrolls.

"No, what does that have to do with—"

"The Hebrew name comes from an actual valley named Ben Hinnom, the sons of Hinnom. Hinnom comes from 'nohem,' which means 'to moan.'"

"The sons of moaning?" Eddie attempted.

"There was a place in ancient Judea, where they would sacrifice children to a most horrible god, Molech. There stood a large, hollow metal idol, and worshippers would light a fire in it until its arms were white hot and then place their child— their own child—on the scorching limbs."

"Oh, God," Eddie winced. "Why?"

"It was a way to receive power," Marlowe said. "There was a fortress with seven rooms. If you sacrificed flour, one room was opened to you, a ram and it was four. But if you sacrificed a child to this god, the seven seals were released and all the rooms were open to you."

"The seventh seal," Eddie pondered. "Isn't that something about the end of the world?"

"Exactly!" Marlowe considered for a moment and picked up another scroll to examine it. "According to the prophecies of St. John the Divine, seven seals are opened to rain down destruction and the final battle for this world."

"Armageddon," Eddie said with a nod.

"You can see how these two predictions use some of the same terminology," Marlowe said. "Through my research I have found that Molech is indeed one of the Great Evil's most ancient identities. This must have to do with the fifth talisman."

"So the fifth talisman, whatever it is, can open the seventh seal. Are we any closer to knowing what it is?"

"Not yet. However, this you will find interesting." Marlowe unrolled a parchment scroll. On it was a very good drawing of the statue of Amatsu Mikaboshi, surrounded by Japanese characters.

"Hey! That's like the drawing I got from Akio," Eddie said.

"Indeed." Marlowe pointed at the letters on either side of the center figure. "And these words warn of an ancient charm that must not be touched, 'lest it awaken the evil deity.'"

"Let me get my copy," Eddie said, got up and walked out to the living room, where he'd left the book, *Talismans through the Ages*. He brought the book into the breakfast room, and extracted the copied drawing.

"Well," Eddie said, "it's like closing the barn door after the horses have—"

A folded brown paper slipped out of the book and fell to the table.

"What's that?" Marlowe asked and picked it up.

Eddie riffled through the book. "I dunno. It was in the book."

Marlowe took in a breath sharply.

"What is it?"

Marlowe looked up at Eddie. "This is virgin parchment, and it is inscribed."

Marlowe turned the paper around and on it Eddie saw a red-brown circle with symbols drawn within it.

"I repeat. What is it?"

"This sigil is used to bind and control demons." Marlowe turned it to stare at the symbol.

"What kind of ink is this?" Eddie tentatively touched the markings.

"It is not ink; it is blood," Marlowe said. "Where did you say you bought this book?"

"At Magickal Cherub. Caleb was copying something when I walked in. Looks like I need to have another talk with Drusilicus' apprentice."

"I believe so!" Marlowe studied the artwork. "This is not the work of a beginner."

"Marlowe, could an enchanter do all these things? I mean, throw Alex into the fire, make that woman do the release spell, all this other stuff?"

"With the right talisman, many things are possible," Marlowe observed. "Is it wise to question him by yourself?"

"Marlowe," Eddie picked up the parchment, folded it and put it in his jacket pocket, "I'm under suspension and suspected of murder. I have to find out who is doing this, or at least eliminate suspects who aren't."

A voice came from the doorway. "Besides, who said he would do it by himself." Luis walked in. He was clean and wearing his wrinkled suit.

"Oh, sergeant, I neglected to clean your clothes. No matter." Marlowe waved his hand and a circle of white light surrounded Luis, starting from the ground and rising to his shoulders. As it passed, the suit became clean and perfectly pressed.

"Man!" Luis admired his outfit. "That's a lot better than dry-cleaning. I didn't have to send it out or even take it off."

"Get some food, partner," Eddie said. "We have a case to solve."

"Yes sir, lieutenant." Luis went over and opened one of the chafing dishes. "Egg burritos! Can you believe it? It's just what I wanted."

Eddie smiled. "Wait'll you try the coffee."

FORTY-ONE

By subway, Eddie and Luis headed downtown to Alphabet City, which gave Eddie a chance to tell Luis about his previous meetings with Caleb. He also mentioned Drusilicus and the night of his initiation.

Luis listened and asked appropriate questions.

For Eddie, it felt good to have his partner to bounce ideas and review the strange happenings of the last few days.

Soon, they arrived at a tenement two blocks from Magical Cherub. They climbed the stairs to a fifth-floor walkup and knocked on the door.

"Who's there?" came a voice to Eddie's repeated rapping.

"Open up, police," Eddie ordered.

A small glass eye opened on the door as a cover was moved, allowing the occupant to peer out.

"Oh, it's you," the male voice snorted.

Eddie glanced down the hall, made sure it was empty, then said, "That's right. Now do you open the door, or do I pull out my staff and huff and puff?"

The door made several clicks and rattles, and slowly opened to reveal Caleb. He was still dressed in black and Luis stared coldly at his piercings.

"Who's the muscle?" Caleb blocked the opening with his arm.

"My apprentice and my partner," Eddie stated.

"We gonna stand here in the hall or what?" Luis demanded.

Caleb took a look over his shoulder then stepped out of the way. "Come in."

Eddie and Luis entered the apartment. It looked as if it hadn't been painted since 1950. The flat-white paint on the ceiling was cracked and flaked. There was clutter and dirt everywhere.

"I mean," Caleb pointed out, "I couldn't keep you out if I wanted to, could I?"

"Kay?" a female voice came from the other room.

Caleb walked to a door slightly ajar from clothes that hung on it. "Hey, babe. You gotta split."

He walked in, there were muffled protests, a quick exchange, then Caleb came out and pulled the door shut as far as the hanging clothes would allow.

"Girlfriend?" Eddie asked.

"Something like that." Caleb had such a smug expression on his face, Eddie felt an overwhelming desire to slap it off.

Easy, he thought, *you didn't become a detective without self-control. You've dealt with jerks like this before.*

The door was opened, and a woman about age thirty-five with fiery-red hair came out, adjusting the blouse she'd hastily put on. She looked at both men.

I know her, Eddie thought.

She gave a quick peck on Caleb's cheek, and said, "Next week?"

Caleb stared impassively at Eddie. "Whatever."

Eddie stepped in the path of the door and put up an arm. The redheaded woman stopped and stared at Eddie. Fear flashed in her eyes.

"I know you," Eddie told her. "You were the woman who led the bonfire on May Day."

"You mean Beltane." She glanced back at Caleb.

"We're with the police," Eddie said.

She flushed and looked down at the floor. "I've already spoken to the police about that poor young man. Imagine, throwing himself in the fire that way."

"Boy, you are way off." Caleb was still focused on Eddie. "She has nothing to do with—"

"I'll be the judge of that." Eddie turned to Luis. "Take her out into the hall, and get her name and vitals."

Luis nodded. "You be okay with the little shit?"

"That's no way to talk about Kay," the woman looked back adoringly. "He's truly magical."

"Yeah, I'm achievin' higher consciousness just looking at him," Luis mocked. "C'mon, miss."

"Actually, it's missus," she said as they exited the apartment. "Look, my husband doesn't need to know about this, does he?"

The door closed.

Eddie looked at Caleb, who leaned against the wall in an offhanded manner. "They find me irresistible."

"Playing with married chicks is dumb and dangerous," Eddie said.

Caleb shrugged. "They're a lot more generous than young girls."

"And easy to manipulate with a few of your toys."

Caleb gave another small shrug. "So what do you want, Newling?"

In one swift movement, Eddie picked the young man up by his shirt and smashed him bodily against the wall.

"Ow!" Caleb yelped.

"That's Lieutenant Berman, punk."

Caleb pulled something from his pocket. There was a gray flash of light. Eddie found his hand forced to release Caleb, and he was pushed back.

Caleb landed on his feet and lifted the golden medallion by its chain over his head. He began to chant in that strange language the wizards used as the golden circle glowed brighter.

Eddie held out his hand and effortlessly his staff flew into it.

Caleb chanted louder as electricity flashed and sparkled around his body.

Eddie was pissed. "Oh shut up."

A blast of red light shot from the tip of his staff and Caleb was thrown across the room, through the door of the bedroom, to land on the bed, the gold charm knocked from his fingers.

The hall door opened and Luis looked in. "You okay?"

Eddie called out, "Our young friend just wanted to play."

The red-haired woman glanced in. "Is Kay all right?"

"He's fine, ma'am," Luis smiled. "I got your information, you can go."

"A-all right," she gave a faint smile. "And you won't call my husband?"

"Not unless it's necessary," Luis said, and the woman turned and quickly headed down the stairs.

"Ooooh, man," Caleb moaned from the next room. "You didn't have to hurt me." He tried fitfully to sit up, then fell back on the bed.

"Hey, I'm a Newling, remember? I don't know what I'm doing." Eddie leaned his staff on the crook of his arm to take out his notebook and pencil. "Now, I need to know where you were yesterday between the hours of ten PM and midnight."

Caleb finally sat up, and put his legs over the side of the bed. "I was around."

"He's playin' us." Luis glanced at Eddie.

"I'm sure he wants to be cooperative. Don't you, Caleb?" Eddie coaxed.

The young man stood up carefully. "I don't have to tell you nothing. I got rights."

"Guess we should run away with our tails between our legs." Luis took a menacing step forward.

"Sergeant, we don't have to waste a lot of energy on him," Eddie said. He held up his staff and a red glow issued from it. It surrounded the young man and lifted him off the ground.

"Hey, you can't do that. I'll report you!" Caleb's eyes grew wide with fear.

"Good idea, right, sergeant?" Eddie ignored Caleb's protests. "Let the young man call City Hall and report that I used my *magic* against him."

"They take those complaints *very* seriously," Luis agreed with a nod.

Caleb began to spin vertically in midair, slowly at first, then with more speed. After about two dozen dizzying revolutions, he stopped with his head facing the floor.

"Oh God," Caleb moaned and put his hand to his mouth, "I'm gonna puke."

Eddie leaned close to the upside-down man. "Now, maybe you want to cooperate? If not, I can show you what I've learned. I should warn you, I make mistakes, especially with transformations—"

"I'll talk!" Caleb blurted, the fear on his face shifting to panic. Eddie surmised that being Drusilicus' student, Caleb probably knew what unpleasant things were possible.

Caleb spun again, this time arriving head up. Eddie waved his staff and the boy collapsed to the floor.

"Were you in the park last night?"

"Yeah," Caleb said. "But I had nothing to do with what went down."

"What do you know about 'what went down?'"

Caleb reddened at this. "It was all over the Internet. Some bigshot hood was killed."

"So where were you, punk?" Luis demanded.

"I got friends, I hang out." Caleb got up off the floor to sit on the bed with an unhappy glance at Eddie's staff. "The park is loaded with places of power. I like to go and feel the energy. It's one of my exercises."

"You know I can compel you to tell the truth?" Eddie told him.

"Yeah, I know," Caleb put his hands up, as if surrendering, though a look of anger flashed in his eyes.

"This look familiar to you?" Eddie withdrew the parchment with the red symbols on it.

"I know what it is." Caleb considered the paper. "It's pretty good. But I do better work."

"I found it in the book you sold me at Magickal Cherub. You were copying something when I came in."

"I copy lots of things. But I don't do parchment." Caleb gave the design another look. "Whatever you use to make a talisman has a vibration. Parchment has a weak one. I prefer metals. I studied jewelry-making."

"It's drawn in blood," Eddie said.

Caleb shrugged. "What else?"

"I have to tell you, there are a lot of questions about you. First of all, we show up and we find you with the girl who released the demon that killed your buddy."

"He wasn't my buddy."

"I know," Eddie replied. "He was your competition to get a staff."

"Quite a coincidence that now you're dating her," Luis suggested.

"I'm not dating her; she comes over for a little recreation." Caleb smirked. "Besides I met her the day Alex died. Nothing wrong with that."

"So he has motive," Luis said to Eddie.

"And opportunity. He could teach the young lady a few spells." Eddie turned to Luis. "Did she look hypnotized to you, sergeant?"

"Could've been," Luis confirmed.

"Now, the other murders involved talismans," Eddie returned his focus to Caleb.

Luis also glared at Caleb. "The lieutenant tells me that's your area of expertise, right, dude?"

Caleb looked as if he'd eaten something distasteful.

"Look, I didn't do it. Alex was always bragging. Said a crazy old wizard told him about the Amulet of Abracadabra."

"Which crazy old wizard?" Eddie insisted.

"He wouldn't say," Caleb protested. "He claimed he was going to find it. He just wanted me to locate the release spell."

"Where have you been since I last saw you?"

"Visiting my mother in New Jersey, okay? I got back in the city last night, called my master, and went to the park. He said it would be good for me to build my energy."

"Wait a minute," Eddie held up his hand. "Drusilicus *told* you to go to the park?"

"He doesn't tell me what to do. He teaches me. You guys don't understand at all. He's my master. I mean, I would die for him."

Luis and Eddie exchanged glances. Drusilicus used Caleb as an alibi and now Caleb was using Drusilicus.

"You know anything else you want to share?"

"Heard a demon made a fool out of you," Caleb snickered.

"Now how would you hear about that on the Internet?" Luis asked, giving Eddie a sidelong look.

Caleb flushed red again.

"You ever get to use a staff?"

Caleb faced Eddie with a serious look. "Now and then my master gives me a taste."

"You ever use his staff without permission?" Eddie said.

"No, he passes the staff to me, and I get some time before it goes back to him."

"How does he do that?"

Caleb shrugged. "He just closes his eyes and concentrates. Then, I feel all this power flow into me. Man, it's like being God."

"Don't let it go to your head, kid," Luis grumbled.

"You don't know what it's like until you take it in your hand."

"How does it return to him?"

"After about five minutes, the energy just flows out of me, and it's done. It's all standard practice, right?"

"Don't leave town," Eddie pointed at the young man. "I will want to talk to you again. You hide on me, I'll hunt you down."

Caleb's mouth grew hard. "I bet you will."

"We'll let ourselves out." Luis moved to the door.

They went back into the hall and walked down the stairs, as Eddie returned his staff to his wallet.

"That thing makes interrogation a lot easier," Luis marveled.

"That was odd about the staff going to him. Marlowe never mentioned training techniques that allow the apprentice to use a staff. He said it was all theoretical."

"Maybe Drew-silly-cuss has his own style," Luis shrugged.

"It could explain why Caleb's charms work so well. What's to stop him from putting some of the staff's energy into them?"

"Can he do that?"

"Marlowe said talismans are like a battery that stores power. We need to talk to Drusilicus."

"Hey, I don't have to start calling you 'master' or anything, do I?"

"I dunno," Eddie considered it. "I might like it."

"Man," Luis shook his head, "that is so *I Dream of Jeannie.*"

FORTY-TWO

They made their way up to Fifth Avenue and found Number 20, just north of Washington Square in Greenwich Village.

They stood out front of the huge structure, an elaborate throwback to another era. It was several stories high and painted white, with large marble columns out front, magnificent balconies, and intricate architectural touches.

"Not bad digs," Luis exclaimed. "Wasn't this built for the Vanderbilts?"

"It *is* pretty fancy." Eddie eyed the building. "Marlowe's house is only ornate on the inside."

"I think this Drusilicus guy needs more attention. He's got this Caleb kid worshipping him."

"Rubs me the wrong way," Eddie grumbled. "I'd like to know if Caleb has a rap sheet. Trouble is we don't have a last name."

"It's Heinz, like the Ketchup," Luis said.

Eddie stopped. "How did you—"

"The old-fashioned way. I looked at his mail box on the way out."

Eddie threw his head back and laughed.

"What? That was easy, Cop 101." Luis was surprised by his partner's reaction.

"I know, that's why I'm laughing. I've been so busy with this wizard stuff, I've forgotten basic detective skills."

"I thought it's what we do."

"I'd better bear that in mind," Eddie noted as they ascended the stairs. "Police skills are my only advantage over the Great Whatchamacallit."

Eddie rang the bell, and a tall man opened the door. He was dressed immaculately in a morning suit, gray cutaway coat, black and gray striped pants, and a silver satin cravat with a matching vest. His gray hair was thinning, and he wore a look of disdain.

"May I help you?" he spoke with a very proper British accent.

"Edward Berman and Luis Vasquez to see Drusilicus Greywacke," Eddie said.

"The master is with guests."

"Look here, Jeeves—" Luis began.

"Actually, it's Howell, sir." The butler looked down his nose at Luis, a difficult process because the immense detective was taller and wider than he.

"Whatever," Luis objected. "I personally don't care if 'the master' is with the Pope. We're NYPD."

Howell was nonplussed. "I shall inform him, sir. Please wait here."

He turned curtly and sauntered out of the room.

"Man, he looks down on you even with his back," Luis said as the butler exited.

"Why was I not surprised ol' Dru would have a butler?" Eddie snorted.

"This whole place is like a stage set. Big house, butler at the door. Like it's all part of the presentation. Why's he trying so hard?"

"I'd like to find out."

The butler returned to the door and held it open. "Mr. Greywacke will see Mr. Berman."

Luis and Eddie stepped forward.

Howell moved to block the door with his body. "Mr. Vasquez has been asked to wait out here," he insisted, and after a short hesitation added, "please."

"Look, you stuffed shirt—"

"Luis," Eddie urged, "it's okay. I'll go in alone."

"He can't do that. We are investigating a murder—"

"Unofficially," Eddie pointed out.

Luis deflated a bit."Yeah, right."

"Where do I go?" Eddie looked to the butler.

"Follow me, sir." Howell led him through the door.

Eddie entered an elaborate hallway, with moulding on the walls and a picture railing that was trimmed with gold leaf. The room looked freshly painted and the walls were the most amazing shade of blue.

Even so, it was much more reasonable in appearance than Marlowe's townhouse. The ceiling was high, but at least it logically fit inside the building.

The butler led him down the long hall and past several shut doors, all with baroque trims, detailed colors, and intricate woodwork. At the end of the hall was a pair of double doors, festooned with more gold trim than all the previous.

"If I may be so bold," Howell wondered. "I understand you are a wizard, sir?"

"Yeah, you too?"

The butler raised an eyebrow, then moved close as if to impart a great secret. "Actually, sir, I'm a werewolf."

"And your name is 'Howl'?"

"H-O-W-E-L-L, sir. Something of a family joke I suspect."

"So, I've heard some supernatural folks are all for the human world being destroyed. Which side are you on?"

"Werewolves in general don't get involved, sir. We only wish to roam free."

"Your job a problem during the full moon?" Eddie asked.

"We manage, sir." The butler opened the door.

Eddie walked into a massive sitting room. There were chaise lounges, sofas with carved wooden legs, and overstuffed chairs, all giving the appearance of restored antiques.

As he entered, Drusilicus stood and turned toward him. As did Eugenia, Ahbay, and Trefoil.

Eddie stopped in his tracks and pondered the situation for a moment. "I guess I missed the memo about the meeting."

"Lieutenant." Drusilicus became the charming host. "I'm glad you're here. Do join us."

He motioned to an empty chair, where Eddie tentatively sat. At the same time the others returned to their seats. Eddie had the feeling he was in the witness seat while a jury watched.

"We were just speaking of you." Drusilicus returned to his own chair.

"Why am I not surprised?" Eddie responded. "By coincidence, my partner and I were just talking about you."

"Ah yes, your *partner*," Drusilicus uttered, and emphasized the word with distaste. "You've chosen the good Sergeant Vasquez as an apprentice, I understand."

"Yes, and he came in very handy when I spoke to *your* apprentice today."

Drusilicus stared. "You met with Caleb, again? Without me there?"

"I was not aware I needed your permission or presence," Eddie muttered. "He was most cooperative."

"That's all veddy lovely." Eugenia seemed very subdued, after the previous evening's encounters. "Edward, we must discuss the situation."

"The situation?" Eddie repeated.

"Yes," Ahbay said apologetically. "We are all concerned."

"About what?"

Ahbay looked at Eugenia and Trefoil for support, then returned his gaze to Eddie. "The incidents that occurred last evening—"

"We were not prepared for the Great Evil," Eugenia blurted out. "I mean, as he is now."

"The way he faced us in the park," Ahbay added. "He was completely unafraid."

"Thass not the way it used to be," Trefoil pointed out.

"And our combined powers were not strong enough to secure him." Eugenia partly rose from her chair. She was more excited than Eddie had seen her. "He should not have been able to transform or escape with four of the Five using a binding spell."

"He shoulda been helpless," Trefoil grumbled.

"This is most true!" Ahbay agreed.

"Okay," Eddie raised his hands as if to quiet the commotion, "so Big Red is pumped up. That means we have to be ready for him."

"Our abilities are weakened." Eugenia returned to her seat and obviously forced herself to remain calm. "Whatever happened in Trefoil's room stole a portion of our powers."

"Add to that," Ahbay advised, "your lack of experience—"

"Right," Eddie jeered, his tone sardonic. "I bet Drusilicus has been very worried about that."

"Lieutenant," Drusilicus admitted, "believe me when I say that I hold you in the highest esteem—"

"Sure you do," Eddie snapped.

"Come on, Eddie," Trefoil said. "You got lucky, but you're in way over your head!"

"I maybe saved all of us last night, Trefoil. Something went wrong in your room, and *I* got us out."

"And then you walked into a trap. You were only rescued by the actions of others," Drusilicus pointed out.

"Look, man, don't take it the wrong way," Trefoil acknowledged. "You think fast on your feet, I'll give you that. But, Abraxas played you for a chump."

"So far, he's played all of you for chumps. He knows what you are going to do before you do it." Eddie looked at each of them. They would not meet his eyes.

"Look, I'll admit the odds ain't good," Trefoil lamented. "I think if we had someone more practiced in the arts, we'd have a better chance."

"And Drusilicus has been after my staff since the night I got it!" Eddie accused.

"Which was only a few nights hence,." Drusilicus's face took on a cruel countenance. "Honestly, lieutenant, I don't see why you resist. The mortal world rests upon the ability of the Five to defeat this creature. Shouldn't we fight him with one who has spent his life mastering the necessary skills?"

"I'll tell you why you shouldn't." Eddie rose from his chair. "Because *somebody* wants me out of the way. Since I was summoned, I have been confronted by people who didn't want me to carry a staff. Then, there are people who don't want me to do anything until I've been trained, and finally there are people who should be on my side and are not!"

On the last statement, Eddie glared at Eugenia and Ahbay, who were much too fascinated with the floor to look at him.

"And speaking of people who say one thing and mean another, Drusilicus. I came here to talk to you alone. But since we are airing our laundry, I wanted to question you about your boy, Caleb."

"Ah!" Drusilicus boasted. "Then he verified my reason for being in the park last night?"

"Not quite. According to him, you suggested he go. It seems odd to me that you would tell him to do something, and then follow him as he does it. A very convenient excuse."

"Lieutenant, I don't know if I like your tone," Drusilicus responded haughtily.

"Let him speak," Ahbay raised his head.

"He also told me you give him opportunities to use your staff," Eddie announced.

The entire energy changed in the room. Eugenia, Ahbay, and Trefoil all shifted their gazes from Eddie to Drusilicus. Drusilicus' face went red for a moment, and he rose a bit from his chair, thought better of it, and returned to his seat.

"It is not uncommon to give an apprentice a chance to have 'hands-on' training," Drusilicus spoke in a flustered tone.

"I have never heard of such a thing," Ahbay's voice was very controlled. "In my day, we taught through reading and exercises to balance the Yin and the Yang. To allow an apprentice such power—"

"I supervised him the entire time!" Drusilicus was now on the defensive.

"Even so," Eugenia gawked, "one is only allowed to wield a staff after one has been initiated. You cannot allow a mere apprentice to—"

"Caleb is gifted!" Drusilicus interrupted. "And he has far more training than this"—he gestured to Eddie—"excuse for a

Newling. Why do we allow him to carry a staff at all, let alone be one of the Five?"

"And so we come to the crux of the matter!" Eddie said. "You just don't like me having a staff, period."

Drusilicus did rise this time, as he was rapidly losing his support. "Do not take me wrong, lieutenant. From what little we have seen, you are an excellent police officer, but you hardly have a background in the metaphysical."

"I didn't ask for the pleasure of sitting in your drawing room —"

"It's an Athenaeum," Drusilicus' voice grew louder.

"Whatever the hell it is, I don't need this. I didn't ask for this honor, and I have to tell you, after dealing with this bunch of two-faced losers, I would be happy to give up my membership to your little group."

"We are offering you that opportunity, Eddie," Trefoil nodded solemnly.

"What I want is a straight answer." Eddie turned to face Drusilicus. "Why were you in the park last night, really?"

Drusilicus hesitated. "I was there because someone called my mirror and told me to be there."

"Who was it?"

Drusilicus exhaled deeply. "Frisha."

"Frisha?" Eddie was taken aback. "When?"

"I'm not sure. I left right after she called. She said not to tell anyone, but she told me she'd had a vision of terrible tidings. There was a chance you could be killed. I walked down to Washington Park and teleported immediately."

Trefoil sat up in his chair. "The old girl *is* a prophetess."

Eugenia piped up, "Whatever inspired her to contact you, Drusilicus?"

"I-I don't know," Drusilicus stammered.

"Why do I get a feeling," Eddie folded his arms, "that there is more to this than you are telling me?"

"What difference does any of this make?" Trefoil argued.

Eddie faced the older man. "It might make all the difference." He returned his glare to Drusilicus.

"Well," Drusilicus looked like a wild animal caught in a trap. "She said that you might be…well, killed…and that I should be there."

"Did she explain any further?" Eddie demanded.

"No, but I assumed I should be there to take up your staff."

"See, that proves the old girl is losing it," Trefoil dismissed. "She was totally wrong. Eddie, you came out of it without a scratch."

"Thanks to Daniel Kraft," Eddie fumed. "And no thanks to you, Drusilicus."

"I arrived as quickly as I could," his face flushed again. "I would have added my arm to the battle, but by the time I arrived, it was over."

"Well, for once I think you've told me the truth." Eddie made his way toward the door. "I'll leave you all in this Athena… whatever you call it. But, I'll add one thing. You can have my staff when you pry it from my cold, dead fingers. So you better decide if you want to kill me or not."

Without another word, Eddie left the room and slammed the door behind him.

There are other ways, thought one of the people who remained.

FORTY-THREE

Late afternoon, Eddie and Luis rode the subway uptown so Eddie could go to Marlowe's, while Luis asked a friend to pull Caleb's rap sheet and get the photos of the stolen Mayan artifacts. They promised to meet at six to make sure Eddie kept his promise to get home for dinner.

Eddie and Marlowe descended the stairs to the underground lair. "Last night, most of what I threw at Abraxas didn't even hurt him. It wasn't until I really got my emotions involved."

Marlowe sighed. "Wizardry is more than mere mental activity. You must set your intention, and you need to *feel* it from the bottom of your feet to the top of your head."

"So why do you all say the ancient words?"

Marlowe shrugged. "Words are power, Eddie."

"Okay, which is stronger, words or feelings?"

"Feelings. After all, words are merely a way to express thoughts and emotions. I must admit, we do not have time to teach you many of the words."

Eddie felt the heavy hand of time as it ticked by; another moment, another hour, and a day closer to the confrontation.

"Let us begin." Marlowe faced Eddie. "I want you to, as they say, do what feels right."

"Don't hold back, Marlowe," Eddie stipulated. "If I'm going to have any kind of a chance, I need to be really ready."

Eddie touched his staff to his suit and the fabric melted, rolled, and changed into his loose-fitting scarlet robe with tall boots.

"Nicely done," Marlowe praised as his garments changed to a hooded cloak. The two men stood, their staffs poised.

With the smallest of gestures by Marlowe, the room changed, becoming dark and smoky, the old man disappeared in the fog.

Eddie coughed from the mist, but did not lower his guard.

It was quiet around him.

Too quiet.

His own heartbeat sounded like a drum in his ears as he looked from left to right through the haze, no longer able to discern the walls or ceiling.

A slight noise to his left. Eddie moved swiftly and as hushed as a whisper.

A huge leopard, the size of a large horse, leapt out of the smoke and shadow. It paused only for a moment, then turned and hurtled directly at Eddie.

Eddie fell back and avoided the creature. He rolled into a crouch, lobster-walked sideways, then raised his staff and yelled, *Out! Out! Damn spot!"*

The creature sprang for Eddie, just as a red beam shot forth from his staff. It struck the feline in midair, and the big cat became nothing more than a thin wisp of vapor.

Not pausing to congratulate himself, Eddie hunched down and shifted his position.

A movement in the corner of his eyes made him spin about.

A shadow rose up and flew toward him, fast.

Eddie looked up to see a large bird, the size of a condor, dive through the air right at him.

He dodged and weaved, as the avian creature burst into flame.

He held up his staff, as the monster spat a blast of fire from its mouth, right at him.

He waved the wooden pole and the flame was deflected to an unnatural, impossible angle.

"*You goin' down!*" Eddie yelled, and hoped he sounded more dangerous than he felt.

The flaming bird tried to rise up, but the light from Eddie's staff surrounded it, and it came crashing to the floor, only to vanish into vapor as it struck.

Marlowe stepped out of the mist next to Eddie, a white beam shot forth from his staff, Eddie raised his own in a quick defense, only to be bowled off his feet by Marlowe's illuminance.

Eddie landed with an "Oof!" as the air was pushed from his lungs. He tried to rise, but decided to lie on the floor and catch his breath.

"What happened to your shielding spell?" The old man stood over Eddie. "You must be able to deflect the most aggressive attack."

Eddie looked up at Marlowe. "I didn't see you move."

"Keep your guard up at all times! Remember, you must surround yourself with your light—"

"I know the drill," Eddie pulled himself to his feet. "Let's go."

Marlowe faded back into the shadows.

They began again. Eddie threw himself into the work with a vengeance. Marlowe created illusions of great and terrible creatures from mythology and nightmares.

Eddie faced each one and dispatched them quickly and completely, as if he'd become a martial arts master and the monsters were nothing more than thin pieces of wood he could split with a well-placed blow.

As they worked, Eddie told Marlowe of the confrontation at Drusilicus' home.

"Time!" Marlowe called out, after Eddie fought a particularly nasty gryphon, using his staff to strike the monster repeatedly in its eagle-shaped head before he vanquished it.

Eddie's breath came hard, a cold sweat over his body. He stepped back and lowered his staff as the fog dissipated.

"So, what's up with the others?" Eddie asked.

"I am shocked, Eddie," Marlowe's form became clear as the room reappeared around them. "You are sure that Eugenia, Ahbay, and Trefoil were actually discussing taking your staff from you?"

"That's what it seemed like. Can they do that?"

"I enabled your staff to be given to any *you* say. There are other ways to part a wizard from his staff, but they are not often used," Marlowe considered. He walked to the raised platform and sat down. "Long ago, there were those who took the power of their staff and twisted it for their own ends."

"Warlocks?" Eddie said.

"Yes, they deviated from the path. They used falsehood to seek dark powers. Over the years, though, the evil among us were defeated."

"And other wizards took their staffs?"

"Usually. But, we found that there were some staves that had been corrupted. Those were concealed and remain unused to this day. We are now much more careful to only find members who seek the enlightenment of themselves and the world, as well as keep the secret of our existence."

"Until I came around."

"It has been many a year since anyone has been summoned," Marlowe sighed.

"So why do you think I was?"

Marlowe smiled and looked at his charge with kindness. "It happens when a wizard dies unexpectedly, which is rare. Each of us chooses when, where, and how to leave this life."

"Chooses? Why would anyone *choose* to die?"

Marlowe stared at the floor a long moment before answering. "It is the way of things, Eddie."

"That's just an excuse, Marlowe."

"Mayhaps." Marlowe still looked at the floor. "There comes a point when, after centuries, perhaps millennia of existence, even a wizard wishes to leave. He has seen all, done all, and lost far too much. At that point, he will choose an apprentice, teach him the arts, then bequeath his staff to him and move on."

"Riftstone didn't."

"He was murdered, yet his staff possessed enough power to summon you."

"For better or worse."

"I believe it was for better, Eddie." Marlowe's eyes grew misty. "You possess courage and a great heart, which shines forth in all you do. You lack knowledge, but not talent."

Eddie nodded solemnly and accepted the compliment. "Yeah, but is it enough to stop the Great Evil?"

Marlowe shook his head. "I pray so. Let's go upstairs, and you can prepare for our voyage to your home."

"*Our* voyage?" Eddie mounted the stairs. "Who invited you?"

"Eddie, I cannot let you go unguarded," Marlowe declared as his clothing melted into a bright-red smoking jacket and dark pants, and his staff shrank into the walking stick. "The attack last night was aimed at you. Doesn't that prove that you are in danger?"

Eddie sighed. "I hope my wife doesn't have plans."

They reached the top of the stairs and came out to the entrance hall where Luis had just entered and stood speaking with Frisha.

"Hey," Luis held a folder aloft, "I got Caleb's rap sheet and those photos you wanted."

Marlowe reached out for the folder. With a glance to Eddie, who nodded his assent, Luis handed them to the old man.

"I'll need a magnifying glass to examine the pictures." Marlowe made his way to the breakfast room.

"Anything important in the rap sheet?" Eddie said.

Luis shrugged. "A lot of juvie stuff, petty theft, underage drinking. Kid's been a problem until about two years ago. Been a straight arrow ever since."

"Probably when he met Drusilicus. He's got talismans, so I guess he doesn't need to steal."

"Or doesn't get caught. I'm goin' for more coffee," Luis said and followed Marlowe toward the breakfast room.

Frisha headed for the front door.

"Frisha." Eddie fell quickly into his professional demeanor.

"Fred!" Frisha turned to smile her mostly toothless grin. "How goest the training?"

"Well and good," Eddie said, surprised that he adapted Oldspeak to his daily conversation, and a bit annoyed by it as well. "I wanted to ask you about last night."

"Last night?" she became tense.

"Yes, you contacted another wizard?"

"Oh! Yes, I didst speak to several." Frisha shyly met Eddie's eyes. "It be a pleasant way to pass the time. I be a lonely old woman…"

"I'm interested in only *one* conversation, Frisha," Eddie said. "One that concerned me?"

"You, Fred?" She looked at her hands for a moment as if considering this.

"Yes, and it's Eddie."

"Are ye sure?"

"Quite. You spoke to Drusilicus, told him I might be killed in the park."

"Aye!" Frisha raised one finger like an exclamation point. "That I did. I received a terrible vision, that thou wert beaten, cast down by the demon that didst kill poor Riftstone."

"Why contact Drusilicus with that information? Why didn't you talk to Marlowe or the others?"

"Oh, it came to me after they wert gone," Frisha's eyes grew wet with tears. "Oh, tis awful, I canna see the future clearly. Not at t'all, and thou canst know the suffering it causes me."

"You say you saw something last night?" Eddie watched her carefully. He wanted to stay aloof and not buy into the old woman's drama.

"Yes, I did. After days of nothing but confused pictures that nary made sense, I clearly saw thee struck down by the demon. So, I did the first thing I could think of."

"Why not come yourself? You could have found Marlowe or the others and arrived sooner."

She stood still for a moment, her mouth moving like a fish out of water. Then she found her voice. "Marlowe said not to leave the townhouse. T'was dangerous!" Her mouth began to quiver in despair. "And thee don't have no idea what t'is like. I be nothing more than a poor old woman and I canst read the future as well as a fortune teller at a carnival."

She let loose with a wail of anguish and threw herself into Eddie's arms and sank into the folds of his tunic.

"Frisha, please." Eddie was uncomfortable with the distraught woman. He preferred to question people in an interrogation room, in a more controlled environment.

"And now, thou hates me for my vision," she bawled. "Oh 'tis a terrible life I have, indeed."

"I don't hate you." Eddie became frustrated at the way this was going. "I'm only trying to find out—"

"Oh, I be a poor, confused woman with no one to help clear me head."

Eddie knew there was no point to continue. He murmured a few words of comfort, then untangled himself from Frisha's embrace. He went quickly into the downstairs bathroom and bolted the door.

He leaned against the door for a moment, tried to enjoy his solitude. Then he pulled off his tunic, noticed the mirror, and placed the garment over the reflective surface.

He tried to pull off the tall boots as he sat on top of the closed toilet, with no avail.

"How did people in the old days take these things on and off?" Eddie muttered. Finally, he grabbed his staff resting near the closed door and transformed the boots and hose back into his pants and shoes.

He washed up in the sink and remade the tunic back into his shirt and suit jacket. When he finished, he stepped out into the hall, cleaned and pressed.

He glanced at his watch to find it now sported Aramaic letters instead of numbers.

"Damn!" Eddie pulled out his cell phone, which used Hebrew on the keys. Eddie exhaled with frustration and walked toward the breakfast room.

"Eddie!" Luis yelled out as he was halfway there.

Eddie broke into a run and bounded through the doorway.

"What is it?" Eddie barked.

"I don't know!" Luis yelled back.

He and Marlowe stood over an unnaturally pale Bankrock.

"When did *he* get here?" Eddie jammed his phone into his pocket, dropped to his knees, and grabbed the wizard by his shoulders.

"Just a few minutes ago," Marlowe said. "He came through the back door, barely able to stand."

"Bankrock!" Eddie carefully got under the man and leaned him up. "What happened? Are you all right?"

Bankrock opened his eyes and looked at Eddie with a start, as if he didn't remember where he was.

"Is he havin' a heart attack?" Luis asked.

"I doubt that," Marlowe blurted. "But, he was most upset and said things that made no sense."

"What were you two doing?" Eddie looked up at Marlowe.

"I was examining those photos of the Mayan artifacts," Marlowe offered.

"We found a bitchin' coincidence," Luis gloated.

"Later." Eddie turned back and shook Bankrock. "Are you sick?"

"No, no," Bankrock croaked. "But I will be if you don't stop shaking me."

"Sorry." Eddie helped him up from the floor and into a chair. "What happened?"

"Yes, my friend, tell me what troubles you so," Marlowe encouraged.

"I have had a vision." Bankrock sat up in the chair. He was still very pale.

"You?" Eddie said.

"He does have prophetic abilities," Marlowe stated.

"Limited," Bankrock corrected. "But this one was so...so... *intense.* I needed to come right over to warn you."

"Slow down, and tell us where you were," Luis said.

"Where I was?" Bankrock squinted at Luis. Then his eyes grew wide. "I was in the park, at the top of Summit Rock."

"A place of great power," Marlowe said.

"What was your vision?" Eddie said.

"I saw a door," His eyes took on a faraway look. "A great golden door held shut by seven wax seals."

"Seven seals?" Eddie exchanged a glance with Marlowe.

"Hear me," Bankrock became very agitated. "The golden door was in a vast temple. There on an awful metal statue was a child about to be given as a blood sacrifice."

"What?" Luis gasped.

"The Great Evil must kill a child to open the seventh seal," Marlowe said in way of explanation.

Eddie shifted his attention back to Bankrock. "But what of it?"

Bankrock grabbed Eddie's arm tightly and eyed him intensely. "You must away."

"I don't understand," Eddie questioned. "Go? Where, why?"

"You, Edward Berman!" Bankrock pleaded. "I did not see clearly, but I am certain the sacrifice offered was a child close to you."

FORTY-FOUR

The traffic on the George Washington Bridge was at a standstill, not an unusual occurrence for a Saturday night at 6:45.

Knowing that did not make Eddie relax, as he sat in the passenger seat of Luis' car, a 1999 LHS that passed its last good day in 2010.

Eddie wanted to go into the park and transport right home. But, Luis, unaware of Eddie's new mode of travel, ran and got his car.

Now, as they sat stuck in traffic, Eddie knew it was the wrong choice. He fought to control the knot in his stomach as he spoke aloud, "We would've missed this if we just left!"

"I needed to make sure Bankrock was all right," Marlowe affirmed from the back seat.

Eddie glanced back at him. "But why did you have to go into the basement?"

"To prepare some necessary precautions."

"Ain't had much luck with that," Eddie muttered.

"I know, Eddie," Marlowe replied sagely. "I prepared something that may help us before the next attack, instead of after."

"Really?"

"I thought it was time to 'think outside the box.'"

Luis sighed deeply. "I guess we should've taken a police car."

"Great way to get fired or even arrested with us on suspension," Eddie replied.

"What does it matter, we're talkin' about your kid!" Luis slammed the steering wheel with one of his beefy palms.

"Calm yourself, sergeant," Marlowe's voice came from the littered back seat. He continued to examine the photograph through a large magnifying glass. "He will not attack before sundown."

"How do you know that?" Luis said.

"The dark forces are not as strong while the sun remains in the sky."

Eddie grabbed his cell phone and pushed the redial button. His home phone number appeared on the screen. At least he hoped it was his home number, because it was still in Hebrew characters. He was greeted by the same busy signal he'd received for the last half-hour.

"Marlowe, is there anything you can do?" Eddie gestured at the unmoving vehicles.

"Much," Marlowe boasted, his head still bent over the photos.

"Great," replied Eddie with hope.

"But not about traffic. We'll have to wait it out."

"Provided we don't suffocate first." Eddie waved away smoke that blew in the window.

"I'm burning a little oil," Luis apologized.

"Smells like you've set fire to a toxic waste dump," Eddie hissed.

"So, why does New Jersey have all the toxic waste dump sites and Washington DC have all the lawyers?" Luis mentioned as he moved the car several feet and stopped abruptly.

"I'm not in the mood," Eddie worried.

"Come on, this is funny, take a guess." Luis had a crooked smile on his face.

Eddie sighed, "Because New Jersey got first choice. Now will you *please* hurry! I can't believe I live so close to the city, and it takes me so long—"

"How did you know the answer?" Luis said, deflated.

"Old joke." Eddie looked to the back seat. "Marlowe, if we get out of the car can we use…other methods?"

"What are you talkin' about, 'other methods?'" Luis asked. "You guys got brooms or flying cars or something? If you could make this car fly that would really—"

"Nothing like that, sergeant." Marlowe kicked a fast food bag out from under his feet. "Eddie, we are almost to Fort Lee. By the time we got out of the car and looked for a suitable park—"

"Yeah, yeah, I know," Eddie grumbled. "Just step on it, Luis."

Luis wondered for a moment about what good a park would be. Then, he moved forward as he tried not to stall his car or smack the vehicle in front of him, even though that temptation grew stronger with each passing moment. He also knew that there was something he was supposed to remember about this Saturday night. Something Maria told him. For the life of him, he couldn't think of it.

Marlowe put down the photo and tapped Eddie on the shoulder. "You were right with your assessment. There was a fourth talisman."

"Why do you say 'was'?"

"It was captured within this pottery." He pointed to the odd symbols that marked the outside of the ancient pot in the photo. "These are warnings to not disturb it, lest a great evil be set free."

"Another spot Abraxas locked away a piece of himself?"

"Worse than that."

"Why? What was in it?"

"A smoking mirror," Marlowe snapped.

"How does a mirror smoke?" Luis now listened as well.

"More likely it was a smoked glass, or obsidian," Marlowe confirmed.

"What's that?" Luis took a glance in the rearview mirror.

"A volcanic rock with a glasslike finish. It can be polished until the surface becomes highly reflective." Marlowe gazed down at the photo. "According to the symbols here, Tezcatlipoca, who was called a young god, probably a wizard, fought the great monster, who cut off his leg. Tezcatlipoca enchanted a mirror to cure the wound and reattach the limb. This mirror gave him the ability to absorb the power of his foe. He stole the great monster's strength and cast him out."

"And stuck a piece of Abraxas *in* the mirror," Eddie guessed.

"Then sealed it in an earthenware jar, with many magickal protections and warnings," Marlowe finished the story.

"And by coincidence, ended up in the only museum physically *in* Central Park," Eddie complained.

"I doubt it was coincidence. Remember, a wizard told Alex where to find the Amulet of Abracadabra. That same wizard surely influenced the right person to have this artifact sent to the museum."

"That warlock is one busy boy." Eddie stared at the windshield, fuming. "And again, everything centers around the park. Why?"

The traffic jam was caused by an overturned truck at the junction of Route 95 and 80. Once past the turnoff for Route 4, Luis made up for lost time and took his car up to its fastest speed, as the engine knocked and pinged.

The worn shock absorbers passed along every bump in the road to the rear ends of the riders. Luis was unaffected, as he was sitting on his own shock absorber, while Eddie and Marlowe were jostled unmercifully.

At 7:24, as the sun neared the horizon, the vehicle arrived at Eddie's house, whereupon it stalled.

Eddie and Luis bolted from the car as Marlowe pulled himself out, kicking fast-food bags as he exited. He glanced with concern at the setting sun.

Eddie noted that his wife's car was in the driveway, but there weren't any lights on in the house. It wasn't night yet, but there *should* be a lamp on.

Eddie reached the front door and pulled it open, with Luis right behind him. The inside of his house was dark, and the quiet scared him.

"Cerise!" Eddie yelled as he entered the house.

"I hope we're not too late," Luis articulated what they both feared.

A heavy weight gripped Eddie's heart. The one thing that mattered—truly mattered—was his family. While he'd been off with a bunch of crazy wizards, he wasn't there to protect them.

"Cerise," Eddie spoke quietly, the fear almost too much for him to bear. His hand went to the shoulder-holster under his jacket, which was empty, his gun having been confiscated along with his shield.

"*Surprise!*" yelled many voices, as overhead lights flashed on, cheap noisemakers bleated and blared. A group of the Bermans' friends and neighbors leapt up from behind furniture and doorways, throwing confetti in the air.

With Cerise in the lead.

Both Eddie and Luis stopped short, blinked, then fell back and grimaced in abject horror, then forced smiles upon their faces.

"I got you, I got you!" Cerise did a little dance reminiscent of James Brown.

William and Douglas tumbled down the stairs as they laughed with delight at their father.

"Man, Dad, we got you good!" William pointed at him. "You looked like you was gonna pass out."

Douglas laughed, his face bright with glee. "I ain't never seen you look so scared, Dad."

Maria, barely five-foot two and almost as round as she was tall, pushed her way through the crowd and ran up to her massive husband and pulled him into her arms to give him a big, wet kiss.

"I tol' my husband to keep his big mouth shut and not ruin the surprise, an' he did it!" Maria crowed.

"That's right." Luis glanced over at Eddie. "It's your surprise party."

"Yeah," Eddie struggled to keep a smile on his face, though it felt pained. "A surprise party…for me."

"Happy Birthday, two days early, baby," Cerise said, pulled him close, and covered his face with kisses.

His sons put a paper party hat on his head that read "#1 DAD" and Cerise led him around the room to meet and greet the guests.

Unnoticed by anyone, Marlowe quietly entered the house and made his way to the kitchen. There was food out on the countertops and guests milled around. Marlowe opened a cabinet and pulled out a small saucepan made of brown glass. He poured in some water and placed it on the stove with a fire under it. He glanced around to make sure no one watched and took out a small envelope and poured the contents into the pan.

"Mr. Marlowe," said a voice behind him.

Marlowe started and turned to see Eleanor Berman, who watched him with her magnified eyes.

"Mrs. Berman," Marlowe beamed at the old woman, "so good to see you again. And please, just call me Marlowe."

"Did Eddie look surprised?" she asked.

"He all but jumped out of his skin, dear lady," Marlowe reported. "I would say he couldn't have expected it less. How are you feeling?"

"I'm good enough." She eyed him suspiciously. "What are you cooking?"

Marlowe looked to the stove and gave a little "oh" as if he just discovered the bubbling contents for the first time.

"That is some...rather aromatic tea," Marlowe began. "In ancient China, when there was a major event, they would brew a special tea for the person being honored."

"But, you aren't Chinese." Eleanor gave Marlowe a glance from head to foot just to make sure.

Marlowe nodded. "But it *is* a lovely tradition, is it not?"

"Well, whatever it is, Marlowe, it don't smell all that good."

"That is as it should be." Marlowe bowed and gallantly kissed her hand.

Eleanor chuckled and made her way carefully into the dining room. Marlowe frowned at how fragile she appeared. He turned his attention back to the brewing herbs. He stirred the bubbling liquid, which now was a thickening brown mass.

The party was soon in full swing as twilight passed into evening. Music blared from the sound system, rock 'n roll and even some hip-hop filled the house as Eddie tried to relax.

He was seriously pumped from the events of the last few hours and the frantic rush from the city. Seeing his family safe—in fact ready to party—was a great comfort.

As Eddie wandered around the party, he found his eyes rested on his sons again and again. He couldn't help himself, after Bankrock's startling prophesy.

He noticed Luis paced with a similar bewildered look on his face.

Eddie would shake hands with guests, say, "Thank you for coming," and other niceties, but it was all a blur. He stayed focused on his wife and children.

People handed him drinks, and he took a sip then put each aside on the nearest table.

He was handed a cup of hot liquid he assumed was coffee, and without noticing who gave it to him, took a sip.

It was horrid.

It tasted like bitter tea with leaves still floating in it, giving him a mouthful of warm foliage. Eddie made a choking noise and barely got the mixture down his throat.

"What in the name of—?" Eddie regarded who gave him the cup.

Marlowe stood next to him, his eyes bright.

"Drink more." The old man pulled at his beard.

"Why would I do that?" Eddie said. His tongue felt coated with fur. He wanted to spit, but controlled himself.

"If you value your sons, do as I say." Marlowe's eyes were intense.

Eddie grimaced and took another swallow. It was no better than the first. "Man, that is *nasty*."

"We'll need it 'ere long. It will keep you awake."

"If it don't kill me first."

Luis noticed Marlowe next to Eddie and moved closer. "You okay?"

"Yeah." Eddie handed the cup to Luis. "Here, drink this."

Marlowe raised his hand. "I did not prepare it for the sergeant."

"If I'm staying awake, so is he," Eddie said.

Luis took a huge swallow, sputtered, and fought to keep the foul beverage in his mouth, and then down his throat.

"Jeezus!" Luis whined. "And I thought Mexican malt was bad. What is this junk?"

Marlowe exhaled, annoyed at the turn of events. "It is a potion," he hissed. "We will need it. Now, both of you, join the party, but stay ready. Odd things will occur this night."

"That's my life." Eddie turned to greet another friend and shake another hand.

Luis went to the makeshift bar outside on the back porch and grabbed a beer, gulped a large swallow to take the foul taste from his mouth.

"Hey." A guest stood next to him and took a beer himself.

"Hey," Luis repeated with a nod. The stranger was a thin black man of about thirty.

"I'm Calvin, Eddie's cousin. You're his partner, right?"

"Yeah." Luis offered his hand. "Luis Vasquez."

Calvin returned his grasp. "I guess we really surprised Eddie, huh?"

"More than you'll ever know," Luis said with a straight face.

"Yeah, well, even as a kid Eddie was a tough guy to surprise," Calvin reminisced. "I can remember when he was eight-"

Luis nodded and took another swallow of beer, then turned back to Calvin, as it was strange that the man stopped speaking in mid-sentence.

Calvin stood, his head leaned to one side, and his eyes closed.

"You all right, man?" Luis asked.

The beer tumbled from Calvin's hand, and Luis recoiled.

"Hey, be careful," Luis said, and with that, Calvin started to fall toward him. Luis caught him, and carefully lowered the slack body down to the wood of the deck.

"You having a heart attack or something?" Luis put his fingers to the man's neck. The pulse was slow, but strong and steady.

Calvin began to snore.

Luis laid Calvin down on the wooden floor of the deck and stood up. "Now *that* was strange," he said to no one in particular.

He turned and walked into the house, expecting to find Eddie and tell him about his cousin passing out.

He stopped in the doorway.

He'd only left the dining room moments earlier, but since then, it was as if a poisonous gas had been released.

People lay about on the floor or asleep in a chair. One guest was sprawled across a large serving plate of food on the table.

"Cryin' out loud." Luis carefully stepped around the fallen bodies toward the living room. "Eddie!"

"This was not unexpected." Marlowe exited from the kitchen. He held a steaming pot, his hand covered with a floral oven mitt.

"What the hell happened?" Luis cried, as Eddie joined them.

"I don't know, everyone fell to the floor—I caught Cerise— what's going on?" Eddie's face creased with lines of concern. "Are these people hurt?"

"No," Marlowe said and stirred the smoldering liquid. "They are bewitched by a sleep spell."

"We weren't affected because we drank that stuff," Luis ventured.

"I suspected this might happen when you gave me the details of Mr. Cuccolo's demise."

"What does that have to do with—"

"Indulge me for a moment, Eddie," Marlowe said as he stirred. "This Cuccolo, he was a thief?"

Eddie stared at Marlowe. "He was a gangster. Yeah, stealing was one of his hobbies."

"And his hand was removed?"

"Yes." Luis' temper began to ignite. "What about all these people?"

"A powerful charm can be made with the hand of a hanged thief. Wicks and wax are attached to the fingers, and with the proper incantations, it can be transformed into a 'Hand of Glory.'"

"So what?" Luis said, and gazed out the windows to see if they were under attack.

"You light the wicks near a doorway of a house, and those within fall into a deep sleep from which they cannot be roused as long as the candles continue to burn."

Eddie looked around the room. "So, nobody's hurt?"

"Correct. You and the sergeant must locate the Hand of Glory. Extinguish its candles and all will wake."

Eddie looked again into the living room where he could see William asleep near his mother. "What about my sons?"

"I shall guard them. You two must find the charm. The spell requires that it be near a doorway," Marlowe said. "Eddie, I think carrying your staff would be a good choice."

Eddie nodded gravely, held out his hand, and the wooden pole obliged. With a gesture, his clothes shifted into the tall boots and tunic with an over-robe. Eddie was amazed how quickly he'd grown accustomed to what would have been strange garments days ago.

With a nod, Marlowe, who still held the bubbling pot, went into the living room.

"C'mon," Eddie gestured to Luis.

"Should we split up?" Luis asked. "Cover more ground?"

"I've got the only weapon." Eddie held aloft his staff.

"I'm big and scary."

"That'll work," Eddie responded, and the pair went out into the backyard. "Let's go for the obvious places: back and front doors."

The two men walked out and across the back lawn, which was beginning to need a good mowing. Eddie was thankful he'd erected the tall, white, vinyl fence, as it blocked prying eyes.

The two detectives, with methodical and well-practiced maneuvers, covered the entire backyard in mere seconds. They met at the back fence and drew close.

"Front yard," Eddie whispered and with a mutual nod, they both made their way around the house from opposite ends.

Eddie peeked out and scanned the front yard, which was empty, except for Luis' and Cerise's cars. He saw Luis' head pop out from the other side, and with a hand signal, they moved toward the front door in unison.

As he approached, Eddie saw that the floodlight over the main entrance was casting an eerie glow that flickered and moved. He stepped up his pace and crouched low, watching Luis mimic his moves, though on a larger scale.

He had a clear view of the entrance. The brick steps rose from the pavement, and on top of the landing sat a strange flesh-colored thing with five small candle flames.

It was indeed a hand.

Cuccolo's hand, severed from his body and now used for a demonic purpose worse than any it performed in life.

Eddie gestured for Luis to stay back as he stood and strode directly at the burning decoration. As he drew closer, he saw each finger did indeed bear a wick with a tiny flame that was unaffected by gusts of wind.

Eddie was about to reach down and pinch out the first wick, when he felt a pressure against his chest. Suddenly, he was knocked backward, as if an invisible hand pushed against him, and fell on his butt.

He was more surprised than injured, and he pulled himself up, taking his staff in both hands to renew the attack.

Luis, however, rushed past him with a roar that would impress any passing rhinoceros, and dove toward the flaming digits, as if to crush the charm with his huge body.

"Luis, no," Eddie warned in a hoarse whisper.

But Luis was already off his feet, launched through the air like a linebacker trying to take down a quarterback in the Super Bowl.

His body stopped its forward motion as if he'd struck a rubber wall and Luis was repulsed.

His huge frame rocketed in the opposite direction. He plummeted to the lawn, kicked up grass, and slid in the muddy earth. It all happened too fast for Eddie to try to break his fall.

Eddie ran to him.

"Luis, you okay?"

Luis raised his head and shook it. "What was that?"

"Something around the hand, to keep us away," Eddie said. "Whatever we throw at it, it sends back with a greater amount of force. I got knocked on my butt, you got flung across the lawn."

"I'm tired of this, Eddie," Luis whined. "How can you bring 'em down when physics don't apply?"

"You were happy about it last night in the elevator."

"That was different. You stopped us from going *splat*."

Eddie stood up and offered a hand to his partner. Luis got up and tried to rub a little of the mud off his pants.

"I can control fire," Eddie realized. "It doesn't matter what's around it, I can turn the flames off without even—"

"*Eddie!*" a cry came from inside.

Marlowe.

"Let's go," Eddie said, and the two men ran to opposite sides of the house.

Eddie glanced through the windows as he went, but he couldn't see anyone standing inside.

Where was Marlowe?

Eddie came around the house to find the huge demonic figure of Abraxas in his backyard, wearing an evil grin. He stood eleven feet tall, red, well-muscled with a goat's legs and feet, and his enormous horns.

In one of his taloned hands he held a limp body. Eddie stopped short and looked up.

There lay Douglas, his younger son.

Action. I have to take action, Eddie thought. *If I freeze up, he's already won.*

Eddie felt every bit of anger within him, from his feet to his head, focused that feeling, then lifted his staff and sent forth a plume of red light that struck the demon in the head, and made him stumble back.

"Stop!" Abraxas bellowed. "I shall kill him."

Eddie made no reply, because with a roar, his partner ran out and dove for the monster's legs.

With a better effect this time.

He caught the giant's calves and the creature fell forward.

Eddie lifted his staff, recalled the feeling of levitation, and focused upon his son. Douglas, asleep and oblivious, rose into the air out of his adversary's grasp.

Abraxas hit the ground and slid in the mud, one of his huge horns digging into the earth, which brought both the demon and Luis to an abrupt halt.

Eddie guided the sleeping boy through the air toward the safety of the house. But another beam of light encircled and pulled him in a different direction.

"No!" Eddie barked and rushed toward his son.

A figure, cloaked and hooded, stood near the vinyl fence. The dark robe was offset against the white background, but the face was in shadows.

"Leave off!" a muffled voice demanded from the robe. "Or I shall kill him here and now."

The timbre of the voice was familiar. He'd heard it before, but who did it belong to?

Eddie withdrew his power and Douglas was surrounded by a gray light as he floated in midair.

The demon smacked Luis away from his leg with one of his massive hands, as if the sergeant was no more than an annoying insect. Luis made a grunt, rolled a few feet away, and came to rest on the damp lawn.

Eddie started toward him.

"*Stay!*" the warlock ordered in his indistinct, gravelly voice.

Eddie froze to his spot.

The demon stood, and with a look to the shadowy figure, plucked the sleeping boy out of the air.

"Where is Marlowe?" Eddie glanced about for the old man.

"What is that to thee?" the cloaked figure said. "Shall we negotiate for the life of your son?"

"Let him go; it's me you want," Eddie said.

"That is where you are wrong. It is your staff I want."

Eddie looked at the wooden pole in his hand, then over at the unconscious Luis, then at the demon who held Douglas aloft.

"Why do you want it?"

"Only the Five can stop us, and they must be united. Without your staff, we have won."

Get him to talk, look for an opening, Eddie thought.

"Aren't you powerful enough with your talismans?" Eddie said.

"I wish to make certain events fall into place."

"What events?"

"Armageddon, of course," the voice sneered. "Enough talk! Surrender your staff or the boy dies."

Eddie glanced at the demon towering over him.

In a hostage situation, the cop in his head spoke, *relinquishing your weapon makes two people dead.*

The demon held the boy like he was a rag doll, and as Eddie watched, he moved his free hand to Douglas' throat.

"Wait, wait," Eddie cried, put his staff on the ground, and stepped away from it. "There, let my son go."

"Fool! You must announce that you give it to me."

"I'm not giving it to you willingly." Eddie glanced at the house. Where was Marlowe when he really needed him?

"Say the words!" the cloaked figure demanded.

"All right!" Eddie gritted his teeth. "I give the Staff of Fire and its power to you."

The wooden pole began to glow red and rose into the air. A flash of red appeared around Eddie, which glowed brightly then shot through the air to the hooded figure and surrounded him.

Eddie's clothes shifted immediately from robes into his suit.

The staff rose into the air and landed in the free hand of the shadowy warlock.

"At last!" he bellowed, and held the staff aloft. The hood turned toward the giant, "Let us go, demon."

"Leave my son," Eddie begged. "That was the deal."

"I don't make deals," he snarled, and with a flash of purple light, the warlock, the demon, and Douglas disappeared.

Eddie fell to his knees as tears stabbed his eyes.

FORTY-FIVE

"What do you mean, you *gave* him your staff?" Marlowe scolded. He held a cloth wrapped with ice to his head as Eddie applied a bandage to a cut in the purplish mass that was once Luis Vasquez's eye.

"I didn't have a choice," Eddie lamented. "My partner was down and my son was in danger—*is* in danger. This is not the time to tell me I made a bad choice. I *know* that!"

His partner sat in the kitchen in his muddy pants with his shirt off, as Eddie checked him over. Eddie had roused him on the lawn and helped him into the house.

A quick search found Marlowe unconscious in the living room, and at first Eddie wasn't sure the old man was breathing. But a few gentle slaps on his cheek brought him around. Then, Eddie helped him into the kitchen and took to doctoring both men.

"Ouch!" Luis said, as Eddie applied hydrogen peroxide to a nasty scrape on his side. He turned to Marlowe. "So, where the hell were you when this was all goin' down?"

Marlowe exhaled heavily. His eye was beginning to swell into a first-class shiner. "I was caught unawares."

"What kind of dumb-ass wizard are *you*, then?" Luis tried to stand, while Eddie pushed him back in his chair.

"Enough! Arguing won't get us anywhere." Eddie turned toward Marlowe. "You're going to have to extinguish the Hand of Glory; I can't."

"Is that wise?" Marlowe said. "No one knows your son is gone. What will you tell them?"

"Hey, you crazy *gringo*," Luis snapped. "My wife is laying on the floor in the living room, I ain't gonna leave her that way."

"Luis," Eddie didn't raise his voice, "calm down." He turned back to Marlowe. "I'll think of something. Luis is right, we can't leave them this way."

Marlowe nodded.

"There is no doubt anymore." Eddie daubed a small abrasion under Marlowe's eye. "We both saw the warlock."

Marlowe hissed with pain. "You *saw* him?"

Eddie's mouth was a hard line. "Yes, and there was something familiar about him."

Marlowe opened his eyes and met Eddie's. "You know who it is?"

"No," Eddie considered, "but the next time I run into him, I will. What I need to know is who has enough power to stop you?"

"I was unprepared, my defenses were not in place. Remember when I struck out at you in practice today?" Marlowe recounted.

"Yeah."

"That was but a small amount of power. I was smote much stronger than thee," Marlowe said sullenly.

"Does Drusilicus or Caleb have the power to take you out? How about Ahbay or Eugenia?"

Marlowe thought for a moment. "I would believe I could hold my own against most. But one of the Five or Drusilicus—he *is* quite adept—"

"I need a simple answer."

"I do not have one, Eddie." Marlowe could not meet Eddie's eyes. "We were outmaneuvered yet again."

"That Bankrock guy was the one who warned you," Luis said. "Could his whole 'I've had a vision' thing be a lie?"

"This warlock is skillful; he could *send* a vision," Marlowe mused. "Especially if the warlock's powers were combined with the demon's talismans."

"Those two were as chummy as peas in a pod," Eddie claimed. "And the demon was definitely taking orders from the warlock."

"We truly are up against something terrible." Marlowe rose. "I shall extinguish the hand."

"Then what do *we* do?" Luis brushed at the mud on his filthy tee-shirt.

Eddie looked at his amazingly dirty partner. "Marlowe, do you mind?" he said with a nod of his head at Luis.

"Hmm?" Marlowe uttered, then noticed Luis's clothing. "Oh, yes!"

Marlowe waved his staff, and the glowing circle of light, like a Hula Hoop, appeared at Luis's feet and rose up his body, cleaning and repairing his damaged clothes.

"Man!" Luis said, "I wish you could heal the bruises that way."

"Clothes are easy." Marlowe touched his own black eye. "I am weakened and cannot even heal myself yet."

"Here's the plan," Eddie announced. "We make sure everyone is all right, call an ambulance if anyone is hurt. Then we go after my son."

"Eddie," Luis observed, "you don' got your staff."

"Doesn't matter." Eddie set his jaw. "I needed it to save the world. Well, now all I care about is saving my son."

"They will not hurt him," Marlowe confided. "Well, not yet."

"Why not?"

"They need a sacrifice."

"That's right," Eddie acknowledged. "The fifth talisman."

Marlowe nodded. "Once they have the talisman, they need to offer a child under the age of thirteen on an ancient altar."

"Why under thirteen?" Eddie asked.

"Why else?" Luis grunted. "Because if he were a teenager, it wouldn't be a sacrifice."

Marlowe gave Luis a dirty look. "In many cultures, a boy becomes a man at thirteen."

"What's all this about?" Luis asked.

Eddie rubbed his eyes and fought back fatigue. "An evil god that expected the sacrifice of children, and will bring the end of the world."

"Oh, glad you cleared that up," Luis said.

"Help the others." Marlowe left the room.

Eddie turned to his partner. "I need you to take Maria and go home."

"No way."

"I can't do this if I'm worried about you. I might get killed, but I would never forgive myself if I took you with me."

"Man, look at you! You're too wasted to go another round with Big Red.

"I'll have Marlowe with me," Eddie said.

"He ain't in great shape, either."

"Right now, we need to help the guests."

"Protect and serve," Luis sighed.

They walked into the dining room, and as if a switch was thrown, people began to stir. They were all caught by surprise, looking up from their various positions on the floor, unsure how they got there.

Eddie and Luis walked through the rooms, helped people to their feet, and asked if they were injured. Most of the guests were merely embarrassed that they fell asleep at Eddie's party. If one considered the speed they all fell into unconsciousness, the only injuries were a bruise or two.

A neighbor who fell into the plate of food needed to be cleaned, but the only damage was to his pride. Everyone felt lightheaded, and Eddie helped Cerise into the kitchen and suggested they serve coffee.

Marlowe looked for Eddie's mother. Eleanor was not downstairs, so Marlowe made his way to the second floor. There, he found her, fully dressed on top of her immaculately made bed.

"Eleanor," Marlowe said, as he touched her hand.

She did not wake with a start, but merely opened her eyes and looked at him.

"Why, Mr. Marlowe," she said, a sparkle in her eyes behind her thick frames. "Visiting me in my room? People will talk."

"Let them, madam." Marlowe was relieved that she wasn't hurt. "What are you doing up here?"

She sighed. "I felt tired and decided to take a little lie down. What happened to your eye?"

"It's nothing." Marlowe was grateful she saved herself a nasty fall. "Are you feeling rested?"

"'Bout as well as I expect to," she said. "Dyin' is no fun."

"I understand you have cancer."

"That's what they tell me," she replied. "I guess it's my time."

"How do you feel about that?" Marlowe asked.

She shrugged. "No one *wants* to die."

Marlowe nodded, but knew it wasn't true. He himself often felt it was time to move on. He'd left too many behind, and his memories were an ache that seldom grew lighter.

"I just think now is a bad time," Eleanor went on. "I mean, Eddie and Cerise, they don't need another burden right now. When they first asked me to live here, I was able to help. Even so, Eddie still hasn't been able to take Cerise on a real honeymoon."

"Eddie told me," Marlowe smiled.

"Didn't have time, him a cop and her a nurse. I understand that. Me and Eddie's father didn't have a honeymoon. I jus' wanted it to be different for my boy. Now, with me dying, they won't be able to get away until the boys are grown and out of the house."

"So, it's not dying you fear," Marlowe questioned, "you just wish it were a different time."

"Yes," her eyes grew wistful. "After all, everybody's got to die, don't they? I just wanted to see my grandbabies all grown up."

Marlowe patted her hand gently. "You are a dear, sweet lady."

"An' you are a silver-tongued devil," she added with a girlish giggle. "We'd better get back to the party."

"Rest for a moment," Marlowe suggested. "May I use your bathroom?"

"Sure, right over there."

Marlowe rose and entered the bathroom, which was a little more than a water closet, but there was a rail around the toilet and sink, which made it wheelchair accessible. The Bermans had planned ahead.

Marlowe turned on the water and checked that he'd closed the door. He stared into the mirror and hissed, "Drusilicus! Drusilicus Greywacke!"

Marlowe called aloud for a good minute, when the silver surface shimmered and Drusilicus stood groggily on the other side.

"Marlowe! It's the middle of the night—"

"Hush! I am at Eddie's house. We have been attacked."

Drusilicus' mouth fell open, and he peered at the bruise around Marlowe's eye. "Who would dare—"

"Never mind that!" Marlowe demanded. "I have a mission for you."

"I am not in the habit of taking orders—"

"Hush, Drusilicus. I need you to teleport to where I am."

"Teleport?" Drusilicus blanched. "That's dangerous, especially if Frisha is right and the future is not stable—"

"Trust me. After all, I am trusting you." Marlowe spoke his plan carefully and slowly as Drusilicus listened, an unusual occupation for him.

A few minutes later, Marlowe came out of the bathroom.

"Who were you speaking to?" Eleanor asked and sat up in the bed.

"Myself, dear lady," Marlowe quipped. "But please, lie down."

Marlowe gently took her shoulder, and at the same time waved his cane. Eleanor fell gently asleep and didn't see the flash of ivory light from the open door to the bathroom.

FORTY-SIX

Within an hour, Eddie had successfully convinced all of the guests to go home. Now, Maria and Luis stood at the door.

"I don' like leavin' like this," Luis said to Eddie.

"It'll be all right, trust me. I'll call you as soon as I have news."

"Okay." Luis glanced to his wife. "We'll talk..."

"Yeah."

There was so much more Eddie wanted to say. Luis once took a bullet, but tonight he had charged an eleven-foot-tall demon to save Eddie's son. His partner was the bravest man he'd ever known.

Luis gave him a bear hug, then escorted his wife to the car.

Cerise sat on the living room sofa sipping coffee, as she watched the Vasquezes' departure. She was beginning to feel like herself again, but the evening's events puzzled her.

"Eddie," Cerise said. "I went up to check on the boys. I couldn't find Douglas."

"I know." Eddie was grateful to see Marlowe walk down the steps. "We need to talk."

"I don't need to talk; I need to know where my baby is," Cerise grew serious. "Strange things are going on here, Eddie, and I have a feeling that you know what it is about."

Eddie bit his lip. "You're right, but it's a long story."

"Is my baby in danger?" Cerise felt her face grow hot.

Eddie glanced at Marlowe. "I have to tell her."

"I thought you would." Marlowe nodded. "And since you gave up your staff, you are no longer obligated to maintain the vows of secrecy."

"I'm not?"

"Technically, no. And, considering the circumstances—"

"What are you two talking about?" Cerise stood, her dark eyes flashing. "I want to know what happened to my guests, my party, and my baby."

"Sit down, Cerise," Eddie said.

"I don't need to sit down!"

"Please," he asked as gently as he could.

Cerise returned to the sofa.

Eddie stood opposite her and put his hand to his head and tried to think how he could summarize the last week of his life in a way that would be coherent, or for that matter, believable. Luis was easy to convince, because Eddie possessed the staff and its power. Now, he needed to tell her without evidence.

"Madame, Eddie has been summoned," Marlowe began, while Eddie struggled to know what to say.

"What?" Cerise wondered.

"You see, baby," Eddie went on, "I was given a…great gift."

"Let me make this easy, Eddie," Marlowe gestured with his walking stick and a mist appeared on the floor of the living room.

"What on earth—" Cerise's eyes became wide.

The fog began to form into shapes, acting out scenes as Marlowe spoke. "Since the dawn of time, there have been those who walk a spiritual path. They have been called many names, but you would know them as wizards."

"How are you doing this?" Cerise reached out to a ghostly figure in robes that dissipated at her touch.

"Cerise, I joined a group of people who are trying to do good things," Eddie explained, as the fog behind him formed into an image of himself in his robes and carrying his staff.

"Your husband agreed to learn of our ways," Marlowe continued, "in order to fight the Great Evil."

The mist rose up and slid into the shape of the demon Eddie fought a few short hours earlier.

Cerise cowered on the sofa.

"But, you see," Eddie offered, "this Great Evil attacked our home tonight."

"I think I would have noticed him, Eddie," Cerise gestured at the phantom version of the monster in her living room.

"I'm afraid not, dear lady," Marlowe pointed out, "because this demon is working in league with a warlock." The demon's shape faded and a figure appeared, cloaked and hooded, with a staff like Eddie's.

For a moment, Eddie was surprised, because the figure in the mist was exactly the same as the warlock he and Luis had faced. If Marlowe was unconscious, how did he know how the mysterious attacker looked?

"This warlock put everyone to sleep except Marlowe, Luis, and me," Eddie told her.

"So we all fell asleep," Cerise frowned, "because of what—a spell?"

Marlowe and Eddie nodded, their eyes fixed on Cerise.

"This is the biggest load of bull I have ever heard," Cerise stormed. "Mr. Marlowe, I cannot believe that you would be a part of such a thing."

Marlowe shrugged, and with a tap of his cane on the ground, it grew into his staff, and his clothes shifted into robes.

Cerise's mouth fell open, and she stared into her coffee cup. "What did you put in the coffee? I'm on LSD, right?"

"No, baby, it's real." Eddie took her arms and pulled her into a standing position. "And these bad guys, they took Douglas."

"They *took* my baby?"

"There was a battle, and your brave friend Sergeant Vasquez tackled the demon," Marlowe testified. "But in the end, they defeated us and kidnapped your son."

Cerise grabbed her husband. "You have to get our boy, Eddie."

"I will, I promise."

"He is in no danger," Marlowe surmised. "They will not hurt him until the day of the solstice."

"I don't give a damn. Eddie, you got to get him back. Right now, tonight."

"Dear lady," Marlowe soothed, "Eddie, as well as I, must rest."

"I don't need to," Eddie vowed. "This is my son we're talking about."

"Eddie," Marlowe stated calmly, "it would be foolish to try to fight the Great Evil when we are weak. It is night, his power is strong. I would advise we search tomorrow and track the Great Evil to his lair."

"How do you suggest we do that? So far you and the others have had no luck tracking him down."

Marlowe nodded. "I assure you we will find your son."

"How?"

"Because I gave both your sons a potion while you were outside looking for the Hand of Glory. I can now trace Douglas to any time, space, or dimension in all of existence."

Eddie stood stock-still for a moment.

"Really?" Eddie considered this, a tentative smile on his lips.

"Really."

"You are one hell of an old sneak," Eddie said with admiration.

"As I told you, I have begun to, as you suggested, think outside the box," Marlowe responded. "But, a wizard has betrayed us, we know not whom. So, no one must know that we can find him."

"You told me," Cerise pointed out.

"You needed to know, to be assured we can indeed find him. However, if Eddie and I went out tonight with our energies drained, it would not bode well."

Eddie and Cerise looked at each other, the tension between them palatable. Eddie thought of his early days as a beat cop, when people from the neighborhood would report a missing child, how awkward and helpless he and the parents felt. It was because there was little they could do but wait.

Cerise's face was drawn as she made a decision. "You have to rest, Eddie."

"But Douglas!" Eddie turned to his mentor. "Marlowe, do you honestly believe we can save my son?"

"Yes, Eddie." Marlowe placed his hand on Eddie's shoulder. "And maybe even the world."

"What is he talking about, Eddie?"

"This demon, the Great Evil," Eddie explained, "if he has his way, he will bring down the apocalypse."

Marlowe continued. "If we do not defeat him, then the whole world will fall to him and his traitorous companion."

Cerise stepped free from Eddie and went to Marlowe. "I am not going to pretend I understand any of this, but I will trust you, Marlowe. I believe you to be a good man."

Marlowe smiled and gave a small bow. His clothes shifted back into a suit, as his staff returned to a walking stick. "Thank you, dear lady."

"Well, you are going to have to put me up," a voice said at the top of the stairs. "Because I have not the ability to go home tonight."

At the top of the stairs stood Drusilicus. He wore a fashionable suit, but no tie, just an open collar. He was a bit paler than usual, and looked haggard with bags under his eyes.

Next to him was Eddie's mother.

She looked ten years younger and didn't wear her glasses. She easily walked down the stairs, not with the gait of a sick woman, but with the confidence of good health.

"Momma?" Eddie murmured as she descended.

"What happened?" Cerise wondered, as the three of them huddled together for a hug.

"That man up there," Eleanor said and gestured at Drusilicus. "He came to my room and, well I'm not sure what he did, but I know that I am cured."

Cerise held Eleanor at arm's length and stared at her. "How is it possible?"

"Eddie faces the most dangerous challenge of his life," Marlowe beamed. "And I thought your family could use one less crisis. It was the least we could do."

Drusilicus chimed in, "Let's not forget who actually did it, shall we? Now where do I sleep?"

Eddie felt his eyes well up as he gave his mother another hug. "Seeing you like this—"

"I still need a good night's sleep, son," Eleanor said. "And so do you."

Marlowe piped up, "I shall sleep down here. Drusilicus, you may have the sofa. Tomorrow will come too quickly and it shall be a full day, indeed."

FORTY-SEVEN

Eddie was sure that sleep would not come, but his body was wiser and he easily slipped into a dreamless slumber until nine the next morning.

Cerise, as well, slept late and they both woke to the smell of breakfast. They came down expecting Marlowe to be at the stove, only to find Eleanor as she cooked enough to feed an army.

"Lots of leftovers spoiled," Eleanor pointed out. "No one cleaned up last night."

Eddie nodded and wandered out to the living room. There, Drusilicus lay on the sofa and Marlowe in the recliner.

He went to shake Marlowe, but saw the old man frowned and struggled in his sleep. His lips moved, and he began to thrash his head side to side.

Eddie leaned closer.

"No, you must not kill him," Marlowe murmured. "All that has been built—it must stand or all is for naught—"

Marlowe's eyes popped open and he raised his hands as if to defend himself.

"You okay, Marlowe?" Eddie said.

Marlowe leaned up from the chair and glanced about the room, as if not sure where he was. "Eddie?"

"Yeah, it's me."

Marlowe exhaled heavily and slowly sat up. It seemed to take a great effort.

"What were you dreaming about," Eddie said. "Last night?"

"No, a battle that happened long ago," Marlowe said. "I failed to save someone. I canst believe I still have that nightmare even after a millennium."

"A millennium?" Eddie said. "Just how old are you?"

"We are both older this morning," Drusilicus grimaced, as he rose from the sofa and adjusted his shoulders. "I should have conjured a proper bed."

"We can't do anything that can't be explained," Eddie said.

"Isn't it too late for that?" Drusilicus uttered in a nasty tone. "Between telling your partner, your wife, and healing your mother, I thought everyone you know was aware. Perhaps we should go door to door and tell the neighbors?"

"I don't want William to—"

"You called me, Dad?" William said from the top of the stairs. He was dressed and looked ready to go somewhere.

"Ah no, William, I was just wondering when you were getting up. We have guests."

"Oh," said the older boy as he walked down the stairs and looked at Drusilicus and Marlowe.

"I will need coffee." Drusilicus headed for the kitchen with Marlowe right behind him.

"Hey, Dad, where's Doug?" the older boy asked.

"He...uh..." Eddie struggled.

Cerise stepped out of the kitchen. "He's spending the weekend at Kevin's." She walked over and handed Eddie a mug of coffee.

William came down the stairs and Cerise grabbed him in a hug.

William tried to move out of her reach. "Come on, Mom, don't get all sappy on me."

"You are my beautiful young man." Cerise didn't let go. "And I love you."

"C'mon, Mom, I just ate." William shook himself free. "Is it okay if I go see Marvin?"

"Marvin?" Eddie thought for a moment. "The kid with the glasses?"

"Earth to Dad," William prattled. "That was five years ago. Marvin is the number one greatest master of all video games."

"Sure, son, that'll be fine." Eddie nodded. "I have to go to work anyway."

"Mom said you were suspended."

"Well," Eddie thought fast, "I'm working on getting un-suspended."

"You keep your cell phone on you," Cerise's voice was firm. "And you call me the minute you go anywhere. Do you understand that? *Anywhere!*"

"Yes, ma'am," William muttered then added in an undertone, "Jeez, it's like bein' in prison."

"What was that?" Cerise burst out, ready to go ballistic.

Eddie, who kept his cool, said in a level voice, "Don't talk that way to your mother, William."

"Yes, sir," William whined. "Can I go now?"

"Sure, but stay in touch, son, please? We mean it," Eddie advised.

"Fine," William headed into the garage to get his bike.

"You have to lighten up, Cerise," Eddie said to his wife.

"I didn't mean to—" Cerise stammered, as tears shined in her eyes. "It just…oh God, Eddie, our boy…"

He took her in his arms. "Sh! I promise, tonight Douglas will be back home where he belongs."

"Marlowe said that you were given one of those sticks—"

"A staff."

"Where is yours?"

Eddie looked at his feet for a moment. "It kind of…well, it was taken from me."

"You've got to get another one," Cerise implored.

Eddie didn't want to tell her the truth. It wasn't as if he could walk to the local *Wizards R Us* and get a brand new shiny one straight from the Forbidden Tree. He decided that to tell her would only make her worry.

They went into the kitchen and sat at the table to join Marlowe and Drusilicus. Marlowe's black eye was healed, which reflected that his abilities had improved. They all ate without speaking much.

Eddie spent the meal watching how his mother puttered about, and was happy that she looked energetic and nimble, up and down, getting this or that.

He looked across the table and met Drusilicus' eye. "Thanks for what you did for my mother."

Drusilicus reddened and regarded his plate. "It was nothing."

Eddie was amazed. Here, outside of the wizard community, divested of his huge house and the need to impress, he acted so differently from the self-important prig he always portrayed.

"My only regret is that you lost your staff," Marlowe sighed.

"Are you going to get him a new one, Marlowe?" Cerise looked at Marlowe, as Eddie nodded his head behind her and hoped the older man got the hint.

"Of course, dear lady." Marlowe rose from his seat and wiped his mouth with a napkin. "In fact, we must go into New York and get him one."

Drusilicus stood and Eddie followed suit. They praised Eleanor's cooking and Eddie gave her a quick peck on the cheek.

As they approached the door, Cerise said in a whisper, "Eddie, you don't have your car."

Eddie glanced toward the kitchen and said, "I don't need one. I'll show you later."

"I'll want to see that!" Cerise replied with a curious grin.

"It's really cool."

"Go save my baby, and take care of my big, black man." Cerise kissed him full on the lips.

Eddie went outside. The day was warm and the sun was bright. Eddie inhaled the sweet air and walked off, behind Marlowe and Drusilicus.

They strolled in silence to the woods. Eddie looked at the fallen branches that lay on the path. He picked up a large one that was about the size of his staff, though covered with bark.

"Maybe if I wish this to be my staff bad enough," Eddie said aloud. "Y'know, will and intent."

The other two glanced back at him.

"That would be most impressive." Drusilicus' staff leapt into his hand. "Shall we away?"

Eddie dropped the branch, a germ of an idea in the back of his mind, but he couldn't quite bring it to the front.

They walked into the trees and Eddie rested his palm on Marlowe's shoulder to make the transition with them. Moments later, they exited a grove near 85th Street and the west side of the park, and walked out through the Mariner's Gate and across the street to Marlowe's townhouse.

"Eddie, I'll get a small hand mirror to bring with us," Marlowe suggested, "in case we need to contact anyone."

Eddie stopped on the steps. The idea had sharpened into crystalline focus.

"Can you give me about twenty minutes?" Eddie requested. "I need to do one thing."

"What? Why?" Drusilicus demanded snottily. Apparently, the teleportation across the Hudson River had returned him to his former nasty state.

"I've got an idea."

"But we—" Drusilicus began.

"Let him go, Drusilicus," Marlowe said. "I must talk with Daniel."

"Humph!" Drusilicus snorted. "That pet vampire of yours—"

"And it will take time to assemble the potions I intend to bring."

"Very well." Drusilicus turned and walked to the door.

"What is on your mind, my friend?" Marlowe asked quietly.

"Maybe nothing," Eddie considered, "but it wouldn't hurt to try."

Marlowe shrugged. "It appears that *you* have become the mysterious one, Eddie Berman."

Eddie walked quickly across the street and up one block to 86th Street, and turned down the transverse road into the precinct. He gave a quick wave to the desk sergeant, who barely looked up, then he went straight up the stairs to the property room.

It was Sunday, and no one took much notice of him; the noise of printers, jangling phones, and raised voices covered his presence.

As he walked into the secure area, he found Hank there like a fixture.

"Hank," Eddie said, a little too jovially, "what are you doing here on a Sunday? I thought the point of being property clerk was the regular hours."

Hank shrugged. "Weekend guy needed a day off. His daughter's getting married."

"Wow." Eddie felt like the smile on his face was painted on. "I'm wondering if you have that cane I signed in last week."

If it could be here, Eddie thought. *No, I must believe it is here. I must want it to be here!*

Hank shrugged again. "I guess so. I locked it away special for you, Lew."

Eddie scratched the back of his neck awkwardly. He focused on wanting the cane to be there. Eddie did bring the cane in from New Jersey that day last week, and when Hank brought out the one in the evidence room, the one in his hand disappeared. Could that happen again?

"Can you get it for me, Hank?"

The property room did most of its business during the week. Being Sunday and early, Hank was alone. He motioned Eddie closer.

Hank spoke softly. "I heard you were suspended, Lew."

"I am, Hank, but I've also been ordered to make sure all of the paperwork on my case is done for the FBI," Eddie lied, his hands open in a "what-can-I-do?" gesture.

"They'd better pay you for the time you come in to do it." Hank reached for the keys on his belt.

"I just have to get it done, Hank," Eddie tried to sound world-weary.

"That's great," Hank said as he went through the keys. "They suspend you, but you can't go until you do the friggin' paperwork. I tell you, it sure is different since I first became a cop. Now every cop has to be one part police officer, one part lawyer, and one part friggin' bureaucrat. Sign the book, Lew."

Eddie signed, as Hank strode out of sight toward the back of the room.

Eddie closed his eyes. *It is here, it is here.*

He could hear Hank in the distance, as he fumbled with the keys, unlocked a door, and grunted at the exertion as he pulled it open.

It is here, it just has to be, Eddie repeated to himself.

The footsteps drew closer.

"You falling asleep on me, Lew?"

Eddie opened his eyes. There in Hank's hand lay the ebony stick with the silver ball at the top.

Eddie gave a small bark of surprise and pleasure, which made Hank stare at him curiously.

"I'm just happy to see it," Eddie tried to calm down and sound businesslike. "It'll make writing my report a lot easier."

Hank held out the stick. Eddie slowly reached out and grasped it. A flash of red light went from the cane into him with a small *'g'zink.'*

Eddie could feel the power as it returned to him, coursed through his veins, and rushed to his brain. He wasn't aware of how much it invigorated him until he held it again.

"What the hell was that?" Hank asked.

"Uh, must've been an electrostatic charge or something."

"Couldn't be," Hank said. "There was nothing to ground it; this stick is wood."

Eddie shrugged, "Thanks, Hank," he waved the cane as he exited.

"He did say ever since he found that stick things got weird," Hank muttered to himself and shook his head. "Now look, even I'm talking to myself."

FORTY-EIGHT

Eddie walked quickly to Marlowe's, the walking stick in his hand. He didn't want to risk trying to transform it until he was in the safe haven of the townhouse.

He knocked on the door. Frisha, who appeared to have taken up residence as the official doorman, opened it.

"Fred!" she blurted. "I hadst a terrible vision of you last evening—"

"Never mind that, Frisha, I need to know where Marlowe is."

"Downstairs with Drusilicus, methinks," Frisha said. "They came in and went straight down."

Eddie held the stick out, closed his eyes, and with the greatest pleasure felt the cane transform into his staff.

Frisha gasped. "Thou hast another staff!"

"No, Frisha," Eddie smiled and held the stick aloft. "I've got *my* staff back."

Frisha drew close and gently touched the wood. "Aye! That you did! I've ne'er heard of such a thing in all me born days. You truly are a most powerful Magus."

"A what?"

"A Magus. 'Tis the name for a gifted wizard," Frisha said. "How did thou do it?"

"A Magus has to have a few secrets, Frisha."

"I must say, it doth change things!"

"It certainly doth. Later, Frisha." Eddie walked across the huge entrance hall and entered the door that led to the marble steps of the basement.

Upon his arrival at the bottom of the stairs, he found the room to be entirely different from his last visit. Instead of an empty, cavernous space, it was filled with tall wooden bookcases. They lined the walls and formed what appeared to be an elaborate maze throughout the room.

"Marlowe?" Eddie called out as he stared up at the tall, heavy racks, which were made from some sturdy wood and stained darkly. Each one was at least twelve feet high.

There were shelves upon shelves, filled with different containers: glass jars, wooden boxes, and elaborate metal canisters. Under each item was a white paper label with words in an embellished hand.

Eddie bent and read a label under a large jar filled with an earthy, brown powder. In the intricate script it read:

Powdered Bat Wing

Eddie lurched back, and looked up at a smaller jar on a higher shelf. A thousand tiny eyes were staring back down at him. Eddie gasped and leaned in to gaze at the label:

Eye of Newt

"Man, they really use crap like this?" Eddie muttered.

"Eddie?" Marlowe's voice came out from behind the rows of bookcases.

"*Yeah*!" Eddie yelled back, as he tried to get a fix on the direction the sound emanated. "Where are you?"

"Walk towards the center of the room, then bear right."

Eddie walked past the huge wooden structures, all filled with the unique vessels, and his eye returned to the handwritten labels.

Each one he saw suggested an ingredient more elaborate and exotic than the last. There were different mushrooms, powders of unsettling colors, and even the occasional container that shook and rattled as if something alive was imprisoned and desperately sought escape.

"Marlowe?" Eddie raised his voice, as he felt he was close to the center of the room.

"This way," Marlowe called and Eddie turned down the row of the huge library to find both Marlowe and Drusilicus. They were both clad in robes, Marlowe's white, and Drusilicus's a light gray. Marlowe carried a small metal cauldron that hung from the crook of his arm by its arc-shaped handle.

"Eddie, you bear a staff," Marlowe gasped.

"I bear *my* staff, the Staff of Fire." Eddie allowed himself a smug smile.

"Didn't you say he lost it in the battle last night?" Drusilicus frowned.

"It seems quite impossible," Marlowe marveled

"In case you haven't noticed," Eddie chuckled, "everything you guys do is impossible."

"It appears," Marlowe sought to regain his composure, "that my student once again accomplishes a thing that the master cannot."

"How did you get it back?" Drusilicus asked.

"Tell you what, Dru," Eddie considered, "you figure it out, and maybe I'll give it to you."

Marlowe laughed. "A dubious gift, if you can take it back anytime you wish. This certainly will foil our adversary's plans."

"Yes," Drusilicus grew concerned, "Marlowe said you faced the warlock last night."

"It wasn't a fair fight. He blindsided Marlowe, then grabbed my kid," Eddie related, as Marlowe went to a specific box, reached in, pulled a small stone and added it to the cauldron he carried.

"From my own encounter, I must concur," Marlowe agreed and set off toward the end of the aisle. "He does not fight according to wizard traditions."

"How do wizards usually fight?" Eddie asked.

Drusilicus stood up straighter. "Challenges are usually met in an open place, where the wizard can meet his adversary face to face."

"This guy ain't interested in your traditions; he's out to beat you."

"And doing it far too effectively," Drusilicus exclaimed, then with a look to Marlowe, added, "no offense."

Marlowe shook his head, "No, no 'tis true enough."

Drusilicus and Eddie followed as the old man continued down one of the aisles. For the first time, Eddie noticed that Marlowe was wearing a conical, pointed hat on his head. It was black velvet and covered with stars and moons.

"Where did all of this come from?" Eddie glanced about, still impressed.

"This is my storeroom of ingredients for potions, Eddie," Marlowe said. "It's not as well-stocked as some, but I make do."

Eddie indicated the towering wooden structures. "Not well stocked? You mean some people have more than this?"

"Oh, yes," Drusilicus concurred.

"So what's with the hat?" Eddie asked, to change the subject.

"It is the Hat of Remembrance, Eddie." Marlowe turned at the end of the aisle and walked up another. He stooped to take a pinch of aquamarine powder from a large jar. "I have collected all of these unique substances over a period of many centuries. Even though they are labeled, I often cannot recall where I put what. By wearing the Hat of Remembrance, I can easily determine each one's location, as well as recall the recipe of every potion."

"But where did all this stuff come from?" Eddie said. "It wasn't here the last time I was down here."

"They are very powerful charms, Eddie. I maintain them in an alternate dimension, so none can find them or use any of them without my knowledge," Marlowe said, and easily stepped to another box where he took a pinch of a puke-green powder that caused an unpleasant smell to waft into the air. "Once you accept the concept of many realities layered upon each other like an onion, it becomes child's play."

"What kind of children do you know?" Eddie quipped.

"Lieutenant, you amaze me," Drusilicus said. "One moment you accomplish surprising things, and the next you can't even grasp the basics of interdimensional storage."

"I'm still tryin' to get down fourth-dimensional physics," Eddie complained.

"Ah!" Drusilicus shook his head in disgust. "I've never been a big fan of it myself."

"That's why your house looks fairly normal on the inside."

"Wait a few centuries," Marlowe said to Drusilicus. "You run out of space. Then you must either create more room or move."

"Admit it, Marlowe," Drusilicus remarked, "you just like having a bigger entrance hall than I."

"There is that." Marlowe placed something that looked like the tooth of a small carnivore into his cauldron. "There, that is all I need."

"Are you sure?" Eddie questioned. "I mean, you don't have a recipe or anything."

"As long as I wear this hat, I can recall any spell, potion, or enchantment I want in every detail," Marlowe affirmed. "Now, we should all step onto the platform."

"Why?"

Drusilicus snorted. "So we don't end up in the alternate dimension, of course. There might not be an atmosphere."

"Oh, there is," Marlowe related as they walked. "But it is frigid and lacks light." He lowered his voice. "Keeps everything nice and fresh."

The three men walked to the raised wooden structure.

"Well, I'm glad you're back to your old obnoxious self, Dru. I was beginning to like you."

Drusilicus sneered, but kept silent.

Marlowe raised his hands and announced, "*Isa Ya! Ri Ega!*"

The room began to shimmer before them, as if a heat haze distorted their view. Then, with a flash of white light, the room was empty once again.

As Eddie stood openmouthed, Marlowe walked to the corner of the platform and reached under it to extract an onyx mortar and pestle. He poured the contents of his cauldron into the stone chalice and began to grind the ingredients.

"You guys are so blasé about all of this," Eddie marveled.

"It becomes an everyday experience, lieutenant," Drusilicus clarified. "That way no one is overly impressed with oneself."

"And when are you going to start doing that?" Eddie pointed out.

"Would you two limit your barbs to when I am not witness to't?" Marlowe pulverized the contents with a firm hand.

"So, what's our plan?" Eddie focused his attention on the older man.

"You and I shall search out your son," Marlowe affirmed. "Drusilicus, I shall ask you to remain here."

"Here? I have appointments—"

"I need someone to observe the houseguests," Marlowe explained.

"Why me?" Drusilicus lamented, not happy with the arrangement.

"Because you have a better chance of seeing if they are doing anything untoward," Marlowe reasoned. "And you are experienced enough to know if they are casting any unusual spells. They trust you."

Which is more than I do, thought Eddie. *Then again, last night he helped my momma. But where was Dru when the warlock attacked? That voice...so familiar...*

Marlowe reached up and touched the hat on his head.

"Oh dear, I forgot to send the hat with everything else." He took it off, folded up the chapeau, and placed it into a pocket of his robe.

They quickly made their way up the stairs.

"Now, remember, Drusilicus, I am carrying a mirror. If you need to contact me, just call."

"Where do you intend to seek him?" Drusilicus asked.

"Is that what the potion is for?" Eddie wondered.

"All shall become clear." Marlowe opened the door to the upstairs. The room had undergone a change since Eddie's arrival. It was still as large, but it was dark, as if black curtains now covered every window.

Marlowe was completely undaunted by the change and called out, "Daniel?"

"No need to shout," Daniel said from the other side of the door, which made Eddie cry out in surprise.

"Sorry," Daniel apologized. The vampire looked very different. He wore a long, black coat that covered his entire body, a black felt hat pulled low over his face and very dark sunglasses. It made his head appear to be floating in midair, the white skin against the dark clothing.

"Thank you for coming down, Daniel," Marlowe said.

"I wanted to tell you right away," Daniel took Marlowe aside. He lowered his voice so Eddie could not hear them as they spoke.

"I still don't know why he keeps him here," Drusilicus murmured to Eddie.

"He seems like a nice guy."

"Vampires are not nice, lieutenant. They feed on blood and live perverse and immoral lives. They want nothing less than *all* wizards destroyed."

"Why?"

"We seek to bring illumination, they wish to bring unending night. Our goals are in direct opposition."

Daniel and Marlowe separated, and Drusilicus reverted to silence. As Marlowe returned, Kraft moved to the staircase quickly and was up the stairs in a few short moments.

"Why didn't he just turn into a bat?" Eddie's eyes followed Daniel.

"Hmmm?" Marlowe said absently, and looked back to the stairs. "Oh! Well, Eddie, a vampire cannot change his form during the day. Whatever shape he is when the sun rises, he remains until it sets."

"So where are you off to?" Drusilicus enjoined.

"Central Park, Drusilicus," Marlowe said, as if it were obvious.

"How could the Great Evil be there...and with a hostage?" Drusilicus seemed concerned. "Greywacke the First created it as a place of power."

"You've said that before," Eddie interjected. "I thought the park was designed by two guys named Vaux and Olmstead."

"That is what your history books tell," Drusilicus puffed out his chest. "But it is a creation by wizards for wizards. That is why the arches are all named for some of our most famous brethren."

"Like Riftstone?" Eddie said.

"Exactly," Drusilicus smiled.

"So, is there a guy named Driprock or Pinebank?" Eddie named two other park arches.

"Driprock is a fine man," Marlowe remarked, "a bit unlucky, but well-respected."

"I was kidding."

"All that has occurred revolved around the park," Marlowe challenged. "The attacks, the stolen talismans—it all took place there."

"But it is a place of power, Marlowe," Drusilicus argued.

"Yes, but a place of power can be used for good or ill. The Great Evil has found a way to use the park for his own dark purpose. Daniel has now given me the final bit of information I needed to find him."

Drusilicus looked dubious, as if Marlowe didn't possess the ability to find a needle in a needle stack.

"And I'm here to help," Eddie affirmed.

"And when did demons become part of your training?" Drusilicus inquired.

"Since last week."

Drusilicus started to say something, thought better of it and sullenly shut his mouth.

Marlowe, as this exchange took place, poured the powder from his mortar into an envelope he pulled from his robes.

"Let us make haste!" he said to Eddie.

As they passed through the door of Marlowe's townhouse, Marlowe's robes and staff changed in the blink of an eye into a tweed jacket, sweater vest, pants, and sensible shoes, and his staff returned to a mere walking stick.

Eddie quickly transformed his staff into the credit card and hid it back in his wallet. However, as he shut the door, he thought he saw someone watching them from inside the house. He glanced back, yet saw no one.

The two men walked across the street into the park through Mariner's Gate. As he and Marlowe crossed the street, Eddie caught a glimpse of someone ducking out of sight with little finesse.

They strolled past the playground and up the incline to reach Summit Rock. They stood near the small stone wall on the asphalt path where they had a beautiful view of the park.

It was a glorious Sunday, and they watched as people flew kites and played softball in the distance.

Marlowe walked to the stone staircase and knelt as he worked his hands through the remnants of a long-dead fire.

"What's this?" Eddie said.

"Ashes of the first sacrifice." Marlowe pulled out a pair of tweezers and the envelope he'd used earlier. He sorted a few pieces that looked like fragments of burned bone and put them in the envelope.

"What's it for?"

"It's the last ingredient of the potion that will track your son."

"What do we need another potion for?" Eddie complained. "Can't you just wave your stick and follow him?"

"Eddie, you must remember, we do battle with one who knows our ways. Therefore, we must augment our abilities."

Marlowe rose and pulled out a small bottle, which held what looked like dirty water. He pulled the small cork, carefully poured the contents of the envelope into it, sealed it, and shook it vigorously.

"So, we dip our staffs in that stuff, and it will lead to my son?"

"Oh no, Eddie." Marlowe uncapped the liquid, which resembled very wet mud. "We drink it!"

Eddie looked at the bottle in Marlowe's hand, and his mouth puckered as he recalled the taste of the potion he'd ingested the previous night.

"Do we have to? I mean, can't *you* just drink it, and I'll follow you?"

"Eddie, I've added a little something special to make it impossible for either a wizard or demon to detect our approach."

Marlowe took a large swig and swallowed the mouthful in one gulp.

"Ah!" Marlowe savored. "I even added extra vitamins, minerals, and a pleasant chocolate flavor."

"Really?" Eddie took the proffered potion.

"Try it!"

Eddie chugged it down in one gulp.

He dropped the bottle, and fell into spasms of coughing.

"What the hell?" Eddie bleated. "That was *awful!*"

"Hmm?" Marlowe murmured innocently as he retrieved the fallen bottle and reinserted the cork. "I may have exaggerated the quality of the chocolate taste."

"You're telling me!" Eddie spat to get the taste out of his mouth. "Man, do I need a Tic-Tac."

"Fresh out." Marlowe took out a small, thin branch from his pocket. "Chew on this."

Eddie put the stick in his mouth. It tasted like birch beer.

"Birch root. Cleanses the palate."

"After that stuff, even chewing a tree tastes good," Eddie grimaced. "I thought wizards didn't lie."

"I didn't lie. I misled."

"You are more slippery than an eel."

"Why, thank you, Eddie."

Eddie chewed on the stick and followed Marlowe as he walked south down from the height of Summit Rock. Then he turned and headed east.

"So what did Daniel tell you?"

"He found the demon's hiding place," Marlowe announced triumphantly.

"What? How?"

"I have been sending Daniel out at night on a special mission to track down Abraxas' lair. It took him days…well, nights. But last night near dawn, he saw the creature return to the hideaway."

"And it's here in the park?"

"Yes," Marlowe said as they followed a walking path parallel to West Drive and over the 79th Street transverse road. "In fact, it is in the heart of the park. I should have realized it at once. Follow me."

Marlowe began to walk with his short, fast stride and Eddie jogged to keep up.

Everywhere Eddie looked he saw people enjoying the park. Some were laid out on blankets on the grass in the warm sunshine, others jogged or walked a dog, delighted to be released from the tiny confines of a Manhattan apartment. Still others merely strolled alone or with a companion, savoring the oasis from rushing traffic and the fast-paced existence only a few hundred feet away.

Without a word exchanged, Marlowe and Eddie turned left and crossed a bridge, landscaped with large stones on the far side of the short span. A sign sat on an ornamental metal pole that read "Bank Rock Bridge."

"Damn," Eddie spat. "Ol' Bankrock got a bridge named after him."

"Hmm? Ah, yes. He made quite a fuss over not getting an arch, so Greywacke named this for him."

"Guess he was a pain even a hundred and fifty years ago?"

"I try not to judge my fellow wizards. However, Bankrock has been much the same as long as I've known him."

They walked up stone stairs carved into glacier rocks and proceeded to the Rustic Arch, a twelve-foot-tall, narrow passageway of cut stones that looked as if it belonged at the entrance of a church and not standing in the middle of a park.

It was too narrow to let them pass through together, so they went one at a time and began to ascend more stone steps up the winding path into the Rambles, wild and overgrown as an untouched wilderness.

Their pace increased; the two men began to resemble race-walkers, as they both moved so quickly.

The lake was to their right, and beyond it tall buildings shot above the highest trees like a mirage that hovered over a desert.

They passed over a tiny rustic bridge, made to resemble a wild collection of intertwining branches, as if it grew naturally, instead of being planned and placed in position.

Although Marlowe moved quickly, his breath was still slow and steady. Eddie was once again impressed by the old man's stamina. He was beginning to get winded and envied the ability to keep going untiringly.

Eddie finally pulled on Marlowe's sleeve, wheezing, "Can we slow down a bit?"

Marlowe's pace decreased to a more reasonable speed, and Eddie fought to catch his breath as they approached another bridge.

"Eddie, you will enjoy this!" Marlowe said. "The view from the Bow Bridge is one of the most spectacular sights in Manhattan."

The path widened out, and a heavily ornamented bridge appeared before them. Eddie could see how it got its name, as it lifted in the center like the graceful curve of a hunting bow. It also occurred to him that it might be named in honor of some guy named "Bow."

The bridge was constructed of heavy cast iron, painted white, the balustrades decorated with a repeating pattern of fanciful, interlaced circles.

They walked over it, and Eddie looked at the water sparkling on both sides, and the panoramic view that allowed him to see two skylines: Fifth Avenue to his left, and Central Park West on his right.

Eddie found it funny that in his day to day work in the park he'd never taken the time to stop and enjoy these sights.

"Are we close," Eddie asked with a sudden concern for Douglas, "or are we going to have to walk the whole park?"

"Right this way, Eddie." Marlowe led him on the path past Navy Hill in silence, and as they turned the corner, Bethesda Terrace appeared before them. The sun shimmered down on the fountain and the fanciful architecture of the grandiose two-level sandstone construction.

Eddie looked at the older man.

"Is *that* where we're going?" Eddie pointed at the terrace.

The path led to the large, round fountain, which was capped with a tall monument where an angel stood atop, as if guarding the fountain below.

"Where else but the 'Heart of the park'?" Marlowe observed. "The monster has been hiding here the entire time."

"Where? In the fountain?"

"Look past it, Eddie," Marlowe indicated.

Eddie shifted his eyes away from the movement of the fountain, but it took effort. The bronze sculpture and the dancing waters pulled his attention so completely, it was easy to believe it was the only thing that should be noted.

Next to it, Eddie saw an elaborate building. Two wide staircases ran up either side, up to street level or down to the lake level. They were massive, heavily sculptured and decorated.

As they drew closer, Eddie could see that the building would have once been called an arcade. It was made from cut stone, and open to the air with seven large Romanesque arches that spanned from the paved ground to the roadway above. On the top was a low wall of pierced stone, and a guardrail to prevent anyone from accidentally falling from the upper deck.

The fountain and terrace were busy in the late morning light. People congregated around the cooling spray of the water. A man strummed a guitar on one of the huge stairways, couples passed hand in hand, and tourists took in the sights from the upper terrace.

Marlowe unhesitatingly stepped on the red brick and granite stones of the walkway past the visitors and right to the open arcade.

They fell into shadows as they entered the building, an open space that lead to yet another huge staircase on the far side of the access road, which ran above their heads.

Two men, who appeared to be in the middle of a transaction, turned angry eyes toward the newcomers. There was an immediate recognition that Eddie was a cop, and the two men hastily left.

Eddie shook his head. He recognized the type as easily as they did him; druggies doing a deal.

He looked up at the ceiling to take his mind off them and gasped.

"Look at that," Eddie pointed at the elaborate mosaic on the ceiling. The colors wove into hypnotic patterns of blues, blacks, yellows, and browns that suggested a museum work as opposed to a display in a dark, empty, outdoor tunnel.

"Ah, yes," Marlowe glanced up and smiled. "Minton tiles, very rare. In fact, this is the only outdoor display of them in the world. The designer, Owen Jones, was a friend of Greywacke, who helped him develop the finishing process."

"They are so beautiful, almost magical," Eddie gaped, surprised he'd never seen this hidden treasure before.

"As a matter of fact, they are magical," Marlowe informed. "What you are looking at, Eddie, is a coded message that only another wizard can translate. This building, Bethesda Terrace, is the spiritual center of the park."

"And these tiles, they tell you something? Maybe where my kid is?"

"I read them as easily as you would read a road map, Eddie." Marlowe indicated the walls around them. "Do you see the niches?"

Eddie's eyes had adjusted to the lesser light of the arcade after the bright sun of the terrace. He could see within the arcade sections of the walls bedecked with three-dimensional arches carved into the sandstone, which mimicked the arches open to the terrace, only smaller in scope. The center of each niche was painted with figures and designs.

Marlowe glanced around, saw they were alone, and gave a delicate wave of his cane, which caused a small ball of light to rise up to the ceiling and light up one of the mosaics.

The light only made the phenomenal artwork more beautiful, with its patterns and sweeping lines.

Marlowe looked back at the wall, and gave one more check up and down the great hall to make sure they were unwatched.

He gestured with his cane, murmured words under his breath. Then he strode to the alcove and laid his hand on the carved arch and pushed.

There was a "click" as if an elaborate mechanism gave way behind the wall, and with a rumble of stone and a sound like rusted hinges, the wall slid back.

Eddie looked out at the entrance arches. No one paid any heed to them. Yet, he had the odd sense that there was someone who watched them.

"Eddie," Marlowe whispered.

Eddie turned to see that the archway had moved back into the wall a good four feet, and a tunnel was on the right in the exposed alcove.

"Come, quickly." Marlowe stepped into the tunnel, and the white light flew down from the ceiling and lit their path.

"Curiouser and curiouser," Eddie said.

He stepped on a huge granite stair and turned into the tunnel. As they walked in, the wall shifted, and the stone moved back to its former position with the sound of rock on rock. The arch became solid, and no cracks or openings existed to show their route.

On Navy Hill, Jason Wilcox lowered his binoculars and wiped his brow. "Where the hell did they go?" he muttered.

He decided to contact his partner, Sam, and get him up here to keep watch. He would also get a team together, probably pull in Conners.

He moved away, unaware that on the nearby Bow Bridge, he was being observed by a figure who carried a large, gnarled wooden staff.

FORTY-NINE

Marlowe shifted his clothes to the more comfortable robes as the wall closed behind them. With a thought, Eddie's clothing shifted as well. His staff appeared in his hand, and a small reddish ball of light rose up to assist in illuminating the path.

The tunnel was constructed of carved stone; in fact, it reflected light like marble, and there were large, elegant arches every fifteen feet. Each one was embellished with carved designs a little different from the last.

"How did all this get here?" Eddie said.

"Greywacke worked with the designers," whispered Marlowe. "He used his abilities to create interdimensional portals throughout the park. I don't know why it didn't occur to me that the Great Evil might conceal himself down here."

"You say Daniel saw him go in here? Did he open that portal and go through the wall?"

"Yes, though I don't know how he gained the ability. Perhaps his warlock helped. I believe he hides in the catacombs."

"Catacombs? There are catacombs *under* Central Park?"

"Yes and no. Going through the arch, we traversed dimensions which brought us into an alternate reality that resides next to our own."

"Do I need to understand what you just said?"

"Not really."

"Good."

They walked through another beautifully appointed archway and into a room that was spherical in design. The ceiling was totally round and rose up at least twelve feet. However, directly in front of them were two tunnels, each going in a different direction.

"I suppose that this is the start of the catacombs?" Eddie asked.

"Yes. And did I mention if we go the wrong way, we'll end up in a maze?"

"Is there a damn Minotaur in them?" Eddie worried.

Marlowe sighed with exasperation. "That's in Greece."

"Good!"

"Besides, the Minotaur died off centuries ago."

"Never hurts to ask. What do we do now?"

"That potion we drank should affect us. Do you feel drawn to one opening or another?"

Eddie stood and assessed the two tunnels. He felt a strange pull, as if he were a piece of metal and there stood a giant magnet nearby. "I feel drawn to the right."

"As do I. Let us go," Marlowe said.

"Is there any creature down there we should worry about?"

"Only Abraxas."

"And he can transform into almost anything."

"Yes."

"It just keeps getting better."

"Keep your voice down," Marlowe murmured. "If our adversaries are down here, they won't be able to sense us, but they *can* hear us."

Silently they continued. The tunnel descended on a subtle incline, and Eddie realized he'd been going downhill ever since they'd walked through the archway. Wherever they were, it couldn't be in *his* Manhattan, as they would eventually run into a subway tunnel or one of the hundred other underground spaces burrowed through the bedrock.

They came to another round room, which subdivided the tunnel a second time. This time they felt a pull to the left, and continued their descent.

After following that passage for a few minutes, they reached yet another round room that contained three tunnels.

Eddie looked to his wrist, but his watch was once again lost in the transition from twenty-first century clothing to wizard garb.

"How long have we been down here?" Eddie whispered.

"It's hard to say. About thirty minutes."

"I thought you always knew what time it was."

"Time passes at a different rate in this place, Eddie."

"So, you think Big Red has been hiding down here since that amulet was dug up?"

"I believe so." Marlowe pulled at his beard. "That's why he was so difficult to locate, being underground in an alternate reality."

"And he still had access to the park."

"Yes."

"Can he do more here? I mean, is he more powerful?"

"With the warlock's help, the Great Evil can teleport, turn invisible, or use any of the powers of one who bears a staff."

"So why did he change into a snake and slither down a drain when we all ganged up on him?"

"He was alone at the time, separated from his warlock."

"Or he was there and didn't want to tip his hand."

Marlowe nodded gravely. "I cannot believe that any we know would choose to work with the demon."

"Well, I saw that warlock myself and he was familiar."

"In any case, we must separate Abraxas from his companion. Working together, united with the power of the talismans, they have the advantage."

Marlowe held up his hand, and they both stopped.

Eddie felt a cool breeze brush past his face.

"We are close," Marlowe whispered.

Marlowe made a quick slash with his hand in the air, and the white light over his head twinkled out. Eddie followed suit with similar results.

Down the tunnel a dim light flickered.

"The light at the end of the tunnel," whispered Marlowe.

Eddie bent close to Marlowe's ear. "How many buildings have you gone in with a perp waiting for you?"

"Well, let's see, there was...then again..." Marlowe stammered. "I believe that the answer is none."

"First mistake a rookie makes is to go into a dangerous situation too cocky," Eddie warned. "Instead, you go in thinking they're expecting you and have a bazooka aimed at the door."

Marlowe considered this for a moment, then nodded. "What do you suggest?"

"We go into the room slowly. You go low and I'll go high. We lead with our staffs, ready to fight, and scan the room before we move into view."

Marlowe shook his head. "Eddie, this is not the way wizards fight. We meet each other in the open—"

"Yeah. Like at my house, where he snuck up on your ass?"

Marlowe was silent for a moment. "I see your point."

"Good. This warlock acts like a thug, we treat him like one. If fireworks start, stay low and concentrate on getting my son out."

Marlowe nodded. "This is really quite exhilarating."

"Stay focused," Eddie hissed. Then, crouching low, Eddie moved forward toward the lit end of the tunnel, his staff out in front of him.

He wished he had his service revolver. Now that would be a surprise for that damn warlock!

Marlowe easily kept up with him and moved as silently as a cat.

They came to an archway, which was another of those round marble rooms. Off to the left, another archway was the source of the light.

Eddie pushed Marlowe down to the crawling position as they entered the room, and on his hands and knees, Eddie moved quickly to frame the other archway.

Peering beyond he almost dropped his staff.

The archway opened on a huge cavern, which Eddie felt was terribly familiar. The ceiling was at least fifty feet above his head and curved, with Astrological symbols painted in stark contrast.

In a flash, he realized what it looked like: Grand Central Station.

Except it wasn't.

If it had been Grand Central, Eddie knew there'd be escalators and ticket booths, as well as merchants selling coffee and flowers, with painted letters on the different archways to indicate how to get to the trains, and paths that led to streets and avenues that framed the enormous building.

This was different. No ticket sellers, though huge archways, wide staircases going in different directions to marble platforms of different sizes and heights that went nowhere. No escalators, though the huge space was lit with cast iron fixtures topped with glowing spheres that contained candles or burning gas. A series of floodlights wound around the room from a cornice twenty feet in the air.

This gave the entire room a confusing appearance, like an Escher print, where your perception of up and down shifted depending on where you focused your attention.

Marlowe peeked out from the far side of the arch.

Directly in front of them was a stairway that descended one flight to a platform, then separated into two sets of stairs on either end, which curved to the floor.

It was in plain view of anyone who watched from the many other high places in the room.

"By Zoroaster," Eddie muttered, which caused Marlowe to look up in surprise.

Eddie crouched low and stayed in the shadows, crab-walking next to his mentor.

"We go down there, and we're sitting ducks." Eddie's eyes scanned the room.

"True," Marlowe nodded solemnly.

Eddie made a gesture, his robe transformed back into a suit and his staff shrank to be returned to his wallet.

"What are you doing?" Marlowe hissed.

"Our only advantage is that we have one bit of information that they don't."

"I don't understand—"

"They don't know I've got my staff back. Let's use that."

Eddie pointed along the staircase to a platform.

"I'm going to go down, right in plain sight, and make a lot of noise. You stay low and move to that platform," Eddie pointed. "Once there, you attack."

"Eddie, to face the enemy without your staff. That is dangerous indeed," Marlowe cautioned.

"All I care is that you get my son out of here, you got that?"

"Yes, Eddie, I do," Marlowe agreed.

"Remember, wait 'til I hit the center of the floor before you move, understand?"

Marlowe nodded.

"Okay, let's go." Eddie rose out of his crouch and swaggered down the steps.

He reached the landing, and the room was silent except for a low moan of a distant breeze echoing in the empty passageways.

"Hello!" Eddie said. "I know you're down here. Olie-Olie In-come-free!"

There was an ominous growl that echoed in the huge cavern, as Eddie walked up another flight of steps that climbed at a different angle.

"Now, don't go startin' an attitude with me, Abraxas. You know why I'm here. You got my kid, and I want him back."

From the corner of his eye, he saw Marlowe slip down the stairs and behind a platform.

"Come on, I haven't got all day!" Eddie shouted. "Or are you afraid to face a guy who doesn't even have any powers? Huh? What did you do? Turn yourself into a chicken?"

His voice echoed in the expansive space, and Eddie could feel he was watched by malevolent eyes.

Eddie saw a flash of blue light, jumped and turned to avoid it. However, it shot past him and struck Marlowe, who toppled to the ground as his staff fell from his hands.

An evil chuckle reverberated off the walls.

A figure walked up the steps of a platform. Red-skinned and muscular, Abraxas rose up like a huge marble statue. He carried a large pole, which had a net hanging off of it, as if he'd been fishing.

Inside the net lay Douglas.

Unconscious—or dead.

No, no, don't even think that, Eddie screamed inside his head.

"So easy to take care of the old man," Abraxas chuckled matter-of-factly. "You just hit him on his left side; he's got a blind spot."

"Give me my son, you sonuvabitch!" Eddie cried out, and ran down the steps toward Abraxas. However, the demon's platform was approached by a set of stairs that were positioned at a ninety-degree angle to the floor.

Eddie rushed up two steps before he lost his balance, then fell to the marble floor with a resounding '*thud.*'

"Why are you fighting us, Eddie?" came another voice.

The sound came from a platform that looked like it hung upside down in midair from Eddie's point of view. On it stood a hooded figure.

Eddie's mouth fell open. The warlock! And yet, he appeared taller than the previous night.

"You took my son!" Eddie struggled to stand up.

The hooded wizard strode down the stairs and onto the platform above Eddie.

"You can have him back," the figured snapped his fingers. "Release the boy, demon."

Abraxas gave a nod, and lowered the pole next to Eddie. The net fell open, and Douglas lay next to him.

Eddie grabbed the boy and checked his pulse. It was strong, and he saw Douglas draw breath.

"He is unharmed. Nothing but a simple sleep spell, which can be removed at any time. I was never going to hurt him. I needed a way to get you here, so we could talk."

The figure walked down the steps, and lowered himself into a crouching position, pulling back the hood of his robe.

Eddie looked up to see Trefoil.

"You?" Eddie said, shocked. "But how...why?"

"I know...questions. Why join forces with a demon? Eddie, it's hard to 'splain it all. But I can show you."

Trefoil held out his hand to Eddie.

Eddie glanced over at Abraxas, who appeared to have lost interest. Then he reached up and took Trefoil's hand.

The room spun out of existence.

The first thing Eddie was aware of was the smell of smoke.

"Where are we?" Eddie asked, rising to his feet.

They were inside a small cabin. Eddie could see pressed dirt under his shoes, and the walls made of large logs, fitted on top of each other and chinked with a gray mortar. The roof was only inches above his head.

Trefoil stood next to Eddie, his staff in his hand. "You are with me in a memory. Nothing here is real. No one can see us and we cannot interfere."

"I've been inside a memory before," Eddie stated. "Why'd you bring me here?"

"To show you the truth, Eddie."

Trefoil walked to the door of the cabin and he and Eddie passed right through.

To mayhem.

In front of them was a huge wooden church engulfed in flames. There was a sign hung from the steeple, which read:

African Methodist Episcopal Zion Church

All Welcome

The sign burned as well; the paint on its surface bubbled and hissed from the heat.

People ran every which way, with bundles in their hands. Some were black, but Eddie caught flashes of white skin. They were dressed in clothing from another era. The men wore long black coats, or a variation of a tailcoat, with vests and white shirts. The women all wore long dresses and covered their heads with hats from a plain wimple to a full bonnet.

White men in strange, long, gray uniforms ran past, and Eddie tried to see who they were. Military officers from a bygone time? They carried billy clubs, but unlike a modern policeman's baton, these were longer and much nastier-looking. Some of the sticks had nails pushed through the head, making a frightful weapon.

Eddie saw the glint of a badge on several of the men's chests.

The uniformed men wore gray hats like a conductor on a train and carried firearms in holsters. But they led with the clubs, yelled, pushed, and knocked down unarmed citizens as if they harvested wheat with a sickle.

"Who are these men? What is going on?" Eddie shouted to be heard above the din.

"They are called 'Keepers,'" Trefoil said and walked through the middle of the bedlam unalarmed. "'Round here we called them the 'Sparrow Police.' They're NYPD, Eddie, and it's October 1, 1857. Today is moving day!"

A big policeman, if that's what he was, marched toward a thin, pale woman with fiery-red hair. He raised his club just as a black man leapt between them. The officer didn't care that his target changed, and struck the black man in the head. The man hit the ground and the woman cried out, "*Husband!*" and dove to shield him with her own body.

"My God, what is this place?" Eddie cried. It looked like a village from a movie of the Old West. A circle of simple homes, well-kept and in good repair around the burning church.

Yet, everywhere he turned people ran, the police pushed, struck, and shoved them on their way. An older black man stood up and raised his cane to defend himself against a man twice his size. The big white man pulled out his pistol and waved the man to go. Crestfallen, the old man took his bundle and slunk slowly off.

Trefoil walked through the chaos as passively as a guide in a museum. "This is Seneca Village. America's first attempt at integration."

"Integration? When was this, again?"

"More than a hundred-and-sixty years ago, right here in New York City," Trefoil said, as he advanced purposely through the escaping crowd. "And these people you see were landowners with deeds to the property they lived on. The newspapers called them squatters."

"Why is this happening?" Eddie asked, as another gray-uniformed thug threw a torch into an empty house.

"It's happening 'cause the landowners are black, Eddie. Not all of them, but most. The city bought up the land around them, then sent the police to close down their businesses. Tonight, the Keepers are here to move them out by force. After all, colored people don't need to own land. And worse, they had the audacity to let Irish and others live amongst them. Some even dared to marry a person of another race."

Eddie was shocked by the brutality all around him, but followed Trefoil as he passed through a door to one of the houses on the far end of the village.

A black woman, her head covered with a scarf, was on her hands and knees in a corner. She turned with terrified eyes, but seeing who came through the door, relaxed.

A slightly younger version of Trefoil stood before Eddie.

Eddie looked to the older man at his side. The Trefoil of his acquaintance stood there in his robes, invisible to all but him.

The younger man stood directly in front of Trefoil in a velvet frock coat, brocade vest, white shirt, with a black satin cravat around the sparkling white collar. His hair was long and curly, but his beard was neatly trimmed and well cared for.

Eddie looked from Trefoil to Trefoil. His Trefoil had aged, but not more than five or ten years in appearance. His hair was still dark-gray and he'd gained only a few wrinkles around the eyes.

"Hear me, do you not? We must dig it up," the woman said with an accent that reflected the Caribbean. "We must use its great power!"

She turned back to the floor and began to remove floorboards.

Younger Trefoil went to her and fell to his knees. He took her hands and pulled her gently to a sitting position.

"Mara, I cannot," he said. "It goes against all I have sworn to protect."

Mara pulled her hands free from his and grasped his coat by the shoulders. "Then go. Go out and strike them dead. I know you have the power to do it."

A woman's scream came from outside, and they both looked to the doorway and listened.

"These people are friends!" she hissed. "They came here to live some place other than slums! They came because of you!"

"They came because of Andrew Williams. I am not responsible," Trefoil said.

"But, you have the power!" she demanded, then let him go. She stood and strode purposely to a wooden armoire. Reaching behind it, she extracted a wizard's staff. She held it out to him. "Use it!"

"I do not—"

"You claim to fight evil," Mara snapped and jabbed her finger toward the door. "There be evil. Smite them where they stand."

The door burst open and two men in uniform crashed into the room, right through Eddie and the elder Trefoil. They held their clubs at the ready.

The woman handed Trefoil his staff, then moved behind him.

The two men were large and brutish; the bigger of the two barely fit his uniform.

"You niggers going to go quietly?" the large policeman threatened, while he tapped his hand with his wicked looking club.

"You have no right," Trefoil said. "We bought this land and it is ours."

"Don't he talk nice, sarge," the smaller man said, giving a crooked smile that showed a history of poor dental hygiene.

"I ain't here to argue with ye," the sergeant said as he moved closer, his eye on the stick Trefoil was holding. "The City of New York has evicted ye, and out ye go."

"You could jus' leave," the smaller man said, and his eyes sparkled with excitement, "or we'll help you on your way."

The big man moved with surprising swiftness and circumambulated toward Trefoil. Trefoil's jaw set, and his staff flashed blue light. Two beams slashed the air, and the men were slammed back against the far wall.

"Yes!" Mara announced triumphantly, a smile growing on her face. She leaned closer to Trefoil and whispered in his ear. "Go, strike them all down."

"It will make no difference," younger Trefoil said, and looked at the two men unconscious on the floor. "Bringing down these men will only make them send an army."

"Then you shall smite an army!" her voice rose ecstatically.

Trefoil shook his head. "I will not. I gave my word to help Greywacke bring his plans to fruition. I came here tonight only for you. Come away with me."

She recoiled from him, her hand to her mouth. "You will not fight? You will let them take my land?"

"We can move on. You and I, together. We shall find another place, rebuild."

"It is no better where e'er we go," the woman spat out.

"Mara, you know the power I wield. I can show you the world." Trefoil tried to take her in his arms.

She pushed him away. "Go with you? Coward! Go and save yourself, if that be your will. If you will not unleash your power, then I shall raise the demon. I can do it! My mother taught me the words."

She fell back to the corner and pulled at the floor boards, which came up in her hands.

"I fight evil, and most of all the Great Evil. You want to unleash him," Trefoil argued.

"Get out!" she stormed. "Keep your word to that white interloper, who only chooses to befriend the rich."

Young Trefoil stared at her a moment as she began to pull away the dirt. He turned, walked out of the room, and shut the door behind him.

Eddie and older Trefoil stood watching as she continued. She clawed the dirt with her hands and dug.

A groan came from one of the officers as he began to regain consciousness.

She gave a cry of triumph and pulled a golden chain from the dark soil. The round medallion sparkled in the light of the oil lamp.

"Now, I have the power to stop them all," Mara rose to her feet. She turned and saw the two men as they got up on their feet groggily.

"What didst ye do to us, bitch?" the bigger man said.

She laughed. "I have far worse for a fat pig like you."

She held up the amulet and began to chant, "*Alsi ku nushi—*"

The air was suddenly charged like the summer sky right before a thunderstorm. A wind blew through the room, and the gold medal began to glow.

"Enough of this." The large man moved forward and brought his club down on her hand.

A horrible cracking noise filled the air as her fingers were broken and the amulet fell. It bounced on the wooden floor and rolled back through the open floorboards and into the dirt.

Shocked, Mara saw it fall. The pain had not yet reached her. With a wail, she leapt at the man.

She never reached him.

One quick swing of the club, and she fell to the floor, as blood poured from her head.

"Oh Jesus," the other man said, on his feet too late to stop his partner. He bent over Mara. "Ye killed her."

"Listen to me." The bigger man looked down at the fallen body. "We were told to get them out. Who cares if a couple o' niggers are dead?"

He reached out with the club and knocked over the oil lamp. It fell to the floor and smashed, fire beginning to spread on the wooden floor.

"There!" the big man said. "We've done our duty in this house."

Eddie and Trefoil followed the men out as the house began to burn.

"The bigwigs said move 'em out. We've gone and done it." The bigger man rubbed his head. He glanced around to see that the area was clear of everyone except the Keepers. The red-haired woman helped her black husband to his feet, and they limped away with a cheap suitcase. Several other houses burned like the one they just left. "The newspapers are controlled by City Hall, no one will know of this."

"All this to build a park." The younger man shook his head.

Eddie stopped and looked at Trefoil, whose expression was grim.

"That's right, Eddie," Trefoil said, tears reflected in his eyes in the firelight. "They killed Mara and destroyed Seneca Village to build Central Park."

FIFTY

Eddie's vision faded to gray, then with a feeling that made his stomach turn, he found himself again on the platform in the extra-dimensional version of Grand Central. Reality—or what passed for it at this moment—had returned.

He stood next to Trefoil, who held his staff and watched him. Trefoil's eyes seemed older than a few moments earlier.

Eddie tried to make his mouth work, but he was overwhelmed. He stared over to see his son still asleep, yet now he had been moved to another platform which hung at an impossible angle to his own.

What if they did that today? Eddie thought. *Just came and took our house and land. Could I protect my wife, my sons, or even myself?*

He shook his head to clear it. "All right, Seneca Village was torn down, and it was brutal. What does that have to do with helping Big Red or stealing my kid?"

"It hasn't changed, Eddie," Trefoil insisted. "Racism, brutality, the horrors men do to their fellow men. I see it every day."

"So do I and that makes me want to change it."

"That's the way I used to think. I have lived as a wizard for over six hundred years. I've been more than a wizard; I've been a black man with a long life. I see it ain't gonna change. Not while mankind is in charge."

"What are you saying?" Eddie shifted his body to put himself between Trefoil and his son in case the conversation went bad.

"Let Abraxas have his way. Give him the fifth talisman, bring down Armageddon. When it's over, we wizards will pick up the pieces."

"That's crazy," Eddie ranted.

"Hear me out, it makes sense." Trefoil clutched his staff. "It'll be cataclysmic, and folks are gonna die. But, not everybody. We start over and guide mankind to a thousand years of peace."

Trefoil turned and gesticulated at the large open ceiling. "It's all clear to me. Mara died, and for what? So Greywacke could create his place of power? So some self-important white developers could feel good about building a park for the common man?" He turned to face Eddie. "So I could get a Goddamn arch named after me?"

"But, Armageddon—" Eddie backed away from Trefoil.

"It's going to happen anyway," Trefoil speculated. "Maybe we're just speeding up the process. Abraxas ain't really all that bad, once you get to know him. He's been around forever, and after forty thousand years, he'll tell you, human beings don't change."

Eddie looked back at the red giant. He sat with his arms folded and his legs crossed. He gave a smile and a shrug to Eddie, as if they were two neighbors exchanging familiarities.

"You'll be safe, and so will your family, I promise. I just want your help. What do you owe the other wizards? They're nothin' but a bunch of crackers, you come right down to it."

Eddie tried to think fast. "People will die."

Trefoil shrugged. "They're mortals; they'll all die sooner or later. You and me, we're gonna live a long time—maybe forever if we want."

"Why me?" Eddie glanced over to Marlowe who lay unconscious.

"I want all of the wizards to join me. But, you think in new ways. You can help me convince them that I did it for all."

"What happens if I don't agree? I end up like Riftstone?"

Trefoil exhaled with a sigh. "That was unfortunate. Riftstone knew that I tol' Drusilicus' apprentice about the amulet."

"So, you killed him."

"Hey, man, it was more than that. He needed to be removed, to weaken the Five, so I could help Abraxas collect the talismans."

"And you faked your own injuries. Why?"

Trefoil smiled and reached into his robe. "All part of the plan, maybe the smartest part."

He pulled out a black velvet bag and held it up. Eddie saw that the demon uncrossed his arms, stood up, and stared at what Trefoil held. "Do you know what this is?"

Eddie glanced over at Abraxas again. "Something that big, red, and ugly wants?"

"You're good," Trefoil smiled. "You know about the robbery of Mayan artifacts from the Metropolitan Museum of Art?"

"You did it?"

"Thass right," Trefoil smirked. "An' I got me a prize."

He pulled a flap open and a flat, black obsidian stone came from the bag, one surface polished to the point of being highly reflective. It appeared to suck the light away from its immediate area, and Trefoil's hand almost disappeared into darkness.

"That must be the Mirror of Tezcatlipoca." Eddie looked upon the polished surface.

"I'm impressed. Now you know the other reason we had to take out Riftstone."

"Yes, a blood sacrifice to activate it," Eddie said. "Like the others."

"Only it was activated with the blood of one of the Five." Trefoil gazed proudly at the dark stone.

"I take it you brought that into Marlowe's townhouse, despite all his protections."

"With your help and Marlowe's. I had it on me in the hospital, and Marlowe brought me and the mirror right in his front door." Trefoil held up the black, round stone.

"That's what caused the fireworks? It absorbed some of our powers?" Eddie reasoned.

"If you hadn't stopped it, this stone would possess *all* the power of the Five."

Eddie began to pace, just like when he was in the station house. "So you put yourself in a coma, so that we'd attempt to revive you, and then that mirror would absorb our powers. You didn't count on me breaking free."

"That's why I want your help, Eddie. You and me together, with Abraxas, will be unstoppable."

Eddie looked at the demon, who now watched the two men fixedly.

"What if this bad boy gets that mirror and decides he wants to take all of us out, you included?" Eddie suggested. "The Five are his only threat. Once he's got the upper hand, you think he's just going to do what you want?"

"It is his destiny to bring Armageddon. He has no interest in us. Once he possesses the fifth talisman, we won't be able to stop him."

"So the mirror is the fourth. What is the fifth one?"

"It can only be used on the solstice, when it is at its full power. All of that energy, three thousand years of it, will be transferred to the Great Evil and whoever helps him."

Eddie looked over at the demon. "Glad you've been holding back, big guy."

The demon shrugged noncommittally.

"So," Eddie said. "Tell you what. Give me the details about the last talisman, and I'll consider joining you."

"That's one jive ass offer, Eddie," Trefoil ridiculed. "Work with me, and you'll see it come to pass. Think about it—a new world, no crime, no murder, and none of the faults of the old, evil human race. A world of the enlightened."

Eddie realized he'd gotten as much information from Trefoil as he could. Now he would either have to commit, or take on Trefoil and Abraxas, with his son a hostage.

"I know you got your staff back, Eddie," Trefoil gave him a wink. "I don't know how, but you *do* keep surprising me."

Eddie exhaled. His one ambush was gone. He needed to change tactics, quickly. "I don't really think you want to hurt anyone, Trey. That's why you used the Hand of Glory at my house. You could have killed everyone, but instead you put them to sleep."

"Figured that out as well, detective? You're putting the pieces together."

"And Yamasuto and Cuccolo—they were crooks, so what if they got killed?"

"Saved the Japanese authorities and FBI a lot of trouble on those two."

"So that's your New World Order? You decide who lives and dies? That's not the kind of world I want, Trefoil."

The smile faded on Trefoil's face. "You got no choice." Trefoil's eyes grew small. He turned to the demon. "Abraxas!"

The giant rose up and started toward them. Trefoil took the bag with the mirror and threw it to the creature, who lunged for it.

"Back, demon!" Marlowe yelled, as he suddenly rose up, staff in hand. A white light lashed out at Abraxas.

Stunned and off-center, the red monster fell back and roared in anger. Marlowe surrounded the velvet bag with a beam of light and pulled it through the air toward him. It floated slowly as the energy was absorbed as quickly as Marlowe sent it.

Trefoil gave a cry and fired a beam of blue light at Marlowe, who deflected it, while he pulled the bag toward him.

Eddie summoned his staff. The wood slapped reassuringly into his hand, as his clothes shifted to his tunic. He didn't want to worry about breaking his phone or losing his wallet in battle.

Eddie raised his staff and shot a red beam at Trefoil, who dodged and sent a blue bolt in response.

Eddie gestured with his newly learned protection spell and deflected Trefoil's ray, which broke a part of a stone step, and knocked Eddie off his feet from the recoil.

"Marlowe wasn't kidding." Eddie rolled over and leapt up.

Trefoil fired another blue ray that pulled and yanked the bag away from Marlowe. They each pulled as if tethered to the bag and caught in an elaborate tug-of-war, the mirror consuming both their energies as they fought over it.

Abraxas regained his feet and leapt between them to snatch the bag out of midair, as easily as if he picked a flower. He pulled the bag open and lifted out the highly polished stone.

Marlowe discharged another ray of white light, but the demon held out the mirror and the beam was pulled off-course to be assimilated into the dark surface.

"I have it! I have it!" Abraxas bellowed, and held it high over his head. A wind began to howl and a distant roar like thunder echoed through the many tunnels.

"Aw jeez," Eddie said to no one in particular. "Not wind again."

A purple glow emanated from the black, flat stone, and energy seemed to flow from the mirror into Abraxas.

"We must stop him, Eddie!" Marlowe hollered. He released another bolt of light, but the mirror merely redirected the beam and incorporated the blast.

"How?" Eddie shielded his eyes as the dust of a hundred years was stirred up and turned into tiny projectiles by the fierce breeze.

"I don't know," Marlowe confessed.

"What about my son?" Eddie shouted.

"I have the boy!" Trefoil yelled. He held Douglas in one arm, still unconscious, his staff in the other. "Join me, Eddie, or he dies."

"You bastard!" Eddie shouted. He took a running jump from his platform and with the wind at his back, he was propelled farther than expected. As if planned, he landed right next to Trefoil.

Without hesitating, Eddie dropped his staff, and drove a fist into Trefoil's right eye.

Surprised by this sudden physical assault, Trefoil released Douglas and staggered back. Eddie took his son and carefully lowered him to the ground, then grabbed his fallen staff.

"Eddie, look!" Marlowe screamed over the din.

There was another figure at the edge of the tunnel. It was someone dressed in the same robes as Trefoil, the fabric flapping madly in the wind, but the hood covered the face.

"Now who the hell is that?" Eddie wondered aloud.

The mysterious figure pointed at Trefoil and croaked out some words that Eddie couldn't hear in the fierce roar of the air. But the voice was familiar. He knew it from his own house the previous night.

The purple energy surrounded Abraxas, and he lowered the mirror, which no longer glowed. The demon seemed to have grown in stature. He looked down on Trefoil as the wind dissipated.

"It seems you've outlasted your usefulness," Abraxas stated simply.

"What?" Trefoil looked from the demon to the figure at the door. He reached into his cloak and extracted a brown piece of parchment. "You are bound to me, demon, by the cartouche on this paper drawn in blood."

"That's not blood, it's marker," Abraxas corrected with almost a kindly look in his eye, as if he'd just told a child that Santa Claus didn't exist.

Trefoil gasped and opened the paper.

Even from the distance Eddie stood, he recognized the symbol on the vellum. It was like the one he'd found in the talisman book and shown to Caleb. Trefoil had made it.

Someone had switched it with a counterfeit.

Trefoil stood paralyzed with shock. "But, our plans—"

"Ah yes, about that," Abraxas shrugged. "Thanks for the help; no hard feelings."

The huge brute held out one of his enormous hands, and purple light danced over the claws at the end of his fingers. With surprising speed, he grabbed Trefoil's head in one hand, his body in the other, and with a quick twist, snapped his neck with a resounding "*Crack.*"

"Murder! Villainy!" Marlowe yelled and rushed forward, his staff raised.

Abraxas turned to face Marlowe, as the cloaked figure bridged the gap between them.

"Let me finish them," Abraxas hissed, and flexed his muscles to prepare for battle. He raised the mirror as Marlowe threw a powerful beam of light. It vanished into the reflective surface.

"Nay," the voice croaked. "We shall kill them all when the time is right."

"I want them dead now. I have enough power to do it."

"I said stay thy hand."

"Surrender, warlock!" Marlowe shouted as he raised his staff aloft.

"Your time is almost up, old fool," the cloaked warlock said, as the demon held up the mirror. There was a flash of purple light, and they were gone. They had disappeared— teleported— together.

Eddie sat down next to his son, relieved that he appeared unharmed. He touched his head.

Douglas' eyelids fluttered, then opened.

"Hey, Dad," Douglas mumbled. "Did I oversleep?"

Eddie smiled. "I always said you could sleep through the end of the world."

Marlowe was breathing hard as he looked down at the two Berman men. "That may occur soon enough."

FIFTY-ONE

The walk back through the tunnels was darker and more difficult than their descent. First of all, it was all uphill, then as they reached the round room where the tunnel split into three, they couldn't decide which way they'd come.

"I am sure it was the left tunnel," Eddie pointed.

"Nay, it was the one next to it," Marlowe concluded.

Douglas spoke up. "Dad, why you dressed like that?"

"It's, 'Why *are* you dressed like that?' Douglas," Eddie corrected.

"It's Doug," was his response. "So how come?"

"Not right now." Eddie looked up each tunnel to see if there was anything familiar. Each one appeared exactly the same.

"When?" Douglas asked.

"When what?"

"When you gonna tell me?"

"Later." Eddie turned to Marlowe. "Great! Now *I'm* not sure which tunnel got us here!"

"Ah, of course." Marlowe handed Eddie Trefoil's staff. "Carry the Staff of Water."

"Why did we bring this?"

"We must give it to one worthy to bear it." Marlowe went through the pockets of his robe.

"Didn't work with Trefoil." Eddie looked back down the tunnel they just ascended. "Was it a good idea to just leave his body there?"

"We could have brought him, Eddie, but I thought the last thing you needed was another unsolvable homicide."

Eddie nodded. "Good point. What's your plan?"

Marlowe pulled a folded cloth from his pocket "I'd forgotten I brought the Hat of Remembrance."

"Is that an oxymoron? I forgot I had a memory?"

Marlowe gave Eddie a dirty look, then unfolded the battered conical hat and placed it on his head. His eyes grew brighter.

"Of course!" Marlowe said, as if it were obvious. "It's the tunnel on the left."

"Didn't I say that?" Eddie glanced at the two staffs in his hand. "Am I supposed to carry both of these?"

"Put your own staff away, Eddie," Marlowe retorted, "and come along!" With that, Marlowe jauntily started up the tunnel.

Douglas said, "Snap! He can walk fast for an old guy."

"Yeah," Eddie added wearily. "We'd better catch up."

Eddie waved his staff and his clothes shifted back to his suit, and then the tall walking stick was returned to his pocket, which left him only Trefoil's staff.

"Dang!" Douglas was impressed. "Dad, tell me how you did that."

"Later." They began to walk.

"That wasn't in any of *my* magic books," muttered Douglas.

They climbed for what felt like hours, and Eddie thought they were hopelessly lost in the underground catacombs. But Marlowe without hesitation knew where to go as they reached each turn.

"Are we there yet?" Doug whined. "I'm getting tired."

"Just a little farther, son."

"Did you rescue me, Dad?"

Marlowe turned and faced them. "Your father risked his very life to save you, young man."

"Dang! Wait'll I tell my friends. My dad rescued me, and I saw a dead guy."

Eddie stopped and knelt next to his son. "Douglas—"

"Doug!"

"Doug," Eddie tried again. "You can't tell anyone what you saw. Only me or your mother."

"But, Dad, I mean, you made your clothes change, and we were in that great big room, and the most amazing thing—"

"I know, son," Eddie put his free hand out in front of him as if he were trying to stop a train, "but what's the first rule of magic?"

Doug thought for a moment. "Never tell the secret."

"Right. So this is like when you do a trick. It's a secret."

Doug frowned and thought about this. "Dang!" was all he could utter.

"Eddie," Marlowe reported, "we are almost there."

"Come on, Doug." Eddie walked up with Trefoil's staff to where Marlowe examined a wall. "So, Marlowe, they just disappeared—poof! How come we have to walk all this way?"

"Teleportation is possible, but to move three people would drain me for hours. The smoking mirror stole another portion of my power. The demon and that other warlock are using that stored energy, as well as the energy from the other talismans."

"I was surprised by the other warlock. I was sure Trefoil was our perp," Eddie said.

Marlowe's mouth became a tight line. "Indeed. Someone who knew Trefoil, yet thought nothing of dispatching him."

"We're right back at square one," Eddie sighed.

"What are you two talking about?" Doug questioned.

"Later," Eddie replied.

Marlowe stepped back from the wall, removed his conical hat, and returned it to the inner pocket of his cloak.

"Here we are!" Marlowe waved his staff. There was a grating sound as rock moved. A part of the wall shifted and sunlight poured into the dark tunnel.

"Quickly," Marlowe warned, "before we draw attention."

Eddie vaulted the short wall and onto the granite step. He reached the ground, then turned and helped Doug.

Eddie looked at the staff in his hand. It had become an old broomstick. As Marlowe stepped through the portal, he was dressed in a suit and carrying his cane. He reached the ground, gave a small gesture with the walking stick, and with a rumble their entranceway was gone.

They stood in the arcade of Bethesda Terrace. People passed, going up and down the stone stairway, unaware that three people had just walked out of a solid wall.

Doug looked at the architecture all around him. "Where are we, a museum?"

"Central Park, son," Eddie said.

"Is this where you work, Dad?"

"I spend most of the time at the precinct." Eddie turned to Marlowe. "Where to?"

"The safest place would be my townhouse," Marlowe said.

"I have to get my son back home. Why don't you call for reinforcements to meet there?"

"Reinforcements?"

"What's left of the Five," Eddie said.

"Is this wise? Your house was attacked last night. The townhouse would be safer."

"No, we have to get Doug home. But, a funny thing…" Eddie peered up at the tile ceiling.

"What?" Marlowe quizzed.

"Every time we have a confrontation with this warlock there is always wind flying around. Who has the Staff of Air?"

"Eugenia," Marlowe responded. "You're not suggesting that *she* is that warlock?"

"I don't know. That raspy voice was meant to disguise something. It *could* be a woman."

"We gonna stay it this old place all day?" Doug pointed at the sunlit terrace. "I wanna see the fountain."

"Yeah, let's go." They walked out into the terrace, which had begun to empty out. Eddie looked at the sun and saw that it sank toward the horizon.

"How long were we…wherever we were?" Eddie pondered.

"Time is relative, Eddie," Marlowe stressed. "Let us say, it was longer out here than it was in there."

"That's as clear as mud."

Doug ran to the huge fountain and put his hand in the water.

"So, rescuing Douglas removes the sacrifice," Eddie put forth. "That's got to put a monkey wrench in their plan."

"I'm not sure." Marlowe shook his head. "I was barely conscious, but Trefoil said he wasn't planning to hurt your son."

"What does that mean?"

"I fear that he intended to select another sacrifice."

Eddie watched Douglas at the fountain somberly. "And it has to be someone under the age of thirteen."

"Yes."

Douglas returned to the two men. "Dad, you got a coin?"

"What for?" Eddie reached into his pocket to locate loose change.

"To make a wish," Doug said and put his hand out. "I only got the half-dollar I use for magic."

"Your son does magic?" Marlowe lifted an eyebrow. "Eddie, what have you been teaching him?"

"*Tricks*, Marlowe," Eddie reassured. "And Doug, it's, 'I only *have* a half-dollar.'"

"Not if you give me more. Come on, Dad, I wanna make a wish."

"You don't believe in that, do you?" Eddie scoffed.

"No, no, encourage the boy," Marlowe recommended. "In fact, you should make a wish as well."

"My wish would be that the three of us be home." Eddie handed Doug a dime, while he took a quarter into his own hand.

Meanwhile, on Navy Hill, a man in jogging clothes lowered his binoculars and spoke into a tiny microphone connected to a surreptitious walkie-talkie.

"I have the subjects in view," Sam told his partner. "They just walked out of the arcade and are standing at the fountain. They have a child with them. African-American, about ten years old."

"Keep an eye on them," Wilcox's voice said into the man's earpiece. "I'm on the move."

It had been a most frustrating afternoon for Wilcox. After he tracked Eddie to Bethesda Terrace and the sudden disappearance of his quarry, he called in Sam to stake out the area.

Sam had searched the terrace and didn't locate Eddie or the odd old man. Now they showed up and had a child in tow. Where did the kid come from?

Meanwhile, at the fountain, Doug closed his eyes and threw the dime into the fountain.

"What did you wish for?" Eddie asked.

"Can't tell, or it won't come true."

"Why don't *you* try, Eddie?" Marlowe smiled.

Eddie shrugged and raised his arm to toss the quarter.

"No, Dad," Doug protested. "You got to do it right. Close your eyes and wish, then throw it in with your eyes closed."

Eddie looked at Marlowe, who nodded. "The young man is correct."

Eddie closed his eyes, wished they were home, and threw the quarter in the direction of the fountain.

The silver disk flew end over end. As it touched the surface of the water, the three men shimmered as if rising heat distorted the air, and were gone.

"What the—" Sam said on Navy Hill and stood up. He lowered his binoculars and glanced about. He had taken his eyes off the trio momentarily to observe the rear end of a bikini-clad young lady. When he shifted back, they were nowhere to be seen.

Wilcox arrived at the upper terrace, slowed to a casual walk, and looked down at the fountain. He spoke into his walkie-talkie.

"Where are the subjects?"

Befuddled, Sam answered, "I-I don't know."

"What do you mean, you don't know?" Wilcox tried to locate his partner on the hill. He quickly spotted Sam in his jogging suit. He walked down the long set of stairs and up to Navy Hill to join him.

"They were there one moment, and now, they're gone, uh, sir." Sam scanned the vicinity.

"Did you keep your eyes on them?" Wilcox looked back at the fountain.

"Yes sir, I mean, I rested my eyes, but only for a second. I have to tell you, it's like they just…disappeared."

"All right," Wilcox commanded, "that's it. I'm going to call the bureau and get a team on the move."

"That'll cause a lot of attention. Is that wise?" Sam shakily pulled out a cigarette.

"Something strange is going on, and I want to know what it is."

"What do you want me to do?" Sam questioned.

"I want you to watch that weird townhouse on Eighty-Fifth Street," Wilcox ordered. "I'm going to put surveillance at Berman's house."

"You're talking about a lot of manpower." Sam lit his cigarette.

"I know, but I think Berman is a part of some kind of conspiracy. If I can prove it, it'll mean advancement for both of us, Sam."

Sam sucked on the white tube and exhaled smoke. "And you get rid of Berman."

"I have to admit, him and his partner kicked out of the NYPD is an added incentive." Wilcox nodded.

The two men smiled.

FIFTY-TWO

"Dang!" Doug yelped.

Eddie opened his eyes to find his own backyard in the place where the fountain stood a mere moment earlier. Eddie gave a small jump of surprise and fought to keep his mouth from dropping open yet again.

"Holy shit!" Eddie said.

"Dad, Mom doesn't like that talk." Doug's face scrunched up in annoyance at his father's faux-pas.

"You see, Eddie," Marlowe smiled. "Much of what you call 'superstition' has a basis in fact."

Eddie looked at Marlowe as if he'd lost his mind.

"Let me get this straight. Making a wish and dropping money in a fountain can—" Eddie stumbled for the right words. "Hey! Didn't you say teleportation uses a lot of power? I don't feel any weaker."

Marlowe nodded. "That's because it wasn't merely your power that made it work."

"Huh?" Eddie said.

"Everything has energy, Eddie." Marlowe opened his arms. "First, the power of the money—and you have to admit, money has no value except the *power* society gives it."

Eddie frowned. "Okay, but that doesn't explain—"

"Second, there is the energy of the fountain, which in the case of Bethesda Terrace was placed in a high-energy location, and then there is the third thing: flowing water. All life on this planet comes from water."

"So one little coin did all this?" Eddie pondered.

"What made it work was that the elements were combined with the strongest force of all: belief. It is belief, will, and intention that creates all things. Being a wizard is more than having magick in you. You have to be aware of the magick in everything, and use what you find."

"Douglas?" Cerise tentatively came out the back door. She broke into a run and made a noise that combined both laughter and weeping, fell upon Doug, and clutched him in her arms.

"Jeez, Mom," Doug complained, "I was only gone a little while."

Yet he found his mother's hug comforting after those dark tunnels and strange occurrences. There was a magic in this, and it was better than any of the tricks he found in his books.

Eddie walked over, fell to one knee, and held his wife and son.

"You did it." Tears spilled down Cerise's face. "You brought back my baby."

"We walked through these *big* tunnels," Doug gushed, "and I saw a dead guy!"

"Come in the house." Cerise smiled through her wet eyes. "Are you hungry?"

"I guess," Doug murmured.

She took her son's arm, and Cerise led the boy in the back door, out of the fading sunlight.

Eddie looked at the broom handle in his hand and turned to Marlowe. "What do we do with this?"

"Find one who can carry it into battle." Marlowe reached into several pockets, and finally extracted a mirror. "Drusilicus."

The glass twinkled, then cleared and Drusilicus' face appeared.

"By Zoroaster!" Drusilicus complained. "Do you know how long I've been waiting by this mirror? I've been in this bathroom for hours. The others are convinced I am unwell."

"Drusilicus," Marlowe went on, "did any one of the others leave the townhouse this afternoon?"

"How should I know? I've been in the bathroom!"

"Dru," Eddie pulled the mirror from Marlowe in a sudden impulse. "We got Doug back."

"That is good news!" Drusilicus smiled. "Did you thrash the demon?"

"We are lucky to be alive." Marlowe regained the mirror from Eddie. "Find the others, then wait for me. Together I shall bring you to Eddie's house."

"So mote it be," Drusilicus said as his image disappeared.

Marlowe returned the mirror to his jacket pocket. "You and your son are home. For safety, I shall enter my townhouse in a state of invisibility."

"You're going to sneak into your own house?"

"It is as you said, the warlock is one step ahead of us. We can assume that Trefoil told of our plans, but it would be wise to act as if we are being watched. I fear the warlock must this night take another child for sacrifice."

"I get it! If you bring the others here, we can watch them to make sure they aren't the one who is helping Abraxas."

Marlowe nodded his head gravely. "By Zoroaster, it is sad when I must look at my oldest associates with suspicion. I shall return as quickly as I can."

With that, the older man walked away and left Eddie alone in his backyard.

Eddie pulled out his cell phone and called Luis.

"Vasquez," came the voice on the other end.

"We got Doug," Eddie said as way of introduction.

"Eddie! That's great, man!" Luis beamed. "I was getting worried."

"Well, I walked through catacombs under Central Park and visited an alternate version of Grand Central."

"Aw, jeez, you're givin' me a headache."

"We found one of our bad guys."

"One? You mean there's more?"

"Get over here. I'll do my best to bring you up to speed. Marlowe and the others will be here soon."

"Oh good, I get to hang wid de Wizard Posse."

"You're my backup. Tomorrow is the final confrontation."

"Okay, I'll bring a change of clothes, in case I have to stay over."

"*Gracias*, partner," Eddie said.

"*De nada*," Luis ended the call.

Eddie walked around his house and headed for the front yard. He was about to turn the corner when something caught his eye and he backed up.

A gray van with tinted glass pulled down the street. It had unusually dark glass, almost black. The side was painted with the logo of "Jersey Power & Lighting."

Eddie wasn't a fully trained wizard, but as an experienced cop he could practically smell a stakeout. And in a van like that, it wasn't NYPD.

Eddie flattened himself against the side of his house and whispered, "FBI."

Cursing under his breath, Eddie returned to the backyard. What was the FBI doing here? Was Wilcox somehow in league with Abraxas, too? That made no sense. However, it would be easy enough for that warlock to manipulate him.

One more distraction Eddie didn't need.

He shouldn't be surprised. Wilcox wanted him to be guilty of something. However, even Wilcox couldn't keep up with all his jumping from place to place.

Eddie considered finding a fountain to *wish* Wilcox away. He decided that would be a quarter well spent.

He walked in the back door of his house and right up the stairs to the bathroom. He locked the door and approached the mirror.

"Marlowe," Eddie said in a loud whisper. "Hey, Marlowe, you there? Yoo hoo, calling Marlowe."

The glass shimmered and Marlowe's face appeared. "What is it, Eddie?"

"Thought you should know my house is being watched by the FBI."

"Oh my! That cannot be good."

"Not for us anyway," Eddie agreed. "Can you create one of those illusions on your way here? They're in a gray van across the street."

Marlowe's face creased in concentration for a moment, then his expression relaxed and a beatific smile appeared. "I think I have just the thing."

"Okay, well, don't turn them into newts or anything."

"Leave it to me, Eddie. You'll know when we arrive."

"Try not to let the entire neighborhood know, okay?" Eddie wanted to tell him, but the old wizard was gone. He spoke to his own reflection.

Eddie noticed he still carried the old broom handle. He walked downstairs to the kitchen, opened the closet that contained the vacuum cleaner, mops, and brooms, and placed it in.

He closed the door and pondered what to do with a second staff. Could he choose who would received it? Could he award it to Luis?

A fantasy passed through his mind of him and Luis, partners for a millennium. Their families might grow and forget them, but they would have each other to depend on, just like always.

Or he could give it to Cerise! They would have a marriage that would last long beyond their own great-great-grandchildren. And both of them could carry staffs and travel the world without concern.

Maybe finally go to Aruba.

Eddie sat at the kitchen table and realized both of those plans were foolish. He'd been *summoned* and was barely able to master the basics of the awesome powers that came with that calling. Tomorrow, he had to fight the demon and warlock who bested Marlowe, killed Trefoil, and outsmarted experienced wizards every step of the way. To give a staff to Luis or Cerise might be emotionally satisfying, but it was a blunder, and the fast track to a quick defeat.

What would that lead to?

The end of the world.

So much rode on the coming confrontation. He might not survive. And if he was dead, Cerise and Luis needed to be able to help each other through the bad times.

"What's the matter, dearie?" a voice said.

Eddie jumped and turned to see his mother as she looked up at him. Her huge glasses were gone, and she appeared years younger.

"Momma?" Eddie said. "Your hair…"

"Oh, I know," Eleanor said, her hand preened her now dark locks. "I went to the beauty salon, got my hair done and dyed. Even got a manicure!"

She held out her polished nails for Eddie's inspection. He smiled.

"I just didn't feel up to taking care of myself. I thought, what's the point?" Eleanor sat at the table. "Now I'm just so much better!" She took Eddie's hand. "And you found our Douglas."

"I had help, Momma." Eddie was suddenly aware of just how tired he was, even though it was only six o'clock.

"What's wrong, Eddie?" Eleanor said. "You can tell your momma."

Eddie gave a wan smile. "It's a long story. These people I've gotten to know…"

"Those strange friends of yours."

"Yeah," Eddie grinned. "They've kind of got me involved in a case. A big case. And I might run into trouble."

"Big trouble?"

"Yeah, Momma."

"An' you're feelin' scared and a bit out of your league right about now, dearie."

Eddie sighed. "You hit the nail on the head, Momma."

"Eddie, all your life you have been able to accomplish anything you set your mind to." Eleanor held Eddie's hand tightly. "You were always doing things that made your father and me ask, 'Where did that come from?' I think it's the same thing now. You have to believe that you are the man for the job. Trust that and trust yourself."

"Thanks, Momma." Eddie smiled, as he heard a car pull up out front.

"Eddie." Cerise came down the stairs. "I think it's Luis."

"How's Douglas?"

"I took him a snack in his bedroom. He's playing away on his Game Boy as if nothing happened," she shrugged.

Eddie rose from the table. "I have a feeling that by tomorrow the entire incident will be much less real than any monsters he kills on that machine."

"I'll get dinner ready. Is Luis staying?"

"Probably," Eddie replied. "And we may have a few more guests as well."

"Now, Eddie," Eleanor chided, "it's not right to surprise your wife with unexpected company. Can I help you, hon?"

Cerise beamed at Eleanor. "Delighted, Momma. And, Eddie, you are my hero. You invite the whole damn neighborhood if you want."

The doorbell rang, and Eddie made his way to the front door. He opened it to Luis' smiling face as he held a large flowering plant.

"Hey, *amigo*," Luis greeted, and switched hands under the pot he held. He leaned close to Eddie's head in a bear hug and whispered, "You see the van across the street?"

"Yeah, I saw it pull up," Eddie whispered back. His mammoth partner released him, all smiles, and Eddie led him into the house. Luis offered Eddie the plant, which had pointed green leaves and small yellow buds that were in little knots like large, deformed berries. "What is that?"

"A present," Luis said. "I didn't get you anything last night. Maria said I should bring a plant."

Eddie took the yellow and green monstrosity from Luis and placed in on the hall table, where it looked large and sad. "What is it?"

"I dunno," Luis shrugged. "I went to the flower store and this spooky guy walked in an' tol' me that it would be a good gift."

Eddie eyed it up and down. "And you bought it, based on that?"

"Yeah, it was like I couldn't help myself," Luis explained. "It *is* kinda ugly, ain't it?"

"Yes, it is. Come on into my office." Eddie led Luis into a small room off the hall. "You're gonna stay for dinner."

"Okay." Luis went in and sat on the small couch, which he filled. Eddie crouched next to him and spoke in whispers. "I don't know if they've got listening equipment or not."

Luis nodded. "FBI?"

"That's my guess. Might be the UCTF."

"Wilcox? Well, a car followed me on the drive over. I picked up the tail in two seconds."

"Marlowe and his guests are coming," Eddie stressed.

"Is that a good idea? With the Feds outside?"

"What else can we do? Marlowe said he'd make a distraction."

"How about a plague of locusts?" Luis suggested.

"I think they're already in that van."

"Hey! That's no way to talk. You're insulting insects up and down the food chain!"

Eddie smiled and they rose, slipped out of the office, and headed to the kitchen.

"Can I get you a beer?" Eddie offered.

"Sure, I'm not on duty," Luis shrugged.

They walked into the kitchen, where Luis greeted the ladies as Eddie went to the refrigerator and grabbed a bottle. Cerise sent them both away so as not to interfere with the meal preparations.

They walked into the dining room, where Luis opened his beer and took a long swallow.

"That's good." Luis followed the statement with a loud belch. Then, he paused and listened. "What's that?"

"What?" Eddie said.

"I hear music."

"Yeah, right," Eddie snickered.

"Eddie, I'm serious. I hear music, like a band."

Eddie listened intently and could hear *something*, though he wasn't sure what. It *was* rather like a marching band, but the music possessed a dissonance, giving it an ethereal quality.

Whatever it was, it grew louder.

"C'mon," Eddie motioned and headed for the front door.

The two men parted the front drapes and peered out. Down the street was a group of people in bright-red uniforms who played instruments that sparkled and shimmered in the setting sun's light.

Luis and Eddie looked at each other, then walked out of the house onto the lawn. They were not surprised to notice that many of Eddie's neighbors did likewise.

"Whaddaya know! It *is* a marching band," Luis chortled.

"That's what it looks like to you?" Eddie asked.

"Yeah. Why? What do you see?"

Eddie stared at the group, then smacked the side of his head with his hand. The marching band, complete with baton-twirlers and drums, faded away, and five rather ordinary people stood in their place.

"Ow!" Luis grunted, puzzled by Eddie's actions. "Why'd you do that?"

"Clears my vision." Eddie did it again. He peered into the distance and saw Marlowe's beard, Drusilicus's long hair, Ahbay's silk vest, Eugenia's dress, and Bankrock's tweed jacket.

Eddie looked at the van and shook his head. If they were videotaping everything that came and went, what would the camera see? Would it show only the illusion, or film the five people who approached?

He didn't know.

The band grew louder as it drew nearer, and Cerise, Douglas, and Eleanor came out the front door.

"Dang!" Douglas bubbled. "It's a band!"

"Hey, nice to see you, little guy," Luis smiled to Doug.

"I ain't so little," Doug squinted up at the big man.

"I'm *not* so little," Cerise corrected.

"You are to me, Cerise," Luis joked. "And, kid, you are practically *tiny*."

Luis bent and picked up the giggling boy and put him on his shoulder.

"Dang!" Doug announced. "I'm as tall as a tree! I can see everything!"

Eddie closed his eyes, then opened them as he tried not to allow the illusion to affect him. But the band appeared as real as could be.

The musicians began to pass their house, and several of the phantasms walked right up on the Berman's lawn and played their instrument directly *at* Eddie and his family.

Almost on instinct, Eddie stepped aside and opened the front door of the house to leave a clear pathway.

"Why'd you do that?" Luis queried.

"Just a hunch." Eddie slapped the side of his head again.

Sure enough, a drummer drew near the house, but Eddie saw Marlowe pass beyond the crowd and through the front door, invisible to all but him. The others only saw the musician who beat his drum and returned to the rest of the band.

The situation was repeated four more times, as Drusilicus, Ahbay, Eugenia, and Bankrock passed from the illusion of the marchers to the reality of the house, while Eddie watched the whole thing.

This required him to slap himself silly, which drew strange looks from both Eleanor and Cerise.

Their mission accomplished, the marching band continued its trek down the street to depart back to the oblivion from which it was called. The Teaneck residents, unaware that they watched nothing but empty air, gave a round of applause before wandering back to their homes.

As family and partner watched the band retreat, Eddie entered the house. He walked quickly up to Marlowe and whispered in his ear, "There are people who might be watching us."

"Don't worry, Eddie," Marlowe didn't lower his voice. "I have taken the liberty of surrounding your house with a protective field. It will disrupt any device, physical or magickal."

"Yes, we avoid dealing with mortal law enforcement," Bankrock approached, a bit miffed.

"There might be bugs in the house," Eddie fretted.

"Your house has vermin?" Ahbay declared, appalled.

"Listening devices, little radios," Drusilicus explained.

"Oh!" Ahbay responded. "These will not work, either."

"No need for concern," Eugenia comforted, "the spell is quite effective."

Eddie exhaled in relief. "That's good. But what if they videotaped the marching band?"

Ahbay and Eugenia turned to Marlowe as if unsure what videotape was.

"No matter," Marlowe beamed. "They will find something is wrong with their equipment."

"If that is all decided," Drusilicus complained, "can we get to the matter at hand?"

"Yes." Bankrock held out his leather binder and began to take notes. "The Staff of Water must be assigned. I want to make certain all regulations are followed to the letter."

"Bankrock, really," Marlowe clucked peevishly. "As Coven Master, I have the power to select a new candidate—"

"It's bad enough that *Mister* Berman was summoned," Bankrock retorted. "I *must* be here."

"It is up to us to select who will bear the Staff of Water," Marlowe said with a nod to the others.

"I hope by this time we all realize whom is the most qualified," Drusilicus boasted.

"Who," Bankrock corrected.

"What?"

"You said 'whom', it's 'who'." Bankrock repeated.

"I don't care if it is who, how, or why," Drusilicus argued. "We must choose!"

"Hold on a minute," Eddie said, "I think—"

Doug stepped into the house and called out. "Mom, there's a bunch of weirdoes in our living room."

Cerise walked through the doorway, and her jaw fell open. She quickly shut her mouth. "Now, Douglas, it isn't polite to refer to your father's guests as weirdoes. You go upstairs, and I'll tell you when dinner is ready."

"Hey," Doug pointed at Marlowe. "I know you."

"That you do, young man," Marlowe agreed with a glimmer in his eye.

"My goodness," Eleanor came in through the front door. "We have company."

"Yes, Momma," Cerise sensed that Eddie was uncomfortable with his mother there. "Can you help me in the kitchen?"

"But I thought I would—"

"In the kitchen, Momma, please," Cerise pleaded.

Eleanor looked from face to face. "Oh, yes, I suppose you'll all stay for dinner." She then hurriedly followed Cerise out of the room.

"Son," Eddie instructed Doug, "you go upstairs like your momma told you."

"Do I haveta?"

"Yes!" Eddie snapped.

One look in his father's eyes made Doug decide not to push his luck. "Dang!" he muttered as an exit line and bounded up the stairs.

Luis was the last one to step through the door. He stopped and stared at the group. "How did—"

"Luis, the marching band was an illusion," Eddie clarified.

"*Must* you tell him that?" Bankrock objected. "The code of secrecy is quite—"

"He's my apprentice!"

"So you say!" Bankrock turned to Marlowe. "Did he fill out the appropriate paperwork?"

"Give it a rest, Bankrock." Marlowe gave a weary sigh.

"Someone close the door," Eddie recommended.

Luis took the doorknob in his hand and began to close the door when there was a sudden flash of light at the threshold.

"What the hell?" Luis bellowed.

All the wizards gestured as their individual staffs flew into their hands at the ready.

Caleb fell into the room. His body was at first somewhat transparent, as if he were a ghost. He then twitched several times and became more solid with each passing second. He sat up quickly and looked fearfully at the ring of staves pointed at him.

"What is the meaning of this?" Marlowe turned to Drusilicus.

"I have no idea!" Drusilicus's face turned beet red. "What are *you* doing here?"

"I was—I was—" Caleb stammered, his eyes darting about the room as he struggled for an answer.

"Isn't this Drusilicus's apprentice?" Bankrock puzzled.

Marlowe lowered his staff, strode to the young man, and with one quick motion yanked a chain from around his neck. The chain pulled Caleb's head forward and then snapped, causing the young man to fall backward.

"I believe *this* is our answer," Marlowe held aloft the broken chain from which a small, bronze-colored disk hung.

"Is that one of Solomon's pentacles?" Bankrock walked over to peer at the sigil in Marlowe's hand. "Oh, I say, nicely made."

"It is the sixth pentacle of the sun, which renders the bearer invisible." Marlowe turned his angry eyes on Drusilicus. "It appears your apprentice followed us."

"From New York?" Drusilicus stormed. "How did he teleport with us?"

"If he placed his hand on one of us, he would have shifted location with the group." Marlowe pocketed the talisman.

"How did he just appear like that?" Luis finally closed the door.

"Simple," Marlowe expounded. "He was not aware of the magical barrier I had placed around the house. He tried to sneak in through the open door, and when he passed through the barrier, it disrupted the power of his amulet."

"Speak, fool!" Drusilicus demanded of Caleb. "What were you doing?"

"I was only watching," Caleb spoke up defiantly. He rubbed the red line on his neck that formed when Marlowe yanked off the amulet.

"To what end?" Marlowe lifted his staff and aimed it at the hapless Caleb.

"I've been watching the townhouse for days." Caleb put his hands up defensively. "I wanted to know what was going on."

"An apprentice spying on his master!" Bankrock was appalled. "This is unheard of!"

"You have no right to keep your betters under surveillance," Drusilicus growled.

"I did it to keep an eye on the cop." Caleb got to his feet with a glance to Eddie. "I thought he was going to blame me for everything."

Eddie drew closer to the young man. "What are you talking about?"

"After you questioned me at my place, I was sure you were going to lay the blame on me for the demon. That's where you were headed."

"Look," Eddie advised, "I don't like the stuff you pull, and I sure don't like your attitude, but I only want the truth."

Caleb hung his head and his eyes darted to the others again. The fear was lessened, but he still glowered like a caged animal.

"How long have you been following me?" Eddie barked.

"Who said I followed you?" Caleb's voice grew sullen.

"How long?"

Caleb lifted his head with a jolt, as if struck. "On and off for the last two days. I put on the amulet and followed you to my master's house."

"You entered my house without permission?" Drusilicus seethed.

"No, I waited outside," Caleb said. "Then I rode in the subway car uptown and hung out."

"Were you watching Marlowe and me leave the townhouse this morning?" Eddie questioned.

"No I didn't get there until about an hour ago. I mean, I couldn't really see much from outside, and I knew I couldn't sneak in—"

"So," Marlowe's tone was still harsh, "you saw myself and the others leave and decided to tag along."

"Well, yeah," Caleb muttered. "I figured if I was nearby and anything went down I could help. Y'know, redeem myself."

"All you have done is demonstrate how truly unworthy you are," Drusilicus announced. "I have grave doubts about whether I should entrust my staff to you at all."

"And why would you be worried about that?" Eddie asserted. "While we are talking about handing out the staff to one who is 'worthy,' I want to state that there is no one I trust more in this world than Luis."

Luis's face opened in a large grin. "Thanks!"

"Oh, great plan," Drusilicus snorted. "Shall we *all* go forth and give our staffs to any we meet? That would guarantee the success of the Great Evil, and the destruction of this world!"

"There is more to this, Eddie," Marlowe added grimly. "Besides our young hitchhiker, I spoke to the others. It appears I made a slight miscalculation."

"What?" Eddie urged.

"I assumed that since tomorrow was the Solstice, the demon would make his sacrifice then."

"And that's wrong?"

"I'm afraid, dear Edward," Eugenia elucidated, "that the Great Evil must assert his power *before* the solstice."

"True," Ahbay added. "He must act when the balance of light and darkness is still in his favor."

"What does that mean?" Eddie asked

"It means," Marlowe intoned, "that the sacrifice to open the seventh seal must take place this very night."

FIFTY-THREE

Eddie stood stock-still, as he tried to absorb the information thrown at him.

"Tonight? Where? When?"

"The when is obvious," Bankrock revealed. "Midnight would be the time all dark and demonic situations occur."

"We do not know where, and have no prophet who can tell us," Marlowe lamented. "Unless you've had another vision, Bankrock."

"I still have no idea where the first came from," Bankrock grumbled.

"Man, we've got to find out," Eddie worried.

"I have tried." A dark expression passed over Marlowe's face. "Again and again, I've reached out to the spirit of the greatest prophet of us all—"

"My teacher," Drusilicus uttered reverently.

"Greywacke the First, right?" Eddie asked.

"Correct," Marlowe said. "I believe it was he who sent me the vision of warning last night."

"Huh! That was a lot of help," Luis snapped.

"Could Greywacke be trying to get through?" Eddie looked from person to person.

"Once a wizard moves on," Ahbay shook his head, "his spirit is beyond the reach of all on this plane."

"And it is against all regulations!" Bankrock added.

The others groaned.

Marlowe began to pace. He seemed to exude a sense of age, as if his many years on the earth had finally caught up to him. "I see now that this has been a subtle plan, which has led us as sheep toward the slaughter."

"Perhaps this might help?" Caleb lifted another chain off over his head and held it out.

Marlowe sighed and said, "Drusilicus, could you take away your apprentice's toys before he annoys me any further."

Drusilicus drew close to Caleb. "Give me your talismans."

"But, master, look at this!" Caleb held out the amulet excitedly. "I made it special."

"Why?" Drusilicus took the silver disk.

"I was led to make it," Caleb lowered his voice. "I had a vision."

At this Marlowe, Ahbay, Eugenia and even Luis turned their heads to look at the young man.

"A vision?" Bankrock interjected. "Are you qualified for vision reception?"

"Well, it came to me." Caleb pushed the disk into Drusilicus's hand.

Drusilicus stared at the silver disk and handed it to Marlowe, who drew in breath in surprise.

"This is the symbol that is upon Greywacke's arch," Marlowe marveled.

"Yes, branches and leaves that form a face," Caleb exulted, almost giddy.

Marlowe held the amulet between his hands. "I sense an energy within."

Drusilicus stepped forward and held his hand high. "More important, if we are to do battle this very night, we must ordain the Staff of Water." He eyed Luis from head to toe. "I would advise we select someone who knows what to do with it."

Luis turned to Eddie. "How did I get involved in this?"

"He could carry the staff." Eddie stood next to his immense friend. "You couldn't find a finer man or a purer heart."

"Wait a minute!" Luis objected. "You wanna give *me* one of those sticks?"

"His grasp of the situation is astounding," Drusilicus sneered.

"Drusilicus, please." Marlowe kept his eyes fixed on the amulet in his hand.

Luis raised his hands in protest. "Hold on. I was willing to be an apprentice or whatever you call it. But I don't *want* one of those sticks."

"Luis," Eddie lowered his voice. "It could be me and you, side by side, like always."

"And have my life turned upside down?" Luis said. "Look, Eddie, I love you, man, but I want to get back to my normal routine. I want my biggest problems to be paying the bills, getting along with Maria, and worrying about my kids. I don't want magic, demons, and all this other stuff."

The group fell silent.

"You...don't want it?" Bankrock finally uttered.

"Hell, no," Luis said, then faced his partner. "But, Eddie, I'm here for you. I jus' don't want to be a player."

Eddie nodded slowly. Luis was right. The night he gained the staff did nothing but make his world more complicated.

"Well, then," Drusilicus announced. "I guess that ends the discussion. There is only one other available candidate."

"I'll get the damn thing." Eddie headed for the door to the kitchen.

As he entered the room, Cerise looked up. "Dinner will be ready shortly. I hope there'll be enough."

"I've never known you to run out of food." Eddie forced a smile.

He hated to give Drusilicus what he wanted, but there truly was no one else. He walked through the kitchen, opened the closet, and extracted the marred aluminum broom handle.

"Is that your new stick, Eddie?" Cerise frowned as she watched him. "It's not as nice as Mr. Marlowe's."

"Well," Eddie said with a shrug, "it's not how it looks, it's the magic in it."

"I believe you've used that line on me before." Cerise gave him a wink.

Eddie grew serious for a moment. "I need to call William. Did he take his cell phone?"

"He's due home any minute," Cerise said, took a pot off the stove, and drained off the water as she held the lid in place.

"I just want to make sure he's all right," Eddie said, heading to the wall-mounted phone.

The back door shut with a crash, and Eddie jumped.

"Young man!" Cerise yelled, without even a look up from the pot. "There is no need to slam the door!"

"Sorry, Mom," William sighed.

Eddie turned and smiled at his son. "Everything okay? You have fun?"

"It was rad, Dad." William offered his fist for his father to bump, which Eddie did.

"Don't start that jive stuff in my house," Cerise said.

"Yes, Mom," Eddie and William spoke in unison, then both laughed.

"Very funny, very funny. Thank you, Edward Joseph Berman, for encouraging such behavior."

"Sorry." Eddie smirked.

"Get out of our kitchen." Eleanor smiled, but her tone was firm. "Or I'll personally whip both your butts!"

"That does it for me, son." Eddie headed for the door. "I know she means it."

"Wow! You mean grandma used to whack your butt?" William followed closely behind.

"Only when he needed it!" Eleanor yelled as they left the room.

Eddie returned to the living room with William, who was startled to find the group of strangers.

"We're having a kind of a meeting," Eddie explained. "You go wash up; they're joining us for dinner."

William shrugged and galloped up the stairs.

"Are you going to stand there or give me the staff?" Drusilicus remarked impatiently.

"What?" Eddie ridiculed, his arms open. "You in a hurry, got another demon to fight?"

"I would prefer it in my hands before dark," Drusilicus confided, then added almost painfully, "Eddie."

"I think I liked it better when you called me lieutenant." Eddie handed the stick to Drusilicus. "Can we do this here?"

Marlowe finally raised is eyes from the medallion, and with a dazed look said, "Let us go out to the backyard."

Everyone rose and followed Marlowe as he walked out of the living room and through the back door just off the kitchen.

"It's very hard to believe about Trefoil." Eugenia shook her head sadly.

"You know someone for centuries," Ahbay deplored, "then you find you do not know him at all."

"I was suspicious of him the entire time!" Bankrock trilled. "The Dark Sleep, indeed."

"Come now, Bankrock," Marlowe commented. "You were as fooled as the rest of us."

"I was being clever," Bankrock stated.

"You're not happy about this," Luis spoke in a low tone to Eddie.

"I don't trust Drusilicus. But, we're out of options."

They walked out past the patio and onto the lawn. One at a time, they transformed their clothing to wizard garb and brought forth their staffs. Only Drusilicus, Caleb, and Luis were still in modern dress.

"Sergeant," Marlowe requested, "may we ask you to stay at the door of the house and keep anyone from interrupting us, please?"

Luis gave a glance to Caleb. "What about him?"

"He must stay," Marlowe conceded.

Caleb gave a bow and said, "Oh thank you, most wise and—"

"Hush, before I reconsider," Marlowe cajoled.

Luis gave a nod and walked back to the house.

"But can't Luis—" Eddie began as Marlowe placed his hand on Eddie's shoulder.

"He cannot be part of this, Eddie." Marlowe then turned to Caleb. "As for you, stay out of the circle until I ask for you."

Caleb bowed and stepped back, a smile on his face.

Bankrock looked at the others. "Shouldn't we assemble the coven? Or bring in the—"

"Silence, Bankrock," Marlowe commanded. "We must take action now. Your staff, Drusilicus."

Drusilicus reached into his pocket and extracted a silver pocket watch. "I kept it in the form my master used before me," he said, and handed the watch to Marlowe.

With a gentle wave, Marlowe transformed Drusilicus' suit into a simple blue robe. Drusilicus held out the aluminum pole and it transformed into a solid staff of wood.

The four other wizards moved into a circle and began the familiar low chant. Eddie found he actually knew the strange words.

Marlowe held up his hands, and the group fell silent.

"Drusilicus Greywacke," Marlowe boomed, "are you here by your own free will?"

"I am," Drusilicus answered, unabashed.

"You are being asked to take in your possession the staff of the element water," Marlowe went on. "Drusilicus Greywacke, are you prepared to accept this heavy burden?"

"I agree."

"Do you swear by your oath, before this honored assembly?"

"I do!"

"Huzzah," the other four said, with Eddie coming in a bit late.

"Do you accept him, upon his oath to join us?"

"We hear and affirm," Eddie, Eugenia, Bankrock, and Ahbay declared.

"Do you accept Drusilicus Greywacke as one of the Five?"

"We do!" came the reply.

"Then as he who carries the staff of the element spirit, I command that the Staff of Water be cleaved unto Drusilicus Greywacke."

"Huzzah," the others chimed.

A proud smile, almost a sneer, appeared on Drusilicus's face.

With a gentle wave, Marlowe's staff sent a beam of white light to Drusilicus's new staff. It was joined by the others, who each projected their own light. The staff glowed blue, and the light surrounded Drusilicus. He closed his eyes for a moment, as the power went into and around him.

They each withdrew their color, and Drusilicus absorbed the blue light within himself and opened his eyes.

"It is done." Marlowe waved to Caleb. "Now, as for thee. Caleb Heinz, step forward."

The black-haired boy walked into the circle. With a wave of Marlowe's staff, his modern clothing shifted into a simple white tunic.

"I thought he wasn't worthy," Eddie hinted, which caused Caleb to scowl at him.

"Hush," Marlowe implored. "Let us begin, my friends."

They chanted a second time. The group went through the words of the ordination again, with Caleb giving the correct responses. Throughout, Caleb beamed. Eddie noticed that he was actually not a bad looking young man when he wasn't busy being sullen.

I hope we're doing the right thing, Eddie thought, *all the way around.*

"There is one caveat I must add," Marlowe put in, after several "Huzzahs" from the group.

Caleb's smile faded.

"Your actions of the past week are suspect," Marlowe accused. "Therefore, as coven master, and bearer of the Staff of Spirit, I command that this staff may be taken from you by my command, if I deem it so. Do you agree to this stipulation?"

"It is a wise enough precaution," Bankrock discerned.

Caleb looked to Drusilicus.

"Agree to it, fool," Drusilicus demanded.

"I-I agree." Caleb's eyes fell to his feet, his face clouded by anger.

"Very well," Marlowe recited. "Then I command that this staff be cleaved unto thee, Caleb Heinz."

The group each passed a beam of light to Caleb's staff. Silver-gray light surrounded Caleb and his body glowed for a moment. It faded and Caleb tried to step forward on unsteady feet.

Eddie drew close and gave him an arm to lean on. "I know how you feel. It knocks you for a loop."

Caleb nodded and gave his head a shake. "I'll be all right. Man, what a rush."

"Dinner," Cerise called from the back door.

With the merest wave of their staffs, their clothing shifted back to modern, and the Five, along with the newest wizard in the coven, walked back into Eddie's house in reverent silence.

"I shall prepare a potion to clear the young man's head," Marlowe decided. "We need every fighter we have this night."

*   *   *

In the van down the street from Eddie's house, Agent Phil Conners was on his cell phone.

"Wilcox," the voice barked over the speaker.

"It's Conners in the surveillance van at the Berman house."

"Have you seen him?"

"Affirmative, sir, we did get a visual on Berman and his partner."

"What are they talking about?" Wilcox insisted, his voice raised in gleeful expectation.

"That's just it, sir, I don't know."

"What!" Wilcox bellowed.

"The craziest thing happened: a marching band walked down the street."

"What of it?" Wilcox was annoyed by this change of subject.

"It was odd, sir," he explained as sweat trickled down his receding hairline. "This band shows up and all of our equipment, I mean all of it, goes down. Nothing works. It took me ten minutes just to get my cell phone operational."

"What caused that?" Wilcox cursed, as if he wanted to add an expletive questioning Conners legitimacy at birth.

The technician sitting next to Conners could hear the question even from where he sat. He turned to Conners and held up his hands to convey that he didn't have a clue.

"We don't know, sir," Conners admitted. "It could be on our end. My only theory is that Berman possesses very sophisticated jamming equipment."

There was a silence at the other end of the phone, then a brief exchange quietly in the background. Conners strained to make out the words.

"Conners!" Wilcox spoke so loud it forced Conners to pull the phone from his ear. "Have you spotted five additional people? Four men and a woman at Berman's house?"

"Sir, we couldn't even video the marching band."

"Spies, that must be it!" Wilcox proclaimed. "Berman is part of a terrorist sleeper cell. Now you listen to me, Conners—"

"Yes, sir," Conners responded.

"You keep an eye on that house, and do whatever it takes to make sure no one goes in or out until I get there. Darkness is falling. I'll send a crew of men to your location. They should arrive within twenty minutes."

"Yes, sir!" Conners said and closed his phone. He looked over at the technician, who still struggled with the computer monitor.

"What's up?" the technician picked up on Conners' excitement.

"It's going to hit the fan tonight!"

FIFTY-FOUR

The dining room table was crammed with more people than it could seat comfortably. The two boys were relegated to eat at the breakfast table, but they did it with few complaints.

Eddie, however, was happy to see that Douglas didn't seem to carry any trauma from his kidnapping and subsequent rescue. In fact, as Marlowe pointed out, the entire incident seemed to fade from Douglas' memory like a bad dream.

Which was fine. Eddie could remember enough for both of them.

Dinner was a smashing success, except for Bankrock, who apparently spent too much time among wizards. He kept giving vocal commands to the dishes, which of course, the dishes ignored. Marlowe corrected him politely and procured what he requested.

Caleb was polite but seemed lost in a stupor. He ate without speaking, a dreamy look on his face.

Drusilicus, for all his pomposity toward Eddie, charmed the women, complimented the cooking and the loveliness of the table setting.

Eddie shook his head. The wizards were a puzzle. They seemed so wise, and yet so foolish about everyday things. And Drusilicus was nice to everyone except Eddie and Luis.

There was more than enough food, and even Luis ate his fill. As Eddie began to collect the dishes, Eleanor took them from him.

"Don't bother, dearie," she said, "let me. I'm so grateful to be able to get around."

"Just don't expect this regularly," Cerise chided good-naturedly as she collected dishes. "You stay with your friends, and we'll clear the table."

Eddie shrugged and sat back down.

"Should we synchronize our watches?" Luis coaxed.

"It's eight-fifty-one," Marlowe said with his eyes partly closed.

"Hey, that's right," Luis looked at his wrist. "You didn't even look at a watch."

"We have no need for such things," Bankrock dismissed.

"We feel the rhythms of the world around us," Eugenia added sweetly.

"Now, if we can only figure out where to go," Eddie challenged.

"I may have an idea, Eddie." Marlowe tugged at this beard. "Tell them about your confrontation with Trefoil."

"If you think it will help," Eddie recalled. "Trefoil took me back in memory to a place called Seneca Village. It was destroyed in order to build Central Park. The police moved in and forced out the residents, even killed a woman."

"Man," Luis frowned. "When did *that* happen?"

"Over a hundred-and-fifty years ago," Eddie said. "The woman had the Medallion of Abracadabra."

"It was thought to be last seen in the West Indies," Marlowe disclosed. "Someone must have brought it to New York."

"Yeah," Eddie concurred, "and it was lost again when the police killed that woman."

"A blood sacrifice that undoubtedly increased the talisman's power," Drusilicus theorized.

The others sat around the table and nodded, even Caleb, although he still looked out of it.

"It lay in the park until Alex and Caleb uncovered it." Marlowe pulled the talisman of Greywacke's symbol that Caleb had created out of his pocket. He looked down at the intricate workmanship, as if he received wisdom from it. "I am now certain of one thing: the final battle must take place in Central Park."

"How do you know that?" Bankrock sniffed.

"Abraxas was released in the park," Marlowe continued, "and the other talismans were acquired there. Even the Smoking Mirror was stolen from the only museum *in* the park."

"We've gone over this," Bankrock stressed, exasperated. "It's a place of power, and the monster is using that power. We need a plan."

The others stared at him.

"Well, *you* need a plan," Bankrock quickly corrected.

Eugenia cleared her throat. "So, could he be gaining additional power from something within Central Park?"

"The fifth talisman?" Eddie ventured.

"We don't know what it is!" Drusilicus admonished.

"Abraxas does," Marlowe contemplated as he held the Greywacke talisman and rubbed it between his fingers. "If we can locate it before midnight, we can put a barrier around it, foil his plan."

"What of the warlock and the Smoking Mirror?" Ahbay said. "Won't it merely absorb our powers?"

Murmurs of assent went up and down the table.

"Not if we can get there before them," Marlowe suggested. "Bankrock, tell me again what you saw in your vision."

Bankrock shrugged. "A huge room with a giant metal statue."

Marlowe thought for a moment, as he stroked the talisman. "To break the seventh seal with a human sacrifice, it would require a shrine."

"Yes!" Drusilicus exclaimed. "That makes sense."

"Problem is, there's no shrine in Central Park," Eddie elaborated.

"It might not be in this dimension," Drusilicus responded.

"He's right," Bankrock agreed. "There are many portals in the park. The arches all contain doorways to their namesakes' residences."

"Wait, what?" Eddie queried. "You're telling me wizards live in those arches?"

"Correct." Bankrock sat up straighter. "I myself reside in a space in an alternate dimension that I can access at my bridge."

"Who says you can't find a place with a view of the park?" Luis quipped.

"If there were a shrine," Ahbay insisted, "it would need to be marked."

Eugenia nodded. "Yes, so it could be located when needed."

Marlowe gave a grunt. "My impression would be to look for an ancient object."

"True!" Eugenia pronounced. "The rites of the Molech are antediluvian, to say the least."

"Can you give us more to go on?" Eddie said, then turned to Luis. "What's the oldest place in the park?"

"I know that." Luis was pleased he could actually add to the conversation. "Blockhouse Number One."

"Say, what?" Eddie frowned.

"We've driven by it." Luis became more animated. "You can see it from the East Drive in the winter. It's that old stone fort on the hill up near 110th Street, built for the war of 1812. It's abandoned, all sealed up."

"I've been there," Caleb said. "Pagans do weird stuff up there on Halloween."

The others looked at him in surprise. These were the first words he had spoken since receiving his staff.

Eddie turned to Marlowe. "What do you think?"

Marlowe rubbed the talisman faster. "It's possible. A location shunned by the public. There could easily be a portal."

"A wizard would not be stopped by a sealed doorway," Ahbay noted.

"Nor a demon," Eugenia added.

Bankrock reached into his binder to pull out a brown parchment. "I don't know if that is one of the listed portals on my official *Magickal Map of Central Park.*"

With one gesture, he flicked it open. It was almost three feet long and one foot wide, and expertly hand-drawn.

"Wow." Eddie was impressed. "That almost looks like the original plans for the park that Vaux and Olmstead came up with."

"It can't be," Luis noted. "That's on display at the conservatory under glass."

"It is an official map Greywacke made up." Bankrock moved the paper about in an attempt to locate the site. "I found it while doing the research Marlowe asked for."

"Hey look," Eddie pointed. "It lists the entrance to the catacombs Marlowe and I were in yesterday."

"There are hundreds of portals." Bankrock ran his finger down the page. "Many are marked, but several stand unnamed."

"Marlowe," Drusilicus considered. "I don't see how this blockhouse would be powerful enough."

"Drusilicus does have a point," Eugenia piped up. "If it is a physical location, it would have to be a site where worship once took place."

Ahbay nodded. "Yes, to make an energetic bond."

Marlowe considered this for a moment. "Interesting, a site where worship took place."

"Is there a church in the park?" Luis said, as he tried to follow the line of the conversation. "I mean, I've seen weddings there plenty of times."

"Are you thinking Conservatory Garden?" Bankrock adjusted his glasses as he peered at the map. "Hm. I see two portals in that location."

"That is our problem, my friends." Marlowe placed the medallion down onto the table. "We have been thinking in a linear way, based upon our current times."

Eddie grinned. "You want to think outside the box."

"Exactly. Do not look where worship occurs today. We seek a place where worship occurred in the time of the Molech."

Caleb, whose eyes were focused on the medallion, suddenly murmured, "Cleopatra's Needle."

"What?" Eddie looked at the boy.

"Cleopatra's Needle?" Eugenia repeated in amazement.

"Hey, I know that!" Luis said. "It's one of those stone things, shaped like the Washington Monument, a…whatchamacallit."

"An obelisk." Marlowe's eyes took on a faraway look rather like Caleb's.

Luis smiled. "Yeah, that's it."

Eddie looked from person to person, feeling a dread permeate the room. "But, that's just a reproduction, put there for show, right?"

Bankrock turned his attention to the map.

Drusilicus shook his head. "No. I was there when it was raised. As Marlowe said, it was the last task my master oversaw. That obelisk is one of a pair, carved to honor Pharaoh Thuthmosis the Third in the ancient Egyptian city of Lunu or Heliopolis. It once was part of the Temple of the Sun."

"Where worship and sacrifice—human sacrifice—took place," Marlowe mused.

"A talisman of great power, indeed," Ahbay declared.

"It was moved by Augusta Caesar to Alexandria in 12 BC," Drusilicus went on. "Then, it was moved to New York in pieces, base as well as obelisk, and erected on its current site in 1881."

Marlowe nodded and slowly rose from his chair. "It makes much sense, my friends. Not only is it thirty-five hundred years old, but even the base it rests on was built over two thousand years ago."

"It lay next to the reservoir when it was erected," Drusilicus said, "which is now the Great Lawn."

"In close proximity to Greywacke's Arch," Marlowe whispered.

Drusilicus nodded grimly. "The place where my master passed his staff to me and then left this plane."

"He died?" Eddie asked.

"Nay," Drusilicus mused. "He merely disappeared."

"This is all speculation." Bankrock raised his head and pointed. "Look, there is no interdimensional portal shown in that location on the map at all."

Marlowe bent close and studied the map. "You are mistaken, my friend. This map doesn't have the obelisk on it at all."

All the wizards bent close and followed Marlowe's finger. It was true, the spot where Cleopatra's Needle sat was empty.

"The portal is connected to the obelisk," Marlowe marveled.

"It is the only explanation that makes sense," Ahbay capitulated.

"So close to Greywacke's Arch," Eugenia shuddered.

"Almost as if to keep watch over it," Drusilicus observed.

"Greywacke made the arrangements to have that stone pillar transported to the park," Marlowe acknowledged. "He never spoke of any danger connected to it."

"That is surprising," Ahbay noted. "One would think, being a prophet—"

"Marlowe," Eugenia pointed out, "such an ancient structure would require enormous power to bring forth its potency."

"Hold on," Eddie raised his hand. "Are you thinking Abraxas stole the other talismans just to have enough juice to access this doorway?"

Marlowe nodded. "To use them as a channel for supernatural powers, they do not have to be specifically good or evil. It will amplify either energy."

"By Zoroaster!" Drusilicus stood and pushed back his chair. "If we are right, then we must away to New York and—"

"Whoa, Dru," Eddie rose up as well. "We need a plan. After all, the obelisk might not be the right place."

"It is the right place." Caleb stood up at his seat. "I can see it."

Drusilicus turned to his apprentice. "You have been a wizard for barely an hour. Do not try our patience."

"No wait," Marlowe said. "When I attempted to reach out to the medallion the boy made, I couldn't read anything. But he seems to—"

"Master," Caleb's face was almost beatific, "I made the talisman because I received a vision!"

Luis' cell phone rang shrilly, and Luis stood, pulled it from his pocket, and began to speak. "Vasquez... Hola, Maria, calm down, I don' understand what you're sayin'..."

Luis quickly left the room, talking as he went.

"Very well." Drusilicus returned to his chair. "We are the Five, whole, complete and unified! We surround the obelisk and seal it from the Great Evil. Then we draw him to us and push him from this world."

"I like your enthusiasm, Dru," Eddie said, "but so far, we've been getting our asses whipped—"

"Eddie," Luis came from the other room, "you gotta come out here."

"'Scuse me." Eddie rushed into the next room. "What's wrong?"

Luis stood and looked out the window through the drapes, still on the phone. "Maria, you have to calm down, you're hysterical, baby. Calm down." He placed the phone against his chest. "Look here, Eddie."

Eddie hurried to the window and looked out. In the dim streetlights, Eddie could see a second power company van join the first. He also saw several other black vans pull up as well. The windows of each vehicle were so opaque he couldn't even see through the windshield.

"What are they doing?" Eddie wondered. "Getting ready for a raid?"

"Eddie," Luis said, "if these guys work for Wilcox, and they are planning a raid, who do you think they have in mind?"

The realization hit Eddie like a thunderbolt. "Us."

"We gotta go," Luis returned the phone to his ear. "Maria, we got a problem here...slow down, tell me what's wrong..."

Eddie returned to the dining room. The wizards were in deep discussion as they argued different protective spells.

"We have to get out of here," Eddie told them. "The FBI is about to raid us."

"What is this?" Ahbay puzzled.

"Federal Bureau of Investigation," Eddie explained. "They have an agent who wants nothing more than to put my privates in a vise and squeeze."

"Well, a tad vulgar," Eugenia said brightly, "but it does make the situation clear."

Everyone rose.

Bankrock fumed. "I told you we avoid confrontations with mortal law enforcement."

"Shall we head for the woods?" Drusilicus proposed.

"We can't go out the front." Eddie grasped Marlowe's arm. "We have to go out back."

"Eddie, even if we go that way, we have to circle the house to get to the woods," Marlowe confessed. "We cannot just transport ourselves from your backyard."

"I got a birdbath," Eddie advised. "Maybe we could wish our way out."

"We would need a larger fountain."

"I would hesitate to use teleportation," Ahbay said. "It would weaken us before the battle, when we need all our strength."

"But we still have no plan of action," Eugenia complained.

"We can't just stand here," Eddie pleaded. "They could move in at any moment."

Marlowe tapped his walking stick on the floor. "Wait a moment! All we need is a distraction."

"So what're you going to do?" Eddie asked. "Another illusion?"

"I have an idea! Let me use your mirror!" Marlowe walked quickly to the small bathroom under the stairs, went in, and shut the door.

As Marlowe left, Eddie glanced at the table and noticed the medallion that Caleb made and Marlowe so recently held was no longer in the center.

"Gone," Eddie whispered.

Just at that moment, Luis fell into the room. He was pale, and Eddie ran to him, afraid he was having a heart attack.

"Luis!" Eddie helped his partner to a chair. "What is it, big guy?"

Luis's mouth moved, yet nothing came out. He stared blankly.

"Is he having a vision?" Bankrock inquired.

"Shall I try a healing spell?" Drusilicus offered.

"Luis, it's Eddie. What is it?"

Luis met Eddie's eyes, and he grabbed his collar in one of his massive hands.

"Eddie, you have to help me," Luis croaked.

"Anything, Luis, you know that," Eddie replied.

Caleb handed Luis a glass of water, which he drank greedily.

"What is it, what did Maria say?" Eddie urged.

"It's Rosita." Luis looked at the floor as he tried to collect his thoughts. "Maria and the kids, they went for ice cream, that's all, just ice cream. On their way home, they ran into this guy—Maria said he was wearing funny clothes, a big cape and a hood—he just came out of nowhere and grabbed Rosita."

"Grabbed her?" Eddie exclaimed.

"Yeah, he held up this big stick, waved it, and just…was gone. Maria is hysterical." Luis bent over at the waist as if he was going to be sick. "*Madre de Dios!* My Rosita, my little Rosita."

Drusilicus put a hand on Eddie's shoulder. Eddie turned and could see that the mocking quality that usually graced his eyes was gone.

"It appears," Drusilicus spoke solemnly, "that our adversary has chosen his sacrifice."

FIFTY-FIVE

Outside of the Berman house, under the cover of darkness, men readied themselves inside their custom vans. Each was dressed in a black knit uniform with a tight-fitting hood. All were equipped with a bulletproof utility vest marked "FBI" in a lettering that couldn't be seen except through night goggles.

Agent Conners moved his goggles up to his forehead and picked up his cell phone.

"Sir, we are in position," Conners informed Wilcox.

"Good! I'm almost there. Has there been any activity at the house?"

"We still can't look in, sir," Conners reckoned. "It must be some kind of jamming device, because nothing on the second van worked either."

"I'm two minutes out." Wilcox hung up.

Conners sat back in his chair. It was peculiar with the second van. He went in and tried their audio and video equipment. All of it worked fine until it was focused on the Berman house. Then the video turned to snow, the remote listening device picked up static, and the cameras locked up and wouldn't take pictures. Conners knew about technology, and couldn't figure out what could freeze up digital cameras.

It would have to be *very* high tech, and what vendor could supply such cutting-edge equipment? The Middle East was oil-rich, but not technologically advanced. Russia? There were some world-class hackers there. But how did that involve Berman?

A black car with reflective glass pulled slowly down the street and parked in one easy movement. Wilcox exited the car.

He strode to the van, and Conners opened the door for the big man to enter.

"Are we set?" Wilcox demanded. He bent his head to avoid slamming it against the roof.

"Yes, sir, there are twelve men in place."

Wilcox looked over at the technician, who sat in a chair and fiddled with a monitor that only showed different shades of gray that moved in annoying patterns.

"Why aren't you suited up?" Wilcox said, and took off his suit jacket as Conners handed him a bulletproof vest.

The technician turned so suddenly his glasses almost fell off. "Me, sir?"

"Yes, you," Wilcox told him. "Your toys are broken. Strap on a vest and play with the big boys."

"Uh…thank you, sir." Sweat popped out on his forehead. "I need to be here, to…uh…make a record."

"Your equipment doesn't work." Wilcox fastened the Velcro straps around his chest and sides to secure the vest.

"Well," the technician swallowed hard, "I should be here in case it starts working again."

Wilcox pulled out his cell phone and barked, "Do the phones and radios work?"

"Yes, sir," the technician replied timidly. "Only surveillance equipment is affected when it's pointed at the Berman house."

Wilcox shook his head in disgust and pushed a button on the phone. "Sam, are you in place?"

"I am, sir," Sam's voice came back. "Right on the corner of Eighty-Fifth Street. I'm watching that townhouse with binoculars. I haven't seen anyone go in or out, but one strange thing occurred. A parade went by about an hour ago."

"A parade?" Wilcox said.

"Yeah, strangest thing. I mean, it ain't a holiday."

"Just keep your eye on the townhouse," Wilcox ordered, and hung up the phone. He then put out his hand, and Conners gave him a hand-held radio. Wilcox clipped it to his belt, donned an earpiece, and spoke into the microphone. "Team one, you ready?"

"Yes, sir," came the reply.

"Team two?"

"In position, sir."

"All right men, let's move!" Wilcox commanded. He noiselessly jumped out the door of the van and pulled his handgun from his shoulder holster. Conners lowered his night vision goggles and followed, a small submachine gun in his hands.

Wilcox could see doors open on the other vehicles, done so quietly the hinges made no sound. In the dim street lights, he watched two trained fighting units move toward the house.

Wilcox chose not to wear a hood or goggles. He wanted Berman to know who would bring him down; the same guy who set him up on the Viper case.

He didn't know that when he tipped off Viper it would get Vasquez shot, but he didn't really feel all that bad about it either. Berman wasn't so smart, and he wanted him to end up on the shit-list. The reassignment to the Central Park Precinct should have humbled him, but here he was again. That man just wouldn't learn.

Now he was going down. Wilcox was sure there was a statute somewhere within the Patriot Act he could use to charge Berman with a crime.

His men began to fan out. The orders were simple: surround the house and move in.

Wilcox signaled through hand gestures to three men and pointed for them to go around to the back of the house.

They nodded and began to rush toward the fenced backyard. Just before they reached the corner of the house, there was a "whoosh" in the air, and one of the men fell over with an "Oof!"

Wilcox touched his radio. "What the hell was that?" he whispered harshly.

"Not sure," hissed a team leader. "Franz, you all right?"

"Something hit me," the man on the ground said in a tight voice. "It packed a wallop."

A shadow moved with another "whoosh" and the second agent fell to the ground with a yell.

"We're under attack!" Wilcox bellowed into his radio, and knelt down. Conners crouched next to him as a man was picked up and thrown through the air.

"Christ!" Wilcox turned to Conners. "What is it, what do you see?"

"Something in the air, only a blur," Conners gulped, as another man fell with a shout.

There was a short blast of muffled machine gun fire, and Wilcox heard a team leader yell, "Hold your fire, dammit, we're in a neighborhood, not a war zone!"

"I can't see what hit me, sir," a voice said in Wilcox's earpiece.

"Run for the house," Wilcox enjoined.

"Which part?" came a murmur in his ear.

"Head for the goddamn front door! Knock it in if you have to." Wilcox rose with Conners and in a low crouch, ran for the front of the house.

"Sir," Conners announced, "I still can't see— Ah!"

Conners rose in the air, a black creature on his chest. The creature itself was perhaps a foot-and-a-half long, but it had *wings*. The wings were at least six feet wide, tip to tip. It lifted Conners and tossed him aside like a rag doll, before rising silently into the darkness.

But Wilcox got a clear look at it, perhaps better able to see it without the night goggles.

"*Bats*!" Wilcox hollered. "My God, the biggest friggin' bats I ever saw."

"Bats can't knock a man down," came a reply.

"These can!" Wilcox shouted. "They're the size of a Buick. *Run*!!"

Staying low, Wilcox sprinted for the door, hearing that hideous "whoosh" followed by a "thud" as a large flying mammal knocked another man down. He lifted his weapon and fired twice in the air.

"Bats," Wilcox muttered. "Why'd it have to be b-bats?"

He focused his eyes on the front door and kept running, as he tried to clear his mind of the frightening images from his youth. There were always bats on the farm, and his brothers told him stories of how they got caught in your hair. He could feel the goose flesh on his arms as he heard another man fall and then another.

He wanted to shoot the obscenities, but they moved so fast, and he didn't want to accidentally hit one of his men. That would not be perceived kindly by his supervisors.

A huge thing flapped by his ears, and Wilcox ducked and dodged, as a yelp of sheer horror escaped his throat. He could feel urine rush down his leg as he lost control of his bladder.

He reached the steps and moved like a bulldozer toward the door, ready to knock it down.

Only the door opened on its own, which made Wilcox stop, fall to the ground, and raise his weapon.

"*Freeze!* FBI!" he yelled. His hands shook so badly the pistol quivered in his grasp.

Eleanor Berman gently opened the door and looked down at Wilcox. "Are you all right, young man?"

"FBI! Put your hands in the air!"

Eleanor obediently raised her hands, a smile on her face. "I don't think I'm very dangerous."

Wilcox rose to his feet quickly and moved to the door.

"I don't want to say anything," Eleanor glanced at Wilcox's crotch, her hands still up, "but I think you wet yourself."

"Where is he?" Wilcox growled.

"Who, dearie?" Eleanor said.

"Berman!"

"Well, I'm Eleanor Berman, if that's any help. In fact, we are all Bermans here—"

"Eddie!" Wilcox demanded, "I want Eddie Berman!"

"He's not here," Eleanor said.

"Sir!" a voice came over the radio. "Possible suspects leaving the area!"

"*Stay on them!*" Wilcox snapped and turned as a huge, leathery wing flapped past his head.

Wilcox screamed like a little girl and dove through the open door into the house.

"Are you all right?" Eleanor asked, as the big man lay on the welcome mat quivering in revulsion.

*   *   *

Eddie looked back down the street as Eugenia, Ahbay, Drusilicus, Bankrock, and Caleb entered the woods.

"I don't think we're being followed," Eddie said to Luis and Marlowe, after his glance down the dark street. "Let's get going."

"Just a moment." Marlowe put two fingers to his mouth and blew a long note. A huge bat swished through the air and landed on the ground. It covered itself with its wings and began to grow in size. The wings changed to arms, and in moments Daniel Kraft stood before them.

"Holy crap!" was all Luis could utter.

"We have them on the run," Daniel confirmed. "I'll call off the others."

"Others?" Eddie glanced at Luis, who was still shocked at Daniel's arrival.

"Yes, I brought along some friends." Daniel smiled, his skin as pale as his teeth, setting off his dark hair and eyes. As he spoke, two other large bats flew to the ground and began to transform.

"I'm glad no one got shot," Eddie said as the two forms became a short man with curly hair and a tall, sultry woman.

"Bullets can't kill us," Daniel remarked.

"Oh yeah," Eddie said sheepishly. "I knew that."

The short man, recently a bat and now fully human-looking, stepped forward with great agitation. "But they sting!"

"You're a vampire?" Luis said to Daniel with a glance at the smaller man. "A *real* vampire?"

Daniel gave Eddie a look that conveyed, "Who is this, and what turnip truck did he fall off of?"

"My apprentice, Luis," Eddie said, as a way of explanation.

"Hey," Luis remembered. "You were the guy who attacked the demon…with the fangs."

The shorter man drew close to Daniel and hissed, "You didn't say we were helping *them*."

"Calm yourself, Tuck." Daniel turned to the man who couldn't have been more than five feet two. "I told you it was all a lark—"

"But we aided wizards!" Tuck spat out the last words. "Our sworn enemies"

"We are grateful for your assistance," Marlowe expressed, his staff at the ready. "I have no wish for conflict between us this night."

The tall woman, who wore a skimpy black dress, gently touched Tuck's shoulders. "It is nothing. Let us go for now. We've had our fun."

She glanced up at Luis like he was the world's largest lollipop. "Unless you'd like some fun, my big man." Her eyes turned an amazing shade of violet, and Luis' mouth fell open hungrily, his own eyes staring. She reached out to wipe the sweat from his brow and brought her fingers to her mouth to taste.

Eddie elbowed his partner in the side.

"Ow!" Luis grunted. "Uh…no…uh…thank you. We got to go."

"The others shall hear of this," Tuck sneered, then faced Marlowe. "No conflict now, wizard. But our time comes soon."

He turned and ran off, his form shifting as he went, and a large bat was airborne and faded into the darkness.

"Lysandra," Daniel addressed the lady, who still stared hungrily at Luis. "Perhaps I have overstepped my place."

"Oh, ignore him, Daniel. Tuck is far too serious." Her eyes immediately returned to Luis. She put a finger under his chin. "If you ever want the experience of a lifetime, my friend, come see me. You might not survive, but I shall make your sacrifice worth it."

She gave a girlish giggle, which seemed very out of place, then leapt high into the air, and flew off as a bat.

Luis gulped hard and shook his head, as if to wake from a dream.

"Daniel, can you join us?" Marlowe implored. "We must go to the park. Cleopatra's Needle is the fifth talisman."

"The obelisk?" Daniel said, his voice filled with awe. "I cannot. It is important to get my associates back to New York. I must keep an eye on them, so they don't end up feeding on some housewife."

Daniel turned, ran in the direction of Eddie's house, became a black remnant in the darkness, and flew off under the beat of huge wings.

"Ohmigod!" Luis gasped. "They all turned into frickin' bats!"

"I thought he was a much smaller bat the other night," Eddie pointed out.

"He was," Marlowe nodded. "Abraxas is not the only one who can alter his size and shape."

The three men turned and trudged into the woods, Marlowe in the lead.

"Do you think Cerise and your mother can handle Wilcox and his men?" Luis asked.

"My momma's tough," Eddie said. He couldn't get Cerise's face out of his mind when he'd told her about Rosita. He saw fear shine brightly in her eyes, but she kept a brave face, and he loved her all the more for it.

"What else can this Daniel guy change into?" Luis finally said as they walked.

Marlowe glanced back at Luis. "Oh, the usual. Many sizes and type of bat. He can become a wolf, though when I've seen him, he looks more like a big dog. And he can dissolve into mist."

"Can he be a snake?" Eddie said.

Marlowe stopped and faced Eddie, a frown on his face. "You think Daniel is in league with Abraxas?"

"I'm asking questions," Eddie responded. "You know, my job? After all, we don't know for sure it *is* a warlock. It could just be someone in wizard robes carrying a stick."

Marlowe turned away and strode into the woods. "Enough."

"You have to consider the fact," Eddie insisted, "that there is a traitor in your midst."

"It's not Daniel," Marlowe vowed adamantly. "I trust him with my life!"

"Isn't that how you felt about Trefoil?" Eddie said.

Marlowe sighed. This thought seemed to tire him. "Yes, it was." He stared up at the dark night sky.

"Someone going with us to that shrine, or portal, might not be a friend. And once they have us there—"

"We must leave that in the hands of the Divine." Marlowe meandered into the woods.

"I hope somebody let the Divine know we need help." Luis followed after Eddie.

"Amen." Eddie placed his hand on Luis' shoulder as they entered the woods.

*   *   *

A voice came over Wilcox's earpiece. "We traced several people to a park, sir."

"How many?" Wilcox said. He was still inside the Berman house, but rose from the floor.

"Hard to say, sir, but we spotted the suspect and his partner going into a grove of trees."

"Are the b-b-bats still out there?" Wilcox stuttered, as he fought to keep his voice steady.

"They seem to be gone, sir."

"Conners!" Wilcox roared.

"Yes, sir," Conners replied.

"Are there injuries?"

"I just had the wind knocked out of me, sir. Some abrasions and contusions, but nothing major."

"Okay. I want all our men to converge on that park."

"Yes, sir," Conners told him.

"Roger that," came the voices of the team leaders.

Wilcox yanked his earpiece out and turned to face Eleanor Berman. He pointed a finger at the older woman.

"Not polite to point, dearie."

"You are under arrest!" Wilcox's voice was a low growl.

"I am the widow of a police officer, young man." Eleanor put her hands on her hips. "If you have charges, they'd better be good."

"Aiding and abetting the escape of a fugitive!" Wilcox announced.

"What fugitive?"

"Your son!"

"Oh, stop! How is he a fugitive? What crime did he commit?"

Wilcox was dumbfounded for a moment. He really didn't have any charges. All he had were suspicions and that wouldn't hold up.

"Well, I—I mean…where did he go?"

"He went for a walk. Is that a crime?"

"We were attacked!"

"By what? I didn't see anything." Eleanor folded her arms.

"You didn't see those giant bats?" Wilcox bellowed.

"Oh those; they're around here all the time," Eleanor gave a dismissive wave of her hand. "You probably just scared them."

"I…scared…*them*?" Wilcox repeated in disbelief.

"Look, young man, why don't you sit down at the table and I'll make you a nice cup of coffee, and you can wait for Eddie to come home and talk to him."

"Cup of—" Wilcox's mouth fell open. This woman was insane, his men were beaten by a bunch of flying rodents, and Eddie was off somewhere laughing about it.

"No, thank you…uh…ma'am," Wilcox gritted his teeth. "I'll be off. Please do not leave the premises, in case I have questions."

"Of course not, dearie, it's dark out there."

Wilcox nodded tightly, opened the door, and left.

"Good night, young man," Eleanor waved as she shut the door.

Cerise walked out from the kitchen and smiled at her mother-in-law. "Good job, Momma."

"I know how to handle slackers," Eleanor heralded. "Oh! I think we are going to need to wash the welcome mat. That boy had hisself a accident."

"I'll take care of it, Momma," Cerise sighed. She went to the kitchen and got a pair of heavy rubber gloves, then returned to the front door. She wasn't wearing shoes, so she quickly put on a nearby pair of bedroom slippers, which bore the face of a bunny on the front and pointed ears that stood above her toes.

She picked up the mat and looked over at the vans, which still littered the street, as the men in black assembled and headed in groups toward the nearby park.

She took the rubberized rectangle with the fanciful "Welcome To Our Home" emblazoned on it around to the side of the house, where stood an outdoor faucet.

She turned on the water and began to rinse the surface. As she finished, she turned off the water and hung it dripping over the nearby fence that separated the Berman property from its neighbors.

"That's that," Cerise muttered to herself, as she took off the gloves and hung them next to the mat. She sighed and leaned against the fence. "Hope you're doing okay, Eddie. I wish I was there with you."

"I desire the same thing," a voice croaked near her ear.

Cerise turned, ready to yell, but a large stick was passed in front of her face, and the scream was frozen in her throat. Her eyes glazed over and her expression became dream-like.

"Yesss," the cloaked wizard hissed. "I think being there with your husband is a fine idea, indeed."

FIFTY-SIX

In the darkness with trees overhead, Eddie wasn't sure when he and Luis shifted from Teaneck to the Big Apple, but he did feel the ground change as he walked out of the trees onto a rocky summit.

"Where are we?" Luis asked.

"Sh!" Eddie hissed. "I think we're near Belvedere Castle." He looked around and got his bearings, deciding they stood just north of the 79th Street transverse road. They were close to one of the park's most fanciful creations. Rising out of the summit of Vista Rock stood a medieval castle with square buildings, a parapet, and even a tower to suit the most demanding princess. It overlooked a small, man-made lake, and matched the rock as if sculpted from the landscape by elves.

Marlowe was still ahead of them, and he turned to look back.

Eddie drew near to the older man and whispered, "Why here?"

"A safe place to assemble," murmured Marlowe. He pointed up at the cut stones that formed a stairway to the castle. "We can observe the obelisk from the parapet, and approach with care."

"Check out the terrain?" Eddie quizzed.

"What's wrong with all of you just waiting for this warlock guy and piling up on him?" Luis challenged.

Eddie turned to his partner. "It might not be healthy for your daughter."

Luis came to a full stop, his eyes instantly wet. "That's right, my baby's there. She must be so scared."

"We shall endeavor to save her." Marlowe placed his hand on the big man's shoulder. "And you shall help!"

Luis nodded and wiped his face with the back of his hand. "I just don' know why they went after her. How did they even know about my family?"

"This dude must've found out I chose you as my apprentice," Eddie whispered as they climbed the steps. "Marlowe, only people in our party had that information."

The group began to climb as short walls rose up on both sides of the stairs. They reached a landing, and the terrace opened before them. They could see clearly in the light of the moon, which was full. The great stones of the castle rose in a square building to their right. The windows were arched and high, and reflected black in the darkness.

They walked in the direction of a small outdoor pavilion. In the dim light, they could barely see the red and yellow paint that was so intricately detailed on the Moorish building. Even so, it wore an exotic appearance.

As they drew closer, Eddie could make out Eugenia, Ahbay, and Drusilicus. There they were: the Five. And Luis as backup. He then realized two people were missing.

"Where's Caleb?" Eddie started.

"What?" Drusilicus replied. "I thought he was with you."

"He was right behind me," Eugenia said, glancing about. "Or so I thought."

"He is a Newling; we should have taken him in hand," Ahbay acknowledged. "He may have teleported elsewhere."

"It's not our fault," Drusilicus bickered. "We were too busy trying to get out of there."

"What about Bankrock?" Eddie peered at the group a second time. "He's missing, too."

"We need to focus, my friends," Marlowe commanded. "Look upon the obelisk."

The group looked off to the east past the body of water below them. The view was spectacular. The full moon was high in a crystal-clear sky. The windows of tall buildings were merely hundreds of floating rectangles of light in the distance.

Directly under the moon, Eddie could see Cleopatra's Needle poking up from the shadows, its pointed head jutting out from the jagged silhouettes of the treetops.

"Look, the obelisk is directly under the moon," Eddie gasped.

"That's just because of where we're standin'," Luis pointed out. "Depth perception, or something."

"No, friend Luis," Marlowe intoned. "The obelisk is indeed in alignment."

"How many centuries did the sleeping forces lie in wait for this night?" Drusilicus declared solemnly.

"You mean this was planned?" Eddie frowned.

"It would appear to be the case," Ahbay reasoned.

"All part of a larger design," Eugenia marveled.

Marlowe spoke with reverent awe. "You see, Eddie, that obelisk was brought from Egypt and put into that particular spot, knowing it would be in perfect alignment on this very night. See how the forces of good and evil work in harmony without meaning to."

Drusilicus nodded. "To think that the object that might destroy all humanity would rest on Greywacke's Knoll."

"It is a mighty fetish," Eugenia agreed.

"Fetish?" Luis blurted. "You plannin' something kinky?"

"No, Luis," Marlowe said, "the older meaning of the word 'fetish' is something that contains great magic."

"I wish we'd known that it was the fifth talisman sooner," Eddie lamented.

"What do we do, Marlowe?" Drusilicus began. "Stand here until midnight? Let us combine the power of the Five and shield the site from the Great Evil."

Marlowe stared off at the Great Lawn, its grass gleaming in the silvery moonlight. "He is right, we must take action, my friends."

The group headed downhill from the castle and due east to follow the footpath. The route was lit by the occasional cast-metal street lamp, the design of which harkened back to gas lights of a century earlier.

They walked past a shadowy figure on horseback.

"Who's that?" Luis asked, as he looked up at the statue holding two crossed swords over his crowned head.

"King Jagiello," Marlowe confirmed. "A Polish warrior, fought the Teutonic forces in 1410."

"Oh, I should've known."

"Keep your eyes sharp and your minds clear," Marlowe warned. "We do not wish to be taken unawares."

"For once," Eddie muttered.

They turned a corner and in front of them, lit only by a single street lamp, stood Greywacke Arch. The opening was not a gentle curve, but pointed in the center. It was made out of hand-carved stones, and the inside of the tunnel was lined with red brick interrupted by patterns of yellow. Around the opening, small fleur de lis decorated every other stone up to the keystone, which was carved with a pattern of interlocking vines.

Eddie stopped cold and pointed, "Whoa! That design on the arch! That was the face that was on the medallion."

"What?" Luis said.

"The design in the center looks like a face."

Luis half-closed his eyes and looked where Eddie pointed. "Yeah, sort of. Some guy with a big mustache."

"That reminds me," Eddie pondered. "Marlowe, when you left the room to call Daniel, I looked on the table and the medallion was gone."

Marlowe shook his head. "I took it not."

"Any of you see where it went?" Eddie turned to the others.

Drusilicus, Ahbay, and Eugenia shook their heads and murmured denials.

"Great," Eddie grumbled. "Then Caleb has it. Any way to track that kid down?"

"Many ways, Eddie," Marlowe confided, "but we must keep to our task for the present. How stands the hour?"

"It's almost eleven." Eddie glanced at his watch. "Hey, I thought you could just feel the rhythms of time."

"I decided it wouldn't hurt to check." The old wizard grinned. "Let us go on."

They purposefully strode up the wide staircase. At the top of the stairs was Obelisk Terrace, with the huge carved stone rising majestically into the night sky, seventy feet high.

"We are hidden by the trees that surround this structure," Marlowe assured. "We should be undisturbed."

"What do we do?" Eddie asked.

"We must form the five points of *Seiman*," Ahbay reported.

"What?" Eddie questioned, uncomprehending.

"In common parlance," Drusilicus translated, "we must create a pentagram."

"I have a compass." Marlowe reached into his pocket. "You all must remain in the positions I place thee." He turned his head to Luis. "Do you know thy task, sergeant?"

"What you said at Eddie's house is that I stay at the bottom of the stairs and let no one up," Luis recited.

"Good, good, now be off." Marlowe waved his hand at Luis, who trudged purposefully down the stairs.

Marlowe held out his small compass and took Eddie by the arm and carefully situated him about ten feet from the obelisk.

"Marlowe, I am still not happy about Caleb wandering off," Eddie protested.

"Lieutenant," Drusilicus said as Marlowe went to him and adjusted his position, "would you please attempt to pay attention to the task at hand?"

"Are you quite sure we are strong enough?" Eugenia worried.

Marlowe stepped to her. "We shall do the best we can."

"I'm veddy certain of that," Eugenia said as Marlowe gently guided her to her spot. "But, our powers were affected that night with Trefoil, and Marlowe, you faced that terrible mirror a second time."

"Banish your doubt, dear lady." Ahbay placed himself across from Eddie. "Doubt will weaken our intention."

"All of you listen to me," Marlowe announced in a commanding voice. "Together we have the ability to face and defeat our foe. The spells we will place around the site will stop our opponent. Let us begin, Eugenia."

Eugenia's clothes transformed to yellow robes and she held out her staff. A yellow beam of light, like a laser, leapt from the top and stretched out to touch the top of Ahbay's rod.

Ahbay's clothes shifted into his green silk *kimono*, and he sent a similar beam of green light to Marlowe's staff.

Marlowe, whose raiment changed from a well-cut suit to flowing white robes, gestured and sent his own ray to Drusilicus' staff.

Drusilicus' Armani suit became an ocean-blue set of robes and he fired a blue light toward Eddie.

It's now or never, Eddie thought. He could feel his clothes altered to scarlet robes and boots. His staff glowed red, and light shot to Eugenia's staff.

They were now all connected, the rays of colored light forming a pentagram that surrounded the obelisk, which began to glow in otherworldly colors of its own.

Marlowe began to chant in that strange language again as a breeze whipped up from nowhere, as if nature itself was affected by their work.

At the bottom of the steps, Luis stood guard. He glanced back over his shoulder at the light show taking place above him.

A shadow approached in the darkness.

"Oh boy," Luis muttered. "And me without a weapon."

He turned to face the figure as it drew closer. He hoped that it was just a New Yorker out for an evening stroll.

But it was someone he knew.

Cerise Berman stepped into the pool of light from the street lamp Luis stood under. Her face wore a blank look, and she stared straight ahead, oblivious to her surroundings.

Luis went to her and noticed that she was wearing bunny slippers on her feet. He gently took her arm, which stopped her.

"Cerise?" he whispered.

Cerise's head slowly turned to face him. She blinked twice and responded, "Luis?"

"Yeah, it's me. What're you doin' here?"

She looked around calmly, then returned her gaze to him. "I have no idea."

In his peripheral vision, Luis saw something move nearby in the darkness and turned just as a beam of light crackled through the air and struck him like a freight train. He spun from the impact and collapsed to the ground, unconscious.

Cerise looked down with her mouth open, and swung about to face the figure in the shadows.

"Go on, my dear," the raspy voice told her.

Cerise's expression became blank again and she began to climb the stairs.

FIFTY-SEVEN

"We don't see any of them, sir," came the voice through the earpiece.

"Damn!" Wilcox cursed. They'd circled the woods in Teaneck for the last half-hour with no sign of Berman, his partner, or any of the other suspects. In fact, the only things in this three-block park were squirrels, groundhogs, and maybe a rabid raccoon.

At least the bats are gone, Wilcox thought with a shudder. *It was weird how they showed up just when Berman made his move.*

He thought back to the night Cuccolo died, how the mobster rose up in the air. It was strange as well because in his memory he had the oddest impression that it was a giant in a Native American headdress that held him aloft.

His cell phone rang.

"Yeah," he barked into the receiver as he pulled off his earpiece.

"It's Sam," the voice said.

"Seen anything?"

"Two people just left that townhouse on Eighty-Fifth Street."

"Who was it?" Wilcox demanded, calming his temper.

"One was a tall African-American woman. The other, some guy all bundled up, with a hood covering his face."

"Where did they go?"

"Into the park. I'm following. Heading for the Great Lawn."

"Stay on them." Wilcox hung up.

He stood there and glanced at his watch. It was just past eleven. He wondered if he should stay here and search more, but his gut told him if he wanted Berman, he would find him in Manhattan.

"Team one and two," Wilcox spoke into his walkie-talkie. "Head for the trucks, get ready to move out."

After they responded, Wilcox called for Conners.

Conners ran over. "Yes, sir?"

"We're leaving. Keep a technician on the house if Berman returns."

"The surveillance equipment is shot, sir," Conners commented. "But he can do it the old-fashioned way—use his eyes, write things down."

"Good! I like your style, Conners," Wilcox said and turned on his radio. "Team One! Team Two! We are going to Manhattan. Stay suited up. I want us ready to move the minute we arrive."

*   *   *

The light that emanated from the obelisk began to grow brighter, hieroglyphics long since eroded away appeared as figures of light dancing up and down the stone sides, and the pyramid on the top glowed a deep mauve.

A beam of light shot forth into the clear night sky, pointed at the moon directly overhead. The ray disappeared as it traveled into space, but in a moment, the moon shifted and began to turn the same color as the obelisk's top.

The ground began to shake and Eddie could feel something move.

"Look!" Eddie cried out, as the ground began to lift and rumble.

The entire terrace, constructed of hexagonal stone tiles, suddenly moved, tossed, and resettled like waves on the surface of the ocean, except on the five points where the wizards stood.

Then, on the west side that directly faced the stairs, tiles began to fall away into a widening sinkhole. More and more shifted, and a stairway rose up from underneath as if slid into position.

"It's the portal!" Drusilicus cried out. "We have opened it."

"I thought we wanted to keep it closed!" Eddie shouted.

"Do not break the pentagram!" Ahbay yelled. "Once Marlowe completes the protective spell, it will be closed forever."

"We wouldn't want that," a voice croaked.

Eddie turned, as the others also faced the cloaked and hooded figure with a staff who stood at the edge of the terrace. Next to the warlock was Cerise, a vacant expression on her face, and of all things, bunny slippers on her feet.

"Cerise!" Eddie cried in alarm, and a cold sweat sprung out on his brow.

"Do not break the pentagram!" Ahbay called loudly as Marlowe chanted faster.

The figure laughed, deep and throaty, and from the robes pulled out the obsidian mirror. The warlock held up the impossibly black stone, and the beams that formed the pentagram began to quiver.

Eugenia's yellow beam was first. It pulled loose from Ahbay's staff and flashed like a crooked bolt of lightning to the mirror. Then one at a time, each of the beams was wrenched out of alignment to be pulled into the mirror, Eddie's last of all.

Eddie felt as if he'd put his foot on the third rail of a subway. Electricity passed through his body and made his muscles quiver and his teeth chatter. He forced his eyes open and looked at the others, saw that their bodies shook as energy was yanked from them. They all cried out in pain and Marlowe no longer said magick words, but howled in agony.

This is the same as in the bedroom, Eddie thought. *Only ten times worse.*

He pulled his hand free from his staff and allowed it to fall to the ground. The glow around him ceased, but Eddie felt as if he'd been struck by a large club. His limbs were loose and trembled, but he forced himself to move.

He rushed to Marlowe, locked his fingers around the old man's hands. Again the sensation that he touched a live electric wire which scrambled his nerves and made the world around him spin out of control. He pried Marlowe's fingers open and knocked the stick from his hand. Marlowe fell to the ground, and Eddie stood for a moment and tried to draw a deep breath.

The warlock still held three beams in his mirror and chuckled mockingly at Eddie.

I know that voice, Eddie thought. Then he fell to his knees and reached into Marlowe's robes. He was afraid that in all of the clothing changes, it might be gone, but his hand brushed velvet, and Eddie pulled out the neatly folded Hat of Remembrance.

"No time for this now," Eddie said, tucked the hat in his belt, and leapt toward Eugenia. She shuddered like a rag doll, but Eddie grabbed her hands, felt the shock, as the smell of ozone struck his nostrils. Her grip was weak and he easily pulled her free from the staff. She fell unconscious to the ground as he moved toward Drusilicus.

"Drusilicus." Eddie dodged under the metal pipe of the short fence that surrounded the obelisk. "Let go!"

Drusilicus was not in control and Eddie was afraid that he was beyond the ability to hear. However, his hand opened, as if by itself, and slowly the stick toppled toward the ground. The blue light ceased, and Drusilicus fell on top of his newly won prize.

Eddie felt so unbelievably tired that he thought his limbs weighed a hundred pounds each. But, without a pause, he dove for Ahbay and tackled the smaller man. The two of them hurtled toward the cloaked figure with the mirror.

The warlock jumped back just enough to dodge the falling bodies, which smacked to the ground in a tumble of limbs.

That surprised him, Eddie thought. *He didn't see it coming!*

The hooded warlock lowered the mirror. "Clever work, Newling."

Eddie rolled off Ahbay, who was out cold. He tried to get up but felt as if every fiber of his strength had been sucked from him. He lay on the cold stone tiles, helpless.

The hooded warlock put the mirror back into his robe and walked to the newly made opening at the base of the artifact.

Eddie looked up at Cerise, who stared blankly as the obelisk continued to glow in a kaleidoscope of colored light.

"Cerise, baby," Eddie sputtered. "Get outta here, run."

She stood oblivious.

Eddie wanted to jump up, help Cerise, fight the warlock, or do anything, but he couldn't even find the strength to stand.

That voice, I know that voice, Eddie thought. His hand went to his belt. He pulled the Hat of Remembrance free, though it also seemed to weigh five hundred pounds.

"Thank you for opening the portal," the warlock croaked, looking down the open staircase, as the obelisk continued its light show of glowing hieroglyphics. "Only the power of the Five could open it. Trefoil and I sought to steal your abilities with the mirror, that was our original plan. But leading you here worked just as well."

The warlock reached into the cloak and pulled out a red snake, which wrapped itself around his hand. He gently dropped the snake into the open stairway.

There was a flash of red light and the sound of heavy footsteps as Abraxas, in his guise as the red demon, rose up out of the opening.

"All is as it should be." Abraxas glanced down the steps.

"Good!" the warlock said.

"Where is the sacrifice?" the demon demanded.

The warlock pulled out a small bottle, and with a thumb, popped the cork. A greenish mist issued forth, and the warlock bent to one knee and poured it onto the ground.

The mist moved and sparkled with inner lights, then began to form a cohesive figure.

Rosita Vasquez appeared from the mist and was lying on the tiled terrace, her eyes closed. She began to breathe and opened her eyes. She started to lift her head.

Eddie rolled over and got on his knees, but couldn't stand. He slowly raised his arms to place the hat on his head.

"Sleep," the warlock said and Rosita's head lowered back to the pavement, her eyes closed.

"Oh, how I have waited for this day," Abraxas trumpeted, and looked at the girl and the fallen wizards, a large smile on his fiendish face. "I stand triumphant as they lay helpless."

"Do not forget who brought you this victory, demon," the warlock said.

The huge devil fell to one knee and bowed his horned head in deference.

The hat on his head, Eddie was surprised when nothing happened. "Great, the damn thing doesn't work."

All at once, a flood of memories came to him, one in particular. He was in Marlowe's living room and found he could recall every detail of the room around him, from each vein of the marble floor to the shade of the wood on the fireplace mantel.

He was listening to someone tell of Trefoil being attacked in the park. Then, she did an impression of the demon, and said, "You've lost your edge, wizard!"

That voice.

"Oh my God," Eddie gasped, the memory clear. "You're Frisha!"

The warlock turned in surprise. Then, with her free hand pulled back the hood of the cloak.

Frisha stood before him, her staff aglow, and her wrinkled mouth broke into a grin that exposed her missing teeth.

FIFTY-EIGHT

Frisha surveyed the terrace, the staff in her hand shone with an unearthly light that reflected on her face and gave her a malefic appearance.

"Thou sees the truth, Eddie Berman," she raised her staff toward him threateningly. "I used a masking spell to cloak my true identity, but I knew it was only a matter of time afore ye found me out." She moved the wooden implement in a gesture of attack.

Eddie closed his eyes, expecting a flash of power from her staff that would kill him. He was too tired to even get out of the way.

A flare of golden light shot past Eddie toward Frisha, who easily sidestepped it.

"Thou hast not won yet, villain," another hooded figure cried out, as he sauntered out from behind a tree. "I knew it would be thee."

"And I knew you would say that," Frisha responded. She turned to the demon and ordered, "Take the child to the temple. Do nothing 'til I join thee to chant the words."

The demon gave a nod, picked up the little girl with one large hand as if she was a toy, walked down the stairs and out of sight.

Eddie turned and glanced beyond the frozen Cerise to see a figure approach dressed in long robes, staff aloft, and a medallion around his neck that glowed with a golden fire.

"Caleb?" Eddie yelped, recognizing the new wizard.

"Nay, Eddie Berman," Caleb spoke with an utterly different voice. "The one you call Caleb is merely my vessel. I am the true master of this staff and this knoll."

"Greywacke!" Frisha growled.

Eddie shot his head from one person to the other as he tried to follow the conversation. "Wait a minute, *the* Greywacke?"

"Yea, verily he is," Frisha jeered. "Or was."

"I knew it would be thee, Frisha. I saw this night a hundred and sixty years ago. Surrender now, old love."

"Old love?" Eddie repeated. "You mean you were, I mean you two, I mean…ugh!"

Frisha's face grew red. "In my day I was quite the beauty, and once worshipped as a goddess."

"That was a *lot* of days ago," Eddie snorted.

"It was my desire that you would choose not this pathway," Caleb-Greywacke effused.

"I saw that you would return, old fool," Frisha taunted. "You should have stayed dead."

"We do not die; we move to a higher plane," Greywacke replied.

"Yeah, your mother." Frisha shot a bolt of energy from her staff.

Caleb avoided the blast and easily deflected it.

Eddie stood unsteadily, grabbed Cerise and pulled her to the ground. He looked at her, shook her, but to no avail. In desperation, he lightly slapped her face.

"What the hell—" she squealed, as her eyes met Eddie's. "I was just thinking about you—"

She interrupted herself to scream as Caleb flung a bolt of golden lightning at Frisha.

Frisha sidestepped, dissipated the discharge, and sent a red beam toward Caleb's feet. The light hit the ground, and the tiles ignited with a *whoosh* of flames that engulfed him.

"Ohmigod!" Cerise screamed. "What's going on?"

Eddie lifted his eyes to see Caleb walk uninjured out of the flames, surrounded by a blue light.

"Cerise," Eddie turned to his wife. "You have to get out of here, right now."

"W-What is that?" she said and gazed up at the glowing obelisk.

"I can't explain now." Eddie pointed to the stairs that led off the knoll. "Head down those steps and keep running until you are out of the park."

"But, I...how did I get here? How do I get home?" Cerise said, and clung onto Eddie. "And where did you get that ridiculous hat?"

Eddie yanked the hat from his head and slipped it quickly into his belt.

"Thou art wasting thy time, Frisha. I am a prophet, and I know what thou doest beforehand," Caleb sneered. He gestured at the obelisk and a hieroglyph of an owl with huge eyes leapt from the stone toward Frisha, its talons bared and its mouth open.

Frisha pulled out the mirror, and the diving bird vanished into its depths.

"Old fool, I see the future as plain as thee. You canst defeat me."

"Cerise, you've got to go," Eddie insisted.

"Should I call 911?"

Eddie glanced at the battling wizards. "Get the damn army if you can."

"Come home to me," she gave him a quick kiss.

"I always do."

She rose in a crouch and scurried down the stairs, the bunny slippers slapping on the pavement as she went down.

Frisha let loose another volley.

Eddie watched Cerise descend the stairs and he crawled to the still figure of Marlowe.

The two prophets started another attack and blocked each other's maneuvers. Eddie shook his head. If both could see the future, there was no way either could win.

The concept made his brain hurt.

He reached Marlowe and tried to rouse him. "Come on, buddy. You've got to wake up, we need help."

Marlowe's eyelids fluttered and his blue eyes opened, not much more than slits.

"What—" he whispered, "we—we were attacked."

"It's Frisha," Eddie said, as there was another blinding flash, Caleb attacking as Frisha parried.

"F-Frisha?" Marlowe attempted to rise. "Nay, nay, it cannot be."

"It is! She and Caleb are fighting—"

"Caleb?" Marlowe murmured weakly.

"But, it's not Caleb. He's been possessed by the spirit of Greywacke."

"I am much confused." Marlowe shook his head.

"Think how I feel." Eddie grimaced.

Eddie pulled Marlowe up and both winced as another scintillation hit the pavement and exploded in the spot Caleb vacated a moment earlier.

"We're in serious trouble," Eddie implored. "The red guy took Rosita down into the temple, and I don't know what happened to Luis."

"The others?" Marlowe fretted.

Eddie looked at the other three. They lay sprawled in different positions about the terrace. "They're out…unconscious, maybe hurt. I don't know, I tackled Ahbay pretty hard."

Marlowe nodded his head and held out his hand. His staff, which lay on the pavement, quivered, then flew into his hand. He leaned against it heavily, barely able to stand.

"Are you up to this?" Eddie scowled.

"I know not," Marlowe quavered.

Caleb focused another blast at Frisha, who reversed it so it flew back at him. Caleb deflected it once again toward Frisha, who easily avoided it, and the energy struck a tree. The leaves all turned brown in an instant.

"What can we do, Marlowe?" Eddie begged.

"Try to get help." Marlowe looked up to a tree and made a chittering sound.

There was movement on the branch of the tree, and Eddie saw a large squirrel peer down at them.

"'Tis Quiptail," Marlowe pointed at the rodent. "Tell him our need."

Eddie glared at the old man. "I don't speak squirrel."

"I am too weary to walk over there. You must talk to him."

Eddie let go of Marlowe and stumbled to the tree. The large squirrel watched him with its beady eyes, ready to run off if Eddie made an unexpected move.

"Quiptail," Eddie soothed. "We need your help. Any of your friends, whoever you got, bring them here, 'cause we need them."

The large squirrel chittered at Eddie, who nodded in reply.

"That's right, bring the whole neighborhood," Eddie said, and pointed at Frisha, still locked in battle with Caleb. "You see her. She killed Riftstone."

Eddie turned and then looked back, and gave the squirrel a bow. "Thank you, good Quiptail…uh…master of squirrels." He felt ridiculous, but decided if he was going to make a fool of himself, he might as well go all the way.

The squirrel chittered, gave a nod, and disappeared into the tree with a flash of motion.

Eddie returned to Marlowe. "I hope that worked."

"You did well, Eddie. I have background coming," Marlowe made a small gesture with his staff.

"I think you mean *backup*," Eddie corrected. Over the noise of the battle, he could hear hoof beats. "What is that? The cavalry?"

He looked up to see a man on horseback mount the steps, two swords aloft in his hands.

The attacker was dressed in coppery chain mail and wore a metal crown on his head. Then Eddie noticed that the man's face was also the same bronze metal, as well as the horse.

"That's the statue we passed," Eddie gaped, "King Jabberwocky."

"Jagiello." Marlowe leaned against his staff wearily. "Quickly, we must use this distraction to get down to the temple and stop Abraxas."

Eddie nodded, and held out his hand to receive his staff, which gravitated swiftly to him. The pair, using their staffs to help them, began to move toward the shrine entrance.

The living statue came at Frisha, who did not take her eyes off Caleb, but gestured and froze the figure with his hands raised, again a mere metal statue.

"Give up, Greywacke or who e'er you be," Frisha threatened. "I possess the magick of the talismans, as well as the power of the Five within the Smoking Mirror. I be the most powerful wizard on this plane."

Caleb leaned against his staff, breathing hard from exertion.

"All of thee, such high and mighty fools," she derided. "Didn't think nothing of old Frisha, did ye?"

"We were in love once—" Caleb coughed.

"I t'weren't good enough for you, was I?"

"You were difficult even in those long-ago days, Frisha. But we ne'er did anything to cause this." Caleb moved to keep her attention as Eddie and Marlowe limped toward the opening.

"Didn't ye?" Frisha scoffed. "I am a prophetess, I know what ye said about me behind closed doors. But thee, despite our affair a thousand years hence, thought me weak, my ways strange."

"Yes, but you have only grown bitter in the last three hundred years or so," Caleb spoke in Greywacke's commanding voice.

"I was ne'er welcome. Look at me now!"

Effortlessly, Frisha turned her staff toward Eddie and Marlowe, and a blast of energy emanated toward them. In a move of surprising agility, Marlowe rolled, grabbed, and threw Eddie and his staff down the open stairs as the brunt of the blast struck him.

There was a tremendous flash of light, and a loud "*boom*" as energy discharged around Marlowe like a bomb.

Eddie looked up and yelled, "*Marlowe!*"

A smoldering remnant of his robe fluttered to the ground.

The old man was gone.

Eddie tried to get up, but instead, his foot slipped and he fell down the steps. He tried to cover his face as his flesh smacked against the hard stone walls and floor. He rolled and rolled, but as he finally reached the bottom of the stone staircase, he struck his ankle against an outcropping and yelped in pain.

His staff rattled down the stairs after him. Using it, he pulled himself up and leaned against it for support. He walked slowly and painfully through a stone arch at the bottom of the steps.

Above ground, Frisha deflected another volley from Caleb.

"Enough of this!" she bellowed, and with a twist of her staff, a bolt of energy went forth aimed at both Caleb's left and right flanks. Each bolt struck at the exact same moment, detonating with another loud "*boom.*"

Caleb fell to the ground, the staff tumbling from his insensible fingers.

"I knew that would do it." Frisha looked down at her defeated enemy. "Apparently, thou art no longer as great a seer as in thy previous incarnation."

She strode purposefully to the top of the temple stairs, "I have seen everything leading up to…"

She glanced around the Terrace, and there was something amiss with the fallen wizards. Her mouth fell open in an unpleasant expression.

One of them was missing.

Eddie!

She looked around a second time. "It cannot be," she uttered in shock. She stepped to the unconscious Caleb, then on to Drusilicus, and Ahbay.

There was a small "*thunk,*" and she turned with her staff raised. An unripe nut lay at her feet.

Something whooshed through the air and struck her on the head.

She spun and looked down to see another nut. She glared up at the trees, where dark figures crawled in quick movements.

"I did not see this," she murmured to herself with a frown. Another nut landed at her feet, and then objects began to rain down on her from all around, as thousands of squirrels threw nuts, rocks, and small branches at her.

She fired beams of light at the attacking rodents, but they moved so fast, she missed. They continued the assault.

She gave a cry of frustration and ran to the opening as she was pelted unmercifully.

She ran down the stairs, as the hieroglyphs up and down the monument, as well as the very top, began to turn dark red.

The color of blood.

Across the Great Lawn, Cerise stopped to pull off the sopping wet slippers. The dew had formed, and the slippers were now heavy with moisture. She couldn't understand how she got here. Without her purse, she didn't have a cell phone to call the police and report the strange fireworks at Cleopatra's Needle.

She was almost out of the park when she noticed a kiosk for a nearby pay phone, probably one of the few left in Manhattan.

As a cop's wife she knew what to do. Dial 911 and announce "officer down" to the dispatcher—that would get an army of police here quickly.

She prepared to run again, but found she had stopped all forward progress.

"Damn!" Cerise said, as she tried in vain to make her legs work. "Now what?"

Her head snapped up, the bunny slippers fell from her hand, and with her expression blank once again, she spun about and headed in the direction of the blood-red, glowing obelisk.

FIFTY-NINE

Wilcox's car pulled over next to the vans parked on Fifth Avenue in front of the Metropolitan Museum of Art. He got out and strode resolutely around the building and onto the path that led into the park.

He pulled open his cell phone. "Sam."

"I'm here," came the answer.

"We're at the museum."

"Okay, come through the arch and head to your right. There's a lot of weird stuff going on. Someone is doing a light show at Cleopatra's Needle. There's a man lying on the ground at the bottom of the stairs. I think it's Vasquez."

"Is he dead?" Wilcox walked faster.

"I'm too far away to tell," Sam replied.

"No point getting injured for him," Wilcox dismissed. "We'll be there in a minute."

Wilcox closed the phone and turned to Conners. "You go on ahead, through that arch and to the right. I'll alert the teams."

"Yes, sir." Conners trotted off, his hand near his holstered pistol.

Wilcox inserted his earpiece and spoke into the radio, "Okay, men, we're moving in. Have your weapons ready, but don't fire unless I give the order."

Sam, smoking a cigarette and still dressed as a jogger strode through Greywacke Arch.

"Hey, Wilcox," Sam gestured. "He's over here."

Wilcox followed and peered at the dark park all round him. "I thought you said there was a big light show."

"There was," Sam said, looking up. "It just stopped and became one color, don't know why. Plus, the street lamps just went out."

On the ground at the bottom of the Obelisk Terrace stairs lay the large figure of Luis Vasquez. Wilcox knelt and gently slapped his cheeks. Luis stirred and moaned.

"You awake, Vasquez?" Wilcox declared.

Luis' eyes fluttered and opened. "Aw jeez, I must have died. Only in Hell would I open my eyes to see you."

"Enough with the wisecracks." Wilcox turned to Conners. "Get him up and cuff him."

"Cuff me?" Luis said, as Conners struggled and gasped to pull the big man upright. "What for?"

"For annoying me, Vasquez," Wilcox goaded.

Conners looked at the big man's wrists. "Sir, the cuffs won't fit."

"Use restraints."

"Man, I hate those plastic things," Luis whined. "They cut into my skin."

Conners dutifully took the flexible plastic strip and put it around Luis's massive wrists and secured them with a metal hook.

Luis grunted uncomfortably, shook his head to clear it, and tried to recall how he ended up on the ground. He'd seen Cerise and wondered what she was doing there.

"You want to tell me what is going on, Vasquez?" Wilcox ordered.

"I was out for a stroll," Luis quipped.

"All the way from New Jersey? You were last seen at your partner's house. How'd you get here so fast?"

Luis shrugged. "I've taken up power-walking. Guess I wore myself out. Thanks for gettin' here before someone thought I was a drunk and rolled me."

"No one would rip you off, Vasquez. You don't own anything of value," Wilcox jibed. "What do you say we have a look up there?"

Wilcox looked around as teams of men arrived dressed in black and in their night-vision goggles. He nodded and they slowly ascended the steps, Conners and another man each holding one of Luis's arms.

There was a huge peal of thunder, and all of the men turned to look as a lightning bolt struck the Great Lawn only a few hundred feet from them.

"Jesus Christ!" Wilcox yelled as a wave of heat washed over them, and the ground opened up where the lightning hit.

"What was that?" Conners yelped.

"Calm down, men," Wilcox commanded, as he sensed fear from his teams. "It was just lightning and it—" His words stopped as his mouth fell slack.

A loud voice echoed through the trees and slopes of the park. "*Come forth!*"

Black smoke issued from the hole in the Great Lawn, as a figure on a white horse rose out of the pit. The horse unfolded a wide pair of pale, feathered wings and took to the air. The rider, dressed completely in a white, monk-like robe and hood, held up a large bow. He pulled a flaming arrow from a quiver on his back and waved it over his head as he flew above the treetops.

"That can't be good," Luis observed, as they all stood agape.

*   *   *

Eddie crouched as low as his swollen ankle allowed and slid into the room. It was brightly lit by a dozen metal braziers containing small fires, which cast flickering shadows everywhere.

The room was as large as the inside of a cathedral. In the center was a round pool of water, what could have been called "a reflective pool" centuries earlier. The walls were made of huge, rectangular, polished stone blocks with elaborately carved symbols. Eddie observed the bas-relief sculptures of snakes, sinister birds, as well as human and demonic figures.

It's all of his different forms, Eddie thought, as he recognized the figure of the giant Native-American Malsum on one stone block and the Shinto Amatsu Mikaboshi on another.

On the farthest wall was a pair of large metal doors, most elaborately detailed. They gleamed, and Eddie guessed that they must be made of solid gold. Six wax seals ran along the center, and Eddie could see a tarnished spot near the top where a seal had been recently removed.

"The door with the seven seals," Eddie whispered. "And one is already gone."

The inside of the building extended upward in a square shape higher and higher. It was like being *inside* a pyramid, each story growing smaller as it rose, with plants hanging down from each level. The stones it was made from were twice as tall as Eddie.

"It's called a ziggurat," a voice echoed from the middle of the building. Abraxas stepped into view in full demonic form near the artificial pond. He came out from behind a metal statue, which was the mirror image of his current persona, with large horns on the head and the heavily muscled body. In the statue's arms lay the tiny figure of Rosita.

"No need to hide, Newling," the demon retorted, as he stared at his burnished doppelgänger. "You are in my domain now."

Eddie stood up, used his staff for support and limped toward the demon. "What did you call this thing? A zig—what?"

"A ziggurat. It's how the Babylonians built the Hanging Gardens, and even further back it was the design for the Tower of Babel," Abraxas gestured at the walls around him. "I know, I was there. I insisted all my temples be made this way." He stared down at Rosita on his statue's outstretched arms. "Mortals used to sacrifice their firstborn to me."

"She isn't the firstborn," Eddie lurched closer.

"She will do." The demon looked a bit pensive. "I remember it so well. It was so sweet, giving me their small ones, in hope of favorable crops and good fortune. To open the seals for them…"

As he spoke these words, there was a rumble and the ground shook under their feet. Eddie moved to sit on one of a series of ornamentally carved marble benches in rows that faced the statue. On the gold door, the next wax seal near the top trembled, crumbled, then fell to the ground.

"What just happened?" Eddie felt fear burn in his throat like bile.

"Not much. A figure called 'War' on a flying red horse has just been released. He will set all of mankind to start to kill each other."

"Not much?" Eddie repeated.

"You have been killing each other for centuries." Abraxas gave a dismissive wave and looked at little Rosita. "I was considered a god by the Assyrians and by the Basilidians, and hundreds of cultures long since dead. I wore a beautiful visage or a terrible one. They adored me, sacrificed their small ones to me, and I took care of them."

He turned to Eddie with anger in his eyes. "Then the wizards got involved. I don't know what their problem was. I could be this form, or one much more pleasing!"

Abraxas spun around and his body changed. The flesh shifted until his body was that of a huge human, the size and perfect proportions of Michelangelo's David, though still red. A pair of feathered wings opened up on his back, also scarlet. He looked down at Eddie with a serene visage, and Eddie stared in awe.

"This is what I was," the huge figure spoke with a voice that was like music, "when I was worshipped, and my name was synonymous with magic."

"Oh leave off, Abraxas," said a voice from behind Eddie. He spun to see Frisha march into the room. "That be ancient history."

"All I ever wanted was to be loved." Abraxas' human-looking eyes brimmed with tears.

Frisha sighed. "I don't understand how one so whiny was chosen to bring the destruction of the world."

Eddie held up his staff, but Frisha pointed hers at Eddie in one quick move.

"Don't try it," she advised. "I knowst what you will do, and it shall not work."

"You killed Marlowe." Eddie's grip tightened on his staff.

"Yes." A gapped smile appeared on her face as she held up her staff to gaze upon it with admiration. "I saw his end in my visions. T'was then I realized how great my power wouldst become."

The demon, still in his angelic form, turned to Frisha in awe. "You have killed the bearer of the Staff of Spirit?"

"That I did!" Frisha boasted. "Nothing left."

"Not even his accursed staff?" Abraxas was overcome with glee.

"Not a splinter." Frisha returned her gaze to Eddie. "The fight is over, Newling. The Five is no more."

"We cannot fail!" Abraxas released a fiendish laugh, his body twisted, and he refashioned into the demon guise again.

Frisha drew closer to Eddie, the head of her staff pointed directly at him. "Put your staff down and kick it away from you."

Eddie did as he was told, and kicked it aside with his good leg.

"May I sit down?" Eddie asked meekly. "I injured my ankle."

"Sit, sit," Frisha allowed, and Eddie lowered himself onto one of the carved marble benches.

"So, what is this all about?"

"It's about the truth, Newling," Frisha smirked.

"And what truth would that be?" Eddie scowled.

"That there be no good or evil. There be only power. And whoe'er has the most, wins." Frisha turned to Abraxas. "Doth the child still sleep?"

Abraxas gave a quick glance at the unmoving Rosita. "Aye."

"I thought you walked the path," Eddie snapped. "You know, improve the world, help mankind, that sort of thing."

There was another minor earthquake. All heads turned to the gold door as the third seal quivered, cracked, and fell to the ground.

"Black horseman is out," Abraxas announced.

"Pestilence?" Frisha asked.

Abraxas nodded. "Now the fun begins."

Eddie tried to rise, but fell back onto the bench.

"Look at ye, you canst even heal thy own leg, Edward Berman," Frisha mocked. "Most who carry a staff know how to do such simple tasks their first day. Yet there you sit in judgment of me."

"I want to know," Eddie demanded.

"I was ne'er accepted as a peer. They thought me crazed and foolish, so I lived that part for them. Little did they know that I would find the true path—the path to power."

"What of Trefoil?"

"Trefoil," Frisha snorted with disdain. "Now there was a fool worthy of the name. A dreamer."

"What do you mean?"

"You heard his ravings! Rebuild the world under the rule of the wizards," Frisha said. "Abraxas, tell him of our shared opinion of that idea."

Abraxas grew serious. "The problems in this world were caused by wizards."

Eddie looked at the monster in shock. "What? They were the great thinkers, the leaders of religions—"

"Yes," Abraxas's voice boomed. "They were terrible! They took my worshippers away with their miracles and their 'Thou shall not worship graven images.'"

"Stay calm, Abraxas," Frisha soothed.

"I was worshipped in every land on this planet," Abraxas continued, "by different names and in different ways, but I was adored. Then the wizards came forth and called my worship an abomination!"

"Must've been bad for you," Eddie noted.

"Bad? They stopped the devotions, tore down my temples, and no longer gave their small ones as a sweet savor unto me!" Abraxas raged, and almost stomped his feet. "The Five came together and chased me from every place. I traveled the world. I only sought a place where I could be worshipped. But they would reveal my true identity, and drove me away again and again. They were against diversity!"

"Diversity?" Eddie repeated dubiously.

"Yes, all this 'the Divine' stuff. Fine for Him, but what about us little guys? I need worship, too!" Abraxas moved back to the great statue and looked down at the child in its arms.

Another tremor ran through the room, and the fourth wax seal shook violently and fell from the golden door.

Frisha sighed. "I do owe some success to Trefoil. He spoke of the amulet, the first step to releasing Abraxas and unleashing his abilities as destroyer of the world. When Trefoil told me of it, a future was revealed to me, in which *I* was the most powerful wizard on this plane. I set that plan in motion. I only needed to tell that ambitious boy Alex about the Amulet."

"What does the fourth seal release?" Eddie stared at the three remaining wax circles that adorned the golden door.

Abraxas considered for a moment. "Fourth horseman, Death. Nice fellow, really, lots of fun once you get to know him. Great at parties."

"And they're out there, attacking the human race?"

"Right here in Central Park," Frisha bubbled. "It was shortsighted of Greywacke to not know the end of the world would begin at his greatest creation."

Frisha walked toward Eddie, her staff at the ready. "You cannot imagine the change this is for me. I lived for centuries under the thumb of others—Greywacke, the coven, the Five. Once I was beautiful and honored. For the last few centuries I ha'e been humored and ignored. When I saw that glimpse of my possible future, I sought it. See how I made it true. I found out about the Smoking Mirror and arranged for it to be shipped to the museum. That was the wisest part of my plan."

"Riftstone died so you could release its power," Eddie said.

Frisha smiled. "So, ye do begin to understand."

"I understand you betrayed Trefoil," Eddie accused.

"Betrayed—a mere word. Trefoil was a means to an end. I shall rebuild the world under *my* rule."

"And I am to be worshipped!" Abraxas stood behind Frisha and glared at Eddie. "Tonight it shall all change."

"Aye!" Frisha exulted. "This night, which has been foretold since the dawn of time and in every culture, will usher in a new era." She turned to Abraxas. "The time grows near. Start the fire in the idol."

"You cannot kill that child." Eddie stood up.

Abraxas looked over in disbelief.

"She will not wake before the fire consumes her," Frisha pronounced, and nodded to Abraxas, who walked behind the metal statue. A flame burst from his extended first finger. He touched it to a pile of wood at the base of the statue.

"You can't," Eddie declared.

"Why not?" Frisha quizzed.

"It's…it's wrong," Eddie stammered.

Abraxas and Frisha looked at each other for a moment, then both laughed.

"If you need a sacrifice, take me," Eddie offered. "I'm a wizard, I'm what both of you really hate. Sacrifice me."

They both stopped laughing and looked at Eddie intently.

"If we burnt his staff along with him," Abraxas spoke in a low voice, "then two of the Five would be no more."

Frisha frowned at Eddie. "Nay, nay, it is not what I have seen."

Another shudder ran through the room, more violent than the last. With one quick jerk, the fifth seal cracked, broke loose, and plunged to the floor in pieces.

Eddie stared at the fallen seal on the floor.

What is happening up above right now? he wondered.

SIXTY

"Form a perimeter!" Wilcox shouted to his men, who pulled close and held on to their weapons.

"This is definitely not good." Luis gazed up at the skeletal shape astride the horse that blew fire from its nostrils. The black hooded figure carried a large scythe and swooped down at the group of FBI agents to wave it just over their heads.

"Stay low!" Wilcox yelled and fired his handgun at the horse and rider.

The weapon made three loud cracks, and three small round bullet holes appeared on the horse's flank. It gave a whinny, exhaled fire, and flew back up into the sky, the wounds disappearing as it went.

"Those things can't be hurt!" Collins yelled to Wilcox.

"Look at the moon," a man cried out, and Luis, Sam, Collins, and Wilcox all turned their heads to see the moon impossibly large and blood red.

"Men," Wilcox fought to control the panic he felt rise in his voice, "we must stay calm and close. I'm sure there is a way to—"

"What's that?" another man hollered and pointed at the huge open crater as it spat fire on what was once the Great Lawn. Smoke was everywhere, and it rolled like fog around them.

Something moved in the mist.

Small figures, hard to discern, climbed out of the pit and walked upright on the ground.

"What is that?" Collins gasped.

"Looks like kids." Sam frowned.

"Keep your guard up," Wilcox ordered in a low voice.

One of the figures made its way through the veil toward them.

"Not like any kid I ever had," Luis said suspiciously.

The approaching creature was the size of an eight-year-old. But it was red, bald, and carried little horns on its head and a pointed tail behind.

"What the—" Wilcox emoted.

The small devil's mouth twisted into an impossibly large smile. It ran to one of the men and yanked a small grenade off his vest in one quick grab.

"Stun grenade!" Wilcox howled and the group fell to the ground as one man, their hands over their heads.

The devil took a few steps back to examine his prize.

There was a sudden *"wham"* as the explosive charge went off in the creature's open hand. The air was filled with a plume of powder, and several of the FBI agents made expressions of pain from the close vicinity to the weapon.

The little hellish thing, however, was unhurt, only surprised. It gave its head a shake, then smiled and danced gleefully.

"Damn!" Luis found his fall to the ground difficult with his arms strapped behind his back. "The little sucker liked it."

It shouted something in a language the men had never heard, as hundreds of shadowy shapes, fresh from the pit, began to swarm toward the federal men.

"Sir," Collins watched the approaching creatures through the sulfurous haze, "we may have a problem."

"You're right. Men, split up!" Wilcox instructed. "You have complete freedom to defend yourselves."

The men began to move off quickly to the right and left and faded into the mist.

"What about me?" Luis objected.

Wilcox looked at Luis square in the eye. "Good luck."

Then, he ran off.

"At least take the restraints off my hands!" Luis shrieked after him, but found he was alone. "Hey!"

Alone in the sense that he no longer had any *human* companionship. Most of the devils faded in the murk after the agents, but a band of ten advanced upon Luis.

"I'm enjoying this less and less," Luis decided, as they drew nearer.

The lead beastie lunged forward and twisted his maw to expose pointed teeth, issuing a low and throaty growl.

"Is that all you got?" Luis said, unperturbed. "You ain't nothing." Luis opened his mouth wide and gave a bloodcurdling animal snarl. "ARRRRRRRR!"

The creatures backed up at this, not used to being on the receiving end of such an outburst. With a quick glance to one another, they decided the large man was too much trouble and ran off.

"Learned that from my mother-in-law," Luis warned the scurrying demons. "She's scarier than you little shits."

"By Zoroaster!" a voice said behind him.

Luis turned suddenly, and there stood Bankrock. The little man wore his wizard robes and carried a staff as he stared dumbfounded at the open pit.

"I believe this is a serious breach in the Magickal Containment Act," Bankrock announced.

Luis noticed that behind Bankrock were three other wizards. "Where the hell you guys been?"

"I sought reinforcements," Bankrock explained. "It was difficult; most had left town."

"Glad you could get here for the fireworks." Luis turned his large body to show his bound hands. "Get these off, will ya?"

His gaze still fixed on the pit, Bankrock made the slightest movement with his staff, and the restraints dropped off Luis's hands.

Luis rubbed his wrists and looked up to see the skeleton on horseback swoop down out of the sky again.

"Hey," one of the wizards with a thick Brooklyn accent said, "ain't that Death? I ain't seen him since the Influenza Epidemic of 1918."

"Maybe you should say hello," Luis suggested snidely, as his temper flared. "Now will you guys do something?"

"What would you suggest we do?" Bankrock's eyes remained on the pit.

"I thought this was the stuff you guys handle!"

Suddenly, the ground shook again and the group glanced up to the sky and peered at the fog to see what happened.

All was silent.

"Guess it's okay this time." Luis faced the stone steps that led to Obelisk Terrace. "Now, let's get up there and help."

Bankrock pulled his gaze from the pit and turned to the others. "Let us see how we can be of assistance, my friends."

The group of wizards quickly climbed the steps and immediately disappeared into the mist.

Luis shook his head. "All-powerful wizards, and they need a sergeant to tell them what to do."

The dirt near his feet shifted a little.

He leaned forward to see what caused it.

A hand shot up out of the ground.

With a yell, Luis jumped back and up several steps.

The skin on the hand was greenish, and white bone could be seen protruding in places. The fingernails were filthy and decrepit. There was another shake and the arm pulled free from the soil. It was covered in old and decayed clothing that may have once been a suit.

Another arm came out, and then a head. The hair was gone, as were the eyes, but there was still skin on the animated corpse's face as it pulled itself free of the soil. The body struggled up and out of the ground that had held it for eons.

"Jeez," Luis grimaced. "People are buried here?" He pulled himself up another step. "Where did those wizards go? Yo, Bankrock!"

The walking dead turned to face Luis with its eyeless sockets. It opened its mouth in a soundless wail as it took a step up the stairs toward Luis.

"Man, you are the last thing I need today," Luis said, as he fought the desire to panic, run, or vomit. He leaned back as the cadaver stumbled up the stairs toward him, then lifted one large foot to the boney chest and gave a strong push.

The already unstable carcass cascaded down the steps just as one of the little devils passed by. It collapsed on the short fiend, and the dead man's head popped off and rolled away.

The devil cursed in its strange language, pushed the remains off himself, shook his little fist at Luis, and ran away.

The cadaver, unencumbered by the loss of its head, rose to its rotten feet and staggered off in a different direction.

Luis exhaled a long sigh and looked over his shoulder at the huge, glowing red obelisk. He muttered under his breath, "Eddie, I hope you are doing something about this."

He started up the stairs.

SIXTY-ONE

Five seals were off that door, and if it opened, Eddie knew it would be very bad for the entire human race.

He regretted his police training never prepared him for such a situation.

There had to be something to give him an edge over his adversaries, as they both watched the metal statue with a look of pleasure in their eyes. If Eddie didn't do something soon, Rosita would be roasted alive.

His hand brushed the Hat of Remembrance in his belt.

Eddie thought of Frisha's fight with Caleb, how easily she avoided his attacks. The only time she looked surprised was when Eddie tackled Ahbay and almost bowled her over.

He felt the glimmer of an idea.

He pulled out the hat and put it on his head.

"What are you doing?" Frisha demanded, her attention returned to Eddie. "What is that?"

It instantly was clear to Eddie. He could remember every detail about the last week, and how time and again Frisha predicted things about him that had been wrong. He surprised her in little ways again and again. She was the one behind the attacks against him, and all of them failed!

"What's the matter, Frisha? Don't you *know* what this hat is? Can't you see it? You didn't see me here in the temple, did you?" Eddie taunted.

Frisha raised her staff. "I have the power to strike you down where you stand."

Eddie smiled and took a step forward, able to recollect each nuance. "Like the elevator. You suggested I use it, and then you were surprised I wasn't killed. And all those warnings, not one of them came true. You can't preordain what *I'm* going to do."

"Yes, I can. I am a seer, and I can prove it!" she raised her free hand and bellowed, "Come to me, my dear."

From the stone archway, Cerise entered, her eyes transfixed dreamily on Frisha.

"Damn," Eddie cursed as his wife drew nearer.

"I knew she is thy wife, which proves my divination."

Eddie shook his head and gave a derisive laugh.

He could easily recall every detail of every moment of the last week. He could recall a cloaked and hooded figure in a tree at his house.

"That wasn't fortune-telling. You were at my house," Eddie boasted. "I got you figured out. You can't see what's happenin' with *me*. That's why Riftstone's staff summoned me. Ever since, you've tried to remove me, kill me, or scare me, but I keep surprising you."

"You speak lies!" Frisha bellowed.

Eddie feinted to his right, and at the last moment dove to his left. A blast came from Frisha's staff, right to the place where Eddie feinted, which missed him completely.

He pushed over the bench, held out his hand, and his staff flew into it.

"That's why you *told* me to use the elevator." Eddie ducked behind the marble. "You didn't know if I would choose it or not. You had to *guide* me."

A flash of light struck the carved stone he hid behind, and there was a cracking sound.

Eddie leapt up and raised his staff.

Frisha pulled out the black mirror in her left hand as she held up her staff with the right.

"Surrender thy staff, or I shall kill thy woman." Frisha pointed her staff toward the mesmerized Cerise, who stood immobile, a puppet under Frisha's control. "You are no threat to me; the mirror has taken most of thy power. Thou hast not the strength to defeat me."

"I may not have the power to stop you—" Eddie shifted his staff and fired a faint red beam at Cerise.

"Ow!" Cerise said, her spell broken. She rubbed her head and looked at her bizarre surroundings. "Now where am I?"

Eddie yelled. "10-33!"

Eddie had yelled the NYPD code for an explosive device. Years earlier, when they were dating, Cerise had drilled Eddie on all the codes as he prepared for his exams. She had memorized them better than her not-yet husband. He prayed she still remembered.

Cerise ducked, and at the same time smashed her elbow into the hefty Frisha, who gave an "Oof" sound. Cerise dove for cover without hesitation, and was quickly under one of the stone benches.

"We must commence the sacrifice!" Abraxas bellowed to Frisha. "There are still two seals!"

"I must say the words. Make yourself useful and kill them!" Frisha pointed at Cerise, who rapidly crawled away. "Her first!"

Eddie jumped up and dodged, as Frisha shot another bolt of lightning at him. Abraxas headed straight in the direction of Cerise as she progressed on all fours toward Eddie.

The demon's anatomy began to undulate and change, his chest bent over as his hands became hooves, and the red fur on his legs spread to cover his entire body.

A giant ram stood only fifteen feet away with the same massive horns as the demon.

Cerise reached Eddie, and he crouched beside her as best he could with his damaged leg.

"What is this place?" Cerise grabbed Eddie's arm. "How did I get here *this* time?"

"Later, honey," Eddie apologized, "stay down."

The giant red ram charged. It bore down on them, huge horns aimed. Eddie was weak and afraid that if he shot a beam of light, it wouldn't have enough kick to stop the charging ram.

Think outside the box, ran through his mind. *How else can my staff be used?*

"Can you do something!" Cerise shouted.

The hat Eddie wore gave him access to every memory he'd ever possessed. A physics lesson from high school flashed through his mind.

"Yes, I can!" Eddie rose and quickly turned the stick in his hand. As the ram drew near, he swung it by the bottom in a huge arc with all his might and aimed at the gnarled spot between the monster's horns.

Wham!

There was a cracking noise as the fierce-looking horns broke and the giant creature's head whipped down to strike the ground. The dazed creature slid onto the bench the Bermans had been behind.

"That not be how a wizard fights!" Frisha shouted.

"Damn straight," Eddie said, as an idea began to form. It was amazing how the hat made his mind so clear.

Frisha let go of her staff, leaned it against her body. She held the mirror aloft with both hands.

No matter what I hit her with, that mirror will absorb it, Eddie thought.

She stood with the mirror outstretched and began to mutter words in the strange language Marlowe used.

Eddie stepped back, as the ram rose unsteadily, stumbled, and fell into the reflecting pool with a huge splash. The water churned and there was a gurgling sound.

"Eddie!" Cerise pointed as a large, winged cat leapt from the fountain and soared up the large center opening of the temple. "What is it?"

"I dunno! A red lion. But it's got...wings!"

Eddie could see a fiery-red mane and huge fangs as the beast flew with what looked like eagle wings, even though each feather was scarlet.

The airborne jungle cat reached the pinnacle of the pyramid-shaped structure, turned magnificently, then dove for Eddie and Cerise.

Eddie didn't have the raw power to take the creature out. Instead, he focused on a small place he could attack.

"Isa Ya!" Eddie yelled. He felt the energy come up from his toes and shoot out at the dive-bombing creature. The light struck it with a flash, and its wings popped off like cheap toys.

The lion's face registered surprise, and it dropped through the air to splash heavily once again into the pool, which sprayed a wave of water over the mirror-holding Frisha.

"No, no!" the old woman bellowed as water crashed down on her and struck the metal statue, raining down on little Rosita, who stirred, but stayed asleep.

The fire in the back of the statue was cooled by the spray of water but continued to burn.

Another tremor under his feet, and Eddie looked up to see the sixth seal crumble and fall off the golden door.

"We are running out of time," Eddie croaked.

"Time for what?" Cerise stood back as the waters appeared to boil from the movements of the demon. "What is it doing now?"

Eddie looked to the churning water, where Abraxas was shifting shape once again to renew the attack.

Eddie stared at Frisha and noted the distance around the pool between them. He could run at her, but she'd strike him down before he got halfway there.

She began to chant those odd words again, the mirror aloft and her eyes closed.

How to stop her?

Eddie gripped the stick in his hand, and the hat brought him to a specific recollection.

The idea burst clear and clean into his brain. *The staff was very well-balanced.*

"Get down," Eddie said, and Cerise dropped behind one of the stone benches.

He focused on Frisha and carefully took aim. As his mind and his muscles recalled forgotten techniques, he cocked back his arm. His eye was on the mirror, as he ignored the pain in his leg, took two large steps, and propelled the wooden staff through the air.

It had been more than twenty-three years since high school track when he last threw a javelin, but the skill was not completely forgotten. The stick rose gracefully, crested ten feet from him, and in a perfect arc, screamed back toward the floor.

The look of astonishment on Frisha's face could not be faked as the staff soared straight toward her. She stood frozen, unable to believe what she saw.

The staff drove right into the mirror and struck it with all of Eddie's strength. There was a loud *"crack,"* louder than shattering glass, as the ancient polished stone fragmented to pieces in Frisha's hands. The stored energy of the mirror was released as a thunderclap.

Colored light streamed out of the shattered pieces: yellow, green, blue, red, and white. Eddie's staff also struck Frisha in the stomach and knocked her to the floor.

The power sparkled, flared, and red light flew about to surround Eddie. He felt as if he'd just had a big meal, a shower, and a massage.

All at once, Eddie knew that since the night they restored Trefoil, he had not been in full possession of the power of his staff. Now, he felt the complete mastery of his abilities, as well as the full extent of his prowess.

Abraxas leapt out of the churning water of the pool. He was now a great red bear, and his muzzle opened in amazement as he looked at Frisha, the broken mirror, and said, "Holy shit!"

"Gee, and that was going to be my pet name for you," Eddie gestured and his staff vaulted across the room back into his hand.

"Maybe we can come to an understanding?" Abraxas suggested with a tentative bear grin.

"Get thee behind me!" Eddie ordered. Effortlessly, a blast of fiery light shot forth from his staff like a charging bull, and the bear was thrown off his feet to the far end of the pool.

Eddie ran as well as his injured leg would allow to the metal statue and held the staff over the increasing fire.

The flames immediately died.

Eddie touched the metal. It was warm, but not yet hot enough to burn. He moved to the front and took Rosita away from the statue, lowering her to the ground in his arms.

She was covered in sweat but didn't appear injured.

Cerise came up behind him. "Is she all right?"

"Yeah." Eddie transferred the small girl into his wife's arms.

There was a splash, and Eddie jumped up. On the bank of the pool was a creature from a bad dream. It had four heads that snarled and growled, and four bird wings on its back that waved and spread to make the creature look bigger. It roared menacingly and crouched to leap.

"Oh, will you just knock it off!" Eddie sent a burst of power from his staff and the creature was shot back into the pool as if from a cannon.

Eddie turned back to his wife and his partner's little girl.

"Come on, Rosita," Cerise said, as Eddie waved his staff over her face. "Wake up. It's Auntie Cerise and Uncle Eddie."

The eyelids fluttered, and then opened. "Auntie Cewise?"

"Yeah, honey," Cerise cooed sweetly. "You all right?"

"It's hot," Rosita whined.

"It's okay, honey, it'll cool down soon," Eddie reassured.

"Wha' happened to my ice cream?"

"We'll get you a new ice cream," Cerise soothed. "Won't we, Eddie?"

"Gallons. Can you sit up?"

She sat up and looked around, and her breath caught in her throat. "It's tha' bad lady!" she pointed with her small finger.

Eddie looked up to see Frisha as she rose, her hair disheveled. She held her abdomen with one hand and leaned on her staff with the other.

Eddie rolled in front of Rosita and fired a bolt of red light.

"Ahh!" Frisha yelled, barely able to raise a defensive charm. The beam struck her and tossed her backward. She stumbled and fell into the pool with a resounding splash.

"Wow!" Rosita said, her mouth open in astonishment.

"Wow!" Cerise repeated.

Eddie turned to his wife and indicated the only exit from the temple. "You see those stairs?"

"Yes," Cerise responded.

"Run up them, don't let anything stop you," Eddie ordered.

She nodded very seriously, and with the girl tightly in her arms, she kept low and dashed off in a zigzag pattern past the many benches in the temple.

Eddie stood up, his staff aloft, and walked slowly toward the pool as Frisha pulled herself out, burbled and spat.

"It cannot be!" Frisha gurgled, as she dripped water everywhere. She looked like a drowned rat. She pulled herself upright with the help of her staff. "I should've seen this!"

"You're the one who helped Abraxas kill Riftstone." Eddie circled her cautiously, as he removed the Hat of Remembrance and returned it to his belt. "Trefoil faked his attack, you two mixed a potion, injected it in his leg to mimic a snakebite, then you show up to tell that story. You did it so Marlowe wouldn't take on Abraxas, and Trefoil could sneak the Smoking Mirror into the townhouse."

"It would have stolen the power of the Five then and there and put ye all into the Dark Sleep," Frisha stood unsteadily, "if not for ye."

"And Marlowe found nothing on Trefoil, because when he came downstairs, you hugged him. You simply took the mirror from him!"

"You were all fooled." Frisha raised her staff. "Who would suspect poor ol' Frisha?"

Eddie frowned, noticed that Frisha looked to his right. He glanced over his shoulder to the pool of water.

As quiet as a whisper, a huge creature was rising from the water. It possessed ten horns on its head, which was shaped like the monster from *Alien*. It opened its maw to expose huge metal fangs that glinted darkly in the light from the brasiers.

Eddie dove to his left, toward the still-warm statue, and spun around, which caused agony in his ankle. He raised his staff and a blast of red light extended from it, engulfing the creature in a sea of flame.

The fire didn't even slow it down, and it continued to rise out of the pool. It stood on the stone floor, at least fifteen feet tall.

Three of the horns on its head fell off, a pair of little eyes sprang forth on stalks in place of two of the horns. Then the monster shook himself, and another stalk came out and lips formed. Eddie could see teeth inside the lips and a voice rang out.

"*Give me my sacrifice! It is my time!*" it bellowed.

"Oh, just give it up!" Eddie said, and with all his concentration, desire and intention, he let loose with the strongest flare of red light his staff had yet produced. It hit the creature and not only slammed it against the far wall, but several feet *into* the solid stone.

Eddie moved fast, spun, and threw up a defensive charm as a bolt of light sent by Frisha struck him.

Eddie felt like a Mack truck ran into him, despite his defense. He crashed backward to the floor and his head spun. Even as he did, he turned his staff and fired a beam at Frisha.

It struck the old woman before she could dodge it or put up a defense. She flipped backward head over heels.

Eddie pulled himself up and looked back and forth at his adversaries. They both lay still. Eddie stumbled to Frisha, grabbed the woman's staff from her hand, and threw it to the base of the metal statue. He grabbed the collar of her robe and pulled her upright.

"Oww! Police brutality," she moaned.

"You killed Yamasuto, you and Abraxas, right?"

"Yes, yes, hurt me not. I'm an old woman." Frisha held her hands up defensively.

"But Cuccolo was your best work. You and Trefoil planned it together, got me in trouble, and almost killed. When that failed, the three of you attacked my house and stole my kid. Trefoil put the 'Hand of Glory' out front, while you took care of Marlowe." Eddie pulled Frisha's arms behind her back. "You didn't kill us at my house or in the catacombs because you needed Marlowe and the Five to open the temple. But you finished off Trefoil because you knew that with the mirror, whoever took his place could be used."

"Yes, yes. Ow! Leave me be!" Frisha shrieked.

"Where are the talismans?" Eddie demanded

"I have them!" Frisha confessed.

"My sacrifice is gone!" a voice wailed, and Eddie whirled around to face Abraxas in his demonic form once again.

Eddie held his staff up. "You are under arrest!"

Abraxas looked at him, puzzled. "You must be joking."

Drusilicus' voice echoed in the chamber. "Mayhaps he is, but we are not."

All heads turned to the stairs, where stood Drusilicus, Ahbay, and Eugenia. They looked haggard, and their hair and robes were in disarray, but each bore a determined and angry face, their staffs at the ready.

At the back of the group stood a singed and rather tattered Marlowe.

"It canna' be," Frisha spoke in awe. "I destroyed you!"

"Only stunned." Marlowe held up a small medallion from around his neck. "I was wearing Caleb's seal of Solomon. The energy of your blast activated it, and I was rendered invisible as well as unconscious."

"No!" Abraxas ran to the golden door which was only held closed by the one seal. He clawed at the wax, but it was solid as stone. "You cannot! Not again. It is my time!"

Eugenia gestured with her staff and a beam of yellow light encircled the demon, who was pulled away from the door screaming in frustration.

Ahbay followed suit with his green illumination. Drusilicus and Marlowe added theirs, as Abraxas struggled. He was lifted off the ground and into the air, encircled in beams of light.

Eddie smiled at his friends despite his own pain, then added the final shaft of red light. The huge demon yelled curses and whined. Then, he began to shrink, smaller and smaller until he vanished completely, and a small piece of metal fell to the ground.

Eddie held Frisha tight and leaned a bit to see what was left. All that remained of the giant demon was a small, gold amulet on the floor. He could almost make out a figure on it: part man, part snake, and part rooster.

There was a rumbling sound as the stone floor shook under their feet.

"The six seals are opened and evil rains down upon the world," Marlowe said. "We must close this portal!"

SIXTY-TWO

Eddie hobbled for the stairway and pulled Frisha along as the temple quaked around them. Benches fell over, braziers went out, and the huge metal statue careened on its side like a drunken man, which pinned Frisha's staff to the floor.

Frisha turned and yelled, "My staff, ye cannot leave it here!" She put her hand out to call the implement to her, but it only wobbled a bit under the heavy idol.

"It is corrupted! Leave it so none shall bear it," Marlowe said, his countenance aflame with anger. He placed a firm grip on Frisha's arms. "Come up the stairs, 'fore I change my mind and leave ye here as well."

"Thought I lost you," Eddie said to Marlowe.

"Not yet, good friend."

"Eddie, your leg," Drusilicus said. "I should heal it."

"Just a sprain," Eddie grimaced. "No time, just help me up the stairs."

He put his arm over Drusilicus' shoulder and they climbed the steps as fast as they were able.

Ahbay was the first to emerge from the adit and step onto Obelisk Terrace. He helped Eugenia up, and both of them aided Marlowe with Frisha, who seemed to have lost her will to fight.

They walked out into a nightmare.

Eddie looked up to see that the moon was now completely full, twice the size it should be, and dark red. The stars were blotted out and the lights in the park were dark.

A great deal of yellow-orange light flickered all about them, and they could see clouds of smoke that hung low over the park.

He peered over at the Great Lawn where the huge hole had opened, and flames shot forth, high into the sky. Ash and debris fell flaming onto the trees and walkways. The air stank of brimstone as hot wind whipped their faces.

"It's about time you got up here," Bankrock said. "We are having a—if you'll pardon the expression—hell of a time trying to keep things under control."

"Later, Bankrock," Marlowe dismissed. "Quickly, we must finish what we started if we wish to renew the six seals."

A gunshot echoed in the darkness.

"Rosita!" Eddie yelled. "Where's Rosita?"

"I'm here, Unca Eddie," the little girl piped up as Cerise stepped out from behind the obelisk's base with the child in her arms.

Eddie hobbled to them and hugged them both.

"Thank God you took care of my big, black man." Cerise kissed him.

"Eddie!" a voice said nearby.

Eddie turned to see Luis leaning against the balustrade of the stairs.

"Luis!" he responded as his large partner galumphed toward them.

"My Rosita!"

"Daddy!" Rosita whooped. Cerise carefully relaxed her grip as the child dove into her father's arms. He picked her up as she squealed and laughed.

"My precious one!" He hugged her as tears stabbed his eyes. "You okay, baby?"

"I'm fine, Daddy," Rosita burbled. "But things were real spooky!"

"Yes, Rosita." Luis kissed her head. "I bet it was."

"What happened up here?" Eddie slipped his arm around his wife.

Luis's hair was being whipped to and fro by the wind, which was heavy with stench. "Four frickin' flying horses came out of the ground and then a bunch of devils. I mean, y'know, like little red guys with horns and tails? They were followed by a big group of rotting corpses."

"I heard a shot."

"That's Wilcox," Luis recalled. "He arrived here with a whole SWAT team, with like the entire Urban Crime Task Force. They're fightin' it out with the devils. And look, we have a bunch of spectators."

He pointed to the top of Belvedere castle. Even with the low fog, Eddie could see the high tower. There, a group of people dressed mostly in black stood and watched. They all had very pale skin and eyes that glimmered in the darkness.

"Who are they?" Eddie asked.

"Vampires," Bankrock hissed. "Believe me, if I had not sent the others into the park, they might have joined the fray against us already."

"Marlowe!" Eddie pointed at the castle.

"Pay them no heed!" Marlowe said, in position at the north end of the obelisk. "We must complete the binding spell, or all is for naught."

A golf ball-sized chunk of ice struck the pavement near them.

"Right," Eddie turned back to Cerise. "Can you, Luis, and Rosita get under a tree?"

"Unca Eddie stopped the bad lady!" Rosita announced.

"Did he?" Luis smiled.

"He sure did," Cerise said, as she led father and daughter to the relative safety of a nearby magnolia tree.

Hail the size of baseballs was now beginning to fall all around, striking the stone tiles with resounding thuds.

Eddie grabbed Frisha, who looked shell-shocked, or possibly *spell*-shocked, and pushed her to Bankrock. "Keep her out of the way."

"I'm a wizard, not a watchman," Bankrock complained, but grabbed Frisha by the arm.

"Eddie," Ahbay spoke loudly, "we must close this portal—"

Eddie ran to his place in the pentagram. Once again, the beams of light were quickly linked from staff to staff. It was much easier than the earlier attempt, as all of them now possessed their full strength. The energy from their staves made the obelisk glow many times brighter than earlier.

Marlowe began to chant as thunder clapped.

There was the whinny of horses, and Eddie saw four different-hued, winged stallions fly overhead. They each took a graceful turn, banked, and flew down into the flaming pit.

"Keep going!" Eddie encouraged.

There was a moaning as the army of half-rotted corpses, some only skeletons, walked, crawled, or stumbled back to different locations and began to burrow into the earth to return to their ancient graves.

Marlowe chanted louder and stronger.

Small red figures ran toward the open hole, as the earth shook and moved. The pit began to shrink in size, and the flames within it began to dissipate.

Marlowe finished his incantation triumphantly.

There was a terrible rending noise, as if the ground beneath them was about to fall asunder, then a bright light came from the opening in the Terrace. With one last shudder, the tiles rebuilt themselves, and the sloping stairs were gone.

Out on the Great Lawn the dirt sealed up and the grass was restored without even a misplaced blade.

Each of the Five released their connection to the others, and the pentagram of light was gone.

The wind faded, the stink dissipated, and the moon and stars shone their correct size and color overhead. There was a flicker, and all of the Central Park streetlights popped on.

Frisha gave a cry. "My staff. I have lost my staff!"

"Served you right if they'd left *you* down there," Bankrock growled.

"By the way, Frisha has the talismans," Eddie told Marlowe.

"What? How could you?" Drusilicus lifted his staff in a defensive pose.

"Fear not," Marlowe reassured. "Without Abraxas, those particular talismans have little power. Take the trinkets from her."

"I presume that is a job for me," Eugenia insisted. Bankrock held Frisha's arms as Eugenia began to go through her robes.

"Leave me be!" Frisha screeched, as Eugenia pulled things from the folds of cloth and hidden pockets.

As Eugenia went through the old woman's robes, Luis, Cerise, and Rosita drew near.

"Fireworks over?" Luis asked.

"I hope so," Eddie groaned.

"You're my hero." Cerise kissed her husband's cheek. "We'll have some fireworks at home."

Eugenia pulled out items and placed them on the ground. "Herbs, a crystal ball…ah, what have we here?"

She held up the jade statue. Even in the moonlight, Eddie could see it glimmer.

"That's mine!" Frisha whined.

"That's nice." Eugenia returned her hands to Frisha's pockets. In only a minute, she located the small box decorated with turquoise.

"I'm afraid I smashed the mirror," Eddie murmured.

"All for the best," Marlowe consented. "As was leaving the Amulet of Abracadabra in the shrine. It has shifted to that other dimension, and it will be very difficult to bring it to this plane again."

"Luis," Cerise asked the tall man, "do you have any idea what they are talking about?"

"I know I don'," Rosita said, which made her father laugh.

Eddie glanced down at the fallen metal statue that lay on the steps of the Obelisk. "Marlowe what about—"

"Oh that." Marlowe raised his glowing staff and waved it in a circle twice. "There!"

A loud whinny came from behind them, and King Jagiello, still on his horse, rode down the steps, shouting something.

"Daddy, it's a metal horsey!" Rosita gushed with delight.

"What'd the statue say?" Eddie asked Marlowe.

"The Polish equivalent of 'Talley Ho.'" Marlowe gave a shrug, as the metallic rider galloped off to return to the stone base that bore his name.

Luis pulled Eddie's arm and pointed. "Look who else is gone."

Eddie looked up at Belvedere castle, and there was not a single figure on its parapets.

"Drusilicus," Eddie indicated the castle, "I saw vampires up there earlier."

"Yes." Drusilicus had a grim smile. "They wanted to see who would win. Probably rooted for the demon." He watched Eddie hobble closer. "Oh! Let me help you with that."

Drusilicus waved his staff, and a pink healing light surrounded Eddie's leg. Eddie stood up straight, his leg no longer in pain.

He looked back at Drusilicus, who gave him a nod.

"Thanks," Eddie smiled.

There was a chittering noise, and the four men turned to see a large gray squirrel sitting on top of one of the stone balustrades that ringed the now-dark obelisk.

"Ah!" Marlowe cheered. "The hero of the day."

Marlowe drew closer as the rodent swished his tail. He made a strange sucking noise that was similar to the creature's own sounds.

"The squirrel's a hero?" Luis frowned.

"Indeed he is." Marlowe looked over his shoulder at Eddie and Luis. "This is Quiptail. He is a very important figure here in the park."

The squirrel rose up on its hind legs and bowed to the group.

"Is that the squirrel I talked to? I thought he took off on us," Eddie began.

"Took off?" Marlowe stood up straight, affronted. "Nay! When Frisha had defeated us, he launched an onslaught and drove her down into the temple."

"Wow!" Luis observed the squirrel with a new admiration.

"All the squirrels do in our neighborhood is raid the bird feeder," Cerise conceded.

Marlowe made a few more noises. The squirrel replied, then, in a flash leapt onto a branch and was gone.

"Ain't that something." Luis watched the retreating rodent in wonder.

"I hope you think so, sergeant," Marlowe remarked. "I promised him that you and Eddie would bring him a very large bag of nuts."

"Look at that, Luis," Eddie quipped. "We finally get an informant that works for peanuts."

"You *must* learn Squirrel, Eddie," Marlowe suggested.

"Maybe later." Eddie felt his wife shiver next to him. He turned to look and realized she had no footwear. "Baby, what happened to your shoes?"

"All I had was those stupid bunny slippers," she said. "I'm cold. Can we go home now?"

Ahbay stepped forward. "Dear lady, allow me to escort you to Marlowe's townhouse. There we can arrange a pair of shoes while your husband finishes his work."

Luis looked at his daughter. "Can you go with Auntie Cerise, sweetheart?"

"I wanna stay wi' you, Daddy," Rosita entreated.

"Honey, Auntie Cerise is gonna call your mommy and let her know you're okay. You wanna talk to Mommy, don't you?"

"I guess," she said sullenly, as Luis handed the girl to Cerise.

Cerise took the child in her arms and smiled at her. Then she looked at Eddie. "I've missed holding a child."

Eddie smiled. "Yeah, our boys are too big."

A dreamy grin appeared on her face. "I always wanted a girl." She walked away with Ahbay.

"Man, watch out," Luis warned Eddie.

"What?"

"That's the look Maria gets when she wants to have another baby."

"Oh, stop," Eddie said to his partner and turned to Bankrock. "I have to tell you, the one who really helped distract the old girl was Caleb. Where is he anyway?"

"I have not seen him, but I do sense him nearby," Bankrock confessed. "You weren't here, Eddie, but other wizards— Claremont, Inscope, Driprock, and I—helped rouse the others and made Marlowe visible again."

"How did you know he was there? I thought he was gone."

"Simple," Bankrock smiled smugly. "I can locate any member of the coven, and even though I couldn't see him, I was aware of his presence. It was only a matter of undoing the effects of the charm he wore."

"I have found our missing member." Drusilicus pointed to a grove of trees.

Caleb was crouched behind a large oak. His entire body was racked by convulsive shudders. His staff lay on the ground and he stared up at the night sky.

Eddie approached slowly. "Caleb?"

The young man looked at him with wild eyes.

"Are you well, young sir?" Bankrock asked gently.

"Am I well, am I well?" Caleb rose slowly. "Did you see? Did you? Fire and hail, devils everywhere, corpses on the move, and some dead guy possessed me!"

"It was the medallion you made; it enabled Greywacke to use you as a weapon against Frisha," Marlowe offered. "You have done well."

"Indeed." Drusilicus threw his shoulders back. "I dare say that it was the most impressive thing any Newling has ever done."

"Hey, what about me?" Eddie said.

"You've had your staff a week," Drusilicus snorted. "He has had his for a few hours."

"Oh yeah?" Caleb reached behind his neck to yank off the medallion that carried Greywacke's symbol. "Well, if this is what it is like to have a staff, you can keep it."

"What?" Bankrock was shocked.

"You heard me," Caleb complained. "I thought it would be cool. A great big power trip. Being like…a god! But it's not. It… it…" he struggled for the right words. "It sucks!"

"But, my boy." Drusilicus reached out to Caleb, who avoided his touch. "This is what we worked for, what you wanted for so long—"

"I don't want it! You guys are crazy, do you hear? I am *so* out of here."

And with that he threw the medallion to the ground and stormed off, the staff left behind as he went.

With a gesture, Marlowe waved his own stick, and the wooden rod that briefly had been Caleb's transformed into a pocket watch.

"I suppose I shall hold on to this, Drusilicus," Marlowe pocketed the timepiece, "until you choose another."

"I doubt I shall." Drusilicus shook his head in disgust. "They are not worth the effort."

Eddie turned to Luis. "You got handcuffs?"

"No, who for?"

"Frisha. She's the warlock," Eddie advised.

"Oh man," Luis complained. "I missed everything."

"Were you okay up here?"

Luis shrugged. "A posse of devils, a rotted corpse who wanted to eat me or something—no big deal."

Eddie frowned, not sure if his partner kidded him or not.

"Eddie." Marlowe came alongside the men. "I have conferred with Bankrock. As we speak, Inscope, Claremont, and Driprock are altering the memories of those who were in the park."

"Yeah, that would be—" An idea grew bright in Eddie's mind. "Wait. Can you choose who forgets and who doesn't?"

"Of course," Marlowe said.

"Then I have a plan," Eddie said wryly. "But first, I have to call my captain."

SIXTY-THREE

Within fifteen minutes, the park was quiet, and on Park East Drive, the flashing lights of police cars arrived in response to Eddie's phone call.

"Berman," Captain Jacobs said as he approached the obelisk from a northern path flanked by a half-dozen uniformed officers.

"Captain, I'm glad to see you," Eddie said.

Jacobs came to a stop in front of Eddie and gave a glance to Luis and the other people who held an oddly dressed woman in purple robes.

"Lieutenant, I want to know what you think you're doing, getting me out here at this time of night." He looked at his watch. "It's past midnight!"

"Sir," Eddie stood at attention, "I called you immediately upon apprehension of our prime suspect in the murder of Mr. Yamasuto, Mr. Cuccolo, as well as the homeless man."

A group of black-clad agents suddenly trooped up the stairs. They carried machine guns hung from straps on their shoulders, but they were dirty, some covered in ash, and all looked dazed.

The uniformed police officers' hands went for their weapons.

"Stand down!" Jacobs yelled to them. "Who are you men?"

"FBI." Wilcox stepped into the light. "We're part of the Urban Crime Task Force."

"Yes, Agent Wilcox, isn't it?" Jacobs said. "What's going on here?"

"I want an explanation, too, captain!" Wilcox demanded.

"An explanation of what?" Eddie said.

"What? That pit…those bats…how…" Wilcox pointed at Eddie. "How that man got here…and those creatures—"

"It was all to catch the killer."

"What?" Wilcox howled. "You are suspended, Berman. You can't even arrest someone for littering!"

"You're right," Eddie agreed. "That's why I called for backup."

"Backup?" Wilcox said, flabbergasted.

"You've heard of that, right?" Luis glanced at his partner. "We always get backup, right, Eddie?"

"That's how I was trained." Eddie shrugged.

Wilcox turned to Jacobs. "Captain, I want to register a complaint. Lieutenant Berman has no right to involve himself—"

"I would not have, sir," Eddie interrupted, "except for the fact that the suspect kidnapped my partner's daughter. We took immediate actions to rescue her."

Jacobs glanced over at Vasquez. "Is that true, sergeant?"

"You bet your ass…uh…sir," Luis said.

"I came here in response to a call from Mister Marlowe here." Eddie jerked his head at Marlowe, whose clothes had been transformed into a seersucker suit that looked very proper. "Mister Marlowe is a witness who was very helpful with information about a homeless woman here in the park. He called to tell me that he'd seen her with a child that matched Rosita's description."

Marlowe smiled warmly at Jacobs.

"You should have called the precinct," Jacobs protested, "not gone after her yourself."

"Sir, I wasn't sure if Mister Marlowe was correct or not, so Sergeant Vasquez and I came merely to observe. However, we found the woman with Rosita Vasquez, and she seemed to be in the midst of some kind of satanic ritual."

Jacobs looked over at Frisha in her strange robes, held tightly between Marlowe and Drusilicus.

"She thinks she's a witch," Eddie stated in a low voice.

"I'm a prophetess!" Frisha announced loudly. "And there's nothing wrong with me hearing!"

"Captain," Wilcox said, "this is all bunk! My partner followed this woman into the park and he saw no child. Only an African-American woman."

Eddie turned to Sam, who still wore his jogging suit, which was now filthy. "See anything unusual near this site?"

"There *were* a lot of weird lights," Sam shrugged.

"The woman worked with an accomplice that is still at large," Eddie intimated. "However, sir, we found these objects on her!"

Eddie took the jade statue and the decorated box from Eugenia and handed them to Jacobs.

The captain turned the objects over in his hand. "That's the missing statue that was in Mister Yamasuto possession."

"Yes, sir. And the box was part of a collection owned by Mr. Cuccolo. I believe all of the murders revolved around a belief in witchcraft."

"That would explain a lot of things we saw here," Collins said. "Strange smoke, odd lights."

"It is my belief that she was burning a large quantity of herbs laced with some kind of hallucinogen," Eddie explained.

Collins gave a nod. "That would explain the smoke we saw."

Wilcox broke into a sweat "When my team got here, we found Vasquez out cold at the bottom of the steps."

"My partner was injured by the accomplice, who remains at large." Eddie waved his hand at Bankrock, Drusilicus, and Eugenia. "But with the help of these citizens, we were able to subdue the suspect."

"I see." Jacobs eyed the group. "Are you all willing to make statements?"

They nodded and murmured assent.

"Well," Jacobs said, "your actions were a bit unorthodox. But as a father, I understand your motives. And you did capture the suspect."

"I don't believe this—" Wilcox groused.

"Agent Wilcox, what were you doing while *my* lieutenant was apprehending this woman?" Jacobs faced the federal agent.

"We were attempting to secure the area." Wilcox waved his arm in the direction of the park. "My teams and I were attacked by demons and corpses!"

"What?" Jacobs glared at him.

"You have no idea what happened out here, captain. This huge pit opened up and there were these four flying horses, one of which was the Angel of Death!"

"Angel?" Jacobs repeated.

"Of Death!" Wilcox said triumphantly. "Then we were attacked by demons—little guys with horns and tails."

"No pitchforks?" Jacobs added wryly.

Wilcox considered this for a moment. "I didn't see any."

"And what about these demons?"

"My men saw it all," Wilcox said and turned to the group of black-clad agents. They looked at their feet and muttered among themselves.

Sam turned to the captain. "It was pretty dark—"

"Come on, you all saw that huge pit," Wilcox pleaded. "I swear, it opened to Hell itself!"

One man stepped forward. "Actually, sir, it's all pretty hazy. I think Lieutenant Berman may be right, there was a lot of smoke. There must have been a hallucinogen in whatever that woman was burning. We all saw a lot of strange stuff."

Wilcox's mouth fell open.

"Agent Wilcox," Jacobs shook his head, "you are not under my jurisdiction, but I find your entire operation suspect. Why were you following my lieutenant to begin with?"

"Berman had something to do with Cuccolo's death, captain," Wilcox stated plaintively. "It made sense to follow him. You didn't see him this afternoon when he disappeared at Bethesda Terrace!"

"Disappeared?" Captain Jacobs' eyebrows raised.

"I'm telling you there was a pit in the middle of the Great Lawn!" Wilcox blurted as he gesticulated toward the open area.

Jacobs looked past Wilcox at the field beyond. "Nothing there now."

"It was Berman." Wilcox was desperate. "He did it and then he made it go away. Look, captain, we were attacked by giant bats tonight, right, men?"

"Agent Wilcox neglected to mention that he and his men raided my house," Eddie interjected.

"He did what?" Jacobs growled.

"We had just cause!" Wilcox whined. "Federal authority gives me the right—"

"Sounds to me like you sent this large team of agents to harass my lieutenant," Jacobs fumed. "And trust me, Federal Plaza will hear of it. Now take your agents and get out of my park."

Wilcox's mouth tightened into a hard line, but he was wise enough to know when to be quiet. He glared at Eddie and Luis, then snapped to his men, "Back in the vans, men."

He turned back to Jacobs and in a tense voice added, "The FBI wishes to apologize for any inconvenience to the NYPD."

He joined his black-clad men and looked as if he'd like to find a dog to kick. They all strode down the stairs and faded into the darkness, doing their own brand of magic.

"What a horse's ass," Jacobs muttered, then looked at Eddie. "Good work, lieutenant."

"Thank you, sir," Eddie said.

"Lieutenant, sergeant," Jacobs chimed in. "Come to my office first thing in the morning, and I'll see that you get your shields and weapons returned. Your suspensions are lifted!"

"Yes, sir!" Luis had a goofy smile on his broad face.

Frisha, who had been standing passively with her head down, suddenly stomped on Marlowe's foot. Marlowe gave a loud "Ow!" and staggered back. She yanked loose from Drusilicus and pulled a sparkling object from a hidden pocket of her robe.

Marlowe and Eugenia cried out, but Frisha lunged at Eddie and jammed a large stickpin into his arm. Eddie bellowed in pain, as two uniformed officers grabbed the old woman and pulled her off of him.

"Didn't see that comin' did ye?" Frisha cackled as the two officers handcuffed her.

Eddie pulled the needle free from his arm. He felt hot and dizzy, and the terrace moved under him.

"Should we get a doctor?" Jacobs asked.

"No, no." Marlowe took the pin from Eddie's hand and gave it a quick perusal. "I have a friend who is a doctor, right nearby."

Marlowe's face swam up in front of Eddie's vision. "Eddie, you must come with me right away."

Eddie was pulled by the old man. He could hear Captain Jacobs' voice, and Luis talked back to him soothingly. But everything else appeared to have the consistency of soft taffy, which shifted and melted around him.

"Eddie, listen to me, you've been poisoned." Marlowe pulled Eddie through the dark foliage. "Try to stay with me. Your life depends on it."

Eddie wanted to form words but his mouth didn't work. He couldn't sense where his feet were and he felt himself falling into blackness.

SIXTY-FOUR

Eddie opened his eyes to see sunlight streaming into his bedroom. He sat up in pajamas, only to find his head hurt so badly that he reached up with the expectation that a manhole cover rested on it.

Despite the pain, he carefully slid to the edge of the bed and stood up. It was his bedroom, in his own house.

He walked to the door, pulled it open, and stumbled into the hall. He was winded and felt like a very old man.

"Eddie." Eleanor rushed up the stairs from the kitchen. "What are you doing out of bed?"

"I...I...how did I...?" Eddie stuttered, annoyed that this small attempt at words was so difficult.

"Ah, the patient is up." Marlowe came up from the kitchen. He wore a red-and-white-striped apron on top of a short-sleeve shirt and long pants.

"What day is it?" Eddie brought his hand to his head to try to quell the pain.

"Wednesday," Marlowe remarked. "Nice to see you up and around so soon."

"Wednesday?" Eddie frowned. "But the last thing I remember, it was Sunday night."

"And you are lucky to be alive, Edward Berman," Eleanor told him. "Now, go back to bed before Cerise gets home."

"Wha—?" Eddie tried to fathom what Cerise would be doing home. "I've got to go to work—"

"You don't have to worry about that." Marlowe guided Eddie in the direction of his room. "You're on vacation."

"Vacation?" Eddie repeated.

"Well, that's what happens when a police officer cracks a big case. Oh, by the way, Frisha confessed. Her public defender filed a plea of 'Not Guilty by Reason of Insanity.' I think the poor old girl will end up in a mental institution for the rest of her life, which will no longer be the augmented life of a wizard. Her powers are gone."

Marlowe gently escorted Eddie toward his bed.

"But how did I get here?" Eddie asked

"Teleported you directly here. You see, earlier that night, I noticed a plant on your table."

"Yeah, Luis brought it," Eddie fought to remember. "Kinda ugly, though."

"You are very lucky he did. It was flowering wormwood. The only cure for the poison Frisha injected you with."

"Wormwood? The plant with the ugly yellow flowers?" Eddie said.

"Yes."

"The same thing showed up in Riftstone's autopsy," Eddie mumbled, and felt as if that was years ago.

"Hmm. I guess he took the wormwood to inoculate himself from Frisha's poison if she had attempted to use it on him."

"Didn't save him," Eddie testified, as Marlowe pulled a sheet over him.

"Yes, and I have a theory about that. Riftstone was a prophet. As I told you a prophet can always see his own end."

"What went wrong?"

"I believe Riftstone saw that he could not defeat the Great Evil. But, he knew that you could. So, he sacrificed himself, allowed himself to be killed, so that you would be summoned."

"Why would he do that?"

Marlowe shrugged. "Mayhaps we shall know in time."

"So, what are you doing here?"

"I was sure my potion from the wormwood would save you, but I decided to stay and keep an eye on you. I had no pressing engagements."

"My head—" Eddie put a hand to his forehead.

"Ah yes, that." Marlowe pulled a small paper packet out of his pocket and mixed some dried leaves in a glass of water on the bedside table. "Here, drink this."

"You're kidding." Eddie observed the brown detritus as it floated in the water. "Why would I ever trust you again?"

"You want the headache to go away?"

Eddie gulped the tainted liquid down, grimaced, and lay back in the bed.

"Sleep some more," Marlowe said. "You'll feel better this evening."

Eddie didn't think he could sleep, but he closed his eyes for a moment. When he opened them, he found the shadows had grown long and the setting sun peeked through the Venetian blinds. His headache was gone, and he felt vitality course through him.

He quickly showered and shaved, got dressed, and walked down into the dining room as Douglas set dishes on the table for dinner.

"Dad!" Douglas put down the stack of plates and ran to his father to give him a hug.

"Hey, son. You guys been keeping the house together while your old man's been laid up?"

"Sure thing, Dad." Doug smiled up at him. "You gave us a scare."

"I'm all right now, Doug," Eddie smiled back.

The kitchen door opened, and Cerise walked out to give Eddie a kiss. She pulled away, and Eddie, in a catlike movement, grabbed her and kissed her again, hard and with passion.

"Dang!" Doug complained. "That's gross."

Cerise parted from Eddie, her eyes half-closed and dreamy. "We'll see about more of that later."

"Without an audience." Eddie glanced to his embarrassed son.

Eleanor came out of the kitchen and walked over to hug Eddie as Marlowe watched from the doorway.

"How do you feel, Eddie?" Marlowe leaned against the doorjamb.

"Great!" Eddie nodded.

"I hope you're up to a dinner party!" Cerise gave Eddie one last peck as the doorbell rang.

"You'd better get it, dearie," Eleanor suggested.

Eddie walked to the door and discovered Luis and Maria on the other side. They both yelled and ran into Eddie's arms.

"Thank you so much for saving my Rosita." Maria had tears in her eyes.

"Couldn't have done it without Luis," Eddie confessed.

"We're naming our next child after you," Luis announced.

"You mean you're—" Eddie stared at Maria.

"No, no," Maria blushed bright red. "We're not expecting."

"But give us a month or two." Luis patted her ample rump.

Maria slapped Luis's hand away and they all laughed.

There was another ring at the door, and Eddie opened it to find Eugenia, Drusilicus, and Ahbay. They each held gifts. Drusilicus brought wine, Eugenia offered flowers, and Ahbay offered a box wrapped in a beautiful Japanese silk textile.

Cerise walked over and touched the shiny fabric. "Ooh. What is that?"

"It is a traditional wrapping, known as *fukusa*," Ahbay said as he offered the gift with both hands. "The gift itself is less formal: *mochi*. That is a chewy rice cake filled with sweet bean paste."

"Why…um…thank you so much!" Eddie said.

"We enjoyed ourselves so much the last time, we thought another visit was in order before we left." Eugenia wore a very fashionable black velvet dress that showed off her figure.

"Without having to be concerned about saving the world," Ahbay added, in an elegant, and quite modern, velvet sports coat. He again had a vest with Japanese symbols, but it was a royal-blue silk and set off the black of the velvet nicely.

"Glad to see you're up and about, lieutenant," Drusilicus greeted. As always, he wore a gray Armani suit and a state-of-the-art tie.

With the breakfast table moved into the dining room, there were enough seats for everyone. The dinner was phenomenal, a creation of Eleanor and Marlowe working together. There was a roast turkey, with side dishes that looked unusual but were very tasty. For dessert, there were two kinds of pie, and a frozen lemon confection with a meringue that was like eating a sweet whisper.

"I am leaving for Europe tonight," Eugenia told the others.

"Are you flying out of Newark?" Cerise asked.

"Something like that," Ahbay smirked. "I must return to Japan and China to resume my duties."

"But you simply *must* come visit," Eugenia told Cerise. "You will be our honored guests."

"When we get a chance," Eddie acknowledged. "I've got to get back to work myself."

"Eddie, you're off," Luis broke in. "Jacobs gave us both two weeks off for solving the case. We are not due back for a week-and-a-half."

"Really?" Eddie considered this.

"Yes, we made the papers, my friend. We got a call from Manhattan North. Captain Seville says he could use the two best homicide detectives in the city. He was talking full reinstatement."

"What about Captain Jacobs?" Eddie frowned.

"He wants us to stay," Luis shrugged. "But he won't stand in our way. He knows the Central Park Precinct isn't the most exciting assignment in New York. It's our decision."

Eddie looked over at Marlowe and the others. "Well, Central Park *is* a place of power. Why don't we stay there, partner?"

Luis smiled. "Fine with me, bro." Maria hugged his arm.

"A week-and-a-half off." Eddie picked up his dishes.

"Eddie, you are the guest of honor." Cerise rose to take the plates from Eddie's hands. "I wanted to make up for your ruined birthday party."

Eddie held onto the dishes and gave her a quick kiss. "That's okay. I want to talk to Marlowe in the kitchen."

The two men disappeared and the dinner party went on, everyone having just one more taste of the fantastic desserts. Eddie and Marlowe reappeared, cleared the dishes, and joined the others.

At about eleven, Luis and Maria said they had to leave, and Eddie escorted them to the door. As they got into their car, Ahbay and Eugenia stepped out of the house.

"It has been quite exciting," Eugenia confided. "I do hope you have a chance to learn how to use your powers more succinctly. I see great things for you, Edward."

"I'll do my best," Eddie promised.

"I am sure," Ahbay volunteered. "Eddie Berman, you have the makings of a great Magus."

"By the way, how come they didn't name any arches after you guys?"

Ahbay and Eugenia smiled.

"Actually, one arch was named for my current persona," Ahbay explained modestly. "Ōbaru can mean egg, but it also means 'oval.' Therefore, Oval Arch is named in my honor."

"And I have always had a fondness for children, though none of my own," Eugenia sighed. "Playmates Arch is the name I requested to honor me."

"Well, it's better than all those 'Flintstone' names," Eddie said. "I guess I'll see you around."

"Blessed be," Ahbay and Eugenia said in unison as they walked down the street toward the park.

"I must be going as well." Drusilicus approached the door. "Though I must say, I enjoyed spending time with your family." Then he added almost guiltily, "They are very—what's the word—genuine."

"How's that?"

Drusilicus looked at his feet. "They don't put on airs, like most of the people I associate with."

"Thanks, Dru." Eddie held out his hand. "I want to apologize for misjudging you—"

"I must admit, I misjudged you as well." Drusilicus took the offered hand in a firm handshake. "You went down into that hole and did what needed to be done. You are already a Magus, lieutenant."

Eddie smiled. "I think you can call me Eddie. Have you seen Caleb? Are you going to give him the staff back?"

Drusilicus thought for a moment. "No, to both questions. In hindsight, I think he's a puffed-up little shit."

"My, my. I could learn to like you, Drusilicus."

"Don't push it," Drusilicus countered, then smiled as well. "Perhaps I have come to see things from a different perspective?"

"See you around?"

"Of *that* I have no doubt, Eddie Berman."

Marlowe came out, as he put on his coat and carried his walking stick. "Well, Eddie. I suppose I shall have to start your regular training soon."

"We've done pretty well so far."

"We've been lucky. No doubt, the Divine guided your hand. But with some practice, you will be prepared for whatever comes."

"I meant to ask you about that plant Luis brought—"

"The one that saved your life?" Marlowe questioned.

"He told me some guy at the flower store told him to buy it. Who was that?"

Marlowe shrugged. "Undoubtably, one who walks the path. We all try to use our abilities to help in whatever ways we can."

"Ask around, will you?"

"I shall." Marlowe gave a nod. "Enjoy your vacation."

"You're sure what I asked isn't a problem?"

"Eddie, it will be my pleasure." Marlowe jauntily swung his cane as he walked off.

"Give my best to Daniel," Eddie yelled after him, "and tell that crazy ghost of yours I owe him a game of checkers."

EPILOGUE

Eddie was mysterious the next morning when he insisted that Cerise call off work until the fifth of July. She tried to protest, but he was so excited, she finally agreed.

Then he told her to pack a bag with beach clothes.

"We can't go on a vacation, Eddie, it would cost too much."

"Won't cost a cent," Eddie assured her.

"What about airfare?"

"Don't need it."

"Even staying at the Jersey shore costs too much, especially over the Fourth of July weekend."

"Just pack, sweetheart, I'll take care of the rest."

"But the boys—"

"Are old enough to get themselves to school for two more days. Momma can handle them. Look at her, she's a new woman. Besides, I already asked her."

"All right, you crazy man, I will pack."

"Good."

At noon she was done. She'd packed light—two small bags. Eddie finished with his own suitcase and smiled at her. He was wearing shorts and a Hawaiian shirt.

"Ready?"

"I suppose. This is so unlike you. You never do things spur of the moment."

"Well, life's short. It's time I did!" Eddie explained.

"You two have a good time." Eleanor held the front door open for them.

"I'll call," Eddie told her.

Eleanor shook her head. "Just go, have fun."

They walked out of the house, and instead of heading for Cerise's car, Eddie turned and headed down the street.

"So where are we going?" Cerise caught up with him. "Are we going to spend a week at the community pool?"

Eddie smiled and hummed to himself. The day was balmy and warm and the sun beat down on them. They reached the small park and Eddie turned toward the woods.

"Is there anyone around?" Eddie asked.

Cerise glanced up the street. "No, I don't think so."

Eddie's smile grew broader. He waved his hand and his staff appeared like a magic trick.

"Hold on to me." Eddie took her arm as they plunged into the woods and ducked under the low branches.

"But where are we going?"

"I made a promise to you," Eddie told her. "I haven't been able to keep it, until now. I thought it was time."

A cool breeze blew past them, and the temperature seemed to drop a little. The light shifted and became less harsh. It was still quite warm, but not the same heat as a few minutes earlier. Cerise looked at the trees and noticed that they were different. They were oddly stilted, and the trunks were fat and round.

"What is happening?" Cerise puzzled. "What did you do to the trees?"

"I didn't do a thing to them," Eddie smiled. "But, they do look different, don't they?"

"Yes, but why—"

They emerged from the trees, and before them was a sandy white beach and an entire ocean of the bluest water Cerise had ever seen. Her mouth dropped open as she watched a sailboat on the horizon.

"It's not possible!" She looked back at their path.

"Oh, yes, it is," Eddie beamed.

"It looks like…like…"

"Aruba."

"Like a postcard. But we can't…I mean…we just—"

"I forgot the good news." Eddie pointed to a huge adobe-style, ten-story building not five hundred yards down the beach. "See that hotel just there?"

"Yes."

"We have the Presidential Suite in that hotel for the next week and a half with all amenities. Everything paid for by our friend Marlowe."

"How could he afford it?"

"He says 'Money is the easiest thing to manifest,'" Eddie said.

"What does that mean?"

"I'm not sure. But I intend to find out," Eddie put down the suitcases and took Cerise in his arms. "Happy second honeymoon."

"A real one!" She kissed him.

He released her, they picked up their bags, and hand in hand they walked off to the hotel as they giggled like newlyweds.

THE END

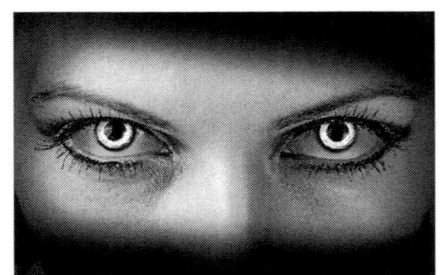

ABOUT THE AUTHOR

Arjay Lewis (aka R.J. Lewis) is an award-winning author, entertainer, and magician. He has experienced every level of show business from street-performing to Broadway.

Arjay's novel, *The Muse: A Novel of Unrelenting Terror,* has won 14 awards in the Horror category including: the 2017 NYC Big Book Award; the 2017 Beverly Hills Book Award; the 2018 National Indie Excellence Award; the 2018 Independent Author Network Book Award; the gold medal at both the 2018 eLit Book Awards and the 2018 Readers' Favorite Book Awards. He also is the author of the *In The Mind* series, which consists of seven novels with more to come.

Arjay's published stories have appeared in *H.P. Lovecraft Magazine Of Horror, Weird Tales,* and *Sherlock Holmes Mystery Magazine.* He also has been published in the anthology *The Ultimate Halloween.*

He has collaborated on several films including: *Down In Flames: The True Story Of Tony 'Volcano' Valenci,* which has won seven Film Festival awards. His screenplay for *Dummy* (co-written with Pamela Wess) was the winning screenplay for the 2017 Garden State Film Festival.

48990427R00385

Made in the USA
Middletown, DE
17 June 2019